TEA & SYMPATHY MYSTERIES

Tea & SYMPATHY

Mysteries

BOOKS 1–3

J. NEW

Tea & Sympathy Mysteries
Book 1–3

Cover design: J. New.
Interior formatting: Alt 19 Creative

Other Books By J. New

The Yellow Cottage Vintage Mysteries in order:

The Yellow Cottage Mystery (Free)
An Accidental Murder
The Curse of Arundel Hall
A Clerical Error
The Riviera Affair
A Double Life

The Finch & Fischer Mysteries in order:

Decked in the Hall
Death at the Duck Pond
Battered to Death

Tea & Sympathy Mysteries in order:

Tea & Sympathy
A Deadly Solution
Tiffin & Tragedy
A Bitter Bouquet

CONTENTS

Tea &
SYMPATHY

A Tea & Sympathy Mystery

BOOK 1

Tea & Sympathy
A Tea & Sympathy Mystery
Book 1

Cover design: J. New.
Interior formatting: Alt 19 Creative

About the Book

**Meet Lilly Tweed. Former Agony Aunt.
Purveyor of Fine Teas. Accidental Sleuth.**

When Lilly Tweed former agony aunt with the local newspaper is made redundant, she takes the opportunity to pursue a lifelong ambition, to open The Tea Emporium in the small market town of Plumpton Mallet.

But with her replacement making a hash of the column, it's not long before she is once again being sought for valuable advice.

When the body of a local woman is found drowned in the river, the contents of her pockets reveal a letter from Lilly and she's unwillingly drawn into the case.

But is it just a tragic accident, as the police think? Lilly isn't convinced, but pursuing her own inquiry means it isn't long before she gets into hot water.

Chapter One

"GOOD MORNING, LILLY. A fine morning." The jogger said as he approached the cyclist.

"Morning, Peter. Isn't it lovely to have the first signs of Spring showing through?" She replied, coming to a stop and causing the grey cat, dozing in his carrier in the front basket, to meow plaintively. "How's Charlotte doing, by the way?"

"Brilliantly, and it's all down to you. I can't thank you enough for your advice. Things are much more peaceful in the house now. Although the music is still louder than I'd like."

Lilly laughed. "That's teens for you, Peter. But I'm glad I could help."

"Well, I for one am relieved you're still on hand to dispense excellent advice, even though you're not with the paper anymore. How's the new shop going?"

"Extremely well, as a matter of fact. Which is an enormous weight off my mind as I sunk almost everything I had into it."

"Excellent news. Long may it continue. And I'm sure it will, considering this country practically runs on tea. And talking of running, I must get on. I'm trying to beat my best time." He said, tapping the Fitbit tracker on his wrist.

"Of course. Actually, while I remember, could you let your wife know the Alice in Wonderland tea set she ordered has arrived?"

"Will do. Thanks, Lilly." He started his stopwatch and set off running again with a last wave over his shoulder.

Lilly Tweed, former agony aunt with the local newspaper now a purveyor of fine teas and owner of The Tea Emporium in the centre of Plumpton Mallet, gripped the bike's handlebars and once again set off down the riverside path on her way to work. Pedalling through the tunnel which passed under one of the major roads from town, she entered the park and took a deep breath. After the dark, cold and wet days of winter, it was a joy to cycle to work again. To see the small buds appearing on the trees and the shoots of daffodils valiantly pushing up through the grass.

She sped along the path, the wheels kicking up the last of the fallen autumn leaves, and turned left up the steep hill at the edge of the park which led to the town. From there, it was a brief journey to the market square and her shop.

Plumpton Mallet was a historic market town with the cobbled square being its oldest part. A firm favourite with tourists who came in their droves to walk through the woodland, picnic on the little stone beaches beside the river, then finish with a meander around the shops and cafes in the square itself.

The Tea Emporium was housed in the old apothecary shop, and although it had had several retailers since then, the interior had remained authentic, with floor to ceiling shelves, and cabinets with row upon row of miniature drawers with dainty brass handles. It was the perfect set up to house Lilly's merchandise and display the range of quirky china she sold.

The exterior was double fronted with large bay windows flanking a recently painted cream door. The door furniture was also brass, including a knocker in the shape of a teapot which Lilly had found at an antique fair years ago and bought on a whim.

She dismounted, leaning her bike against the window and retrieving Earl unlocked the door and entered.

❦

INSIDE, LILLY RELOCKED the door and let Earl out of his carrier. He sauntered across the wooden floor, stretching each individual leg in turn, then jumped up to his favourite spot, the window. Delicately avoiding the items on display, he walked on silent paws to his bed and curled up. It was an odd place for him to choose, but it was the position he obviously felt safest and happiest, and there was no doubt about it: having a cat in the window certainly made people stop and look. Earl Grey was good for business.

He'd turned up barely a week after she'd opened, a thin, filthy and flea ridden bag of bones with a scar on his nose and a chunk of his right ear missing. Lilly hadn't a clue how he'd ended up on the streets, but he wasn't doing well. She'd promptly taken him to the local vet for a check-up and adopted him immediately. It had been touch and go for a while, but Lilly had poured all her energy into saving him. That, along with his fighting spirit, had seen Earl over the worst and well on the way to recovery. Now he was as much part of the shop as she was, and her first order of the day had been to install a cat flap in the storeroom door at the rear of the shop. There he had access to food and water as well as a litter tray and another bed. But he still preferred the window.

Lilly repositioned the **Help Wanted** sign in the other window, then began getting ready for the day ahead. The Tea Emporium had only been open for just over two months, but word had spread quickly thanks to some free advertising for its former employee in the Plumpton Mallet Gazette. Now though, it was necessary to take on her first member of staff.

After she'd gathered the post, the morning newspaper and set up the rest of the shop, she turned to the last job, decorating her bike. On the pavement outside she chained the bike to an old post and hung the open sign on the handle bars. She filled the basket with colourful pots packed with spring flowers and fixed another flower basket on the seat. Her last job was to put up the **Tea of the Week** sign. She'd chosen Echinacea because of its benefit to improving cold, flu, and sinusitis symptoms. Perfect for the time of year. That done, she went back inside and brewed herself a cup of Ginkgo Biloba, known for improving both brain function and vision, and perused the paper while waiting for her first customer of the day.

The front-page story was a rehash of one that had run previously, with very little in the way of updates. There had been a break-in at the local university and various small, but high cost pieces of equipment and a number of pharmaceuticals had been stolen from the labs. So far the culprits hadn't been found even though there were continuous interviews being carried out with students and teachers alike. Popular opinion was the drugs were being sold to addicts somewhere out of town. Lilly could almost hear the tone of derision in the piece at the failings of the police to solve the thefts. The author wouldn't be doing themselves any favours by making an enemy of the local police officers. She glanced at the byline and noticed Abigail Douglas had written it; the new agony aunt. Lilly had heard rumours that the column wasn't doing well, was Abigail trying to set herself up as an investigative reporter instead?

When the small local paper had been taken over by a much larger concern, they had offered Lilly redundancy. The new owners already had an agony aunt who apparently intended to move to Plumpton Mallet, and Lilly suddenly found herself middle-aged and unemployed. It was a terrifying prospect but was just the push she needed to try to make a go of a long-held dream; to open her own tea shop. If she didn't grab the opportunity now, then she knew she never would. A combination of her redundancy money, the majority of her savings and a small loan from the bank and she had secured the premises. Two months later, it looked as though it was paying off. There wasn't a day when she wasn't busy.

She turned to the page where the agony aunt column usually was to find it absent. Lilly had worked hard on her column and through good advice, a genuine desire to help and her interest in people, she had turned what was to all intents and purposes a 'filler' into an integral part of not just the paper but the community. She sighed, it saddened her to find it was no longer popular, but it wasn't her concern now she had her own business to look after.

She was just disposing of the paper when the shop bell tinkled. Time to get to work.

ᗉᗉᒪᗉᗉ

HER FIRST CUSTOMER entered and announced themselves with an almighty sneeze.

"Kate, you poor thing."

"Sorry, Lilly. Can you help? I'm getting nowhere with my cold medicine, I think I've become immune to it, and I want to see if something more natural will work."

"Of course, have a seat and I'll put the kettle on."

Kate took one of the bar style stools at the counter while Lilly selected several samples.

"Is it a cold or more sinus symptoms you have?" Lilly asked, putting a teacup and saucer in front of Kate.

"Sinus problems, although I'm just getting over a nasty cold as well."

"Do you have a sore throat at all?"

"A little, although not as bad as it was."

"Well, both Mint and Echinacea will help with the sinus problem. As will Ginger, and it also helps relieve congestion. If you have an infection, then Thyme will help. I've also just got some Japanese Kuzu tea, which helps with cold and sore throats."

"So many to choose from. What do you suggest?"

"I'll brew you a cup of Echinacea, I think that's the best for the sinus problem and as *Tea of the Week* it's on special offer. Have you eaten, Kate?

"Yes, I had porridge for breakfast."

"Good. You mustn't have this tea on an empty stomach. You can have a cup two or three times a day until you feel better, but don't take it for more than ten days. Also ginger will help fight any infection and reduce inflammation, so you could take some for later if you want?"

Lilly let the tea steep in the small teapot for three minutes, then using a decorative strainer, poured a cup for Kate. She took a deep appreciative breath and smiled.

"It smells lovely. Hope it tastes as good."

She took a sip and nodded. Within five minutes she'd finished the cup.

"I feel better already. I'll take it and some of the ginger as well. Thanks, Lilly."

With her purchases wrapped, Kate asked Lilly if she mended tea sets?

"It's the handle of one of the cups which has come off. I'd like it mended as it belonged to my mum."

"I'll need to see it before I can tell you if it's possible. Can you drop it in some time when you're passing?"

"Yes, I'll do that. Thanks, Lilly. See you soon."

After Kate had left, there was a steady stream of customers. It actually was busier than usual, which Lilly was thrilled about. She hurried from customer to customer, brewing tea samples, teaching about remedies, wrapping up sales and dispensing personal advice on occasion. She was still being sought out as an agony aunt. By eleven o'clock the shop was packed and Lilly was wondering how she was going to find time to replenish what she'd sold from the stock at the back, when a young blonde woman entered.

Lilly sized her up and came to the conclusion she was neither local nor English. She was of athletic build, slim, tanned and radiating health with hair tied in a high ponytail, wearing jeans, trainers and a white tee shirt under a faded raspberry hoodie advertising a well-known brand of soft drink. She returned Lilly's smile, showing perfectly straight and white teeth.

"Welcome to The Tea Emporium."

"Hey, thanks. You're Lilly Tweed, the owner, right?" The girl replied in an American accent.

"Yes, I am. Are you looking for anything in particular?"

"Oh, I'm not here to shop," she replied, thrusting an envelope into Lilly's hands.

Opening it, Lilly found an application. "Oh, you're looking for a job?"

"Sure am," she said, sticking out her hand and shaking Lilly's with a strong, confident grip. "My name's Stacey. Stacey Pepper. I just started at the university and am looking for something part time. You're looking to fill a part time position, right?"

With the sign in the window, Lilly could hardly say otherwise. "Yes. But do you know anything about tea, Stacey?"

"I know it's brewed in a kettle, but that's about it. I'm a quick learner, though."

"Actually, the tea is brewed in a teapot," Lilly gently corrected her with a smile. "The kettle is used for boiling the water, which is poured into the teapot."

"Right! I think it's an English versus American terminology thing. But don't worry, I won't forget again."

"Perhaps you're right. Well, I'll be sorting through the applications this evening and..."

"Oh, drat it!" a man's voice rang out just as the unmistakable sound of smashing china reached Lilly's ears.

ᙇᘿᘒᘒᘓᖭ

"*L*ILLY, I AM so sorry," an elderly man said with a combined look of horror and shame. "Don't worry about it, Jeffrey. It was an accident."

"But that's twice in as many weeks! You must let me pay for it this time," he said, reaching for his wallet with a shaking hand.

"Honestly, it's not necessary," Lilly began.

"It is, you know. I insist."

While Lilly had been speaking with Jeffrey, Stacey had taken it upon herself to start picking up the bits of broken china.

"Stacey, be careful!" Lilly said. "I don't want you cutting yourself. I'll deal with it in a minute."

"I don't mind. Where's your mop and broom?"

Lilly sighed. "In the back storeroom, just behind the door, you'll find the dustpan and brush and a mop and bucket. Thank you."

While Stacey busied herself cleaning up the mess, Lilly rang Jeffrey's payment into the large antique till. Then she had an idea. A few days before, a company rep had come in and left some product samples with her. Now, normally Lilly didn't like plastic products, they were harmful to both the environment and the wildlife. All her merchandise was sold in paper bags or cardboard boxes. However, these she would make an exception for as they were recycled plastic. She dug one out of the box under the counter and set it in front of Jeffrey with a smile. A beautiful deep teal with a gold rim teacup and saucer, styled like its china counterparts. It was so perfectly put together that unless you knew, it was almost impossible to distinguish between it and the real deal.

Jeffrey shook his head. "I don't want to have another mishap, Lilly."

"You won't. I promise. Pick it up."

Jeffrey did so, then broke out in a huge grin. "Well, I never. Isn't that amazing? I would never have guessed."

"Would you like refill?"

"I would indeed. My usual please, Miss Tweed."

Lilly laughed and reached for the Fennel, known to help brain function. The first time he'd broken one of her cups, Jeffrey had confided that he'd been diagnosed with early onset Parkinson's disease. The tremors had caused him to lose his grip. There was little Lilly could do in the way of help, but Jeffrey was adamant the Fennel tea was alleviating his symptoms and who was she to question it?

With Jeffrey sorted out, Lilly made a note to order a few more of the plastic range of tea cups for her samples. They would be a lovely alternative for those elderly customers who had trouble gripping and lifting a heavier china version. It seemed Jeffrey had the same idea.

"I say, Lilly, do you sell this range? I'd love to have a set at home. Much more practical."

"It's something new I'm trying, so I can add your order to mine, Jeffrey. I'll have to confirm the price for you, but it shouldn't be too expensive."

He made a vague gesture with his hand, dismissing her concerns. "Whatever it is, it will be cheaper than constantly breaking and having to replace the china ones. Order me a set of six would you, my dear?"

By the time that was done, the mess was cleaned up, everything had been returned to the store room and Lilly had several other customers to serve. She had no idea what had happened to Stacey. Ten minutes later she got her answer as Stacey came over with arms full of merchandise she was carrying for a customer. The older woman was laughing at something the younger girl had said and thanking her profusely for her help.

"Anytime," Stacey replied.

She's acting as though she already works here, Lilly thought with amusement. For the next hour she didn't have time to think about the confident American girl. There were simply too many customers in the shop to deal with. She did notice that Stacey stood to one side, observing and making notes in a small notebook. She was obviously keen.

Shortly after lunch and with the shop now empty, Lilly had time to grant the girl a more formal interview. She brewed them both a cup of Rooibos, a red tea from South Africa, and took a seat at the far end of the counter.

"Well, you've certainly got my attention, Miss Pepper," Lilly began. "But what do you think qualifies you to work in my shop?"

"Honestly, not much. Although I am good with people. But I'm willing to learn like I said before. And I'm a quick study."

"And do you drink tea?"

"A bit, although nothing like the stuff you have here. My dad's actually a Brit, from London, but I've spent most of my life living with my mom in the US. I decided to apply to college here and was accepted. It'll give me a chance to get to know my dad better."

Lilly smiled and nodded but remained silent. She'd learned that if you kept quiet, people were inclined to fill the silence. It was a good way to get to know more, and Stacey obliged.

"My parents divorced when I was five," she continued. "Mom's old job meant she travelled a lot, it's how she met my dad. They lived in London for a while, but after the divorce she took me with her back to the States. Dad is pretty much a once a year call on my birthday kind of parent."

"I'm sorry, Stacey."

"Hey, it's no problem. We're cool. He was pretty pleased to have me move over here to go to school."

"Divorces can be nasty, though. I went through one myself a few years ago. It was fairly civil, but of course there were no children involved."

"Nah," Stacey said, waving Lilly's comments away. "As far as I know, they get along fine. Better now they aren't living together, actually."

"Well, that's positive at least," Lilly said just as Earl made an appearance and jumped straight into Stacey's lap.

"Hey there," she exclaimed, scratching his ears. "What's his name?"

"Earl."

"Earl, and he's grey. So, Earl Grey like the tea, right?"

Lilly nodded, pleased she had picked up on the intended pun.

"Cute. So, um... do you have any questions for me?"

"No, I don't think so. But you really were a great help today and Earl seems to like you."

Stacey grinned expectantly. "I love animals. So, you're considering me?"

"How about a trial run?"

"Awesome!"

"All right. I'll get some leaflets together for you to study on the types of tea I offer and their health benefits. We can discuss your hours once you've been through them. Do you have any other questions?"

"Only about that little letterbox out the front. I saw some of your customers using it and wondered what it was for?"

Lilly explained her former job as an agony aunt with the paper. That even though she no longer worked there, many people still wanted her advice and had taken to coming to the shop instead.

"Sometimes they come in to chat over tea, but others have problems which are more private, so I installed a letterbox outside. The letters drop into the basket inside and I collect them each day and take them home to answer them."

"Cool!" Stacey said. "I just love this place. I think I'm really going to enjoy working here."

Chapter Two

COUPLE OF HOURS later the day was over and Lilly began the process of shutting the shop. She moved the signs and flowers from the bicycle display back inside and put Earl in his carrier. After taking out the day's takings and balancing the receipts, she transferred it all to the safe in the storeroom. It had been one of her best days so far. Not least she suspected because of Stacey and her way with the customers. She certainly knew how to sell.

Her last job was to remove that day's letters from her agony aunt basket. "Four today, Earl," she said to the cat. "Let's get home and see how we can help."

As she locked the door and put Earl in the bike basket, she felt the wind begin to rise. Dark clouds were beginning to roll in over the moor. "Looks like rain. We better get a move on otherwise we could be drenched before we get home."

Retracing the morning's route, Lilly was just at the end of the park when the first light drops of rain began to fall. They quickly turned into a deluge, soaking her to the skin and plastering her unruly hair to her face.

"Good grief," she said, picking up speed, eager to get out of the wet. "Where did this come from?" Earl, tucked up comfortably in his warm carrier, didn't respond.

Ten minutes later, she stopped outside her cottage gate. Snug in its cloak of trees with views over the river, it was part of the nature reserve a short distance North East of the town centre. An incredibly picturesque setting, even with the gloom of an impending storm. Leaving her bike in the shed, she retrieved the cat and dashed inside.

After she'd fed Earl, she put her dinner in the oven and went for a long hot shower while it cooked. An hour or so later, warm again and nicely full, Lilly settled down with a cup of chamomile tea and the agony aunt letters.

The first was from a local teenager discussing problems at school. Struggling with mounting responsibilities and social pressures, Lilly advised the youngster to confide in parents and teachers, or if that wasn't possible, at least discuss the issues with her friends, who were most likely in the same situation. She also recommended some books and on-line resources which would help. The main thing for her to understand was that she was not alone, and that there were always solutions to be found. She signed off by saying if the girl wanted to talk face to face at any time, then Lilly could be found at the shop.

The second was a brief note from a gentleman looking to start his own business. However, he had some concerns regarding the landlord of the building he wished to lease.

During her time at the paper Lilly had amassed a number of professional contacts, including someone at the local council who dealt with Landlord Registration in the locality. She also gave the name of a solicitor who could look over the lease. Her final piece of advice was to seek out and talk to the other tenants of this landlord and get their views.

The third note was simply a suggestion card. She kept them on the counter in the shop and used the letterbox outside to receive them. It helped keep the privacy of those with a genuine problem, as no one noticed who was posting what. She put it to one side and turned to the final letter, fully expecting it to be something simple to deal with. She was wrong.

ISS TWEED, THE letter began.

You're my last hope. If you can't help me, then I don't know what I will do. I think I'm being followed and I'm frightened. My doctor says I'm paranoid, and it's part of my illness, but he's wrong. Someone has been in my home when I'm out and my husband is having an affair, I'm sure of it.

"Oh, Earl, this poor woman."

Lilly put the letter down and rubbed her eyes. This was much more than she could deal with. She wasn't a doctor or a psychiatrist and had no official qualifications to call upon. The woman was obviously suffering some sort of mental health breakdown and needed professional help. The writing was messy and hurried, as though the author were trying to get everything down while they were lucid enough to remember it. It flitted from one statement to the next with no cohesion, and there were several wet splotches across the page too. Tears, Lilly thought sadly. The woman was in dreadful emotional pain. She picked up the letter and continued to read...

> *They say I'm imagining it all, but I've been taking my tablets, and it's still happening. I don't know what to do. Am I seeing things, Miss Tweed? It's hard to know what's real and what isn't when my senses have failed me so many times before. I know I've been a burden to those around me. Perhaps this is their way of getting rid of me for good? To make me think I am crazy after all. But I don't feel safe anywhere now, even in my own home.*
>
> *What shall I do, Miss Tweed? Can you help me? I don't know who else to turn to because I feel I can't trust anyone. They're all lying to me.*
>
> *Please write back.*
> *Carol Ann Hotch.*

Lilly made herself another cup of tea, the first forgotten about and now cold. Then settled down to write a reply to Carol Ann.

It took over an hour and several attempts before she was happy with what she had written. She finished off by saying she would be more than willing to meet with Carol Ann either at her home, the tea shop or any other place Carol Ann felt comfortable. She was not to think she was alone and without support. She wasn't. Lilly would help in any way she could.

Once finished, she gathered the three letters together and hopped on her bike to take them to the post box at the end of the lane. The final letter had been the most urgent one she'd ever received, and she wanted the reply to get there as soon as possible. The postman would pick up at seven-thirty the next morning, so Carol Ann should have her reply the day after. Lilly just hoped she'd agree to meet.

⸎

*I*T HAD BEEN three days since Stacey Pepper had waltzed into Lilly's shop and practically demanded a job, and Lilly was very pleased with how things were going. The day after she'd been sent home with the information leaflets, Stacey had returned having memorised most of it and promptly set about sampling the various teas in order to get a better handle on the tastes.

Day three and Lilly had the official paperwork for her employment together and work schedule sorted out. Stacey was assisting customers and even making recommendations, but if she was unsure, she always turned to Lilly for assistance. This was a big plus in the girl's favour as far as Lilly was concerned. Never be too proud to ask for help or conceited enough to think you know it all.

Without being told, Stacey had also changed her casual outfit for a smart white polo shirt and black trousers, similar to what Lilly herself wore. The long, black, bibbed aprons with The Tea Emporium logo on the front pocket in gold, finished off the look.

"I have to say I'm impressed," Lilly said as Stacey returned from helping a customer to her car with not one but two full tea services, and another on order.

"Really?" she replied, a huge grin on her face.

"Really," Lilly assured her. "I can't believe how much you've picked up in only three days. If I'm being honest, yesterday I thought you were just using it as an excuse to gorge yourself on all my tea samples before I saw your notebook."

Stacey laughed. "I wouldn't do that. But I need to know what they taste like to sell them."

"So what are your thoughts? Do you have a favourite?"

"I like a lot of them. I didn't realise tea could taste so great and be good for you. But I think my favourite is the Chamomile. It tastes like apples and honey."

"It does. Although the trick with that one is not to leave it steeping for too long otherwise it starts to taste bitter. And that reminds me, we're running short of both the chamomile and the ginger. Could you pop upstairs and get some more?"

"Upstairs?"

"Yes, there's a flat above. Just go out the back and there's the entrance door to the left." Lilly said, handing over the keys.

"I didn't realise you owned that too."

"It's just storage at the moment, but at some point the plan is to get it organised and rent it out."

"Hey, my organisation is great. If that's the goal, then I'm happy to make a start on the back storeroom. I think with a bit of rearranging I can fit a lot more back there."

"I might just take you up on that, Stacey. Thanks."

A few minutes after Stacey had left, Lilly spied a young man hovering outside the shop window. A student, she thought and was proved right when he turned and she spied the university logo on his sweatshirt. He looked exhausted. Unruly hair as though he'd just crawled out of bed. Dark circles under his eyes and a haunted look. She poured a cup of recently made peppermint tea, good for relieving stress, and took it out to him.

"Hi. Sorry, I didn't mean to make you jump. You look like you could use this."

He stared at her blankly for a moment, then took the cup with a smile.

"Thanks, that's kind of you. You're the owner, er, Lillian Tweed, is that right?"

"Yes, but call me Lilly. Lillian is my Sunday name."

"Yeah, I've got one of those too. Frederick. Frederick Warren, but known as Fred."

"Nice to meet you, Fred. Is there anything I can help with? I don't want to interfere of course if you're just window shopping."

"No I... well, actually a friend told me about your letter box. You helped her when she wrote to you and..."

"Do you want to come in, Fred? The shop's quiet at the moment."

He paused for a moment but eventually nodded and followed her in, clutching his tea cup and saucer as though his life depended on it.

(eeleg)

*L*ILLY TOOK FRED down to the far end of the counter away from any shop browsers and refilled his tea cup.

"I love your shop," Fred said. "Really vintage looking. It's like going back to the past."

"And that's exactly what I was aiming for. It seemed fitting, not only because of the age of the town and the building, but because tea has been used as a medicine for thousands of years."

"Wow. I didn't know that."

"There's a well known Chinese proverb which says, *'Drinking a daily cup of tea will surely starve the apothecary.'*"

"It looks a bit like an old chemist shop, actually."

Lilly smiled. She wouldn't push the boy to speak to her about personal matters if he didn't want to.

"It used to be. Well, you're welcome to stay as long as you want. Drink your tea and relax a bit. If you want to talk, I'm here. If not, that's fine too."

Lilly moved away and grabbing a tea towel began to dry the recently washed cups and saucers.

Fred cleared his throat, then suddenly blurted out, "My girlfriend's pregnant."

No wonder he looked as though he hadn't slept for a while. Doubtless he could see his future disappearing before his eyes.

"That must be very difficult for you, Fred. I expect it feels as though the world has just ended, doesn't it? But believe me, it hasn't. Things are never as bad as they first appear. There is always help. You've made the first step by coming here. Talking with someone else will give you clarity. Have you talked to your girlfriend about your feelings?"

He shook his head. "She doesn't know I've found out. I thought she would have told me, but she didn't. I don't know what to do."

"Well, she could be afraid to tell you. Have you been together long?"

"About a year."

"I can't tell you what to do, but I feel the first step would be to sit down and discuss it with her. You obviously care or you wouldn't be feeling so wretched about it."

"But it's not mine."

Ah, that shone a completely different light on it. Not only was he dealing with the shock of the pregnancy, but the heartbreak of finding out his long-term girlfriend had been with someone else.

"How can you be sure?"

"Because we've never... you know," Fred said, blushing furiously. "She wanted to wait, and I was fine about it. Obviously she just took me for an idiot."

"You don't know that for sure, Fred. How did you find out?"

"I found the pregnancy test in her dorm room bin. Positive. I thought it belonged to her house mate at first. Then she asked me to grab her phone from her bag one day and there were some, I don't know, vitamins I think. You know, for pregnant women."

Lilly nodded.

"She's had some doctor appointments recently and... well I couldn't keep denying it then, could I? I knew."

"I can't imagine how tough this must be for you, Fred. You've got some difficult decisions to make. Do you still want to be with her?"

"I thought I did, but now I'm not sure. I mean she cheated on me, which is bad enough, but she's carrying someone else's child. I'm twenty two, Miss Tweed, I don't..."

Fred's voice wobbled. He was close to tears.

"I understand, Fred. You don't have to explain it to me. But, if I can offer one word of advice, it's this: talk to her but be gentle, she'll be scared herself. It's no use waiting because it will just drag on and on otherwise, which isn't healthy for either of you. Tell her you know she's pregnant and probably scared and see what she has to say. And if you need to talk at anytime, you know where I am. Don't shoulder all this yourself, Fred, there's help and support if you know where to look."

He nodded, giving a wan smile. "Yeah. Thanks for listening, I appreciate it."

"Anytime. I mean it."

"Hey, can someone give me hand?" a muffled voice called from the store-room door.

Frederick jumped from his seat and hurried over to help Stacey with several boxes.

"Oh, thanks."

"No problem."

"Hey, you go to the university, right? I think I've seen you around the campus."

"Oh, yeah, you're the American. Um, Pepper or something?"

"Stacey Pepper. And you?"

28

"Fred Warren," he said politely. "Well, I have to go. Nice to meet you. Thanks for the tea, Miss Tweed."

"You're welcome, Fred," Lilly said as he left the shop.

"Was he here to buy tea?"

Lilly said nothing.

"Oh, I get it. He was consulting your alter ego. I won't ask any more. So, there were a few chamomile and ginger teas to choose from. I didn't know which one you meant, so I brought them all."

"Sorry, Stacey. It's these two I should have been more specific."

"No problem. I'll take these back upstairs."

"And after that, do you think you could use your organisational skills to get the back room in better shape?"

"Absolutely!"

Lilly was very pleased to note Stacey didn't push her for information about her consultation with Fred. As an agony aunt, she was privy to many secrets and people trusted her not to gossip. Thankfully, it looked as though Stacey was the same.

She looked up just as the bell above the door rang and a familiar face walked in.

"Archie Brown!" she exclaimed, pleased to see him. "I wondered when I'd get a visit from you."

"Sorry it's been so long, Lilly." He said, removing his Trilby hat and giving her a peck on the cheek. "It's a busy life as a crime reporter, you know."

"Have a seat and I'll get you a drink. What do you fancy?"

"Anything to take the edge off and stop me wanting to throw things."

Lilly raised an eyebrow. This was unlike the Archie she knew. She perused her tea selection then nodded, picking a passionflower blend noted for helping with stress. She chose Rooibos for herself and with both teas made she asked him how life at the newspaper had been since she'd left.

Archie sighed. "Awful, if I'm honest. Abigail Douglas, your replacement, is a complete nightmare. She's ruined your column and unfortunately has discovered people are still writing to you. She knows about your letterbox outside and she's on the war path, I'm afraid."

Chapter Three

"I REALISED THERE MUST be a problem when the column was missing from the paper, but it's hardly my fault. I installed the letterbox because I was getting so many letters. I thought it would trickle off once they got used to Abigail. Looks like that's not going to be the case though, doesn't it?"

Archie scoffed. "Well, it's hardly surprising considering she's unintentionally 'outed' a couple of people in the column already. Infidelity and fraud, would you believe? Didn't go as far as actually naming them, but gave enough clues so that they'd be recognised by their nearest and dearest. People won't write in to her if she's going to splash their problems all over the paper."

"But she can't do that, Archie! Doesn't she realise this is a small town? You can't walk six feet without bumping into someone you know."

Lilly broke off for a moment to serve a couple of customers who had come in for their regular supplies.

"Try telling Abigail that," Archie continued once Lilly had returned. "She's from a bigger concern, remember. Dealing with large cities where people don't know their neighbours and sensationalism sells papers. Her advice is dreadful. She's peddling gossip rather than genuine advice. Between you and me, I think she wrote the last few herself. But don't repeat that."

"Of course I won't. So, if the column is failing, what's she doing?"

"She's after my job."

"What? I saw the article about the thefts at the University, but I thought she was just covering because you were so busy."

"Oh no. She went behind my back. Unbelievable isn't it. Apparently the agony aunt thing was just to get her foot in the door. She's always wanted to be a crime reporter. Says she's got *unique skills*, whatever that means, and fully expects to win awards and have the nationals fighting to give her a job. She's completely delusional if you ask me. She can't get a decent quote anywhere because no one will talk to her, so she exaggerates."

"I'm sorry, Archie. Is there anything I can do to help?"

"See, that's why I'm here. For a bit of tea and sympathy."

Lilly laughed. "You know, that would have been a great name for the shop."

"And talking of the shop... you've done a superb job here, you know. I'm so pleased you were able to put the redundancy money to good use. I don't know why I felt so worried for you. You've got a knack for bouncing back."

"I've had a lot of support from the community though, Archie. The place wouldn't have worked without them."

"Don't sell yourself short, Lilly. There's a reason you've got their support. You're a good person and they like you. You give sound advice and never gossip. Plus, your tea is excellent." He said, draining his cup.

"Do you want a re-fill?"

"Yes, but I'd better not. Look, there's another reason I dropped in."

"Oh?" Lilly questioned, raising an eyebrow. Archie's expression had changed. She'd seen that look before when he was working on a serious article. "What's happened?"

"It's not common knowledge yet." Archie leaned closer, his voice dropping to a whisper. "But there's a body been found in the river."

Lilly gasped. "A body?"

Archie nodded. "I've a contact at the police station, as you know. The body of a woman was found early this morning by a couple of joggers."

"What happened?"

Archie shrugged. "It could have been an accident, or maybe suicide. I don't have much information at the moment. I expect the autopsy will be done over the next few days and we'll know more then. But be prepared for a possible visit from the authorities. I wanted to be the one to tell you first."

"Me? But why would they want to see me? Wait, was it someone I know?" A nervous knot had formed in her stomach and she suddenly shivered.

"I assume so. There was a letter from you found in her pocket."

*L*ILLY COULDN'T HELP but breathe a sigh of relief. "Someone needing advice, then? Do you have a name?"

"Carol Ann something. Hang on..." he said, fishing in his pocket for his notebook.

"Hotch." Lilly finished for him.

"Yes, that's right. You do know her then?"

"No. I never met her but I won't forget her name in a hurry. She wrote to me asking for help and naturally I wrote back. It was a really alarming letter, Archie. The poor woman was convinced she was being followed. That someone was breaking into her home. She was frightened for her safety but was told she was being paranoid. Now she's dead."

"The police are aware she had mental health issues, but I can't get anyone to talk just yet. Reading between the lines, I believe they're thinking it's either an accidental or deliberate overdose of her medication. Of course until we get the post-mortem results back it's all speculation."

"Do you think she would have written to me asking for help if she was planning to commit suicide?"

Archie sat back, arms folded while he thought. "Undoubtedly it does seem odd," he said finally. "But by the same token, she obviously wasn't in her right mind. I've yet to speak to the husband but according to my contact he's been worried something like this was going to happen for a while."

Lilly got up to brew herself another cup of tea. Passionflower for herself too, this time. She was feeling twitchy and anxious as a result of Archie's news.

"I feel dreadful," she said. "I should have reported her letter to the proper authorities, rather than write asking her to meet then waiting for a response."

"Lilly, you can't blame yourself for what happened," Archie said sternly. "Thinking that way is ridiculous. You'll make yourself ill. You did the only thing you could."

"I don't even know what she looked like. I could have passed her in the street. She could even have been in here and I wouldn't have known."

"Well, I can help with that." Archie reached into his coat pocket and withdrew a photograph. "A copy from my friendly police officer."

Lilly took the image. Staring back at her was a youngish attractive woman with shining strawberry blond hair, holding a small white dog. A Pomeranian, she thought. She looked happy and content. Without a care in the world. She didn't look like someone so unhappy with life that they wanted to end it. But then depression was a hidden disease. Appearances could be deceiving, and this was nothing but a single snapshot of her life. She quickly took a photo with her phone and offered the original back to Archie.

"No, it's fine. You keep it, I've got another."

"Hello," said a voice behind them.

"Oh, Stacey. I didn't hear you there. Archie, this is Stacey Pepper. She's just started working with me. Stacey, this is Archie Brown, head crime reporter with The Plumpton Mallet Gazette."

"Nice to meet you, Archie. Are you here for some tea? We have something for every occasion and most ailments you know. This one for example..."

Lilly smiled at how easily Stacey had turned the conversation to business and listened as she explained in detail the various teas and their health properties. Archie looked at her briefly and grinned, but played along, asking sensible questions with a keen interest. Having worked with Lilly for so long previously, he knew almost as much about tea as she did, but understood this was important to Stacey.

While the discussion continued, Lilly tuned out and turned back to the photograph of Carol Ann Hotch. *Something isn't right,* she thought. *I understand the assumption that it was accidental. It might very well have been, but I can't see a woman taking her own life so soon after writing to me so desperate for help.*

She sighed and put the photo back in her pocket. There were customers to serve. But as the working day drew to a close, the nagging doubt wouldn't leave her. She had an inexplicable feeling something was dreadfully wrong.

❧

*L*ILLY HAD ALREADY sent Stacey home as she had a test to study for and was in the process of closing up when there was an almighty crash of thunder which rattled the windows and the heavens opened. Great sheets of rain poured down from the awning above the shop as the storm took hold, producing a waterfall so dense you couldn't see the square beyond. Luckily, she'd already brought in her bike and the plants.

"Right, Earl, it looks as though we're getting a taxi home. I have no intention of cycling in this."

Earl was weaving a figure eight around her legs, so she scooped him up and put him in his carrier. With a final check, she grabbed her coat and exited through the back door where she'd arranged for the taxi driver to pick her up. To her surprise, she spotted Stacey in the main town car park, which was behind the shop, her head under the rear of the vehicle. It was an old Beetle which had definitely seen better days. In places, the original blue paint work had worn down to the metal.

"Stacey!" Lilly shouted through the wind.

Stacey looked up and seeing Lilly, slammed the boot, locked the car and rushed over.

"Hey."

"What are you still doing here? I thought you'd gone home ages ago."

"My car won't start. I thought I could fix it, but I'm clearly no mechanic. Serves me right for picking up the cheapest ride I could find. Didn't even have the decency to break down when the sun was shining."

Lilly laughed. "Well, I've just called a taxi. There was no way I was cycling home in this downpour; Earl would never have forgiven me. You can share it."

"That would be wonderful. Thanks so much. Oh, here it is, right on time."

The driver pulled up as close as he could and the two women jumped in the back seat, Earl between them. "Crazy weather," the driver said.

"You're telling me," Stacey replied. Peeling layers of wet hair from her face.

"So, where to, ladies?"

"We'll get you home first, Stacey," Lilly said. "You're soaked to the skin."

Stacey hesitated slightly. "It's okay. You probably live closer than I do."

"I insist." Lilly didn't know the girl well but as her employer she felt responsible.

Stacey gave the driver her address and Lilly then understood her initial reticence. The area was on the outskirts of the town, the less salubrious part made up of cheap accommodation and the odd shop rapidly going out of business.

Once they'd arrived, Stacey fumbled in her purse for her part of the fare, but Lilly said no, it was on her. At that moment Earl chose to be sick.

"Oh, Earl, you poor thing. What's caused that? Is it the storm? Stacey, would you mind if I brought him in to clean up?"

"Sure, no problem."

Lilly paid the taxi driver, and they both hurried over to the building Stacey called home. Originally it would have been a large single townhouse, but the planners in their wisdom had decided that making it into four cramped flats was a good idea. Stacey's was on the top floor at the back, under the eaves.

While the young girl went to change out of her wet clothes, Lilly released Earl and filled a bowl of water for him. Then cleaned the carrier, leaving it on the draining board to dry. While she waited for Stacey, Lilly observed her surroundings with dismay. The flat was in an awful state. Wallpaper that looked as though it had last been in fashion in the mid sixties was peeling away from the walls. There were signs of mould in the upper corners and in several places water was leaking in from the roof and Stacey had laid out various pots and pans to catch the drips. Unfortunately, due to the storm raging outside, they were currently mini waterfalls. It was damp and unattractive, although Stacey had tried to liven it up a bit with plants.

"Sorry about the state of the place," Stacey said when she returned. "It's temporary. I needed somewhere close to school, and this was the first place that was available."

"It's not you who should be apologising, Stacey, it's your landlord. At the very least, the roof needs fixing."

"It only leaks when it rains," Stacey replied with a grin.

"I have news for you. This is England. It rains a lot. Have you told your landlord how bad it is?"

"Yep. I've emailed pictures and videos, too. She says she'll get it sorted as soon as her builder has some time. But honestly, I'm planning to get out as soon as I can. It's one of the reasons I pushed so hard for the job. I want to get somewhere closer to town."

Stacey made a pot of coffee and they sat at the small Formica-topped table while Earl curled up on an easy chair nearby.

"Do you think your father could help you with a better place to live?"

"I've only spoken to him once since I arrived in England." She said sadly.

Lilly could tell there was more to the story but didn't want to push too much.

"Oh, has he been busy?"

Stacey shrugged. "I don't know. Actually, I don't know my dad at all, really. I told you I came here to get to know him better, and that's true. But... it wasn't exactly part of his plans."

"He didn't know you were coming to England?"

"He knew. I don't think it was something he wanted, though. I think he was pretty content with things the way they were; namely me being a million miles away and him sending a card with money in once or twice a year. When I told him my plans we talked on the phone some, but he didn't seem all that eager to get together. So, to answer your first question, no, I don't think dear old dad would help me with a better apartment."

"I'm sorry, Stacey."

"Hey, no worries. I have an awesome stepfather. A great role model actually, and he really loves me and my mom. I was just hoping dad would be a bit more excited that I was here. But, whatever. His loss, right? I'm here to get my degree. That's the important thing."

"Good for you," Lilly said, finishing off her coffee. "You know, if you want more hours at the shop..."

"Yes," Stacey said quickly. "I definitely want more hours at the shop. As long as it doesn't interfere with school, I'll take as many hours as you can give me."

"Wonderful. I'm sure we'll work something out that suits us both. In the meantime, do you think you'd be okay opening up on your own tomorrow?"

"Definitely! You can count on me." She said taking the keys from Lilly.

They chatted a bit longer, then Lilly lifted a sleeping Earl and put him in the now dry carrier. By the time she got back outside the taxi she'd called was already waiting and half an hour later she was back in the warmth of her own cottage.

Setting the table for dinner, she was in the process of collecting up the agony aunt letters to transfer to her files, when she spotted the one from Carol Ann Hotch on the top. Regardless of what Archie had said, she still felt partially guilty at not being able to help the woman before it was too late. Then she saw something she'd missed previously. On the reverse of the paper, discreetly printed at the bottom, was a business address for *Dr. Jorgenson. MD. Psychiatrist.*

"That must be her doctor, Earl." Lilly said to the disinterested cat.

A quick on-line search revealed the office wasn't far from the centre of Plumpton Mallet, on one of the side streets. It was also open for another twenty minutes. A quick phone call later and she had an appointment set up for the following morning.

"What?" Lilly asked the cat who was staring straight at her. "Don't look at me like that, Earl. I just want a few answers to set my mind at rest, that's all."

Earl stalked away, tail held high. Lilly swore he shook his head at her in disgust.

Chapter Four

THE NEXT MORNING Lilly woke with a start, thinking she'd overslept as the sunlight poured in through the curtains. Then, remembering Stacey was opening up, she sank back into her pillow with a sigh of relief hoping for a rare lie in. The rest was short-lived, however, because a moment later Earl jumped up on the bed and started meowing in her ear. It was obviously time for breakfast.

Once she was ready to leave, Lilly momentarily contemplated leaving Earl at home. At a good clip, it was at least a half an hour walk to The Tea Emporium, and she didn't really want to take her car as it was such a lovely day. But Earl was much happier at the shop with people, and she'd never left him alone before. So putting him in his carrier, she took him with her.

Arriving at the market square, Lilly was pleased to note Stacey had set the bike outside and decorated it as she herself did. Inside there were several customers, some browsing, a couple with baskets full of merchandise and one looking through a catalogue with Stacey trying to choose a tea set.

Lilly opened the carrier and released Earl, who gave a languorous stretch before occupying his bed in the window.

"Good morning, Mrs Erickson," Lilly said as she passed Stacey and the woman she was helping.

"Oh, Lilly, there you are. I was surprised not to see you this morning. But don't worry, Stacey has been a great help. She's helping me find a tea set for my daughter-in-law. And I think we've found the perfect one."

Lilly gave Stacey a wink. "Well, that's excellent news, Mrs Erickson. Stacey has a very good eye when it comes to the china and is very knowledgeable about the teas."

"Oh, she's a credit to you, that's for sure."

Lilly made her way to the till to serve those wishing to buy, but with that done, for the first time since she'd opened the shop she found herself with little to do. Checking the vintage train station clock on the exposed brick wall opposite, she decided she may as well set off for her appointment. It would be better to take a leisurely stroll and arrive a little early. Once Stacey was free, she explained her plans.

"No problem, I can manage here."

"You've done an excellent job here this morning, Stacey. Thank you. I shouldn't be more than a couple of hours, but I'll have my phone if you need me. I'll pick us up some lunch on the way back."

Stacey grinned. "Sounds good to me. Thanks, Lilly."

The spring sunshine had brought both locals and tourists out in their droves, and the town centre was awash with people shopping, chatting with friends and soaking up the warmth while having coffee and pastries at the pavement cafes. Because of the shop and her former job, Lilly was well known in Plumpton Mallet and spoke to several people on her way through the square. Stopping to chat briefly with her fellow shop owners who were making the most of the weather by either, cleaning front windows, hanging their flower baskets or sweeping the broad pavement. There was a distinct holiday buzz about the place, and Lilly found herself walking with a spring in her step as she approached the doctor's office.

On the wall outside the double story building was a discreet brass plaque; **Dr Jorgenson MD**, the same as the notepaper on which Carol Ann had scrawled her letter. Inside, contrary to the hustle and bustle she'd just walked through, was an oasis of calm. Peaceful, with warmly upholstered furniture, deep pile rugs and several large potted ferns. Comfortable chairs were positioned around an unlit but working Victorian fireplace, and on a half moon console table in the side alcove a tinkling water feature was displayed. Occasional tables sported a variety of magazines, and a discreet rack was filled with leaflets advertising various support services.

Lilly approached the desk where a secretary was busy at a computer.

"Hello, may I help you?"

"Yes, I have an appointment. Lilly Tweed, I telephoned yesterday."

"Yes, of course. One moment." She reached into a drawer and handed Lilly some new patient paperwork to complete.

"If you'd like to take a seat, the Doctor will be with you shortly."

Lilly sat down and filled out the paperwork, secretly wondering how much a single session was going to cost considering her appointment was a ruse. She'd just signed and dated the final sheet when a smart but casually dressed man appeared. "Miss Tweed?" he asked politely as she stood up.

"Yes, that's right."

"I'm, Dr Jorgenson. You can leave your paperwork with Sarah. Come on through."

Lilly took a deep breath. There was no going back now. Fingers crossed the doctor wouldn't be angry at her subterfuge.

೦ ೦ ೩ ೦ ೦

TAKING A SEAT in a comfortable, warm office which was as well appointed as the reception area, Lilly observed the doctor. He looked to be in his mid-forties, the same as her, with a shock of blond hair. A legacy of his Nordic heritage, she thought, judging from his name. He spoke with no discernible foreign accent, so she assumed he was several generations removed from the original Viking settlers. He took a seat opposite, pen and notepad poised on his lap.

"So, what brings you here today, Miss Tweed?" he asked kindly. "Perhaps you could start by telling me a little about yourself?"

Lilly returned the smile. "Well, I've lived here all my life. I used to work for the local paper but now run The Tea Emporium in the market square."

"Do you know, I thought I recognised your name. You used to be the gazette's agony aunt, is that right?"

"Yes, it is. In your line of work I don't suppose you agree with agony aunts, do you?"

"On the contrary. I believe there's a place for them providing you're not attempting to diagnose or treat serious illness. That's my job," he said with a smile. "I used to read your column as a matter of fact, professional interest you understand, and found it to be honest and frank with good advice. I also happen to know if you came across something you weren't able to deal with, you'd advise the writer to seek professional help."

"Oh?" Lilly said, surprised he seemed to know so much about her.

"A couple of the doctors at the local health centre are friends of mine," he said by way of explanation. "Sadly, I can't say the same for the woman who took over from over you. I'm surprised people are still writing in."

Lilly nodded. "Actually, that's really the reason I'm here. Not actually for myself. When I left the paper, I found people still writing to me. So much so in fact that I installed a letterbox at the shop for that purpose. I got one very recently that disturbed me greatly and discovered it was written on the reverse of your surgery note paper. I naturally assumed she was one of your patients?" She reached into her pocket and pulled out the letter, passing it to Dr Jorgenson.

He took his glasses from his top shirt pocket and read the letter. "Oh dear. Yes, she is one of mine. I've been working with her for a number of years and thought she was doing well. This letter seems to suggest she may have relapsed. I have an appointment with her next week, but in light of this I think I'll ask Sarah to move it forward. Thank you for bringing it to me."

Lilly realised he had no idea his patient had died. And now it was suddenly up to her to break the bad news.

"*D*R JORGENSON, I am so sorry, but Carol Ann is dead. She was found drowned in the river yesterday."

She'd definitely taken him by surprise. He stared at her slack jawed and wide eyed for a moment, then said, "Are you sure?"

"I'm afraid so. I have a reporter friend at the paper who came and told me. My reply to her letter was found in her pocket, you see. I assumed the police had already been to talk to you."

"No. No, I haven't heard a thing. Although I expect they will turn up at some point. Was it an accident do you know?"

"Possibly, although the police think it may also have been suicide," Lilly answered. "I was curious about whether you believed she would take her own life having treated her? I mean, you must have known her better than anyone I would have thought. Was she suicidal?"

"Doctor-patient confidentiality doesn't allow me to discuss Carol Ann with you, Miss Tweed."

"I think someone killed her," Lilly blurted out, much to her own surprise as the doctor's.

"I beg your pardon? Why do you think that?"

"Read her letter again. She was afraid for her life. Regardless of whether or not her fears were justified, she certainly didn't want to die. Why would she write to me in fear one minute and pleading for my help, then take her own life so soon afterwards? It doesn't make sense to me."

Dr Jorgenson got up and poured a glass of water from the crystal carafe on the sideboard. Lilly declined one when asked.

"What exactly is your interest in Carol Ann, that you felt it necessary to seek out and schedule an appointment with me, her therapist?"

Lilly sat back and sighed heavily. "Honestly? I feel guilty and somehow responsible. I feel as though I should have done something more than just write back asking her to meet with me. I should have reported her letter, or gone to find her. Perhaps if I'd done more I could have prevented her death?"

"Assuming you're not the guilty party and I'm sure you're not, that would have taken some foreknowledge of the crime. You're obviously perceptive, but I don't think you're clairvoyant, Miss Tweed. Perhaps it would be wise to schedule an appointment for yourself after all."

Lilly smiled grimly, unsure whether he was being serious. "Maybe."

"Look, I shouldn't discuss a patient with you, there are obligations with regard to confidentiality, ethical more than legal now that she is deceased, but I don't want you blaming yourself. If it sets your mind at ease, Carol Ann was a very disturbed individual."

"So you do think it was suicide?"

"If not an accident, which I think the more likely, then yes, it's possible. She'd been diagnosed with paranoid schizophrenia many years ago, long before she became my patient, that's common knowledge. And I concurred with the findings of my colleague. It's a complicated illness and one where rational thought is absent a lot of the time."

"But she was obviously afraid of something, or someone. Do you know what or who it was?"

"To be honest, it would depend on what day you asked her. But there was a recurring name mentioned; Monica."

"Who is Monica?"

"I'm not actually certain she exists at all, Miss Tweed. When her name first came up I asked her husband about it. He said they had met someone of that name at a function quite a while ago but had never socialised together again after that. It seems Carol Ann may have created a fictitious person in her mind, a nemesis if you like, but given her a name of someone she had met in real life. It was a delusion I was working through with her."

"Thank you for telling me. I know you didn't have to."

"I hope it makes you feel less responsible for what happened."

"I still feel unsettled about the whole thing," Lilly admitted. "Moreover, I don't believe she took her own life. But perhaps it *was* nothing more than a simple accident."

"Let's hope so, Miss Tweed. The alternative doesn't bear thinking about. Now, you've still got," he looked at his watch.

"Twenty-five minutes of your session left. Perhaps there's something I can help you with personally?"

❦

AFTER LEAVING DR Jorgenson's office Lilly was surprised to find herself feeling a bit better, in terms of her own involvement, regarding what happened to Carol Ann. It had, despite her insistence to herself that it would not, turned into a therapy session. Dr Jorgenson had a deep and soft melodious voice which had a definite soporific effect. She'd found herself relaxed, a rare occurrence, and comfortably discussing things she hadn't thought of in years. They'd spoken of her recent job loss and the risk she'd taken opening the shop. Her worry that it may not continue once the novelty had worn off. They'd even touched on the subject of her divorce nine years prior. It had been an amicable split, but there were aspects of it, which she hadn't fully admitted to herself, that bothered her even now. "Crikey, he's good," she muttered to herself as she left the premises. While she didn't see herself returning for any more therapy sessions, having reached a point in her life where she felt reasonably content and confident, she believed she had made a new friend of sorts in Dr Jorgenson.

Back in the market square Lilly stopped at her favourite bakery and cafe for two baguette sandwiches and some caramel slices for lunch, then returned to the shop where Stacey was, once again, handling things as though she had worked in the shop for years rather than just a matter of days.

"Lunch is served, Stacey," Lilly said, handing her the paper bag. "Just pop mine in the fridge, will you? I'll take my break when you're finished."

"Thanks, I'm so hungry. Are you sure you don't want to eat first?"

"No, you go ahead. You've earned it."

While Stacey was at lunch, Lilly busied herself with serving customers and restocking items which had sold. When it was her turn to eat, she had an idea.

After her appointment with Dr Jorgenson, the one thing which had stuck in her mind was the name Monica. While the doctor was inclined to believe she was a figment of Carol Ann's imagination, Lilly wanted to prove it one way or another and a good place to start was on-line. Almost everybody had a social media presence nowadays and after a bit of searching Lilly found not Carol Ann herself, but her husband, Joseph Hotch. It seemed he used his page primarily for professional purposes and shortly after she'd sent a friend request it was approved. This allowed her to look at his friend's list.

While not a very common name, she did find three people with the name Monica and set about searching each one individually, looking for the most likely candidate. Joseph Hotch was an architect, and his posts on the subject garnered quite a lot of interest. Two of the women had shared and commented, but there was no level of personal detail that would suggest they knew him socially. The third, however, a young woman named Monica Morris, lived locally and had commented on several of his personal posts. She was a university student, studying chemistry, and was a member of the college hockey team. If the Monica character that Carol

Ann had mentioned to Dr Jorgenson was in fact a real person, then it seemed likely this was the one.

She decided to pay a visit.

Chapter Five

"STACEY, I'VE GOT to pop out again. Will you be all right for a couple of hours?"

"Sure, no problem."

"Well, I've got..."

"Your phone if I need you?"

Lilly laughed. "Right. I'm obviously sounding like a broken record."

St John's university was a lengthy journey from the shop, so Lilly took her bike and cycled home to fetch her car. She only used it in foul weather these days or when she had a large shop to do, preferring to either walk or cycle, but the older model Mini Cooper painted in racing green, while not modern and a bit of a rattler was still reliable.

Twenty minutes later she parked in the university car-park and was walking across the tarmac to the principal building when she heard a voice calling her name. Her stomach sank.

"Abigail," she muttered. She'd only met the woman once when she handed over her job at the paper, but she'd recognise that grating voice anywhere. It was like fingernails on a blackboard. She turned and almost laughed.

Abigail was dressed in a knee-length white trench coat, tightly belted with the collar turned up, and high heeled black boots reaching up to her knees. But the cherry on top was the black fedora set at a rakish angle over hair which had been back combed to within an inch of its life. She was older than Lilly and, it had to be said, looked perfectly ridiculous. Archie was right she was after his job. But unlike Archie, she obviously felt that dressing like a female Sam Spade would automatically turn her into an investigative reporter.

"I thought that was you, Lillian."

"Hello, Abigail. How are things?"

"Well, I was going to say I can't complain. But actually I can. It's about that agony aunt letter box outside your shop. I want you to remove it. It's not your job now, dear, it's mine and you're making things difficult."

It wasn't just the ludicrous demand that astounded Lilly, but the condescending tone in which she spoke. Especially when she referred to her as 'dear.'

"I'm afraid I can't do that, Abigail. People are still writing to me for advice. But if they stop, then I'll be happy to remove it. I'm sure you agree that's fair?"

There wasn't much Abigail could say to that. But she was the sort of person who had to have the last word. "We'll see, dear. But I suppose we should bury the hatchet. I so dislike unpleasantness."

Hatchet? What hatchet? Thought Lilly. *I didn't realise there was a hatchet to bury.*

"Right. Well, anyway, if you'll excuse me, Abigail, I have to get on."

"I'll walk with you, dear. It appears we're going in the same direction."

Lilly sighed inwardly. She really could do without Abigail trailing after her. Then she had a sickening thought.

"What exactly are you doing here?"

Abigail smirked. "Hot on the trail of a clue, Lillian. I expect you already know about the body that was found? Yes, I thought you would. Anyway, I think I've found a connection between the dead woman and the university. So what do you say to that?"

"You're doing investigative journalism now?"

This wasn't quite the response Abigail had been expecting, but she gamely carried on. "Yes, of course. Being an agony aunt is rather demeaning when you have high skills elsewhere. I really should play to my strengths."

Lilly gritted her teeth. Had Abigail really no idea she'd just insulted her?

"So, Lillian, what are you doing here? Come to sell your tea in the staff canteen?"

Good grief, was there no end to the woman's vitriol? "Actually, I'm here for the same reason as you. I too found a connection between the university and the deceased woman."

Abigail stopped walking. "What? You're not a journalist. You don't even work for the paper anymore. So what do you think you are doing investigating?"

Lilly paused, wondering how much she should tell Abigail. But then again, she didn't actually know very much at all. She was here on a whim due to a gut feeling that something was amiss. She wanted to satisfy her curiosity more than anything and put to rest the uneasy feeling that she could have done something to prevent the woman's death. She wasn't really investigating; she had no experience with that sort of thing anyway. Abigail, however, did at least work for the paper and obviously something had brought her here. So, what harm could it do to be truthful with her? She took a deep breath and, although it might come back to bite her, decided to share what she knew.

"I feel somewhat responsible. You see, Carol Ann wrote to me asking for help a few days before she was found in the river. She was very upset and distressed and,... Wait a minute. If you're here, you can't think it was an accident or suicide either. You're certainly not here to write an obituary. Am I right? What made you think it's something suspicious?"

Abigail blushed and shrugged. "Reporter's intuition, I suppose. I always did have a good nose for a story."

"Rubbish! What do you know?"

"Well, how charming!" Abigail said crossly, folding her arms in defence. "Fine, if you really want to know, I met her in the waiting room at Dr Jorgenson's. He's my therapist. I spoke to the woman a few times, and while completely off her rocker, I don't believe she was suicidal. Happy now?"

Lilly softened her tone slightly. "Were you and Carol Ann friends?"

"No, of course we weren't. What a ludicrous suggestion. The woman was as mad as a box of frogs. But, I swear, if you tell anyone I've been going to therapy..."

"You're not the only one who has therapy, Abigail. Millions of people benefit from having someone to talk to, particularly a stranger. It's much easier with a qualified professional than family or friends. You should know that being an agony aunt. As a matter of fact I was there myself only this morning."

"Oh, really? I see. Well, never mind that. I really must insist you leave the investigation to me, Lillian. You're not cut out for this line of work. Please, leave it to the expert." And with that parting shot, she began to stalk away.

Lilly called out to her retreating back. "If you're worried I'm going to step on your toes, or heaven forbid, beat you to the punch, don't be. I have no intention of writing an article independently and sending it to the Gazette. Although I could if I was so inclined." She added belligerently. It was a childish retort, but the woman had really got her back up.

Abigail rounded on her so fast she nearly lost her ridiculous hat. Lilly took a step back in surprise as the furious woman strode towards her, jabbing a finger in her face.

"You know there was a reason you were let go from the paper and replaced, Lillian Tweed," she hissed. "Professionalism. A real professional would have done something about that letter you received from Carol Ann. What did you do, exactly? If only she had written to me instead, then she... Well, I think you get the point. Stop meddling where you don't belong."

Lilly felt as though Abigail had punched her in the stomach. How dare she! Okay, it was nothing she hadn't already berated herself about, but she took exception to hearing it spewed forth in such a venomous and derogatory way. She was just on the verge of retaliating when they were interrupted.

"Is everything all right over here?" the voice of a young man asked. In Lilly's anger, she almost didn't recognise him. It was Frederick Warren, the student she'd helped at the shop earlier in the week.

"Thank you for your concern, young man. I'm afraid this lady was becoming hostile with me, but it's nothing I can't handle myself. You can be on your way." Abigail replied, with a dismissive wave of her hand.

Fred glanced quickly at Lilly, then back at Abigail.

"No, it's all right I'll stay."

"Young man, you are obviously too obtuse to take a hint so I will spell it out for you. We were having a private conversation. Go back to class."

"Actually, I think I'll stick around. My classes have finished for the day."

"Well, how rude! Who do you think you are?"

"Frederick Warren," he said with a grin. "I'm not bothering anybody by being here. I'm not bothering you, am I, Miss Tweed?"

"Not at all, Fred."

"Oh, for heaven's sake. So you know each other. Very amusing." And with that, Abigail stormed off.

Lilly laughed. "Thanks for rescuing me, Fred."

"No problem. What was that all about if you don't mind me asking? It seemed pretty heated."

"Nothing much. She blows hot and cold and thinks I want her job, which is nonsense."

"She's a bit of a tartar, isn't she?"

"Good grief, Fred, where did you hear an old fashioned word like that?"

Fred shrugged. "It was a favourite of my Gran's. I never really understood what it meant until now."

Lilly laughed. "Well, it's a favourite of mine again now, too. So, how are things with you, Fred?"

"Better, actually. I took your advice and my girlfriend, well ex-girlfriend now, had a long talk."

"So, you broke up?"

"Yeah, it was necessary, and we both agreed it was for the best. I was kind and supportive like you suggested, and I think she really appreciated it. I did tell her I thought she should talk to the baby's father as soon as possible. I'm not one-hundred percent sure, but I don't think he knows she's pregnant yet."

"Well done, Fred. You should be proud of yourself."

Fred shrugged. "So what are you doing here?"

"Just visiting, nothing exciting."

"Okay. Well, I better get to class or I'll be late."

"I thought your classes were finished for the day?"

"No. A little white lie. I didn't want to leave you on your own with that woman."

"Nicely done. Thank you, Fred. Tea's on me next time you're in town."

"You're on!"

She watched as Fred sped off to his class, wondering at his ability to lie so easily and convincingly, then made her way toward the main building. It was time to find Monica Morris. Preferably without bumping into Abigail again.

※ ※ ※

*L*ILLY DIDN'T KNOW where to start in her search for Monica, but as luck would have it, one of her regular patrons at the shop was in the reception area carrying an official looking clipboard as she entered.

"Hello, Janet. I didn't know you worked here, I thought you'd retired?"

"Hello, Lilly. You're a long way from town. Yes, I'm one of the administrators. Been here for, oh, it must be going on four years now. I found retirement didn't really suit me once I'd lost Reg. Not enough to do to fill in the days. I was a student here many moons ago, and when the job came up, I decided to apply. I didn't expect to get it, of course, but was thrilled when I did. It's been a Godsend quite frankly. So, are you wanting help with something?"

"I'm looking for a student, actually. She's a member of the hockey team if that's any help?"

"I assume she's written to you for advice? We do have a qualified counsellor on the faculty but of course some students prefer to seek outside help."

Although she felt a tad guilty, Lilly didn't put her right.

"I can't tell you where a specific student might be, but the girl's hockey team are all housed in G-Block. Just follow the path round the side of this building and it's directly behind. Someone there should be able to help you."

"Thanks, Janet. Pop into the shop sometime, I've a new blend of Oolong I think you might like."

"Lovely. I'll do that, I'm almost out of my usual blend. Would you mind signing in before you go to G-Block, Lilly? Anyone who is visiting is supposed to do so at reception."

"Oh, are they? No, of course I don't mind."

Lilly followed Janet to the reception desk where she signed the visitor's book, giving her name, the date and time. She listed her reason for visiting as seeing a student resident in G block on a private matter, which Janet authorised by co-signing. Tellingly, Abigail had not yet signed in.

She then exited the building and followed Janet's directions. Five minutes later she found herself outside G-Block. Jogging up the stone steps, she opened the main door and only narrowly avoided being knocked over by a short girl carrying a tall box.

"Gosh, I'm so sorry. I didn't see you. Can't see much of anything actually," she giggled.

"Don't worry, you missed me," Lilly said, taking in the hive of activity inside. "Are you getting ready for a party?"

"Yes. The ten-year reunion for past students. It's chaos as normal, but it usually works out all right in the end. Are you an old student?"

"Actually, Janet in admin just sent me over. I'm looking for Monica Morris?"

"Oh, right. She's in the common room. Just through that door over there," she indicated with a toss of her head. "She's the one in charge so you can't miss her."

"Thank you."

The common room was huge, at least the size of a tennis court, Lilly thought. With sofas and easy chairs arranged around tables and shelves full of books and board games. A television was secured to a bracket and hung on the wall opposite a large sideboard which was currently being filled with polished glasses. A large trestle table at the opposite end was being assembled by three girls with another waiting to lay a pristine white table cloth. And in the corner several students were blowing up white balloons with the number 10, in gold, emblazoned across the front. *Now,* thought Lilly, *where is Monica?* Due to the photographs from her on-line profile, Lilly knew what the girl looked like; tall, slim and very attractive with long chestnut hair. She spied her a moment later in the corner looking officious with a clip-board. As the girl with the box had told her, she was obviously the head organiser.

Lilly wandered over.

"Monica Morris?"

The girl glanced up, dark eyed and demure. "That's me. Can I help you?"

"Actually, I was wondering if you could spare me a few minutes? Is there somewhere we can talk in private?"

"Is it about the reunion?"

"No, it's something else. Not related to the university."

"Oh. Well, all right. I could do with a break, actually. Let's go outside it's quieter there."

She scribbled some additional notes, Lilly catching a glimpse of all the fine details which would make the reunion party a well-oiled success, then handed her clip-board to another girl explaining she'd be out in the garden if needed and exited through a side door at the back of the block. Lilly followed her into a lovely flower garden with several picnic tables and they sat down.

"It's really lovely out here, do the students maintain it?"

Monica nodded. "There are full-time gardeners for most of the property, but this area is looked after by volunteers from the agricultural courses mainly, although other students get involved, too. She took a small paper bag from her pocket and offered Lilly a ginger chew.

"No, thanks."

"So, how can I help? Sorry, what did you say your name was?" Monica asked.

"Lilly Tweed."

Monica eyed her curiously. "Do we know each other? I don't recognise your name?"

"No, we haven't met before, I'm..." it suddenly occurred to Lilly how odd it would look to appear out of nowhere asking personal questions. She would hardly have clout as a former agony aunt and current shop owner. So, with the recent spat with Abigail forefront in her mind, she just blurted out the first thing that came to her. "I'm a reporter. I was wondering if the name Carol Ann Hotch means anything to you?"

Monica started. "Is this some sort of joke?"

"A joke? No, not at all. I'm quite serious. You do know her, then?"

"Yes, I know Carol Ann. She's crazy."

"I'm sorry to have to tell you, but she's also dead, I'm afraid."

"Dead? Really? Oh, my god, I'm so sorry. Maybe I shouldn't have said that, but she's been harassing me. It's been pretty scary, actually. I had to call the police, eventually."

"Can you tell me what happened?"

"Look, I'm really not comfortable about being mentioned in the paper or anything. It's been really stressful and if I'm honest, my studies have been affected. It's made concentrating difficult when I've been constantly looking over my shoulder. I just want to forget about it and pass my exams." Suddenly her brown eyes widened as a memory obviously occurred to her. "Wait, was it her they found in the river?"

"Yes, it was," Lilly nodded. "How did you hear about it?"

"Some of the guys in my class were talking about a suicide or something, but they didn't know who it was. I wasn't really listening, just caught a few snippets, but it's not exactly a common occurrence round here, is it? I literally just put two and two together as you were speaking."

"Monica, while I was doing some research I found out, obviously correctly, you may have known Carol Ann, it's the reason I'm here. I'm hoping to learn more about her. If you don't mind me asking, how did the two of you meet?"

Monica sighed heavily and gazed off into the distance. Lilly wondered if she was going to change her mind about talking to her. Fortunately, she finally shrugged and turned back.

"I met her about a year ago at a reunion, here. Her husband was a former student, and she came with him. We hardly spoke at all during the event, but I must have made some sort of impression because she was fixated with me after that. Since then, I've been getting some crazy calls from her. Then last week..." Monica paused, seemingly reluctant to carry on.

"What happened last week?" Lilly urged gently.

"God, I hope what happened wasn't the reason she died. Did she really kill herself?"

"We don't know that for sure as yet. It could just as easily have been a tragic accident. Go on, Monica. Tell me what happened."

"She broke in here, smashed a window in the middle of the night and started screaming and shouting. She was completely hysterical. It woke everyone up. We called security and they escorted her off the premises. We didn't press charges or anything. I mean, it was obvious she wasn't in her right mind, but I messaged her husband and told him what had happened. I did say if she did it again, we'd make it official with the police and get a restraining order. I feel really awful about that now."

"What day was this?"

"A couple of days before she was found. Look, I know you'll be writing an article, but I don't want to be in the paper, okay? If she killed herself because of me then... well, you know what gossip's like, I'll get blamed even though it's not my fault."

"Don't worry, I'll keep your name out of it," Lilly assured her. "But I'd like to have a chat with some of the other girls. Maybe one of them would be willing to give me a quote instead?"

"Yes, maybe."

"Just one other thing. Do you know why Carol Ann was so fixated with you?"

"Seriously, I have absolutely no idea. Maybe I reminded her of someone else? That's the only thing I can think of because I didn't know her."

Lilly nodded. "Okay, thanks for your time, Monica. I'll let you get back."

✇

*L*ILLY SAT IN the garden for a moment after Monica had gone back inside collecting her thoughts. It seemed likely that Carol Ann had seen something in the girl that wasn't really there. Something traumatic from her past, perhaps, that had been brought to the fore on meeting Monica. A mannerism, a look, or the way she talked that reminded her of something or someone else. Lilly was pleased she'd managed to find the right Monica, but it was obviously a dead end. She got up and decided to walk through the gardens, which enveloped the building on three sides.

There were large swathes of lawn, some rising to form small hillocks where Lilly could imagine students gathering in the summer months to socialise or study. Large trees would give much needed shade on hotter days and the flower beds, where new shoots were just poking through, would be a riot of colour and scent. It was a lovely space, very calm and relaxing.

She continued to walk the pathway around the block and came across a boarded-up window at the side of the building. No doubt the one Monica had referred to. On impulse, she tried the nearby door and found it unlocked. It led directly into a large kitchen where several students were preparing food.

"Hello," said one of the girls. "Are you lost? This is for students only you really shouldn't be here."

Lilly saw another girl pick up a rolling pin, ready to swing if it became necessary. Obviously the break-in had left them nervous and wary of strangers. Understandable, she thought.

She held up her hands placatingly, "Don't worry. Reporter. I'm investigating the break-in last week. Were any of you here at the time?"

"I was," the girl with the rolling pin said. "I'm Tracey Scott."

"Do you mind if I ask you a few questions, Tracey?"

"So long as you don't mind me rolling the pastry while we talk. I've already ruined one batch of quiches."

"You're baking for the reunion, I take it?"

"That's right. We're all studying catering and hospitality. These events go towards our degree qualifications."

"So, the woman who broke in, Carol Ann, had she ever done anything like this before?"

"She's never broken in before. But that's where she got in if you're interested," Tracey said, pointing to the boarded-up window. "It was pretty frightening, I can tell you. It was the middle of the night and sounded really loud. She threw a brick through it and then climbed in. By the time we all got down here she was just standing here screaming and crying. Hands and knees covered in blood where she'd cut herself on the glass. I called security and another girl, Olivia, tried to calm her down and made her sit at the table before she hurt herself further. Or one of us. She was rambling a lot and shouting. It was a total nightmare."

"What was she rambling about?"

"Monica, she's one of the students who lives here."

"Yes, I've just been talking to her outside, actually."

"Right. Well, this woman was accusing Monica of stealing from her. Monica didn't know what she was talking about, but her presence was making Carol Ann worse. Really agitated, so we told her it would be better if she left. She waited in the common room until security came and took Carol Ann away."

Lilly glanced round the rest of the girls who were all doing other chores but listening closely. Once Tracey had finished, one of them spoke up.

"It was the first time she broke in, but it wasn't the first weird thing she did. She's shown up here before, walking around looking for Monica. We've told her she shouldn't be here, but that just made her angry. She would wait outside Monica's classes and follow her back here. About a month ago we reported it to the university security, and they started keeping an eye out for her. All visitors are supposed to sign in at reception, but it's hardly ever enforced. And it's closed at night, anyway. I think things have improved a bit since Carol Ann broke in though."

Lilly shook her head. "I didn't realise how serious it was."

"Well, breaking in was the most serious," Tracey said. "Before that, she'd just sent letters here and walked around the grounds. I think she called Monica a few times too, and she was getting really stressed about it, so we made sure she wasn't left on her own. I don't get why Carol Ann had it in for Monica, she didn't even know her. She's obviously got a bit of a screw loose. I feel a bit sorry for her if I'm honest, but it was really disturbing for all of us, especially Monica."

"Yes, I can imagine. Well, I think that's all I need. Thanks for your time. Good luck with the event."

Lilly exited the same way she had entered and paused outside the broken window. It was quite high up and glancing below she realised Carol Ann must have rolled the heavy rock in place to give herself an added boost. *She really had been determined to get in*, Lilly thought as she tried to lift the rock herself. In doing so, her pulse quickened when she saw a glint of metal. Scratching away the earth, she revealed a ring with two keys attached. On the disk were the engraved initials C.A.H.

"Carol Ann Hotch," Lilly said softly, shoving them in her pocket.

Should she try to find out what they unlocked?

A S LILLY WALKED back to her car, a quick glance at her phone made her realise just how late it was getting. She'd spent much longer at the university than planned and hadn't intended to leave Stacey at the shop on her own for so long. She hopped in her car and the radio came on as she started the engine. A traffic report announcing that due to an accident, the road she would normally take back to town was closed.

Of course it is, she thought. She'd better phone the shop.

"The Tea Emporium, Stacey speaking."

"Stacey, it's Lilly. I'm heading back now, but there's been a traffic accident on the main road into town so I'll have to take the scenic route. Can you manage for a while longer?"

"Yep, no problem."

"Okay, I'll be back as soon as I can."

"No need to rush. We don't want you getting in accident as well."

"My car doesn't go that fast, to be honest. See you soon."

As she pulled out of the car-park, her thoughts turned to the keys she had found. There was no doubt they belonged to Carol Ann. They were her initials and found under the rock which she'd used to boost herself through the university window. But what would they open? One was a standard Yale door key, so a house or a flat somewhere most likely. The other was much smaller, more solid and old fashioned. She had no idea what that could access. She was relieved to have found them first, though. Just as she'd been leaving, she'd heard the unmistakable voice of Abigail coming from the kitchen. However, Tracey and the other girls were in no mood to repeat themselves and flatly refused to talk to her. By now Abigail would have realised that Lilly had beaten her to it, and knowing her would be incandescent with rage. She full expected the woman to seek her out and give her a mouthful. Oh well, there was nothing she could do about it now. Her main concern was whether to hand in the keys or use them to further her investigation. It was a matter of ethics, and Lilly wasn't altogether comfortable with the way her brain was thinking.

Chapter Six

TEN MINUTES LATER, as she turned onto a long and straight stretch of road on the outskirts of town, a fancy car whipped around her right side, overtaking at a dangerous speed and in front of on-coming traffic.

"Idiot. No wonder there are so many accidents," Lilly said out loud to the reckless motorist.

She tapped the foot on the brakes to avoid getting too close as the errant driver tried to overtake another car, only to be met with a truck coming the other way. They swerved back in too close to the car in front and instinctively slammed on the brakes to avoid a collision. But Lilly didn't realise the brakes had been depressed as there were no red lights. She immediately slammed on her own, but it was too late. She clipped the bumper, causing it to spin ninety degrees and come to rest sideways across the lane. The driver's side window facing her.

"You've got to be kidding," Lilly exclaimed as she came eye to eye with a furious Abigail Douglas.

She'd never in all her years of driving been involved in an accident, and it took a short while to calm down and stop shaking before she had the presence of mind to turn on her hazard warning lights. The car which Abigail had tried to overtake had also stopped, and the driver had got out. Waiting by the passenger side of his vehicle, his warning lights flashing to alert other motorists from both directions there was an immediate hazard and to slow down. He'd be a good witness, Lilly thought as she took a deep breath and opened her door.

Abigail was already at the back of her Porsche, assessing the damage. "My car! You've hit my car. You did that deliberately, Lillian Tweed! I'm calling the police."

"Honestly, Abigail, I didn't even know it was you. Are you all right?"

"No, of course I'm not all right. Look at my car! What were you thinking?"

"Calm down and stop shouting at me. It was you who was driving like a maniac," Lilly said.

She went to the rear of the vehicle and saw the bend in the back bumper. It would need fixing, but it was hardly catastrophic. By the same token, her own car, apart from some missing paintwork, was miraculously unscathed. They had both been very lucky.

"Is that the police? Yes, I'd like to report an accident on the university road going into Plumpton Mallet. Yes, that's the one. This stupid, idiot driver just drove into the back of me and damaged my car," shrieked Abigail into her phone.

Lilly rolled her eyes. If Abigail was going to be so melodramatic, she'd be better waiting in her car for the police. She began to walk that way when she heard Abigail screech behind her.

"She's trying to leave! Wait, let me get her number plate," she shouted, running behind Lilly's car.

"I'm not trying to leave, Abigail. Don't be so ridiculous. I'm going to wait in my car so I don't have to listen to you shrieking like a banshee. And you hardly need to take note of my number plate details when you know who I am."

Back in her car, Lilly wound down her window slightly so she could still hear what Abigail was saying, and rubbed her neck. It was aching a bit. No doubt she had a bit of whiplash from the collision.

Abigail was now on another call. "Yes, of course, *that* Lillian Tweed. How many Lillian Tweeds are there in Plumpton Mallet?" she snarled. "So, I'll be late back to the office…"

Lilly picked up her own phone and sent a quick text to Stacey saying she'd been delayed. No point telling her truth and worrying her. Then she sat back and waited for the police to arrive. Ten minutes after Abigail had called, a police car pulled up behind Lilly's Mini and a familiar face got out. Sergeant Bonnie Phillips. She was Archie Brown's contact at the station and Lilly's friend. She also had a colleague with her, a younger officer who, after speaking with Bonnie, went to get a statement from the driver of the third vehicle who was still patiently waiting a few metres up the road.

"So, would you like to tell me what happened?" Bonnie asked Lilly. But before she could draw breath, Abigail interrupted.

"She drove into the back of my car. Look at the damage! I want her arrested."

"It's, Ms Douglas, isn't it? Abigail? Well, I was speaking to Miss Tweed, here. I'll get to you in a moment."

"It's all right, Bonnie. Take her statement first. I'll wait."

Lilly leant against the bonnet of her car while Bonnie took Abigail's statement. After several *'it was her fault's'* Lilly tuned out. She came back to the present as the police officer told Abigail to start her car, turn on her lights and depress the brakes.

From the rear of the Porsche, Bonnie confirmed the brake lights were out.

"With limited damage to your vehicle, I suspect these were faulty at the time, causing Miss Tweed to hit your car. Is that correct, Lilly?"

"Yes. I had no idea she had braked until it was too late."

"What rubbish," Abigail hissed. "I've only had this car a few weeks there can't be a fault such as you suggest."

"Are you calling an officer of the law a liar, Ms Douglas?"

Abigail spluttered, realising the trouble she was getting herself into, and backtracked a little. "Well no, of course not but..."

"I will be writing you a vehicle defect rectification notice for your faulty lights. I suggest you take the car to Dan's garage immediately and get them fixed. Ah, one moment, my colleague is beckoning."

Lilly watched Bonnie walk up the road, fully aware in her peripheral vision that Abigail was shooting daggers at her, but she refused to meet her gaze. After a brief conversation with her colleague and the witness, both police officers returned and the other driver left.

"Ms Douglas, having spoken to the witness and received his sworn statement, it is apparent you were driving erratically. You will shortly receive a summons to court to answer to the charge of careless driving."

"What?" Abigail staggered back, all colour draining from her face.

"Abigail," said Lilly, stepping forward. "For goodness' sake apologise. If this gets as far as court, you could lose your license. If that happens, then you could lose your job as well."

Abigail stared at Lilly as though she didn't understand what she was saying. Lilly turned to Bonnie.

"Bonnie, is this Abigail's first offence?"

Bonnie checked the police national computer from her tablet, "Yes, it is."

"Would you be prepared to let her off with a warning? There's been no one hurt, thankfully. She'll take the car to be fixed immediately she leaves here. Your colleague can even drive her car himself straight to Dan's garage. And she'll promise never to do it again. That's right, isn't it, Abigail?"

"Yes, that's right," she said, finally coming to her senses. "I apologise, officer, I was in a rush to get to the office to file my article before the deadline and wasn't thinking properly. It won't happen again."

Lilly looked at Bonnie, waiting for her response.

"You're lucky to have such an understanding friend, Ms Douglas, that's all I can say." Bonnie said eventually, much to Lilly's relief. "I suggest you take your car to be fixed now. You'll have fourteen days to provide proof to us that your lights are in full working order. You're free to go but consider this a warning. If I find out you've gone over the speed limit by as little as one mile per hour, I'll throw you in the nearest cell. Understood?"

"Yes. Yes, of course. Thank you, officer." Abigail stammered and hurriedly got in her car.

They watched her drive away, and then Bonnie turned to Lilly. "You're far too nice for your own good, you know."

Lilly shrugged. "I fully admit she is a pain in the rear end, but I don't want her to lose her job, Bonnie. Yes, she's conceited and thinks a lot of herself, but sometimes that means there's an underlying feeling of inferiority. It's possible her brash and boastful personality is a result of something in her past. Apart from her taking over my job at the paper, I don't know anything about her. Who knows what's happened in her life?"

"You're giving her the benefit of the doubt, you mean?"

Lilly nodded.

"All right, I'll accept that knowing you like I do, but remember you can't take everyone's problems on your own shoulders, Lilly. You're under no obligation to help the likes of Abigail Douglas, she, and people like her, need to be responsible for their own actions and accept the consequences accordingly."

"I know. It's a fault of mine. I'm working on it. So, how are things with you? I've not seen you since I left the paper.

I'd thought you'd have popped into the shop for a cuppa before now?"

"I thought so too, but we're a bit short staffed so I've more on my plate than usual. What with that, studying for my detective exams and now this body being found, I've hardly had time to breathe. Archie said he told you about Carol Ann Hotch when we found your letter in her pocket?"

"Yes, he did. That's why I've been out today. I found a connection between her and the university."

"The break-in at G-block, you mean? Yes, a colleague was on call for that. It's not the first incident involving Carol Ann, though."

"Oh? Anything you can share with me?"

"She called us out on her landlord a few times. Accused him of breaking into her flat in the early hours."

"Was there any truth to it?"

Bonnie shook her head. "None that we could tell. It's difficult when all you've got is a *'he-said-she-said'* dynamic. There was no sign of forced entry and what with Carol Ann's medical history, it was difficult to believe what she was saying was true."

"That's really disheartening, Bonnie."

Bonnie nodded. "So, why exactly are you getting involved with this death? It was either a tragic accident or suicide, as far as we can tell so far."

"Look, don't take this the wrong way, I'm not telling you how to do your job. But I don't think it was either. There are some things that don't add up. It's just a..."

"No, please don't say it, Lilly," Bonnie groaned.

"A gut feeling."

"You know, gut feelings and hunches are for books and television? It doesn't happen in real life. In real life we follow the evidence."

"I did say don't take it the wrong way. Apparently, Abigail Douglas thinks the same as me."

"I've known you long enough not to take it the wrong way, Lilly. I hope you'll take what I'm about to say in the same vein: Remember which one of us is the police officer."

LILLY LEFT BONNIE a few minutes later, with the police officer promising that if she heard anything that would shed new light on Carol Ann's death then she would let either Lilly or Archie know. But anything Lilly was told was not to be used as an excuse to go dashing about investigating. She might like her afternoon tea and tisanes, but she was neither Marple nor Poirot and shouldn't forget it.

She drove directly back to the shop rather than picking up her bike from home. She'd already been away much longer than intended and felt bad that she'd left Stacey to run things on her own. She parked up beside Stacey's broken-down car and dashed in the back entrance, going through the storeroom to the main shop.

Inside, Stacey was efficiently floating from customer to customer, dispensing advice on various teas and brewing samples. She rang up sales from several customers while Lilly grabbed her own apron and joined her behind the counter.

Eventually, with the shop almost empty, Lilly apologised for taking so long.

"No problem," Stacey said. "I've managed. So what happened?"

"I got into a car accident. I'm fine and so is my car, so don't worry."

"Oh, wow. I'm sorry. I won't ever joke about that again."

"I doubt you hold that much power in the cosmos, Stacey," Lilly laughed. "Anyway, while I remember, here are the details of a garage who can mend your car. Dan's an old friend, so he'll either tow it home for you or take it back and fix it, whichever you want. But if you mention my name and the fact you're a student, he'll give you a discount."

"That's cool, thanks so much. I was wondering what I was going to do about it. I'll give him a call now."

Despite the accident and being away from her business for so long, Lilly felt she'd accomplished quite a lot. She'd certainly learned a lot more about Carol Ann Hotch and also had the keys she'd found currently burning a hole in her pocket. Should she use them or give them to the police? She'd had plenty of opportunity to hand them over to Bonnie earlier, so why hadn't she? Perhaps because Bonnie was convinced there was nothing suspicious about the death? It was a dilemma and one she'd need to think about seriously. Hopefully by the time it came to closing, she'd have made her mind up about how to proceed.

*B*ACK AT HOME she fed Earl then heated up some lasagna for herself. Taking her plate and cup to the table, she turned on her laptop and with Carol Ann's letter by her side, made a search for her address. It didn't take her long to find the building. A former bijou hotel owned by a single landlord had been converted into eight flats. As many of the larger properties on the periphery of the town had been, sadly. They obviously were no longer financially viable as single resident dwellings.

It wasn't a part of the town she'd had much reason to visit previously, being at the opposite end to both her home and her shop, but she knew vaguely where it was. She quickly snapped a picture on her phone, then took her empty plate to the sink.

"So what do you think, Earl? Bonnie's right, I'm not a police officer, but there's something niggling at me about this case. I mean, Carol Ann wrote to me asking for help. I have her keys in my pocket. What harm could it do just to check her flat and see if there's something inside that would help determine what happened to her one way or another?"

Earl jumped onto the counter and giving a loud meow, head-butted her arm. She reached out and scratched his ears, feeling the immediate purr reverberating beneath her fingers.

"Yes, you're right. I've already made my mind up, haven't I?"

A few minutes later Lilly had changed into jeans and a warm jumper. She grabbed her fleece from the hook in the hall and shouting goodbye to Earl, locked up and grabbed her bike. If the on-line map was correct, there was a short-cut she could use which would avoid the main roads and end up not far from Carol Ann's home.

She turned left outside her garden gate and rode to the top of the lane, then took another left to join the pathways that ran alongside the river. Ten minutes later, she turned right onto a cycle trail that ran through the woods. It was still light enough to see even with the overhead canopy of Evergreens, but her return journey would have to take another route. Obviously there was no light source through the woods and it would be foolhardy and dangerous to attempt to cycle through it in the dark, and it would be too far to walk even if she could see where she was going. She cycled for a further fifteen minutes, then not far from the exit and close to the road where Carol Ann's building was, she was forced to stop when her phone rang. It was Archie. She dismounted and continued on foot, pushing the bike to her destination while they talked.

"I don't know how you did it, Lilly, but your instincts were bang on."

"In what way?"

"I've just got word from Abigail. The wretched woman muscled in on my investigation again by answering my phone and pretending we were working together. Can you believe her cheek? Anyway, at least she had the decency to share what she'd found out. It was the autopsy results on Carol Ann. She overdosed."

"Ah, okay. That's really sad news to hear, Archie. But why does that mean my instincts were correct? My thoughts were the opposite. I didn't think it was suicide, but if it was an overdose after all..."

"Well, that's the thing," Archie said, his excitement at genuine news palpable. "There were abrasions inside her mouth and some other indicators that she wasn't alone. Bruising, etc. I can't give you all the official medical terminology. But, to cut a long story short, Lilly, someone forced the tablets down her throat. You were right all along. The police are now treating it as murder."

"**I** KNEW IT!" LILLY exclaimed. "There was something about this whole scenario that just didn't feel right. Oh, poor Carol Ann... I can't begin to imagine what she went through. She must have been terrified."

"So, tell me, what do you actually know? I just got an earful from Abigail when she got back to the office. Did you really crash into her car?"

"Oh, for heaven's sake. What's she been saying?"

"That you both got into an accident coming back from St. John's. She suggested you may have done it deliberately."

"Well, quite frankly that's a lie, Archie. She was driving like a lunatic and her brake lights didn't work. She made an emergency stop having tried and failed to overtake the car in front with traffic coming the other way, and I ran into the back of her. It was a complete accident and one I had no hope of avoiding. I don't suppose she told you that Bonnie was about to arrest her for dangerous driving, which would have meant she could have lost her license, her job and possibly gone to prison?"

"No, it must have slipped her mind to share that nugget of information. So Bonnie attended the scene did she?"

"Yes. And it was only the fact that I persuaded her to let Abigail off with a ticket and caution that she was allowed to go at all."

Archie barked out a laugh. "You are much too nice, Lilly Tweed."

"Bonnie said the same thing. I'm beginning to think you're right now you've told me Abigail is blaming me. A charming way to repay a favour isn't it? I hope no one believes her."

"Don't worry, they don't. We've got the measure of Abigail Douglas. But I'm curious what you two were doing at the university in the first place?"

"I went there trying to track down someone Carol Ann may have known," Lilly explained. "I subsequently found out she broke into student accommodation; G-Block and caused a scene. I think Abigail had uncovered details of the break-in and had gone to ask about that."

"But you went to talk to someone specific? Who?" Archie asked. "Give me a leg up on Abigail, would you? She's really starting to annoy me the way she's barging in on my job. I'm running several investigations at once, while she's only got this case, so she's beating me to the punch on this one every time. She's making me look incompetent."

"I don't mind helping you, Archie, but you must give me your word that you won't let this girl know you got her name from me? And more importantly, that her name won't appear in the paper? She made me promise her, and she's been through a lot already with Carol Ann. She's already falling behind on her course work due to the stress, and I think she's pretty close to breaking point. For some reason Carol Ann was utterly obsessed with her."

"Cross my heart, Lilly. And a good newspaperman never reveals his sources."

"Okay, her name is Monica Morris."

"Thanks, Lilly."

"Excuse me, can I help you?" a voice said. Lilly had arrived at Carol Ann's home a minute or two previously and had been leaning on the palings surrounding the communal garden at the front while chatting with Archie. She turned and came face-to-face with a stocky, florid looking man with a stern frown.

"Archie, I've got to go. Let me know if anything interesting turns up."

"Likewise. Bye for now, Lilly."

She hung up and warily faced the man in front of her, sincerely hoping there wouldn't be any trouble.

Chapter Seven

"**H**ELLO, DO YOU live here?" Lilly began.

"Why, are you looking for a flat?"

"Sort of. I'm looking for Carol Ann Hotch's place?"

The man's frown deepened. "What business do you have with Carol Ann?" he asked sharply.

"She recently passed away…" Lilly began, but the man interrupted her.

"Yes, I know. The police informed me this morning. I'm Barney Darwin. I own the building. Are you with the police?"

"No, nothing like that. My name is Lillian Tweed, Carol Ann wrote to me shortly before she died."

"You're the agony aunt for the paper?" he said.

Lilly nodded. "I used to be."

"Yeah, I thought I recognised the name. I wrote to you once. Long time ago now. Anonymously, but you helped me out. It was great advice, actually."

"I'm glad I could help you."

"So, what are you doing here, Miss Tweed?"

"Well, as I was saying, I received a letter from Carol Ann shortly before she was found in the river. She was asking for my help, but she died before we could meet. I'm trying to get some answers, I suppose. I understand from a police sergeant friend that she gave her landlord some trouble in the past. That would be you, would it?"

Barney sighed heavily and stuck both hands in his jacket pockets. "She was a nice woman, but she had some problems. Paranoia, seeing things that weren't there, that sort of thing. She was a little crazy, to be honest. I expect you know all about that? She called the police on me two, maybe three times accusing me of breaking into her flat. Which was ridiculous. I don't have any business being in one of my tenant's homes unless they need something fixing. And then I make an appointment."

"What made her think you were breaking in?"

"Miss Tweed, if I knew, I'd tell you. Sometimes I'd see her in her garden at the back and she'd randomly shout about how she'd seen me in her kitchen during the night. No truth to it, but she believed what she was saying because she was ill, so I couldn't really blame her. She had hallucinations apparently, normal for the problem she had, where she would see or hear things that didn't exist outside her own mind. I put it down to that."

"It must have been a nuisance for you?"

He shrugged. "Yeah, but the police were pretty understanding after it happened the first time. It got on my nerves a bit, sure. You never know what other people might think, do you? Even though it wasn't true it could easily have ruined my reputation. You know how the saying goes, no smoke without fire? But in this case, there was. Luckily folk realised it was all in her mind and she couldn't help it. It was her illness. She once told me she thought the paperboy was a government spy, I mean how ridiculous does that sound? But she was unstable, especially if she forgot to take her tablets. I was always sorry I couldn't do more to help her, but she was suffering from paranoid delusions."

Not that paranoid, Lilly thought. *Someone did kill her.*

"I was hoping you'd let me into her flat," she said, cutting to the chase.

Barney was visibly surprised at the question. "What? No, of course I won't, it's private property. Besides, her husband is coming along shortly to start clearing the place out."

Lilly nodded. "Yes, of course, I understand. I was just looking for answers, that's all."

"Well, you won't find them here, Miss Tweed. I suggest you go home and leave things to the police."

"I suppose you're right," Lilly said with a smile. "Thanks for your time, Mr Darwin."

She gripped the bike's handlebars and began to wheel it away from the railings, up the road. Out of the corner of her eye, she watched as the landlord approached and entered the front ground-floor flat.

He obviously hadn't realised it, but he'd given Lilly a clue as to which flat had belonged to Carol Ann. The large

Victorian building had been broken up into eight flats; four on the ground floor, two at the front and two at the back, mirrored on the second floor. The front ground floor flats shared the communal gardens, but the ones on the ground floor at the rear had their own. There were only two of them, and Barney had mentioned seeing Carol Ann in her garden. Lilly only had to try the key in two locks to find the one she wanted.

She wheeled her bike around the side of the building and leant it up against the wall. Creeping to the edge, she peered around the corner and discovered high fencing surrounding the plots. At the end there were two tall wood gates, one for each flat. The first flat had a light on, which made Lilly's job much easier.

She carefully opened the gate of the second garden and tip toed down the path to the door. The flat, as expected, was in total darkness. Taking the Yale key, she inserted it into the lock. It turned with a satisfying click. She was in.

*F*OR OBVIOUS REASONS she didn't dare turn on any of the lights, but there was a torch function on her phone which would work well. She had entered straight into a small galley kitchen. She shone the torch around briefly, but there was nothing much to see. No cups or plates in the sink, nothing on the worktops except a white microwave, a silver kettle and matching toaster. The cupboards revealed the usual things a kitchen would house, but there was nothing that would help her.

She moved across the central hall into the room opposite, a lounge with a window looking onto the garden, framed in faded green and blue chintz curtains. Again the place was pristine, almost austere. One double seat sofa and a matching armchair in grey cord. A nest of small tables and a plain blue rug in front of a gas fire. On the chimney breast was an old art deco style mirror hanging from a picture hook by a chain. There were no knick-knacks or photos. No books or magazines. Nothing personal at all. It was the least homely home Lilly had ever been in, and she wondered how long Carol Ann had actually been living here?

She returned to the small hall and found the bathroom, again almost empty. A couple of green towels hanging over the bath and a bottle of shampoo in the corner. A bar of soap, a toothbrush and a toothpaste tube on the sink. The mirror faced cupboard above was completely empty. No sign it had ever been used at all, which Lilly found odd. Finally she entered the last room at the rear, which was the bedroom. Even here it was apparent Carol Ann had not really settled in. There was a single photograph in a silver frame on her nightstand, a picture of her in happier days with a handsome, dark haired man who she assumed was her husband.

The wardrobe revealed a neat but sparse row of clothing. Lilly diligently went through the pockets but came up empty handed. Shining the torch on the floor of the wardrobe, she found something far more interesting. A small steel safe. Crouching down, she examined it further. Pulling to the side a little metal disk revealed a key hole. One that would take a small, old-fashioned key. Lilly smiled and brought out the keys she'd found at St. John's. As she'd hoped, the small one unlocked the safe.

Inside, she found an antique pocket watch and a single photograph. She closed the safe and took the items to the bed where she could get a better look. Shining the torch on the photo, she was shocked to discover it was of none other than Monica Morris, smiling happily with a small white dog in her arms. A Pomeranian.

"I've seen something like this before. I know I have. But where?" Lilly muttered. Then she remembered. She grabbed her phone and began hurriedly scrolling through the images until she found the one she wanted. It was the photo Archie had given her of Carol Ann Hotch. The one where she was holding a small, white Pomeranian dog.

"No wonder Carol Ann was so obsessed with her. All that following her around and accusing her of being a thief. Monica must have stolen her dog."

Suddenly she caught a familiar noise. One she really didn't want to hear. Someone had just unlocked the front door and entered the flat. She hurriedly stuffed the photograph and the watch in her pocket and dashed to the bedroom door. Peering out, she saw a man crossing the hallway from the kitchen to the lounge. Heart pounding, Lilly stepped back into the bedroom, intent on finding a way to escape. Too late she realised there wasn't a window. She was trapped.

*L*ILLY TOOK A deep breath. Breaking and entering 101; be confident and pretend you belong there. She'd read that somewhere. It was probably nonsense, but what did she have to lose?

The light turned on and the man jumped back in shock, bumping into the hall wall.

"Hey! Who are you? What are you doing in my wife's flat?"

"Mr Hotch? I am so sorry, I didn't know you were coming. I'm Lilly Tweed, your wife wrote to me just before she died. Please accept my condolences for your loss."

There was a moment's pause as he considered her words. "All right. But that still doesn't explain what you're doing in here. How did you get in?"

"The door was unlocked." Admittedly she shouldn't have lied, but it was instinctual. Besides, there was no going back now. "I shouldn't have come in, I know, but..."

"No, you shouldn't. I've come to collect her belongings, but you still haven't told me what you're doing here?"

"Your wife wrote to me, like I said. I used to be the agony aunt with the Gazette. In her letter she sounded terribly distressed and I wrote back asking to meet so I could help. Apparently my letter was found in her pocket when she was pulled from the river. I've been distraught about the whole thing and was just looking for answers about what happened. I thought there might be something here that could help me. It's for my own peace of mind, really. I just wish I'd been able to help her."

Joseph's expression softened slightly. Now she looked at him closely he looked exhausted and grief-stricken.

"Believe me, Miss Tweed, you're not the only one. I shouldn't have let her move here. I knew she shouldn't have been alone for an extended length of time. That she wouldn't cope. But she was so insistent, and my attempts at trying to dissuade her just made things worse. I should have come and got her sooner."

"Why was she here, if you don't mind me asking?"

There was a momentary tension in his jaw as he gritted his teeth. Lilly was afraid she'd intruded too much, but then he relaxed again and replied.

"We were separated. For about a year now. She's been fighting a losing battle with schizophrenia for a long time and her paranoia was gaining ground. If I'm being honest, I was growing frustrated with it all. I needed a break, so when she packed up and told me she was leaving, I eventually gave in and let her go. I should have made a better effort to stop her, I knew if she left home she'd forget to take a medication, but I was thinking of myself. It was selfish and now I'll have to live with the guilt of knowing she would still have been alive if only..."

Lilly could see the pain and guilt etched in the man's face. Mental illness was incredibly difficult for a partner to deal with, and Joseph Hotch had obviously been living with it for a long time. Watching his wife spiralling out of control must have been heartbreaking. It was hardly surprising he wanted a break from it all.

"I know it sounds a bit hackneyed, but you can't blame yourself. Someone is responsible for taking Carol Ann's life. That's the person you should blame."

"You know the police think it's murder now, then?"

Lilly nodded. "I have a friend at the station."

"It made more sense to me when they told me it was suicide. I don't know what to think now."

"Do you know anyone who would want to harm your wife, Mr Hotch?"

"No one at all. She was a bit of a nuisance when the demons took over, but I can't imagine anyone wanting to kill her. She had such a good heart and always meant well when she was taking her medication. I can't understand why anyone would want to hurt her. Surely Carol Ann should have evoked sympathy and compassion? Even at her worst, she wasn't a threat."

"Unfortunately, people are often fearful of things they don't understand."

Joseph nodded. "I suppose so. Look, I need to get on now, I appreciate you listening, and your kind wish to help my wife, but you really have no business being here. And this is a job I would prefer to do on my own."

"Of course, I'll get out of your way."

She left the bedroom and returned down the hall to the kitchen. Joseph Hotch followed her. At the back door she hesitated a moment, wondering if she should ask a final question. Carol Ann's letter had mentioned her husband, but this was a tricky situation. The man was in mourning for a murdered wife. But at the same time, he was also a suspect. She didn't know him, so how volatile was he? What should she do? It was Joseph himself that made up her mind.

"Is there something else, Miss Tweed?"

Lilly opened the back door and stepped into the garden before turning back. She needed the security of being able to run should it be necessary. She took a deep breath and spoke.

(celeo)

"**A**CTUALLY, YES, THERE is one more thing and believe me when I say I'm really sorry to have to ask it, but in your wife's letter to me she mentioned an affair. Were you cheating on her, Mr Hotch?"

Lilly had never witnessed a person's complexion go from sallow to puce in the blink of an eye. Clearly this was one question too far. She retreated up the garden path as Joseph Hotch took a threatening step forward and yelled at her.

"How dare you! Get out before I have you arrested and don't come back."

"I'm sorry," Lilly stammered just as the door slammed shut.

She could feel the adrenaline pumping through her body as she bolted round the side of the building back to her bike. She wanted to put as much distance between herself and Joseph Hotch as possible. She shook her head, disappointed in herself as she mounted her bike and set off home. She could have, *should have*, handled it much better. She'd already irritated him enough simply by being in his wife's flat in the first place, but he'd been gracious enough to answer her questions. He was grieving, and now she felt awful for pushing him to that level of anger. Her timing really had been terrible, she'd added another layer of unnecessary anguish when he was already going through the most dreadful difficulties. However, Joseph Hotch was still a suspect. In fact, he was the prime one. Lilly knew the police would always look to family members first before widening their search. Could Carol Ann's disease have pushed him over the edge? Made him angry and bitter at what he saw as his wasted life, caring for someone who was so ill that a chance of a normal, loving relationship was never going to happen? Enough to want to free himself from the burden without divorce or the associated public shame of abandoning a sick wife?

As she road home the long way, she also realised Joseph Hotch hadn't answered her question. Carol Ann was sure her husband had been having an affair, but did her accusation have any merit considering her mental health issues? Perhaps she had confronted him and he'd killed her in order to keep her quiet? If so, who was the other woman? Could the mystery woman be the guilty party? It was just another layer of confusion for Lilly to try to peel back, and her head was spinning.

Perhaps Joseph Hotch was exactly what he appeared to be, a mourning husband who had done all he could to take care of and protect a very sick wife. He had been wracked with guilt when he'd admitted to his desire for a break, yet had stayed with her for years trying to help. It was a level of dedication Lilly couldn't help but admire.

Her mind then turned to Carol Ann's landlord, Barney Darwin. Everything he had said sounded perfectly plausible. But what if he was lying? Bonnie had said there was no proof he had broken in. It was his word against Carol Ann's. But on the other hand, there was nothing to say he hadn't either.

Were her delusions the reason Carol Ann had been a perfect target? Had Barney taken advantage of the fact no one would believe her when he was accused? Her flat had looked to Lilly as though it had never been a home. There were no personal items that would make it such. Maybe Barney had been letting himself in on a regular basis and taking her things to sell on, secure in the knowledge that no one would ever find out?

By the time she got home, she was mentally and physically exhausted. She was looking forward to a relaxing bath and an early night. Perhaps in the morning things would make more sense.

It wasn't until she hung up her fleece that she remembered the photograph and pocket watch she'd taken from Carol Ann's safe. She closed her eyes and rested her forehead on the wall as her stupidity took hold. She'd just stolen potential evidence in a murder inquiry.

Chapter Eight

*N*EXT MORNING LILLY transferred the photo and watch from her fleece jacket pocket to her bag, making a mental note to call Bonnie about them later. She decided to take the car to work. After all the cycling she'd done the previous evening, her legs ached too much to do it again today. Besides, with Stacey's car in the garage, she could give her lift home if needed. It would save her having to spend her wages on taxi fares.

Once again, she parked in the rear car-park and entered through the storeroom door. Inside the main shop she saw Stacey standing at the front door waiting to get in. She'd returned the keys to Lilly previously, but if she was going to be first to arrive, then it would make sense if she had her own set.

She let Earl out of his carrier where he promptly made a beeline for his usual spot, then opened the front door, locking it again after Stacey was inside. There were still twenty minutes to go before they opened.

"Morning, Lilly," Stacey said brightly. "I was expecting to see you on your bike like always."

"I brought the car this morning so if you need a lift home later just let me know."

"I don't mind taking a cab."

"I know you don't but you're going to have a garage bill to pay shortly and taxi rides add up. The offer's there if you want it."

Stacey grinned. "Yeah, that would be great, actually. Thanks, Lilly."

They both went straight to work getting the place ready for the day. Restocking items, checking the till float and straightening the displays. While Stacey ran a quick duster around the shelves, Lilly boiled the kettle. It had become a morning routine to brew a different pot of tea for just the two of them in a morning. She would either quiz Stacey on what she had learned, or if it was a new tea would talk her through its health benefits and history while she wrote down the details. It was a ritual they both enjoyed.

At nine-o'clock on the dot, Stacey flipped the sign to open and unlocked the door.

"I'm going to work in the shop this morning," Lilly said. "Would you be okay working on clearing and organising the back store room and the upstairs flat?"

"Sure. I love doing that stuff."

Lilly was kept busy for most of the morning with both regular customers coming in to restock or pick up orders, and much to her delight several new ones. She'd recently taken delivery of a new product line; three and four tier vintage sandwich and cake stands, perfect for afternoon tea. She'd placed one in the window that morning and already had sold all but two. She scribbled a note to order more.

At lunch time Stacey popped to their favourite bakery for sandwiches and ate in the back room first, but made Lilly promise she wouldn't peek in the storeroom. She wanted it to be a surprise. So an amused Lilly took her lunch across to a bench in the square and ate there.

A hectic afternoon followed and Stacey took time from her tidying up to help in the shop. About an hour before closing time the rain started and with the shop empty of customers Lilly was finally allowed in the back to see what had been accomplished.

Stacey stood in the door way to keep one eye on the shop while Lilly stared at the scene before her. The place was unrecognisable from the chaotic mess it had been that morning. Shelves were rearranged and stacked with merchandise, all neatly labelled, so it was easy to see at a glance what products were running low.

The small staff kitchen had been scrubbed and the table where they ate their lunch was adorned with a colourful table cloth, which Lilly recognised as being part of the upstairs flat. Stacey had even made a cosy corner for Earl with his alternative bed lifted onto a small table. Lilly knew cats preferred to be up high, it gave them a good vantage point from where they could spot any dangers. And as if to prove the point, Earl sauntered through to the back room and jumped straight in, beginning to paddle and purring loudly.

"Well, that's a first!" Lilly exclaimed. "Stacey, you have done a fantastic job, I hardly recognise the place."

"Hey, I loved doing it."

"Let me go and have a look upstairs too, then we can close up."

The upstairs was just as pristine as downstairs. All the products had been removed and were now where they should be, in the storeroom. It was a tremendous effort, and Lilly was incredibly grateful to Stacey for doing so much work. It was something she'd been putting off for a while, being too tired at the end of a working day to tackle such a big job. But now it was done, she'd make sure it stayed that way.

"Well done, Stacey. Seriously, that is a load off my mind." She said once back downstairs. "Let's close up and I'll take you home. You've earned it."

⟨ₑₑₗₑₑ⟩

"DO YOU WANT to come in for a coffee?" Stacey asked when they arrived outside her flat. Lilly smiled. "That sounds lovely. Is it okay if I bring Earl?"

"Absolutely, he's part of the family."

In the kitchen, while Stacey put the coffee pot on, Lilly let Earl out and sunk into a seat at the table. She noticed there were signs Stacey had tried to improve the place since her last visit. The peeling wallpaper had been glued, the mould spots scrubbed clean, and several sample pots of paint, in dusky pinks and greens, were sitting on a shelf.

"You've been busy here, too. I like the paint colours."

"Yeah, doing my best. The paint reminds me of home. They're my mom's favourite colours." Stacey said, handing Lilly a mug of coffee. "Not sure how much I can improve it, though. I'd rather spend my time finding a better place, but they're either out of my price range or just as bad."

"I had a thought about that, actually. You'd prefer to be in the town, I think you said?"

"Definitely, but prices in town are way out of my budget."

"What do you pay here?"

"Five hundred pounds a month, with bills on top. It's cheap compared to other places, but you get what you pay for, I guess."

"Good grief, Stacey. You are definitely paying more than this place is worth. It's a bit of health hazard to say the least. And if I'm honest, I'm not really happy with you having to live here. My plan was always to rent out the flat above the shop when it was cleared out. Which you've managed to do now. Would you be interested?"

"Wow! Yes, of course I would. But I can't afford the rates in town, even with my grant. I've trawled everywhere looking, believe me."

Lilly shrugged. "The rate is what I would say it is, I own the whole building. At the moment it's a waste of potential as it's not earning me anything. So how about you pay the same as you do here?"

"Are you serious?"

"Don't get me wrong, Stacey, it's not wholly altruistic on my part, although I really would like to see you get out of this hovel. I would benefit greatly from having the person renting the flat also working in the shop, but it would make you easily accessible if I needed additional help at any time. You'd need to consider whether or not you'd be happy living above where you work and the fact that I may call on you at a moment's notice because you'd be so near."

"Are you kidding me! I'd love it! But are you sure? I mean, I know you could rent it out for twice as much as you'd be charging me."

"Of course, I'm sure. Though in exchange, I may ask you to open up on your own some mornings? What do you say?"

Stacey jumped up, tears of joy in her eyes, and gave Lilly a fierce hug. "Thank you so much. My neighbour is a nightmare, plays music at all hours. I can't wait!" she sprang back and knocked Lilly's bag off the table, scattering the contents.

"Oh no. I'm so sorry. Got a bit excited there. Let me get everything." She passed the bag back to Lilly and on hands and knees began collecting the items. Keys, lipstick, a pen, diary and eventually the watch.

"Oh wow! I can't believe you have one of these."

"What?" Lilly asked, holding out her hand to take the pocket watch from an amazed Stacey.

"It's a Patek Philippe. My stepfather got one when he retired from the company he worked for. They're worth about eight thousand dollars on average. More if it's a special edition type. How long have you had it?"

"Eight thousand dollars?" Lilly squeaked. "Are you sure? How much is that in pounds?"

"About six thousand, I think."

"Oh no..." Lilly's stomach dropped. She'd stolen a pocket watch worth a small fortune. She was surprised the police hadn't already come knocking on her door.

"Lilly, what's wrong?"

Lilly explained everything, from being at the college and finding the keys. To entering Carol Ann's flat and discovering the safe.

"When I heard the door open and footsteps coming down the hall, I panicked and just stuffed it in my pocket before I had a chance to think. I'm such an idiot. Joseph Hotch must know Carol Ann had the watch if it's that valuable, and surely he's realised by now it's missing from the safe? His first thought is going to be that I was the one who stole it."

"Maybe he thinks she sold it or something? Besides, you've got the keys, right? There may not be another one to the safe so he can't open it."

"Actually, Stacey, that's a very good point. But I still can't risk holding on to it. I meant to call Bonnie, my police friend, about it today, but we were so busy it slipped my mind. I need to return it and own up to what I did before it all gets out of hand. I really didn't mean to keep it."

"Man, I can't believe my boss is a cat burglar!"

"Stacey!"

Suddenly they both burst into uncontrollable laughter. *The whole thing was so ridiculous you had to see the funny side,* thought Lilly.

"So, was that the only thing you pinched?"

"No, actually," Lilly said with a blush, which made Stacey giggle even more, reaching into her pocket for the photograph and handing it over.

"Wait, I think I know her. I've seen her around campus with that little dog before. I can't remember her name though. She's a year or two above me."

"Monica."

"Yeah, that's it."

"When I was at St John's the other day, some of the girls said Carol Ann thought Monica had stolen from her." She reached into her bag and brought out the photo Archie had given her. "Have a look at this."

"Oh, wow. It looks like the same dog. You think she stole the poor woman's puppy?"

"I don't know. It seems a really cruel thing to do and I can't think why she would do it. Plus, she wasn't exactly hiding it, was she? I think I'll go to the university in the morning and ask Monica about it, see what she says."

"You want me to open up?"

"No, it's all right. I'll need to drop Earl in at the shop before I go."

"Well, be careful. You don't want to get in any more trouble."

*

THE SUN WAS shining the next morning and while she would have preferred to bike to work, it would have to be the car today if she was to visit Monica at St John's as planned. She parked in the rear car park and grabbed Earl's carrier, entering through the store room. She was just unlocking the front shop door when Stacey appeared.

"Good morning. Great day, isn't it? So glad the sun is shining it means we should be busy."

"Let's hope so. Oh, and while I remember, I've brought the spare shop keys for you." Lilly said, handing over a key ring with a miniature floral china teapot hanging off it.

"Awesome! Thanks so much, Lilly."

"Look after them. They are the only spares I've got."

"No problem. But maybe we should see about having another set cut, just in case?"

Lilly nodded. The girl was right, and she made a mental note to get it done sometime this week.

They spent twenty minutes setting the shop up and chatting briefly over a cup of chamomile tea with honey, then it was time for Lilly to go.

"I shouldn't be too long, but if I'm delayed for any reason, I'll let you know."

Once again she parked in the same place she had previously, and where she'd had the unfortunate run in with Abigail. It had obviously disturbed her more than she'd thought as she found herself looking over her shoulder more than once. Fortunately Abigail didn't appear and Lilly, having once again signed in at reception first, made her way to G-block unmolested. On the steps at the front of the building two female students were comparing notes, text books and highlighter pens in hand.

"Hi," Lilly said. "I'm looking for Monica Morris, is she around?"

"Still in chemistry class, but she should be back soon. You're welcome to wait inside if you want?"

"I appreciate that, thanks." She made her way into the entrance hall. The place was much calmer than her previous visit, and the common room, fully set up for the reunion now, was thankfully devoid of people. Settling on a small sofa, she waited for Monica to arrive. She wasn't alone long.

"I can't believe you had the gall to come back here," a tremulous voice said a few minutes later.

Lilly stood up. "Monica..." she began. Obviously the girl had learned the truth.

"You're not a reporter, are you? Another woman turned up shortly after you left the other day, asking the same questions. We told her we'd already spoken to a reporter, but she made out she didn't know who we meant. I never mentioned your name, but I got the feeling she knew it was you, anyway. She left eventually, but I decided to look you up and found you were sacked from The Plumpton Mallet Gazette months ago. You were only the agony aunt and got replaced when the paper was bought out. So why are you even asking questions about Carol Ann Hotch?"

Lilly took a deep breath. "You're right, Monica, I shouldn't have said I was a reporter. It was a spur-of-the-moment decision so as not to alarm you and one which I now regret. But I needed to speak to you about Carol Ann. Yes, I was the paper's agony aunt for many years. I wasn't sacked but was made redundant. However, many people still write to me for help. Carol Ann was one of those people. Her letter upset me a great deal, but before I had a chance to help she was found dead. I've felt dreadful about it ever since."

Monica sighed then carelessly threw her bag then herself on the sofa. "You should have just told me."

"Yes, I know I should. Would you have still talked to me if I had done, though?"

"I don't know. Maybe. So what do you want now?"

"I've recently come across something about Carol Ann and wondered if you could help me with it?"

"You know, I am so tired of hearing that name. I just want to forget about her. I don't know anything. Really, I don't."

"Could you just look at a couple of photos for me?"

"Okay, fine."

Lilly handed over the first picture, the one of Carol Ann. "This was given to me by a friend at the paper. And this one was found in Carol Ann's flat." She handed her the second picture of herself with the dog.

"She had a picture of me?" Monica said, looking at Lilly in shock. "Why? That's really disturbing."

"Well, I think it's because of the dog you're both holding. One of your house mates said she'd been accusing you of stealing something from her. Was it her dog?"

"What? No, of course not! Why would I steal her dog? That's ridiculous. Is that what she was so upset with me about?"

"I think so." Said Lilly. "Is that not the case?"

"No, it's not even the same dog." She held up the picture of herself and pointed to the dog. "This is Pipsqueak. My dog. It took me ages to name her, but she lets out a little squeak when she's excited. It suits her. She lives with my parents most of the time as I can't keep her here." She thrust out the other photo. "The dog in this picture would be much older now and actually died about a year ago. These pictures were taken ages apart. Carol Ann was a crazy woman who missed her dog and obviously wanted mine. I can't believe this is what it's all been about."

"They look exactly the same."

"Of course. They're from the same breeder."

"So, you just happened to choose the same breeder as Carol Ann, only years apart?" Lilly asked, a slightly sceptical tone in her voice. "That's a bit of a coincidence, wouldn't you say?"

"It wasn't a coincidence at all, actually." Monica replied with strained patience. "I met her husband here, remember, at one of the reunions? Well, he's the breeder. He showed me some pictures of the puppies he had available and I fell in love with Pipsqueak and got her."

Lilly clasped her hands, staring at Monica. "You didn't tell me all this when I spoke to you. You seem to have more in common with the Hotch's than you let on."

"I hardly know them. Look," she said, counting off the points on her fingers. "I met them at the reunion. Joseph told me about the puppies. I asked to see them. He showed me photos, and I chose one. That's it."

Lilly sighed. "So, you think Carol Ann convinced herself that the puppy in your picture was her old dog that had died?"

"I have no idea. I don't even know where she got the picture. All I know is she started following me around, accusing me of stuff I didn't do and making me really uncomfortable. I tried to ignore it because it was obvious she was ill, but it got worse. The break in was the last straw, and I called security.

Look, I'm sorry, but I don't want to talk about it anymore. If you have any more questions, then I suggest you talk to her husband. I have to study."

Lilly watched as Monica got up and strode purposefully from the room. A moment later she heard footsteps running up the stairs. She leaned back, feeling deflated. She hadn't learned much more at all. The fact Joseph Hotch bred dogs could be easily proved, but how did that help in regard to Carol Ann's death? She couldn't work out a connection, and if she was honest, it hadn't moved her investigation forward in the slightest. *And I don't think I'll get anything more out of Monica,* she thought.

She was about to leave when she noticed Monica's bag beside her. The girl had been in such a rush to leave she'd forgotten it.

⸎

*L*ILLY QUICKLY GLANCED to the door to make sure she was alone, then turned back to the bag. *Don't even think about it!* Her mind warned her. But her curiosity was too strong. Gingerly, she lifted the flap. There was the usual paraphernalia associated with a student; notebook and pens alongside a study book. A pink purse was tucked in the bottom next to a packet of mints, the ginger chews the girl had offered Lilly the first time they'd met, vitamins and a lipstick. But it was the letter that made her catch her breath. A letter she had no business having.

Her mind was working overtime as she carefully withdrew it from the bag. Suddenly she heard clamouring voices and a multitude of footsteps on the stairs. Quickly, she stuffed the letter in her pocket and left the room. The students she'd met on the way in had gone, so she hurried down the steps unseen and jogged to her car. Safely inside, she took out the letter and began to read.

Carol Ann,

I insist you stop this ridiculous and dangerous behaviour and come home immediately. I don't know what you think has happened, but you must know it's not real. It's all in your mind. Have your therapy sessions taught you nothing? You're making a fool of yourself, not to mention embarrassing me. If you carry on the way you are, you're going to get yourself in serious trouble and I won't be able to help you then. I had another call from the university. What on earth were you doing? You must leave that poor girl alone before she has you arrested. I'm getting tired of it all, Carol Ann. For everyone's sake come home before I'm left with no other choice. I don't want to do something I'll regret.

Joseph

It certainly wasn't a love letter, which had been Lilly's first thought. It also painted a rather different picture of Joseph Hotch from the loving, caring husband who would do anything to help his wife. Mind you, she'd seen him go from sad and dejected to furious so fast it had made her head spin. He obviously had a temper.

She folded the letter and slipped it into her bag alongside the watch and photo. "You're fast turning into a kleptomaniac, Lillian Tweed." She muttered.

She mulled over the letter and the information about the dogs Monica had given her for a while before making a decision and reaching for her phone. She should at least confirm the dog story. Scrolling through her phone contacts, she reached the letter J. If anyone could confirm it, it would be Dr Jorgenson, Carol Ann's therapist. He'd given Lilly his private number when she'd been to visit him so, providing he wasn't with a client, he should answer himself. He did.

"Miss Tweed?"

"Yes. Hello, Dr Jorgenson. I'm sorry to bother you. I wondered if you had a minute to answer a question I have about Carol Ann?"

There was a heavy and slightly exasperated sigh down the line. "Miss Tweed, as I explained before, I really can't discuss my patients with you."

"I know, but it's not about Carol Ann per se, it's about her dog."

"Her dog? You mean Scooter?"

"I don't know it's name. Was it a small white Pomeranian?"

"Yes, that's right."

"What can you tell me about it?"

"He was a gift from her husband and she adored him. They went everywhere together, and she really looked after him well. Having something else to care for made her look after herself better. Scooter was totally reliant on her you see, and she loved him. He was almost like her child, actually. He died about a year ago, I think. Hit by a car, unfortunately. It was extremely traumatic for Carol Ann, as you can imagine. It was one of the primary causes of her relapse."

"A year ago? So, that would be around the time she and Joseph separated?" Lilly asked.

There was a distinct pause. "Yes, I suppose that's correct. Is that all, Miss Tweed, I have a client due?"

"Just one more question if you don't mind. Do you know if Joseph Hotch bred Pomeranians?"

"Yes, he did, that's how Carol Ann got Scooter in the first place. Miss Tweed, what on earth is this about?"

"I'm not sure yet, Dr Jorgenson. It may mean nothing. But I appreciate your help. Bye for now."

She ended the call and sighed. So Monica was telling the truth about the dog. Perhaps Carol Ann, unable to face the fact her little companion had died, had seen the student with a dog which looked exactly like hers and convinced herself Monica had stolen him. With her history of mental illness and a sudden trigger like the death of her beloved pet, it was more than plausible that she'd fabricated the theft in her own mind and convinced herself it was true.

The obsession the dead woman had with the student had, Lilly thought, been answered, but she still had more questions. Why did Monica have a letter from Joseph to his wife? What was the motive for Carol Ann's murder? And most important of all, who had killed her?

She needed to return the pocket watch to Joseph Hotch rather than the police, she decided. Maybe she should ask him about the letter at the same time? She'd need to think about that. It would probably be better just to hand it over to the police and have done with it. She started the car and pulled out of the car park. First things first, she needed to get back to the shop.

Chapter Nine

SHE STOPPED BRIEFLY on the way back to town to pick up a lunch of cheese sandwiches and cartons of hot tomato and basil soup for her and Stacey. The day was warm but after her encounter with Monica she was in need of comfort food.

"Hey, you're back. And with my favourite lunch! Thank you. So, how'd it go?"

There was only one customer browsing, and she left shortly after, so they ate their lunch together at the counter and Lilly brought her up to date.

"It turns out that Carol Ann's husband is a dog breeder on the side. He gave his wife one from a litter several years ago and Monica bought hers from a more recent litter."

"So, they're not the same dog?"

"No, although they obviously look very similar. Unfortunately, Carol Ann's dog was killed by a car about a year ago. It seems the event was so traumatic she got it into her head that Monica had stolen him when she saw her with an almost identical animal."

"Man, that's really sad. Poor dog and poor Carol Ann. But at least you found the answer to the mystery."

"Yes, but it's got me nowhere. Honestly, Stacey, I don't know why I thought I could investigate this myself. I must have been out of my mind. I know my certainty that it was neither an accident nor suicide was proved right, but the post-mortem confirmed that, anyway, so what exactly have I achieved? All I've done is scare poor Monica, antagonise Joseph Hotch, and get on the wrong side of Abigail. Not to mention trespassing and petty theft. I've decided to give back the watch and photo to Carol Ann's husband and contact Bonnie about a letter I've discovered, then leave the professionals to get on with it. I am not cut out to be a detective."

"Yeah, you're probably right," Stacey said. "Don't beat yourself up about it. You did your best. Oh, head's up, we've got customers."

Lilly grabbed the empty food wrappers and made her way to the store room bin while Stacey greeted them. On her return she came face-to-face with two people she hadn't expected to see, either in her shop or together. Joseph Hotch and just behind him, Barney Darwin.

*J*OSEPH GLANCED UP and locked eyes with Lilly. "You!" he exclaimed.

Lilly gave a tentative smile. "Mr Hotch, welcome to my shop."

"Your shop?" he said, clearly surprised. "I've heard good things about the place recently. I didn't realise you owned it. I should have made the connection sooner. I was in town for lunch with a friend today, trying to take my mind off things. We decided to call in. I believe you've already met Barney Darwin?"

Oh, dear. "Yes." She nodded in the landlord's direction. He replied with a scowl.

"Can I brew you a sample of anything? I've got a green tea with Jasmine, which is a good stress reliever. Or perhaps a dandelion root. It helps to boost serotonin levels?"

He eyed her carefully. Perhaps he realised how much thought she'd put into the teas she'd just recommended? "I'll try the dandelion. Thanks."

She boiled the kettle, left it for a few minutes so it didn't scald the tea and reduce its flavour, then made a ritual of setting out the bone-china cup and saucer, brewing, timing and finally pouring the tea through a silver strainer into the cup. She slid it across the counter with a smile.

After several sips, he nodded. "I like it. I'll take some, please."

She weighed and measured two-hundred grams. Poured it into a vintage style biodegradable box filled with bleach free tissue paper and closed it with a Tea Emporium sticker. She also included one of the information leaflets.

"It's on the house, with my compliments."

"Oh, thank you. But, there's no need."

"I know, but I'd like to all the same. Mr Hotch, I owe you an apology."

"I seem to remember you already did that."

"Well, yes. But actually I have an additional confession to make."

She glanced around the shop to make sure they weren't overheard. Stacey was dealing with several customers, one of whom was piling the counter with items intended for purchase, but she glanced in Lilly's direction every so often to check on her. Others were asking questions and Barney Darwin was standing a few steps away with his back turned, studying the china cabinets.

"I really am very sorry and I hope you'll forgive me," she began in a low voice. "When you walked in on me at the flat the other day, I was holding a pocket watch I'd found. It was pure instinct when I heard your footsteps. I'm afraid I just shoved it in my pocket. I forgot all about it until I got home and I've been carrying it around ever since. I need to give it back to you. I never meant to take it in the first place."

Joseph scowled. "You know, I wasn't happy that you broke in in the first place. Now you're telling me you stole something?"

"I didn't technically break in," Lilly began.

"Yes, if I remember rightly, you said the door was unlocked. Barney, however, is convinced it wasn't. So what's the truth? Come on, Miss Tweed, considering the way you've acted recently, you owe me at least that much."

Lilly's stomach curled with anxiety. She was caught. Stacey was assisting a customer at the other side of the shop, but she was quite aware that both Joseph's tone of voice and body language had changed from politely pleasant to mildly threatening. Lilly took a deep breath. Honesty was always the best policy; she needed to own up to what she had done.

(cclco)

"THE TRUTH IS, after Carol Ann wrote to me, I wanted to know what happened. I thought there was more to her death, and I didn't think the police were taking things as seriously as they should. I decided to start investigating myself, which I realise now was a monumentally stupid idea. I'm not cut out to be a detective. But while I was snooping, I came across a key ring and keys. I need to return those to you as well."

"You have Carol Ann's keys?" Joseph asked sharply.

Lilly nodded. "I'm sorry. I should have returned them when I found them, but I was hoping there would be something in her flat that would point to who had killed her. I had no intention of keeping them I was simply looking for clues."

Joseph deflated. It was obvious he had no more energy left for a fight. Leaning his elbows on the counter he said, "I don't suppose I can accuse you of breaking in if you had the keys, but it was still poor behaviour. When I walked in and found a complete stranger going through my wife's things, I was livid. I shouldn't have raised my voice. I understand why you panicked. But what you did was wrong."

Lilly breathed a sigh of relief. She hadn't expected Joseph Hotch to be so tolerant. In fact, he had every right to be incredibly angry. Perhaps she hadn't given him as much credit as he deserved.

"Thank you for understanding. I know the pocket watch is worth a lot of money."

Joseph scoffed, and then whispered, "Actually it's worthless. It belonged to Carol Ann's father and his father before. She was convinced it was real and I expect at one point in time it had been. But somewhere along the line a copy was made and I expect the original was sold. I had it appraised a few years ago, and it was confirmed to be a replica. I didn't tell Carol Ann, of course, it would have broken her heart. That's if she even believed me. But it meant a lot to her, and I'd like it back."

"Of course, I'll go and get it." Lilly said, also keeping her voice low. "I must say I'm extremely relieved to know I haven't been carrying around thousands of pounds worth of watch."

She hurried into the back store room where she'd left her handbag. She felt a huge burden lift now she'd come clean. She'd been worried sick over how Joseph Hotch was going to react when she revealed she'd taken the watch, but it couldn't have gone any better.

She hurried back to a waiting Joseph and opened her bag. It was then that she remembered the letter.

Chapter Ten

$\mathscr{S}$HE TOOK OUT the watch and put it to the side, just as the customer added several more items to her pile, practically obscuring it. She took out the letter, hesitating for a moment. "I'm really sorry to have to ask you about this," she said. "Especially when you've been so kind about everything else... but I found this letter..."

"What letter?" he asked, holding out a hand. Lilly passed it across. "I was hoping you could explain to me why you would write something like this to her?"

He took a minute to read it through, then handed it back. "I didn't write this. I don't know where you got it or who did write it, but it certainly wasn't me."

"But it's addressed to Carol Ann and signed by you?"

His face flushed an angry red. "Look, Miss Tweed, I have been very patient with you thus far, but if you are accusing me of something, then I suggest you come right out and say it."

"I'm not accusing you of anything, Mr Hotch, I'm just trying to find answers."

"Well, you're looking in the wrong place. Now, give me my wife's watch."

Lilly reached out for the watch, frantically searching in among the customer's boxes, but it was no longer there. "It's gone!" she exclaimed just as she saw Stacey hurtling through the shop.

She stared, rooted to the spot for the short time it took Stacey to launch herself at Barney, knock him into the door-jamb and throw him into an expert headlock.

"Stacey!" Lilly shrieked and bolted round the counter to the door.

"Drop it, you thief!" Stacey snapped, and Lilly spied the watch falling from Barney's meaty hand just as he had recovered his wits enough to fling Stacey to the floor.

"Barney!" Joseph shouted in shock as he rushed over.

Barney dove for the watch, but Lilly kicked it out of his reach. He responded by giving her violent shove into a stack of shelves, causing heavy tins of tea to fall and roll across the shop floor. As Barney made a second attempt to bolt for the door, Stacey grabbed an errant tin and flung it at his head. It made impact causing him to stagger into another shelf upsetting a display of teapots. One fell and shattered with a sound like gunfire. This was the final straw for poor Earl who bolted from the window, hackles raised, hissing and snarling in fear.

"You stupid..." but before Barney could finish, Joseph grabbed the watch and savagely kicked Barney in the knee, sending him down. Earl leapt towards Barney's face, claws out, leaving a long scratch down his cheek as he used his head as a jumping off point, before fleeing to the back store room in terror.

"Stupid Cat!" Barney shrieked, reaching for the laceration, his hand coming away covered in blood.

Joseph threw his friend to the floor, putting a knee on his back, and glowered at Lilly.

"Call the police," he demanded.

❦

*L*ILLY TELEPHONED THE police and then went to check on Earl. He had calmed down and was curled up in the bed Stacey had made for him.

"When done, Earl," Lilly said, stroking his head. "Salmon for tea, I think. You deserve it."

Back in the shop, the customers who had witnessed the entire thing were being taken care of by Stacey. She'd brewed them all a calming tea and had rung up and packaged their purchases, ready for when they would be allowed to leave. All of them were more than happy to wait and give witness statements.

Lilly wandered over to where Joseph was still guarding Barney and Stacey joined them a moment later.

"I saw him take the watch right off the counter and try to walk out with it," she said.

"Are you all right?" Lilly asked, concerned. "You took a nasty fall."

"So did you. But, yeah, I'm fine."

"Well, please don't make a habit of tackling shoplifters, my heart nearly stopped."

Stacey laughed. "Sorry. I didn't really think about it, just acted. I hate thieves."

The police car arrived a moment later and Bonnie got out, walking over to the shop with a stern look on her face.

"Oh, Bonnie, I'm so glad it's you."

"What happened? Is everyone all right?"

"Yes, we're all fine. This man tried to steal a watch and Stacey tackled him. It got a bit fraught. He knocked both Stacey and me down and frightened Earl, who scratched his face." Lilly succinctly explained.

"Well, I'll need to take statements from everyone. So I suggest you put the closed sign up and lock the door." She turned to her colleague and spoke in hushed tones. He nodded, handcuffed Barney and put in him in the back of the police car before taking a seat behind the wheel to wait for Bonnie.

"Right. I take it these people are your customers who happened to be here at the time, is that correct?" Bonnie said, gesturing to the end of the counter.

"Yes. They were happy to wait to give you their statements."

"I'll start with them so they can be on their way, then come back and speak to you three."

Lilly, Stacey, and Joseph sipped newly brewed drinks at the other end of the counter while Bonnie went about her job.

"I'm sorry about your friend," Lilly said to Joseph.

"I don't understand it. He obviously knew about the watch, but why attempt to steal it?"

"He must have overheard me telling you that I had it. But he missed the bit when you told me it was a fake."

"Is that what this has all been about? A damned pocked watch?"

Lilly had no time to answer as Bonnie chose that moment to join them.

"You can let your customers out now, Lilly. I've got what I need for the moment. We'll take full statements at their homes. I've made them promise not to talk to anyone about what happened for the time being."

Lilly looked out of the window and saw there was quite a crowd gathered outside. Word had obviously spread quickly. She sighed, it wouldn't be long before a reporter was on the scene.

"Stacey, could you let everyone out then lock the door?"

"Sure."

"I think I know why he stole the watch," Joseph said to Bonnie. "Miss Tweed, was about to return it to me and he overheard part of our conversation."

"And you are?"

"Oh, sorry. Joseph Hotch."

Bonnie was brought up short. "Carol Ann's husband?" she asked, giving Lilly a brief sideways glance.

"That's right. Barney was my wife's landlord. We were separated. Barney was supposed to be keeping an eye on her for me."

"You think your wife told her landlord about the watch?"

"She must have done, officer. He wouldn't have known about it otherwise. I certainly didn't tell him."

"I'm afraid this changes everything. It's possibly connected in some way to the death of your wife, Mr Hotch, and as such will need to be passed on to the lead detective. It's not my case. I will take Miss Pepper's statement now, but then I'm afraid the two of you will have to come to the station to be interviewed. Would you like me to send a car?" Bonnie directed this last question to Lilly, who shook her head.

"No, I can drive us both. The last thing we need is to be seen driving off in the back of a police car. Is that all right with you, Mr Hotch?"

"Yes. I don't have transport with me; we came in Barney's car."

"Stacey, can you hold the fort here until I return? There's no need to open if you don't feel up to it. I expect the place will end up full of people who are just being nosy and wanting to know what's happened rather than serious shoppers."

Stacey grinned. "And that's a perfect time to sell them something," she said. "Don't worry, I'll be fine."

Fifteen minutes later, with a certain amount of trepidation, Lilly and Joseph were on their way to the police station.

*A*T THE POLICE station they gave their names to the desk sergeant and were shown to a small waiting area. Windowless and devoid of personality, Lilly found it gloomy and depressing. The chairs were grey plastic and very uncomfortable and there was nothing in the way of reading material, unless you counted the dramatic crime posters on a nearby notice board. Joseph sat morose and silent, nursing a vending machine coffee that looked like sludge. Eventually he leaned forward and deposited the untouched paper cup on the scarred table in front of him.

He reached into his pocket and brought out the watch, turning it over in his hands as though seeing it for the first time. "Of all the stupid things... is this really the reason my wife was killed?" Lilly knew better than to interrupt. He was speaking more to himself than to her. "She reported Barney to the police before. I didn't believe her."

Lilly's mind went back to the day she had hit Abigail's car. After Bonnie had sent her on her way, they'd both talked about Carol Ann. She recalled Bonnie mentioning that she'd reported Barney to the police for breaking into her flat. Barney had naturally denied it, and as there was no proof it had been put down to Carol Ann's mental illness and increased paranoia.

"You knew she'd called the police about Barney?"

"Yes. First time it happened they brought him here, and he called me." Joseph said. "I came down here straight away and talked to the police, explained the situation about how my wife was ill, delusional. At the time, I thought I was just cleaning up another one of her messes. I didn't think for one minute that Barney had actually broken into her flat. This whole time I thought he was looking out for her."

Lilly tried to reassure him. "At the risk of repeating myself, you can't blame yourself. Given her history, it makes sense that you'd believe Barney, especially as there was no proof and that Carol Ann may not have been taking her pills."

Joseph slipped the watch back into his pocket. "All over a stupid watch, which isn't even the real thing, just a clever copy."

"Yes, but Barney didn't know that, did he? He thought it was worth a lot of money. How did you and Barney meet?"

"I used to breed small dogs and his niece wanted one. He came to me. It was years ago, but we kind of became loose friends after that. Occasional drinks at the local pub, a couple of football games, that sort of thing. We weren't best friends, but we were close enough that he called me when Carol Ann showed up wanting to rent one of his flats. She didn't know Barney, you see, and wasn't aware we knew each other. I thought it was the perfect way to... well... give myself a bit of a break while simultaneously giving her some independence, and with someone to watch out for her in case she needed help. Someone who could also keep me informed about how she was doing. And to think he was taking advantage all this time! It sickens me to my stomach, it really does."

"I really am sorry about what's happened," Lilly said. "Especially my part in it all. I got rather sucked into it after Carol Ann wrote to me. I should have just left well alone and let the police do their job."

"Well, if it wasn't for you we wouldn't have caught Barney," Joseph replied.

"Does this mean you forgive me for taking the watch?"

He shrugged. "I suppose it must."

From the corner of her eye, Lilly spotted movement. She glanced over and saw Bonnie enter the hall from a door at the back marked private. She made her way towards them, a stern look on her face.

❦

BOTH LILLY AND Joseph stood up instinctively, leaning forward in anticipation of what news Bonnie had to tell them.

"What did he say?" asked Lilly.

"Has he confessed?" said Joseph at the same time.

Bonnie held up both hands to halt the onslaught of questions before they came. She took a seat opposite and turned a page in her notebook. Lilly and Joseph sat back down and waited for her to speak.

"No, he hasn't confessed as such. He's adamant he had nothing to do with the death of your wife, Mr Hotch, although at this stage I wouldn't expect him to admit to any involvement. He's keeping tight lipped in that regard but has given us an alibi for the time, which we are in the process of checking now. However, he has made an interesting admission about the watch."

"Oh?" Joseph said.

"He says he bought the watch from Carol Ann, but after he'd paid, she refused to give it to him."

"Then he's lying. Carol Ann would *never* have sold that watch, it meant too much to her."

"Did he break into her flat looking for it, then?" asked Lilly. "Is that what Carol Ann meant? Her letter to me said she was sure someone else had been in her home while she'd been out."

Bonnie nodded. "Yes, he's admitted to entering her flat while she was out. On a couple of occasions in the early hours she was actually there and caught him. Several times he entered, apparently, looking for the watch he's adamant he bought from her. He couldn't find it, though."

"That despicable... is there any proof he paid for the watch?" Joseph asked. "Did you find a receipt or a note or anything? We have a joint bank account so I can check the statements if that's any help?"

"He said he paid cash."

Joseph threw up his hands in despair. "Well, of course he did! It's just a web of lies to try to get himself off the hook."

"How much did he say he'd paid for it?" Lilly asked.

"Five-hundred pounds."

Lilly glanced at Joseph, wondering if he realised the implication. He was frowning, but she wasn't sure if he'd put two and two together as yet. His mind was probably clouded with anger at the thoughts of Barney Darwin entering his wife's home while she slept.

"He's even more of a louse than I thought he was then." She said, eventually. "Carol Ann thought the pocket watch was the genuine article and would have told Barney so. He therefore thought it was worth thousands, yet only offered a meager five-hundred for it. He was taking advantage of and hoping to profit from a very ill woman."

"That utter..." Joseph swore loudly, then jumped up and began to pace from one side of the small area to the other. "That's his motive, isn't it? He killed my wife because she wouldn't give him the blasted watch. He had plenty of opportunity to work it all out because they lived in the same building. A building he owned and had all the spare keys for. Gain her trust and slowly make her think she was going mad, then make himself the one who she'd turn to. Dear god, I should have believed her." He returned to his seat, dashing away tears before they could fall.

"What about his alibi, Bonnie?"

"Lilly, I can't really discuss that with you. Suffice to say we're following it up, but it's a bit shaky."

"Okay. But off the record, do you think Barney killed Carol Ann?"

Bonnie stood up and Lilly did the same. Joseph remained sitting, emotionally exhausted, but likewise interested in what Bonnie's answer would be.

"It's not my call, Lilly, you know that. This isn't my case. But, off the record, I think we've probably got our man. He clearly had a motive and as her landlord would have known her routine. As you said, Mr Hotch, he would have been able to spend the time gaining her trust and alienating her from her friends and family. But, you both know as well as I do that none of this means anything unless we can prove it."

Lilly nodded. "Yes, of course."

"All right. I need to go back in now. I only came to double check whether Carol Ann would have willingly sold the watch. Someone will be with you in the next fifteen minutes or so to take a formal statement."

After Bonnie had gone, Lilly sat back down and turned to Joseph. "Are you all right?"

He shook his head. "I don't know. I trusted someone who I thought was a friend to look out for my wife. Now it looks as though he not only took advantage of her, but probably killed her. I've got so many different emotions warring with each other that all I can feel is a numb shock."

"Can I get you anything from the machine? Tea or coffee or something to eat?"

"No, I couldn't stomach a thing, thanks."

"Look, Joseph, I know this is a bad time, but I need to ask you about the letter?"

"Letter? What letter?"

Lilly rooted around in her bag and brought out the letter she'd found when she'd spoken to Monica.

"I'd forgotten all about that," he said wearily. "But, I told you I didn't write it. It's not my writing, look." He brought out his wallet and showed Lilly several examples of his writing. On a cheque, a shopping list and his signature on the back of his credit card. It didn't match the letter.

"Well, someone did, and we need to find out who. Because it makes you look culpable."

"**D**O YOU THINK Barney could have written it?" Joseph said.

"Barney?"

"Yes, to implicate me?"

"No, I don't think so. I found it at St John's. One of the students there had it, a girl called Monica Morris. You know her, I think?"

"No, I don't... oh, wait, yes, she had one of my puppies. I used to breed Pomeranians, and she took one from me, Pipsqueak. It was a while ago now, though."

"This one?" Lilly asked, pulling out the photograph of Monica with her dog.

Joseph stared at it for a moment before letting out an uncomfortable sigh. "Where did you get this?"

"Your wife's flat," she replied, handing it to him. "It belongs to you now. I had heard Carol Ann was upset when she saw Monica with her dog?"

"I don't know anything about that. She was grief stricken because her own dog had been killed by a car. Maybe she thought this dog was hers. What was she doing with this photo?"

"How did you and Monica meet?"

"At a reunion at St John's. The three of us, that's Carol Ann, Monica and myself, got talking and the conversation turned to dogs. I said I bred them and she wanted one. That's it really."

"You didn't meet up at all, other than when she collected her dog? Socialise maybe?"

"No, we did not. I had no contact with her after she took the dog and I don't think I like what you're implying, Miss Tweed. They've caught the man who murdered my wife, and I really think you should stop with the amateur sleuthing. Just leave it to the professionals before you make things worse."

Lilly didn't have a response to that. He was right, she needed to let this whole investigation go and get on with her own life. Joseph Hotch was under enough strain already without her making it worse. With perfect timing, a police constable came through to escort them to separate interview rooms and they said their goodbye's.

Almost an hour later Lilly had completed her statement and made her way back to the reception area. There was no sign of Joseph Hotch. He had either left before she had or was still being interviewed. It was probably for the best, Lilly thought.

She glanced at her phone and saw a text from Stacey confirming they'd had a great number of people in the shop after she'd left. A record day for sales, but she'd not breathed a word about what had happened. She'd apparently locked up and left Earl asleep in the window. After a short time in the back room, he'd decided it was safe to venture back out to his favourite spot.

In the car on the return journey, Lilly's mind wouldn't rest. There was something Joseph Hotch had said that was important. Something that didn't seem quite right, but try as she might, she couldn't remember what it was. She decided to do something totally unrelated to the case. Forget all about it in fact and hope her subconscious would do the work. It would come to her, eventually. And she had the perfect project to keep her mind busy.

Chapter Eleven

*S*HE MADE A quick detour on her way back to the shop to visit fellow trader Jim Carmichael. He owned the DIY and hardware shop on the outskirts of the market square. The shop sign was turned to closed, but peering through the glass-fronted door she could see him still at the counter. She knocked and waved as he looked up.

"Lilly, what a nice surprise. Come on in."

"Hi, Jim, sorry to turn up so late, it's been a bit of a rush today."

"No problem. I'm in the middle of a stock take so will be here for a while yet." He locked the door behind her and they made their way to the small kitchenette at the back. "I was just making a cup of tea. Do you want one?"

"No, I'm fine thanks, Jim. I've come for some paint, actually."

"Then you're in the right place, but don't tell me you're doing up the shop again?"

"No, that's perfect as it is. It's for the flat above. I'm renting it out to Stacey, the girl who works for me, but it could do with a bit of an upgrade."

"Any ideas about colours? I've got a good range, but if you want something in particular, I can mix it for you. Shouldn't take long."

Lilly gave him the colours she was thinking of and between them they looked at what was available on the shelves. None were quite what Lilly had in mind, though.

"You know, for the age of the building I think you wouldn't go far wrong with the heritage range." Jim said, handing her a colour chart.

"Oh, these are perfect." She said, indicating the two colours she had been thinking of.

They spent the next ten minutes choosing everything else Lilly would need, including rollers, paint trays, brushes and paint for the ceiling and woodwork.

"Okay, I'll get this lot sorted out for you and deliver it to the back door in about an hour with the invoice. How's that sound?"

"Perfect. Thanks, Jim, I appreciate it."

On the way out, he asked her about the trouble at the shop earlier in the day.

"You heard about that did you?"

"It was the talk of the town all afternoon. You're all right though, are you?"

"I'm fine. It was a case of opportunistic theft, that's all. It just got a little heated, but Bonnie came and sorted it out.

I don't think he'll bother us again." Lilly said, not wanting, nor in fact able, as per the police order, to give too much detail. No doubt the full story would come to light in the coming days.

"That's a relief to know. Right, I better get on with your order. See you shortly."

Back at the shop, Earl raised his head as soon as he heard the key in the door and came to weave himself round Lilly's legs when she entered. She scooped him up and gave him a cuddle.

"Well, Earl, what an exciting day you had," she said to the purring cat. "Glad to see you're back to your usual self."

She popped him on the counter while she read the brief note Stacey had left. She'd cleaned up the breakages, re-stocked those items she'd sold and balanced the till, putting the days takings in the safe. Lilly checked the total on the till receipt and was amazed. It had been the best day she'd had since she'd opened, and that included the launch day. It was amazing what a bit of drama could do. It looked as though everyone who set foot through the door to gossip had been sold something by Stacey. The girl really was an excellent salesperson.

"Come on Earl, let's go and see about getting the flat sorted out. But first a treat for you."

She always kept a few tins of tuna or salmon in the staff kitchen for Earl, just in case. Having filled up his bowls, she left him to it and exited the back door in time to see Jim drive up with a car full of decorating supplies. Unlocking the door, he helped her carry everything upstairs to the flat.

Jim looked around, and then nodded. "The paint is a very good choice for this place. It will be beautiful when it's finished. It's good to see all the original features are still here, too," he said, indicating the ornate coving, ceiling rose and picture rail. "So many of these old places have been stripped of their history. Right, I'll leave you to it, Lilly. Give me a call if you need anything else."

"I will. Thanks, Jim."

Alone, Lilly sent a quick text to Stacey thanking her for her hard work, then rolled up her sleeves, snapped on rubber gloves and set to scrubbing the place from top to bottom. Time to make the place sparkle.

*W*HEN SHE'D BOUGHT the building, the upstairs flat had been in reasonably good condition, just neglected. It was clean, though dusty, but there was no water damage as the roof had been repaired by the previous owner and the old sash windows were in excellent condition. There was also some furniture; a double bed base, wardrobe and chest of drawers in the bedroom. A small dining table and two chairs in the kitchen and two wing back armchairs in the lounge. It was certainly enough for Stacey who had no furniture of her own. Lilly would purchase a mattress for the bed and she had a few pairs of spare curtains at the cottage she could use.

She was up the ladder cleaning the glass shade in the bathroom when her phone rang. It was Stacey.

"Hey, Lilly, just got your message. It was a great day after you left, so many people came in to find out what was going on."

"It looks like they all went away with something too."

"Yeah. Although it wasn't difficult to sell anything, they loved everything you have. I definitely think we got quite a few new regular customers out of it. So how'd you get on with the police?"

"Not much to tell, really. We gave our statements, and that was it. We didn't see Barney at all. Are you okay after your fall?"

"I'm fine. It looked worse than it was. Where are you, it sounds really echoey?"

"I'm up a ladder in the flat bathroom. Hang on, I'll move to the lounge."

"Wait, are you cleaning up there? I'll come and help if you want?"

"Okay, if you're sure? That would be a great help. Do you need a lift?"

"No, I've just got my car back. It was the fan belt, so all fixed now. I'll see you soon."

Lilly had finished in the bathroom and was already half-way through scrubbing the kitchen when Stacey turned up. She didn't see her but heard a squeal and a moment later she came rushing in. "You bought paint! And my favourite colours. Thank you so much, Lilly."

"It needed painting anyway, so I may as well use the colours you like as you're the one moving in. It's going to look great when it's finished."

"I can't wait. Right, let me get to work in the living room."

An industrious two hours later and the whole place was clean and ready for the new paint. It was too late, and they were too tired to begin decorating, so Lilly suggested a cup of tea in the shop to wind down before going home. "I need to get Earl, anyway."

Over a hot cup of Chamomile infused with lemon balm, the discussion inevitably turned to Carol Ann Hotch and Barney Darwin's part in her death.

"So, he murdered her just so he could have her watch?" Stacey said incredulously.

"He said he bought the watch from her and she wouldn't give it to him even though she'd taken his money. But I suppose it amounts to the same thing."

"You don't believe he bought it?"

"No, I don't. There's no proof he gave her any money, and he's admitted sneaking into her flat to try to take it. From what I can understand, he entered when she was asleep and woke her up a couple of times. Poor woman must have been scared out of her wits when she saw him."

"Man, that is all kinds of messed up. What a worm."

"I think he was intent on stealing the watch, but whether he killed her for it, I can't say. There's no proof of that either at the moment. Then there's this letter I found, which doesn't fit in with anything so far."

"What letter?"

"I found it at St John's when I was speaking with Monica. Written to Carol Ann by Joseph, but he denied writing it, and when we checked his handwriting, it wasn't a match. But who did write it, and why did Monica have it?"

"Yeah, that seems strange. What did Monica say?"

"I haven't spoken to her about it yet. I slipped it out of her bag when she left."

Stacey smirked. "Cat burglar Tweed strikes again."

"Embarrassingly, yes." Lilly admitted with a wry smile. "But I won't be doing it again."

"Well, the only one who can answer your questions is Monica."

Lilly nodded in agreement. "I'm not looking forward to it considering how we left things, but I'll need to visit her one last time if I want answers."

"I thought you were going to let the police deal with it from now on?"

"So did I, Stacey. In fact, Bonnie told me to do just that. But I need to find answers to my questions, otherwise I just won't be able to sleep. I'm honestly not sure if they've got the right man. And if they haven't, then we need to find the right one."

Chapter Twelve

THE FOLLOWING MORNING, after helping Stacey get the shop up and running, Lilly headed back to the university with the intention of having another conversation with Monica about the letter. She didn't suspect Monica of having anything to do with Carol Ann's death, but it was very odd that she had a forged letter from the deceased's husband in her bag.

Perhaps someone had slipped it in there without her knowing to make her look culpable? It was practically common knowledge that Carol Ann was fixated on Monica, so it wouldn't take much of a stretch of imagination to point a guilty finger at her and make people believe it. But who would be in a position to do such a thing?

She drove on, lost in thought. It was a beautiful day with real warmth in the spring sunshine and the bright yellow heads of newly opened daffodils swaying in the gentle breeze. But Lilly hardly noticed. She had so many other things on her mind. The police may be confident they had their suspect in custody and part of her knew she should just let it go, but her stubborn side insisted there was more to find and Barney's motive seemed absurd to her.

Whoever had killed Carol Ann had done their research, they knew about her medications, her mental illness. Which, admittedly, Barney also did, but they had been smart enough to make it look like an accident or suicide. There had been some clever thought behind it and Barney, to her mind at least, didn't seem clever enough to have committed the crime. He'd tried to steal the watch in broad daylight in front of several people, for heaven's sake.

Plus, if he knew she was already dead, then he'd had plenty of time to enter the flat and find the watch before the police turned up. He could even have taken the safe out of the wardrobe. It was quite heavy, admittedly, but it wasn't large and not bolted in place. He could have taken it away on a dolly trolley to work on at his leisure. Carol Ann resided on the ground floor so it would have been easy enough, then he could have spent some time trying to get inside before returning it.

Let's face it, Barney not only owned the building but he lived in it. As landlord he legitimately could enter the other resident's homes without raising suspicion. If he had covered up the safe and wheeled it around the building to his own ground floor flat would anyone have raised an eyebrow? Lilly thought not. She shook her head. The more she thought about it, the less sense it made.

She parked and was halfway to the accommodation block when she realised Monica would most likely be in class. She changed direction and took a seat at a bench under the shade of an oak tree, halfway between the classrooms and G block. Hopefully Monica would pass this way and she would be able to intercept her.

Quarter of an hour later she was just about to give up when a flood of students poured out of the main building. Lilly scanned the crowd and almost at the end of the sea of people spotted Monica leaving the chemistry lab and walking towards her, head down, looking at her phone. She had a backpack across one shoulder and in her free hand carried her hockey stick.

Lilly stood just as she reached her. "Monica."

The girl glanced up, her mild expression changing to one of disgust as she realised who it was. "Oh no, not you again. What do you want now? Why can't you just leave me alone?" She shoved her phone in her pocket and strode away down the path. Lilly hurried along beside her.

"Actually, I've come with some news. I thought you'd be interested to know that the police have someone in custody for Carol Ann's murder."

"What?" she said, coming to a sudden halt. "That was quick. Who was it? Do you know?"

"It's not important because I think they have the wrong person and they're going to realise it soon."

"So, you still think you're better than police? Can't you see how arrogant you sound?"

Lilly ignored the jibe and continued. "There are some things which don't add up, and I think you can help me fill in the gaps. I know Carol Ann discussed you regularly with her therapist and the general opinion was that she was obsessed with you for no reason. You thought that too."

"I still think that."

"When I first talked to you, you acted like you hardly knew Carol Ann or her husband, yet you had one of his puppies and were able to personally message him when his wife broke into G block."

"So?"

Lilly's stomach suddenly flipped over as she remembered that elusive comment of Joseph's which she'd failed to grasp the importance of at the time.

"You said it took a while to name Pipsqueak. You didn't name her straight away. Joseph Hotch told me once you'd taken her home you and he never saw each other again."

"We didn't. What is this all about?"

"When I showed him the photograph of you and your dog I got from Carol Ann's flat, he knew your dog's name immediately. How would he know that unless you'd been in touch?"

"I don't know, maybe he saw me around here with her. It's not a secret what I called her."

"Perhaps, but I don't think so, Monica. Then there's this letter." Lilly pulled the letter out of her pocket. "This letter, supposedly from Joseph to his wife, was in your bag. But the thing is I compared it to Joseph's handwriting. It's not his."

Monica snatched the letter from Lilly's hand and looked at it. "You stole this from my bag! I ought to call the police right now."

"I agree. Go ahead," Lilly said. "Because I know you're the one who wrote the letter, Monica. I feel stupid for not noticing it before, but that's your handwriting. I saw it on the clipboard the day we met and it matches perfectly. The question is why did you forge this letter to Carol Ann?"

"You're as crazy as she was. I didn't write this!" Monica shouted. "And I'm calling security right now."

Lilly took a step back as Monica raised her hockey stick. If she didn't try to calm her down, things could get very nasty. Then she saw a familiar face coming to her rescue for a second time. Frederick Warren reached out and gently pushed Monica's arm down, lowering the stick. "Monica, what's going on? What are you shouting about?"

Monica prodded a finger at Lilly. "This crazy woman stole something from my bag and is now accusing me of stuff I didn't do."

"Are you sure, Monica, it seems a bit unlikely?"

"What? You're accusing me of lying?" she hissed at him, eyes flashing dangerously.

"No, of course I'm not, but you can't just go around accusing people of stealing, Monica. Maybe you should go back to halls and calm down, all right?"

"I wasn't the one bothering her!" Monica spat, but Frederick stood his ground. "Fine! Take her side." Monica yelled at him then stormed away.

Fred stood for a moment staring after Monica, a look of concern on his face. Then he turned back to Lilly. "What was that about, Miss Tweed? You seem to get into trouble a lot around here."

"Thank you, Fred," Lilly said. "That's the second time you've rescued me from a heated discussion. Hard as it probably is to believe, I'm not the type who goes looking for trouble."

Fred gave a grim smile in response, then looked down and kicked an errant stone across the path into the grass. "Look, Miss Tweed," he said, a slightly irritated note in his voice. "I appreciate the advice you gave me, and I don't want to sound rude, but you needn't be concerned about my private life. It's all sorted out now."

"Fred, I'm sorry, but I have no idea what you're talking about."

Fred blinked in confusion. "Monica," he said. "She's my ex-girlfriend."

❦

LILLY SPENT A few minutes reassuring Fred that her reason for speaking with Monica was totally unrelated to her being his ex, then phone in hand and heart pounding as she realised how things were fitting together she raced back to her car, dialling Archie's number as she went. She'd had all the clues and couldn't believe it had taken her so long to work it out.

She briefly wondered if phoning Bonnie rather than Archie would be better, but then dismissed the idea. Bonnie had told her that she should leave the investigation to the police and not get involved. If she went to her now, she'd be admitting she hadn't taken any notice. There was also the matter that if she were proved wrong, and realistically that could very well be the case, then she'd be wasting Bonnie's time. Archie was well placed to do some semi-official investigation work and could then pass his findings onto Bonnie himself. This seemed to Lilly to be the best plan all round. Unfortunately, Archie wasn't answering his phone. She left a brief message.

"Archie, it's Lilly. I need you to call me back as soon as you get this. I've just discovered something important regarding Carol Ann Hotch's murder. I'm almost sure they've got the wrong person. I'd like your input on what I've found out. Please, call me as soon as you can."

She hung up, turned round and came face to face with Abigail Douglas.

"Abigail."

"Lillian. So, you've got a lead in the murder case, have you?" she asked, nostrils flaring. "What are you doing still investigating? You don't work for the newspaper anymore, nor are you a private detective. None of this is any of your business, yet you still insist on poking your nose where it doesn't belong."

"And you know what, Abigail? I could say the same about you. You're supposed to be the paper's agony aunt, so what are you doing following this story?"

"Trying to keep a roof over my head! It's all right for you, you've got a successful business, but what about me? Thanks to you no one is writing in to the paper anymore and..." she stopped suddenly, choking on her words as tears pooled. She grabbed a hankie from her pocket, dabbed her eyes and blew her nose.

Lilly was shocked at Abigail's sudden vulnerability. She was such a stony and inflexible woman normally. Pecksniffian her mother would have called her. But on closer inspection she realised there were telltale signs that things were obviously very wrong. The smear of mascara on her cheek, the silver roots showing in her normally perfect coiffure, and the red lipstick on her front tooth.

"Abigail, are you all right?"

She shook her head and sniffed. "No, not really. They're talking about getting rid of my agony aunt column. If I can't transition to something else, it will be too late. I'll be out of a job."

"I'm sorry to hear that," Lilly said.

"I uprooted myself for this job, you know? Gave up everything and now, just a few months later, it looks like it's all been for nothing. And worse, I've nowhere else to go. I've been following the Carol Ann Hotch case closely. Doing my due diligence, following up sources in the hope that if I write a good story, I'll be able to prove to the editors that I know what I'm doing. But no matter what I do you get there first. Please, Lilly, it's not your job, but it's everything to me. My last chance. Would you please share what you know with me?"

Lilly stared dumbstruck for a moment. She didn't recognise this contrite, apologetic and polite Abigail. Things must be really bad at the paper. However, she felt she should really be providing this information to Archie, not only because he was her friend but because he was the newspaper's official crime reporter. She didn't owe this woman anything. Still, a part of her felt somewhat responsible for the shaky predicament Abigail now found herself in.

"Okay," Lilly said at last. "I'll help you, but you must promise me something first."

"What?"

"Before you write one word, you must share what I'm about to tell you with Archie. In fact, you could partner on the article as Archie has also been working on it. Longer than you or me actually, so he deserves this break as much, if not more than anyone. Do you promise to tell him everything?"

"Yes, all right," Abigail said, albeit a little reluctantly. "I suppose it's the right thing to do."

"Okay. Well, I'd rather not discuss this in the university car park, there's a cafe not far from here where we can talk."

"Good idea. I could do with a strong cup of coffee. You can drive and then drop me back off here to collect my car. Seems silly to take two, don't you think, what with the price of petrol nowadays."

Lilly rolled her eyes at Abigail's audacity. Then again, having seen already how carelessly she drove, did she really want to be a passenger with her behind the wheel? The answer was a resounding no. She unlocked the mini and invited Abigail into the passenger seat. Hoping the conversation wouldn't be reduced to a slanging match. You could never tell how things would pan out with Abigail Douglas.

HOLLINGBECK FARM WAS about a mile outside St John's university on the top moorland road with views of Plumpton Mallet nestled in the valley below. A working dairy farm, the owners, Judith and Richard Fosdyke, had diversified when the price of milk had fallen below sustainable levels.

The conversion of a long, low stone barn to a cafe and restaurant had taken nearly a year once planning had been approved and had become an almost instant success. Popular with walkers, hikers and cyclists in particular, it catered for special events such as birthdays and weddings as well. It was also one of the local outlets that sold Lilly's tea in their cafe.

"I didn't know this was here," Abigail said to Lilly as they exited their vehicles. "It's got awards too. Look at those plaques on the wall."

"Yes, it's very popular. There's a lovely garden at the back which will give us some privacy."

The entrance to the rear garden was through the main cafe and as they made their way past tables, the majority of which were full, a jolly looking woman in a floral apron waved at Lilly from behind the counter. "Lilly, I didn't know you were coming today. How are you?"

"I'm well thank you, Judy." She introduced Abigail and explained they were looking for a quiet place in the garden.

"Of course, you go right ahead. I'll send Bethany out with a menu shortly."

Out of earshot Abigail hissed, "Do you know everyone, Lillian?"

"Not quite. See that man over there in the corner?"

Abigail peered in the direction Lilly indicated. "Yes?"

"Well, I don't know him."

"Oh, very droll."

Over tea and toasted crumpets underneath an arbour which provided both shelter and privacy, Lilly laid some ground rules.

"Firstly, what I'm about to tell you is only what I have discovered and put together myself. There's no evidence as such. You won't be able to use a lot of it before it's proved otherwise you could find yourself in court. Again."

Abigail ignored the thinly veiled reference to her previously close call with the local courts, but her face flushed angrily.

"I'm familiar with both the libel and slander laws, Lillian. I wouldn't dream of writing anything which could get either myself or the paper in trouble. Now, tell me what you know."

Lilly replenished their tea, then began with how Frederick Warren had turned up at the shop one day worried about his pregnant girlfriend.

"The young man who was so rude to me?"

"He wasn't rude to you, Abigail, but yes, that's him."

"So, he got his girlfriend pregnant."

"No, someone else did. She was having an affair with a married man. I didn't realise who Fred's girlfriend was until just now at the university, although I should have done. The clues were there. She offered me a ginger sweet when I first met her, which helps with morning sickness. And there were vitamins in her bag."

"So, who was the married man?"

"I think it was Joseph Hotch."

"Carol Ann's husband!" Abigail squeaked. "Oh my word, this changes things. How do you know? And who is the girl?"

"It's Monica Morris."

"The one Carol Ann was obsessed with? Of course! I spoke to her before. Although thanks to you getting in there first, it took all my powers of persuasion to get the most meagre details from her."

Lilly bit her tongue, ignoring the jibe. She was determined not to rise to the woman's barbs. Abigail continued, scanning her notebook.

"I managed to confirm she adopted a puppy from Joseph Hotch a while ago. Told me she met him at one of the reunions."

"That's right. No one knows she's pregnant, so tread very lightly with that information."

"So, what exactly is your theory, Lilly?"

"Joseph has an affair with Monica. I don't know when it started, not long after they met and she got her puppy, I would think. Carol Ann in her letter to me said she thought he was having an affair. She left him and moved out to a flat of her own. On account of the affair, or for some other reason, I don't know. Regardless, the affair carries on and Monica ends up pregnant. Joseph doesn't know she is by the way, but Fred found out and after a heart-to-heart chat they decide to break up. Monica then realises she's going to be on her own when the baby comes and it's a frightening thought. She's young and scared, understandably, but Joseph has already ended the affair as he wants to reconcile with his wife. Carol Ann is the one thing standing in the way of a proper relationship with Joseph and a future for her and the baby."

"Oh, gosh, Lilly. You think Monica killed Carol Ann?"

Lilly nodded. "I find it very difficult to believe, but it's beginning to look that way, isn't it?"

"But how? The autopsy report said she was drugged, causing a fatal overdose."

"Do you remember the story you wrote about the break-in and theft at the laboratory at St John's?"

"Of course."

"Can you remember what was stolen?"

"A number of high value apparatus which I can't remember the names of, those small enough to carry away at least. The place was completely ransacked, so it was difficult to piece together exactly what was missing for ages. But there was a lot of pharmaceuticals taken... Oh dear, yes, now I see where you're heading. You really think Monica was smart enough to do this?"

"Her major is pharmaceuticals, Abigail, she spends a lot of time in the labs studying. She knows them like the back of her hand. She'd know when they would be empty, the codes for the doors and the locks on the cupboards. I also think she'd be clever enough to take a multitude of items and an array of different drugs in order to camouflage what she really intended to steal. It would be difficult to connect the murder with the theft at the lab then. The only point I'm not sure of is the fact that Fred broke up with her *after* the robbery, so that would mean she was planning the murder for quite a while before she suddenly found herself single."

"Maybe..." Abigail began, tapping her pen against her teeth while she thought. "She was sure her boyfriend would dump her when he found out she was pregnant?"

"Yes, that's a distinct possibility. Fred, told me they'd never slept together, Monica wanted to wait apparently, so there's no way the baby could have been his."

"Mmm. But do you really think she was deciding to kill Carol Ann so far in advance?"

"Honestly? I don't know. But why else would she steal the drugs?"

Abigail snapped her fingers and immediately went into reporter mode. Speaking in headlines. "Desperate times call for desperate measures. A young, single student with bright prospects finds herself pregnant by a married man, who has already hinted his intention of returning to his wife, and suddenly her future is in ruins. Penniless, shunned by her parents and unable to find a job. What would you do for money?"

"You think she was planning on selling the stolen drugs?"

"I do. It's what I originally wrote in my article, if you remember."

This thought had not occurred to Lilly, but she could see it held some not insignificant merit. "You know, I think you might be right, Abigail. Monica knew she would be needing money, so stole drugs with a high street value that could be easily sold on. But when Fred broke it off with her and Joseph decided to try again with his wife, she was suddenly alone. She decided to use the resources she already had at her disposal to get rid of Carol Ann, leaving the way clear for her and Joseph to have a future, especially when she told him about the baby."

Abigail grinned and snapped her notebook shut. "Excellent work if I say so myself. Now I've just got write it."

"You'll need more than just speculation before you put anything in print, Abigail. All we've managed to do is talk through our ideas, putting them together with what we already know and making them fit the crime. It's not enough. There needs to be definitive proof. And don't forget to let Archie know what we've discussed. That was the deal, remember?"

"Of course, dear. Now, I'll just go and pay a visit to the powder room. I'll meet you back at the car."

Typical, Lilly thought as she watched Abigail sashay her way back inside. *Leave me with the bill.* But she couldn't be bothered to argue.

（ℓℓℓ）

*T*HE RETURN JOURNEY saw Abigail back to her usual tactless and slightly acerbic self, and Lilly switched off. By the time she pulled into the university car park, she'd just about had enough. Then they saw Abigail's car.

"My car!" she screamed. "Look at my car. It's only just been fixed!"

The windscreen had been smashed along with both wing mirrors and there was a huge dent in the bonnet. Lilly and Abigail jumped out of the mini and rushed over.

"Who would do such a wicked thing!"

The answer came almost instantly and Lilly just had time to yell, "Look out!" and grab Abigail's sleeve to pull her away before she was struck by Monica's hockey stick.

"You nosy witches!" Monica yelled before throwing back her arm, ready to take another swipe with her stick.

"Move!" Lilly snapped, shoving Abigail. The two of them bolted between their vehicles as Monica made another swing. Thankfully she missed them both but the momentum continued and she struck the passenger side window of Abigail's car with such force it shattered.

"My car!"

"Forget your car, Abigail, just run!"

Monica continued to swing and yell at them as they charged across the car park. Running blindly with no idea where they were headed, they dashed down an alleyway between two buildings. A dire mistake. It was a dead end, and they had nowhere left to run. They turned back to the entrance just as Monica appeared, panting slightly but still brandishing her hockey stick.

"She's going to kill us with that stupid stick," Abigail sobbed, clutching Lilly's arm.

"You two," Monica hissed. "Are going to ruin everything."

"Monica, let me help you," Lilly said gently. "I know you wrote that letter to Carol Ann. It was to try to drive a wedge between her and Joseph, wasn't it? So she'd believe he thought her a burden and an embarrassment?"

Monica nodded once but stayed silent, continuing to stare with utter hatred at Lilly.

"That bit at the end, about him not wanting to do something he would regret? It was supposed to make her think he would have her sectioned, put in a mental institution wasn't it?"

"Lilly, what are you doing?" Abigail hissed. "Shut up or you'll make her even crazier."

But Lilly knew she needed to try to calm the girl down. Keep her talking so they could either disarm her or get away. She shrugged Abigail off and took a step forward.

"She realised it was you who'd written it though, didn't she?" This was a complete guess on Lilly's part, but an educated one.

Monica gritted her teeth. "Yes. She recognised my writing from the reunion invitations. It was a stupid mistake. Next thing I know, she's here looking for me. Wanting to talk to me about it. About me stealing her husband. Said she was worried about me. Can you believe it? The local crazy woman worried about me!"

"So you drugged her?"

Monica shrugged. "It wasn't difficult. I just added a little something to her tea while we talked in the garden. It relaxed her. I suggested a walk. It was easy to get her down to the river after that."

"Then you forced her to take an overdose of the medications you stole from the lab."

Monica scowled. "Well, aren't you the clever one? It was easy, she was so high she practically drowned herself. But you won't be telling anyone else." She stepped closer, brandishing the stick, a look of crazed menace in her eyes.

Lilly felt Abigail once again grab her arm. "Stand your ground," Lilly muttered. "And we can try to get that hockey stick away from her..." Abigail whimpered as Monica came nearer, getting ready to swing.

Chapter Thirteen

*L*ILLY FELT LIKE a caged animal as Monica came nearer. "We go at her at the same time," she whispered to Abigail, who looked far from keen on the idea. Unfortunately, Monica wasn't giving them any other option. It was clear she was determined to keep her secrets, even if meant beating two women to death with a hockey stick. Though how she thought she was going to get away with it, Lilly had no idea. She'd obviously been pushed to breaking point and was no longer rational.

Lilly moved forward and let out a brief sigh of relief when Abigail followed her lead. Monica swung directly at them but was momentarily taken off guard when both Lilly and Abigail lunged forward. The hockey stick connected with Abigail's shoulder, but Lilly had already grabbed Monica's arm, which slowed down the swing and lessened the impact.

"Ow!" Abigail yelled, grabbing the stick and wrenching it from the girl's hands. She threw it to the ground.

"That's enough, Monica," Lilly said in a firm tone, still holding her arm. She was about to try to calm things down when Abigail decided she'd had enough.

Furious at the damage to her car, having to run in fear across a car park and being cornered like an animal and threatened, she lashed out, violently pushing Monica who slipped and fell to the ground. She was on the verge of kicking her when Lilly pushed her aside. "Stop it! You can't go around kicking people, Abigail! And she's pregnant, remember."

Stopping to squabble was a big mistake because as soon as they were distracted Monica rolled over, snatched up her hockey stick and stood up. "Look out!" Abigail yelled just in time for Lilly to avoid being smacked on the back of the head.

However, their positions had reversed, and they now found themselves with a free run out of the alley. They turned and bolted back the way they'd come.

"Where is everybody?" Lilly wheezed as they dashed across the deserted car park.

"Let's just get back to the car and call the police," Abigail gasped.

Lilly quickly glanced behind them and saw Monica on their tail. But she must have damaged her ankle when she fell, as she was limping. By some unspoken agreement, they made their way to Lilly's undamaged car first, only to find she'd not got her keys.

"I must have dropped them back there."

"You can't go back for them. Quick, we'll have to take mine. Get in."

Lilly grabbed the handle and yanked open the passenger door, only to see the glass from the window on the seat. She slammed the door, opened the rear one and launched herself across the back seat. "Quick, go!" she yelled, just as Monica reached them.

Abigail threw the car into drive and peeled out of the parking space to the sound of squealing tyres and the smell of burning rubber. Lilly, who hadn't had time to put on her seatbelt, went crashing to the foot well, bashing her elbow as she did so.

"She's following us," Abigail cried as she accelerated, causing Lilly, who'd just crawled onto the seat to fall sideways and bang her head on the door.

"Abigail, will you calm down! Let me get my seatbelt on."

Abigail slowed down a fraction, enabling Lilly to get strapped in.

"Lilly?"

"What?"

"You don't suppose Monica has a car, do you?"

*L*ILLY FUMBLED IN her pocket for her phone, her intention to call the police.

"Abigail, drive to the police station, I'm calling them now." She switched on her phone. "Oh, no. I must have pocket dialled Stacey by mistake."

"Never mind Stacey, whoever she is," yelled Abigail. "Call the police, she's right behind us! Good grief, I can hardly see a thing out of this windscreen."

Lilly turned to look out of the rear window, and sure enough there was a small black car speeding in their direction. "Put your foot down," she shouted, now wishing they had remained at the university and tried to get to a classroom rather than turning this into a high-speed car chase. The likes of which had never been seen in Plumpton Mallet in all the years she'd lived there.

Abigail accelerated, speeding down the road towards the outskirts of town when a red traffic light caught them. She tapped the brake. "Are you mad? Don't stop" Lilly shouted from the backseat. "She's gaining on us."

"Right... right." Abigail stammered, speeding through the light.

Lilly turned back just in time to see Monica following them through the red light and another vehicle slamming into her from the oncoming intersection. "Stop!" Lilly yelled, recognising the other car. "That's Stacey."

Abigail slowed down and pulled over to the side of the road. Lilly tossed her phone at her. "Get the police and an ambulance here, now," she said. Abigail fiddled with the phone, her hands shaking so much she could barely hold it, but Lilly didn't notice, she was already out of the car and running back up the road towards the accident.

Monica's car had been flipped upside down. Stacey, on the other hand, seemed relatively unscathed as she exited her vehicle. The front end was bashed in as a result of the impact, but considering the force with which she'd hit, the damage was remarkably little.

"I can't believe you just walked away from that impact. Are you all right?" Lilly asked, noting the nosebleed and the cut above her eyebrow.

"I'm good. My car's too old for airbags, apparently, but the seatbelts are just fine."

"What are you doing here?" Lilly demanded. It came out sharper than she'd meant.

"Are you kidding?" Stacey said. "You called me. I could hear you and knew you were in trouble, so I closed the shop and headed out after I called the police."

Lilly pulled the girl in for a quick hug. "You're amazing. Thank you." She said. Then turned to Monica's car.

They hurried over, kneeling on the road by the driver's side window. Monica groaned.

"Monica, stay still an ambulance is on the way."

Lilly knew better than to try to move her. There was no smoke and no smell of petrol, so the car wasn't in imminent danger of catching fire. She held the girl's hand and talked to her gently.

"My leg..." Monica gasped.

"Try not to move, you'll be out of here very soon. I promise."

Cars were braking all around them, completely blocking the crossroads as people stopped, exiting their vehicles in an effort to either see what had happened or to help. Several were on phones reporting the accident to the police, but thanks to Stacey's earlier call they were already on their way and a couple of police cars and a two ambulances arrived a few minutes later.

"My baby." Monica cried, her free hand resting on her stomach. She turned to look at Lilly, the crazed look she'd had before had completely vanished, replaced with fear. She looked like a terrified child, and Lilly couldn't help her heart twist in sympathy.

"Try not to worry, Monica. The ambulance is here. They'll take good care of you both."

Monica took a last look at Lilly before breaking down in tears. "I'm sorry. I'm so sorry."

⸙⸙⸙

ONCE THE POLICE were busy calming the chaos and trying to clear the scene of onlookers and their obstructing vehicles, Abigail got out of her car and walked over to the crash. She'd managed to find a notebook and pen and was about to speak to Monica, who had been extracted from her vehicle and loaded onto a stretcher, when a fierce look from Lilly made her think otherwise. She slipped her notebook in her pocket with a contrite look. But as usual, she had to get the last word.

The ambulance was about to set off with Monica in the back, when Abigail informed a police man that the girl had attacked them with a hockey stick and caused massive damage to her car. A confirming nod from Lilly and he elected to travel to the hospital with Monica.

A paramedic from the second ambulance was busy talking to Stacey.

"You need to get to hospital too," he said, shining a light in her eyes. "You've got a mild concussion."

"No, sorry. I can't afford it."

"Stacey," Lilly said. "It doesn't cost you here like it does in America. You need to get yourself checked out, okay?"

"Oh, right? I forgot. Yeah, okay, I'll go. I am a bit dizzy."

"I'll come and see you shortly."

Stacey handed over her car keys to the waiting police officer and moments later was in the second ambulance on her way to hospital. Lilly surveyed the scene with a combination of horror and sorrow.

"Dreadful isn't it." Abigail said, coming up behind her.

Lilly nodded in agreement.

"I mean, how on earth am I to do without my car? The insurance process takes so long, and no doubt I'll be given some inferior model to use in the interim. It's already cost me a small fortune in repairs recently."

Lilly stared at her, aghast. Luckily, she was saved from speaking her mind as Bonnie drew up in a police car and came over.

"Lilly, I heard on my radio about the accident and came as quick as I could. Are you both all right?"

"Yes, we're fine. Just a few bumps and bruises, mainly."

"Speak for yourself," Abigail retorted. "My car is a complete mess. Not to mention I was nearly bludgeoned to death by a hockey stick wielding maniac."

Bonnie raised an eyebrow. Lilly quickly shook her head.

"Right. Well, we'll need to take full statements from you both. Abigail, if you'll go to my colleague over there, please. Lilly, I'll take yours."

"Can you give me a lift back to St John's?" Lilly asked Bonnie once Abigail had gone. "My car is still there, and I lost my keys in the car park."

"Yes, all right, we can talk on the way."

Bonnie executed a perfect three-point turn, then let out an exasperated sigh. "So, which part of *don't get involved* and *leave it to the professionals* didn't you understand, Lilly Tweed?" She demanded as they journeyed back to the university.

"Ah, you're angry with me?"

"Of course I'm angry with you, you could have been killed. What on earth did you think you were doing?"

Lilly laid her head back, closed her eyes, and related the entire story from start to finish. Bonnie had reached their destination long before Lilly had completed her story, so parked up and listened in silence. Eventually, Lilly opened her eyes and sat up. "So, that's what happened."

"God, Lilly. Don't ever do anything like this again. You've been very lucky. So, you're saying Monica Morris confessed to killing Carol Ann Hotch."

"Yes."

"And she was responsible for the laboratory thefts, too?"

"Yes, I think so. She didn't deny it when I asked her, anyway. The stolen drugs are the same as those Carol Ann was forced to overdose on."

"I'll need to radio all this in and make sure she has a twenty-four guard at the hospital at the very least. You go and find your keys and I'll come and help in a minute."

"Don't worry, you go and do your job, Bonnie. I can get a taxi if I have to."

"Okay, if you're sure?" Bonnie paused. "Look, I'm not condoning what you did, Lilly, but it looks like you've solved a couple of cases for us. So, thank you."

"Does this mean I'm forgiven?"

Bonnie smirked. "Of course. Just stay out of trouble."

It didn't take Lilly long to find her keys, they were in the alley where the main scuffle had taken place. She scooped them up and walked wearily back to her car. She was just unlocking the door when her phone rang. It was Archie.

"LILLY, WHAT'S THIS I hear about yet another car crash? Abigail's just called, claiming she's got the scoop of the century."

Lilly laughed. "A bit of an exaggeration, but yes, it's a big story as far as Plumpton Mallet is concerned. Actually, come to think of it, it's a pretty big story anywhere, so may even end up in the nationals."

"You've got to give me the scoop first, Lilly," Archie said, but Lilly hesitated.

"You've really put me on the spot here, you know, Archie. I don't want to be in the middle of you two. I told Abigail what I knew because she was here and had almost worked it out for herself anyway. I made her promise that she would tell you everything first though so you could put the article together between you."

"The only reason she was there at all, was because she swiped all my notes!" Archie cried down the phone. "She thinks I don't know, but I've been putting all this together from the start and the only way she'd make those connections is through my hard work. I tell you, I'm just about at the end of my tether with that woman."

Lilly gasped. "She stole your notes? Oh, Archie, I'm sorry I had no idea. That really is beyond the pale. Is that how she found out about Monica?"

"How did you find out about Monica?"

"Hang on, let me get in my car and I'll tell you everything."

For the second time in an hour Lilly went through the entire sequence of events, stopping occasionally while Archie asked questions and confirmed sources. At the end, Archie let out an appreciative whistle.

"Wow, Abigail was right, that's some story."

Lilly wasn't exactly a fan of Abigail, she'd taken Lilly's job at the paper and gone out of her way to make her life difficult because of the agony aunt letter box outside her shop. Now it turned out she'd also pinched Archie's notes. But on the other hand, Abigail had broken down and told Lilly how desperate she was. That must have taken some courage for a woman like her. She couldn't afford to lose her job and in no way did Lilly want to be even partly responsible for that if it happened.

"Archie, I've told you everything and you now know exactly what Abigail does. You're on a level playing field. But please, will you try to work it out with her? She's worried sick she's going to lose her job, and she has nothing else to fall back on."

"And so she should be," said Archie tetchily. "Her agony aunt column is a disaster, and the investigative pieces she did on the university break-ins were very poorly constructed."

"That may be so, Archie. Not everyone can write as well as you. But you have to admit she was right about the drug dealing side of the thefts. Why not take this opportunity to let her learn from a master, Archie? She actually has quite good instincts when she puts her mind to it. And she enjoys running around and following up leads. She could be an asset to you if you let her."

Archie sighed dramatically. "Oh, all right. Here's what I'll do. I'm going to talk to Abigail, and I'll suggest we co-write the main article together. I'll also inform her that I know she took my notes. So she'll have to say yes to my very magnanimous offer. However, after that I want an exclusive interview with you about your role in solving the case, okay? Just you and me over a cup of your delicious tea."

Lilly laughed. "Yes, okay, I'll happily do that for you. Although, a glass of wine in the local pub would be a welcome change to tea."

"Done!" Archie said. "I might even treat you to dinner."

"Now that sounds like a proper plan. Listen, I've got to get to the hospital and see how Stacey is. She got quite banged up saving our bacon. I'll call you when I leave and we can discuss where to go for that dinner."

"All right. I hope Stacey's okay. See you later, Lilly," he said, and hung up the phone.

*I*T TOOK LILLY half an hour to get to the hospital. Then another ten minutes to find a parking space, find the right change for the meter, get a ticket to put on her dashboard and walk back to the A&E department. At the desk she was told to wait and someone would come and get her when Stacey was able to receive visitors. She was assured, however, that the girl wasn't severely injured. The doctor's were purely keeping her under observation for the time being.

She wandered over to the seating area just as Joseph Hotch rushed up to the counter in a frantic, dishevelled state. She turned and hurried back.

"Joseph, what are you doing here? Are you all right?"

"Lilly, do you know what's happened? I got a call saying there'd been an accident?"

"Yes, I was there, I'm afraid. Who called you?"

"Someone from here. The ward sister, I think. She, Monica that is, gave my name," he paused, looking sick and wretched. "Lilly, is Monica pregnant? Do you know?"

She studied him for a moment and saw the guilt along with the pain. There was no denying he knew her now. He must have realised how pointless it was. "Yes, she is."

"And she did it, didn't she? She killed my wife?"

"Yes. She confessed to Abigail and me earlier. I'm so sorry, Joseph."

He staggered to the nearest chair and collapsed into it, head in hands. Lilly followed and sat beside him.

"It's all my fault," he sobbed.

"No, it's not. You can't blame yourself for what Monica did, Joseph. She's an adult and accountable for her own actions."

"I would have taken responsibility for the child and looked after them both, if only she'd told me. She didn't have to hurt Carol Ann. Oh my god, what have I done?"

Lilly sat with him while he poured his heart out. Telling her about the difficult life he'd had with Carol Ann as her mental health deteriorated. The flattery he'd felt when a young woman had shown an interest in him. *He wasn't the first man who'd had his head turned by a pretty girl*, Lilly thought. *Nor would he be the last*. But this affair had ended in the ultimate tragedy and ruined many lives. The ripples of which would be felt for a long time. It would take Joseph Hotch years to put the pieces of his life back together.

Lilly sat with the distraught man for over an hour. Eventually the crying ceased, and he began to pull himself together.

"What are you going to do, Joseph?" she asked gently.

"I don't know," he said, wiping his eyes. "I have no idea what to do. I can't think straight." He looked up at her, "I don't suppose you have any advice, do you?"

Lilly thought for a moment, then nodded as an idea took hold. "I think I might have some if you're willing to listen."

Chapter Fourteen

IVE MINUTES AFTER she'd opened the shop the next morning, Lilly was surprised to Stacey walk in. She'd told her at the hospital, when she'd eventually been allowed to visit, not to bother coming in, to rest until she felt better.

"Stacey, what are you doing here? Are you all right?"

"I feel fine, don't worry."

"Well, you don't look it," Lilly said, peering at the two black eyes Stacey now sported.

Stacey waved her off. "It looks worse than it is."

Oh, to be young again, Lilly thought. She'd had a restless night with her swollen elbow and the bruise on her temple where she'd been thrown around in the back of Abigail's car.

"Well, you must promise me you'll go home if you start to feel poorly."

"I will. I've got pain medication from the hospital so I should be okay."

At nine o'clock Lilly turned the shop sign to open, and the day began in earnest. Customers were still coming in to discuss the theft, and Stacey brewed tea samples and tisanes and deftly sold them merchandise before they left. At ten o'clock a car Lilly didn't recognise pulled up outside and Abigail Douglas got out. She rushed to the agony aunt letter box, stuffed something inside, then returned to the car. Driving away without even a glance through the window.

How curious, Lilly thought as she went to retrieve what Abigail had posted. It was the morning edition of The Plumpton Mallet Gazette. She unfolded it and emblazoned across the cover was a candid shot of herself at the site of the accident speaking with a police officer. She hadn't even realised someone had taken it. The headline read; **Local Teashop Owner Turns Super-sleuth.** Lilly's cheeks burned as she turned to page three where the story continued. The by-line read *Archie Brown* and just below that *with Abigail Douglas*. At the bottom scrawled in red pen was a note. *Thanks, Lilly. AD.*

"Well, I'll be," she said out loud, smiling. Archie had told her he'd informed Abigail the only reason he was agreeing to a co-written article and not having her demoted or sacked for stealing his notes, was because Lilly had vouched for her. Thanks were completely out of character for Abigail. Perhaps there was still a chance the two of them could get along after all.

She closed the paper, she'd read it properly later, and turned back to the shop, surprised to find it was almost full.

She'd been so engrossed in the article she'd shut out her surroundings completely.

"Sorry, Stacey," she said when she got back behind the counter. "I didn't realise we'd got so busy."

It turned out the place was packed because everyone who'd read the paper that morning had decided to turn up at the shop and congratulate its proprietor and her lovely American sales assistant. Several of them had papers tucked under their arms and were insistent on reading out sections and peppering her with questions as to how she'd managed to solve the case. Stacey insisted on getting photographs of everything for social media, encouraging patrons to do the same if they had accounts. "It will put this place on the map!" she told Lilly with a grin. She was quite happy to have her photo taken with two black eyes, so how could Lilly refuse when all she had was a bruised temple and cheekbone in a fetching shade of violet?

Eventually there was a brief lull and while Stacey retired to the back room for lunch, Lilly took the opportunity to read the article in full. It was clear Archie had done his research. The story was well written and full of detailed information, most of which she had provided over an excellent dinner and a bottle of wine the previous evening. He must have worked through the night to get the article written in time for the morning edition.

Abigail had interviewed Stacey over the phone while she was at the hospital, so had included a couple of quotes from her. Archie, as well as formally interviewing Lilly, had even managed to speak briefly with Joseph Hotch.

The first half of the article was mainly concerned with how Lilly had pieced together clues and eventually realised who the murderer of Carol Ann Hotch was. For her part Lilly had told Archie most of it was dumb luck, but he'd waved away that idea. It mentioned Bonnie as being an integral part of the investigation, complimenting the local police and their efforts, despite the original incorrect assumption that Barney Darwin had been the guilty party due to his attempted theft of the victim's pocket watch.

With no proof that he hadn't bought the watch from Carol Ann, and with the watch safely back with Joseph, he had been released with a hefty fine and a warning. His reputation in tatters.

But it was the second half of the article which interested Lilly the most. Apart from a broken leg, Monica had come out of the accident in one piece. But more importantly, her baby was unharmed. Joseph had taken Lilly's advice and had spent a long time talking through the future with Monica, and they had agreed he would be raising his child alone. Monica would be serving a long prison sentence, and it was likely the baby would be an adult if and when she was ever released. She had therefore willingly signed over all parental rights to the father. While it wasn't in the paper, Joseph had shared with Lilly the fact that if it was a girl, he would name her after his wife.

She knew Joseph had a lot to work through; the consequences of his decisions and actions had had a catastrophic outcome, so she'd taken the liberty of handing over Dr Jorgensen's details to him. Whether he sought out the doctor was up to him, but Lilly felt sure he would.

She sighed, wondering what would become of them all. Then folding the newspaper put it under the counter. It was time to turn her attention back to her proper business. Several customers had entered.

Lilly knew everyone who ventured in over the next half hour, apart from one older gentleman who had positioned himself in a corner and hadn't moved the entire time she was busy serving. Eventually it was just the browsers who were left, so she approached him with a smile.

"Hello. Can I help you with anything?"

He glanced round the shop. "I was looking for someone. But perhaps she's not here today?"

"Who is it you're looking for?"

"Stacey Pepper. I do have the right shop, don't I?"

"Yes, she's at lunch at the moment, though. Sorry, who are you?"

The man gave Lilly a fixed look. "My name is James. James Pepper. And I need to speak with my daughter."

If you enjoyed *Tea & Sympathy*, the first book in the series of the same name, please leave a review on Amazon. It really does help and you'd make the author very happy.

A Deadly
SOLUTION

A Tea & Sympathy Mystery

BOOK 2

About the Book

**Meet Lilly Tweed. Former Agony Aunt.
Purveyor of Fine Teas. Accidental Sleuth.**

It's the height of summer and Lilly has been asked to demonstrate at a local book club. Not only is this her first event, but it's for the crème de la crème of the town's residents, a member of the aristocracy and a wealthy heiress included.

When the proceedings get underway Lilly notices underlying tension and competition between the members and it's not long before tragedy strikes. The heiress is found dead.

As a prime witness Lilly is asked unofficially to help solve the crime, but with motives galore, animosity running rife and all the women having spent time alone with the victim, the culprit could be any of them.

The more she digs the murkier it becomes, and she soon realises appearances are deceiving when it comes to the rich and titled of Plumpton Mallet.

Chapter One

*L*ILLY TWEED, FORMER agony aunt now purveyor of fine teas at The Tea Emporium in Plumpton Mallet's market square, was currently sitting in Psychiatrist Dr Jorgenson's office. She had met him a few months prior when she'd made a phony appointment in order to question him about one of his patients. A woman who had died in what Lilly thought were suspicious circumstances. He'd been very gracious regarding her subterfuge and had answered those questions he could, within the remit of his profession, but toward the end he'd cleverly brought the conversation round to Lilly herself. Through their conversation she discovered she had been harbouring negative feelings and some fair amount of guilt regarding her divorce several years prior.

He'd recognised immediately she had been swallowing her emotions and putting on a brave face which as the years had gone by had become second nature. It had come as a complete surprise to Lilly, however. She and her ex-husband had eventually fallen into a platonic relationship, more house mates than partners, and had become lazy in their romantic endeavours, taking each other for granted, and they had naturally drifted apart. While one party wasn't to blame over the other, Lilly had shouldered more than her fair share of responsibility for the failed relationship. Alongside the proverbial, 'is it me?'

Falling out of love, they had gone their separate ways before the apathy could become animosity, and in the main it had been with little tension. He had moved away from Plumpton Mallet, making it easier for them both to move on with their lives. Yet, there was still something about the experience that had been quietly gnawing away at her, and it had taken Dr Jorgenson to make her see it.

He'd also made a diagnosis which could transform into something of a more serious nature if not addressed; compassionate empathy disorder. Lilly had never heard of it, but once Dr Jorgenson had explained what it was, she'd recognised it in herself immediately. It had come to the fore when she'd become reluctantly involved in solving the death of the local woman who had been the doctor's long-term patient.

"So what exactly is compassionate empathy disorder?" she'd asked when he'd first brought it up.

"Well, empathy itself is a significant human capability. It allows us to connect with one another, as well as recognise, understand and share in emotions."

"So, being able to react with compassion to what someone else is going through?"

"Exactly. But in some cases the person is very sensitive and highly tuned to others' emotions. This can result in 'empathy burnout,' which is when you become emotionally exhausted and completely overwhelmed by taking on everyone else's problems."

"And this is what I have?" Lilly had asked.

"Not quite yet, it's borderline, though. It would seem you do have difficulty regulating your emotions. If there isn't that boundary, then you risk taking it all on and going the other way. That's to say you tend to stop feeling so empathetic. Your empathy becomes your kryptonite, if you like, and can start to cause you harm. It's a challenge to step back from, but that's something I can help you work through."

It was at this point that Lilly had welcomed the opportunity to address her issues with the doctor, and regular therapy sessions were set up. He went on to explain in more detail the disorder.

"There are three categories of empathy; **Cognitive;** where you can place yourself in another's shoes, understand and relate to their emotions and react in an appropriate way. **Affective**; where you share the feelings another is experiencing. Becoming one with their emotions if you like. And finally, **Compassionate;** this incorporates both of the other types, making you want to take action and relieve the other person of their suffering. It's partly what made you such an effective agony aunt."

Over several sessions, they went on to discuss at length the emotional cost of Lilly's involvement in the death of Carol Ann Hotch. She had found herself several times mired in the guilt and emotional well-being of all those concerned.

From the victim herself, her husband, and the perpetrator. Even Abigail Douglas, the woman who had taken over her agony aunt job at the paper and was known to be an extremely difficult personality, didn't escape her innate feeling of compassion.

But it was Stacey, an American student and her employee, who had eventually come to her and Abigail's rescue at the eleventh hour, that she felt most responsible for. And it was to her that the conversation turned today, during her fourth session with Dr Jorgenson.

৫৫৫৫৯

"SO, TELL ME how things are going with Stacey? She's been with you a few months now." Lilly shifted in her chair and reached for a glass of water on the side table, taking a sip before answering.

"Well, now that the summer holidays are here, she's taken more hours at the shop as she's not got classes. She really is an excellent employee and the customers love her. I had been worried initially about her lack of knowledge regarding what I sell, but she's learned so much since she came to work for me. She said when she first applied that she was a quick study and she was right. My fears were totally unfounded. I couldn't be more pleased."

Dr Jorgenson smiled. "I expect her being on summer break has afforded you more free time than you're used to since you first opened?"

"Absolutely. I try not to take advantage of her and still spend most of my time in the shop. It is my business, after all. But I am a bit worried about Stacey."

"Worried? In what way?"

"It's her father," Lilly said. Wondering if she was about to be ticked off for getting involved in matters that weren't her concern. "She has dual citizenship and grew up in America with her mother because her father was unreliable. She chose to come to a university in England in order to get to know him better, yet he kept her at arms-length for the longest time. He didn't seem to want anything to do with her. He lives in London, I think I've mentioned that before?"

"It's a long way from here. Has he been to visit at all?"

"Not at first, but ever since the newspaper headline ran about how we solved Carol Ann's case, he turns up quite regularly."

Both Stacey and Lilly had ended up on the front page of The Plumpton Mallet Gazette when it was discovered they were instrumental in solving the case. Stacey had two black eyes, the result of a traffic accident which had ultimately ended a high-speed car chase, the likes of which the small town had never seen before, and saved Lilly's bacon. Along with that of Abigail Douglas who was driving the car being pursued. The sight of his daughter's injuries on-line had spurred Mr Pepper into action, and he'd immediately caught the first available train and landed in Lilly's shop the same afternoon.

"What is it that concerns you, exactly?" Dr Jorgensen asked after a lengthy pause. He never seemed to ask a question that he didn't at least suspect she already knew the answer to.

"I suppose I'm worried it's not sincere," Lilly said. "Stacey and I have become quite close since she started working for me, as well as also renting the flat above the shop, and I naturally care about her welfare. Mr Pepper has a tendency to let her down quite regularly whenever they make plans, and I'm worried it's causing her some stress."

The doctor made some notes then asked, "Have you tried to get to know Mr Pepper at all?" without looking up.

Lilly sighed. "No, not really. To be honest, I haven't actually wanted to. I find him quite taciturn and a bit belligerent."

Dr Jorgenson nodded as though that was exactly what he expected her to say. "Do you think perhaps, Lilly, the reason you are so concerned about the relationship between Mr Pepper and his daughter is because you are using Stacey as a stand in for your own lack of family in the area? Specifically, the fact that you and your ex-husband never had children of your own?"

Lilly started in shock. Her stomach dropped and her heart thumped. Then she frowned. She sometimes wondered why she came to see a man who kept holding up a mirror to her like this. Her parents had passed away, and she'd been an only child. While she'd grown up in Plumpton Mallet and had many friends, it was true she lacked a strong family connection. Drat it!

"I don't *believe* that's what I'm doing..." she said, then shook her head. "I don't know, maybe I am." It was a disconcerting admission.

"Don't get me wrong, Lilly, I think the relationship you've developed with Stacey is to be admired. There's nothing wrong with being a role model for the girl, and from what you've told me that's the kind of relationship you've developed. My concern is that Stacey already has both a mother and a father. Her own family drama to juggle. But it's her responsibility, not yours. It's wise not to overstep the mark and intertwine yourself in another's family matters."

Lilly folded her arms and looked down, tracing the pattern in the carpet with the toe of her sandal.

"Yes, you're right," she said eventually. "I don't want to overstep, Stacey and I have a good relationship, but I must remember that what's going on between her and her father is their business. I think being the agony aunt for Plumpton Mallet for so long has sometimes made me think people value and want my opinion or help more than they actually do. It's an issue of pride, isn't it? Another reason why I was sceptical initially about the idea of counselling. It was partly the irony of an agony aunt needing the services of a shrink."

Dr Jorgenson laughed. "It's good you recognise that about yourself." He closed his notebook and put his pen in his shirt pocket. The signal that the session was coming to an end.

They both stood up and Lilly grabbed her handbag from the adjacent chair, putting the strap over her shoulder.

"So, tell me, what's life been like since you became the most famous woman in Plumpton Mallet?"

Lilly chuckled. "Very strange. A couple of days ago I was away from the shop and Stacey told me later that four different people had come in looking for 'The Super Sleuth.' I've gone from being a local tea shop owner to a point of gossip or interest for over half the town. And beyond, actually. It's weird having people turn up at the shop wanting autographs or their photo taken with me, like I'm a character in a mystery book. It was over three months ago, yet people are still eating it up like it was yesterday. Even the tourists are aware of it. So much so that The Tea Emporium has now been added to the must see stops on the town tour."

"That must have been good for business?"

"It really has, and believe me I am not complaining, it's just not something I'm used to. Stacey loves it all though, and is now in charge of all our social media, which again has had a very positive effect on trade."

They'd walked as they talked and now found themselves at the door. Dr Jorgenson opened it for her and Lilly stepped out into the sunshine.

"I'll come and visit your shop soon," he said. "I'm an avid tea drinker."

"You wouldn't be British if you weren't," Lilly replied with a grin.

"Indeed. I need to find enough time to dedicate an hour or two in my pursuit of a perfect cup of tea."

"Well, you'll be made very welcome. You can try any sample I have. I'm sure we'll find your next favourite blend."

Lilly thanked the doctor and made her way down the small path. At the gate she turned left and within a couple of minutes was back out into the town centre, a few minutes' walk from the market square and her shop.

◈

THE SUMMER WAS now in full swing and the town centre was a hive of activity. Tour buses arrived daily, disgorging excited passengers eager to discover what this quaint little market town had to offer, and Plumpton Mallet had everything they could want.

The river, running along the outskirts of town, was flanked by large fields and small stony beaches, perfect for picnics, with designated areas for both swimming and fishing. The woods, a mass of bluebells carpeting the floor in the spring, were a joy to walk through in summer. Full of squirrels and songbirds and if you were very lucky, the odd deer. And the large green park with its avenue of trees, a play area for children and a pub with a cafe and outdoor seating at one end was immensely popular. As were the colourful rowing boats moored at the side of a quaint stone jetty, in the shadow of an ancient humped-backed foot bridge which took you over the river to the fields at the opposite side.

At the other side of the town were the moors, popular with walkers and hikers. Turning into a mass of purples and green in spring with the heather in abundance, it looked like an old master oil painting viewed from the town's market square nestled in the valley below. It was one of the most popular images for both photographs and on the postcards the town sold to tourists.

The cobbled market square was where Lilly's shop, The Tea Emporium, was situated. A prime position in the centre of the long row of historical shops that flanked one side, double fronted with a cream door in the centre. It looked both inviting and exciting. It also had the one thing none of the other shops had; a sleeping cat in the window. Earl Grey had been a stray who had wandered into the shop a week after it had opened and never left. Lilly adored him, especially because the scar across his nose and the missing chunk of his ear spoke volumes. Proof he'd had it tough on the streets but had survived.

Her bicycle, parked outside the shop and festooned with hanging baskets, looked an absolute picture, and several people had stopped to pose next to it to have their photos taken.

Inside, she checked the basket where her agony aunt letters, posted through the letterbox outside, were collected, and finding several tucked them under her arm. As her eyes adjusted to the dimmer light, compared to the blinding sunshine outside, she spotted Archie Brown, crime writer and her old colleague at the paper, having tea at the counter with Stacey.

Chapter Two

IT WAS RARE Lilly got a visit from Archie these days. With his additional workload due to the paper being taken over by a larger concern, a primary reason for Lilly being made redundant, he didn't have a lot of free time. But she was always happy to see him on those rare occasions when he did have enough for a cup of tea and a chat.

"Ah, the wanderer returns." Archie said with a smile. "We were about to give you up for lost."

"Hey, Lilly," Stacey said from the other side of the counter where she was brewing samples for some waiting customers.

Lilly smiled and spoke to several shoppers on her way through the shop, pleased to see it so busy.

"Hello you two. Nice to see you, Archie. What brings you in? Crime at an all-time low?"

Archie scoffed, "I wish. Actually, I was looking for some repair work," he said, pointing to a little teacup on a velvet covered board at the end of the counter. It was the area Lilly used for examining damaged items for repair. Fine china, delicate as it was, had a nasty habit of being mishandled and damaged, so this was an additional service she offered her customers. She'd taken numerous night classes and become very adept at it, but she only touched those items that weren't antiques or highly valuable.

"Let's have a look," she said, going behind the counter and searching through a drawer for her combined light and magnifying glass. After a close examination, she deemed it an easy repair. "There are no bits missing so a good adhesive, a light sand and a touch up and it will be as good as new."

"Excellent," Archie said. "I'm very fond of that tea set."

"I'm glad to hear it since you bought it from here."

"Best set I've ever owned, but I admit I should treat it with a bit more care. Now what's this little repair going to cost me?"

"Consider it a gift for a friend, Archie. It won't take me too long."

"Very kind of you, Lilly, thank you. Although I suppose you do owe me a favour."

Lilly raised an eyebrow. "Oh? And why is that, Archie Brown?"

"Two words," he said, holding up his fingers before folding his arms. "Abigail Douglas."

Lilly groaned. "What's she done now? And why is it my fault?"

"You persuaded me to let her co-write that last article. The greatest headline and story we've ever had. Since then, she's been the biggest headache you can imagine. She has ideas so far above her station I'm surprised she's not short of oxygen. Which actually would be a big improvement, come to think of it. She's driving everyone at the paper crazy with her demands for all the biggest projects, but especially me."

Lilly cringed. Abigail had started investigating the Carol Ann Hotch case behind Archie's back. She'd even swiped all his carefully researched notes. Because so few people wrote to the paper for Abigail's agony aunt column now, she had acted out of desperation and fear that her job was in jeopardy. However, Abigail had also been a great help to Lilly as she sought the truth and as a result Lilly had insisted Archie co-write the article with her, to give her some help and job security.

"I'm sorry," Lilly said. "Is she really that bad?"

"Think of the worst it could be, then multiply it by ten," Archie said bitterly. "I honestly thought after we'd helped her get her name on the byline, she'd settle down and be grateful. Unfortunately, it wasn't enough to persuade the big bods she had the skills, so they didn't back her up. She's returned to doing her agony aunt column, which doesn't amount to much, and the odd human interest piece, which she's not very good at either, unfortunately. Not enough interest, sympathy or motivation for the reader. She's taken to demanding a position on the investigative journalism team, and I'm not going to put up with it anymore. She's already stolen evidence from my desk once."

"Couldn't she have been fired for that, Archie?" Stacey asked.

"At the time, yes, if I'd reported it. But there's too much water passed under the bridge now. Not to mention I let her co-write the article in the first place. I wouldn't have a leg to stand on. Has she given you any more trouble, Lilly?"

For a long time Abigail had been a thorn in Lilly's side, insisting she remove the letterbox from outside her shop as it was interfering with her job. The fact people preferred to write to Lilly had not crossed her mind, she was insistent that Lilly was doing it deliberately to make her look like a fool.

"Honestly, since the article ran, I haven't heard from her. She knows I'm the main reason she was allowed to co-write it in the first place, so I imagine that's why she's left me alone as long as she has."

"Lilly's getting a lot more agony aunt letters though," Stacey said. "Since you mentioned the letterbox in the article, Archie, people have been writing in from everywhere. There's at least three or four new letters in it every day now."

"That's true," Lilly said, nodding.

"You always were good at it. A lot better than Abigail Douglas, that's for sure."

"Thanks, Archie. Stacey, could you hand me an order form for repairs, please?" She glanced up when Stacey didn't respond. She was staring at her phone while sending a text. "Earth to Stacey!" Lilly said, a little louder, and Stacey jumped.

"Sorry, what did you need?" She asked, stuffing her phone in her pocket.

"A repair order form."

Stacey located the paperwork and handed it over. Lilly filled it in, asked Archie to sign in then sent Stacey back into the storeroom with the form and the cup. There was a designated shelf with all the repairs Lilly had to do that week. She watched as Stacey disappeared before turning to Archie.

"She's been a bit distracted lately. I think something might be going on. I might need to talk to her about it."

Archie stood up, stretching his back, then grabbed his hat from the counter and put it on. "Don't prod, Lilly. She's a student and probably doesn't want you nosing into her private business. You're already her boss and her landlord, you don't need to be a parent too."

"Yes, all right, Archie," she huffed in response. She thought back to her conversation with Dr Jorgenson. If Archie was pointing it out too, she wondered if she really was guilty of prying too much. It was difficult not to be concerned when there was something so obviously amiss.

❦

STACEY TOOK A while to return from the back room, and Lilly suspected it was because she'd been on her phone again. She elected not to mention it. Stacey had always been a highly personable and productive employee, and it shouldn't be necessary to introduce a no phone policy. It should be a given during work hours unless it was an emergency. Yet, for the past couple of days, Stacey had been glued to her phone far more than usual.

Lilly couldn't help but think that Stacey's out of character behaviour had something to do with her father's reappearance in her life. She clearly had a lot of baggage where James Pepper was concerned, and the way he'd acted when the girl had first come to England was, to Lilly's mind, downright insulting.

But then again, it was hardly her job to judge. He *had* come rushing to Plumpton Mallet when Stacey had been injured, so in his own way he did care. Lilly idly wondered if Stacey would consider moving down to the capital to be closer to her father. The thought worried her, but she shouldn't try to stop her if that's what she wanted. Her thoughts were interrupted when the shop door opened and a familiar face entered.

"Hello, Mrs Davenport, nice to see you again."

Elizabeth Davenport was a rotund woman of indeterminate age who was always dressed to the nines regardless of what her plans for the day were. She walked with a dignified elegance that spoke of socialites of a bygone era and tilted her head back as though looking down her nose at those around her. Comical looking considering her short stature.

"Miss Tweed," she said in reply. "How have you been, my dear?"

"Very well, thank you. Is there anything I can help you with?"

"Just browsing today. Your shop has been the talk of the town recently, and I'm rather ashamed to admit I haven't been in since you first opened. You've added to your inventory I see, those gift hampers are new. I'll have a good look round and perhaps will pick up a little something for myself before I leave." She concluded, before making her way to the rear of the shop to admire some of the silver tea spoons and cake slices.

Stacey, who'd returned from the back and was now standing near Lilly, whispered, "She sounds like the Queen of England."

Lilly smiled but warned Stacey to hush. Stacey grinned in response.

The shop bell tinkled once more and several well-dressed women entered together. Lilly recognised the woman in the lead immediately. She touched Stacey's shoulder and leaned over, whispering. "That's Lady Defoe. Be as professional as possible while she's here, please."

"Me? Professional? Always," Stacey replied, shoving her phone in her pocket, as though she knew she'd been anything but by being glued to it for half the day. "So, like, a real Lady? As in Lord and Lady?" she whispered.

Lilly nodded. Plumpton Mallet may be a historic market town, but it was one of the most sought after places to live in the north of the country, and counted among its residents several members of the aristocracy.

"Welcome to The Tea Emporium," Lilly said as Lady Defoe caught her eye.

The woman smiled politely. "You have a very beautiful shop."

"Thank you."

"Oh, would you look at these adorable teapots? This one is in the shape of a welsh dresser, and look at this one, tea and honey with a beehive as the lid. I've never seen anything like them. They really are exquisite." She said to her friends, who agreed unanimously.

Lilly was a wise woman. She knew if Lady Defoe made a purchase it would mark her shop as the most fashionable place to buy and consequently bring in an influx of new and very wealthy customers. She stood back, watching Lady Defoe carefully to see what piqued her interest, and waiting for an opportune moment to offer her assistance.

*L*ILLY GLANCED IN Stacey's direction and found her gawking open-mouthed at the ladies across the shop. She was utterly mesmerised by Lady Defoe's presence. She had become so adept regarding the teas and other British customs that Lilly had forgotten how alien some things still were to her. There were obviously no members of the aristocracy in the states.

"Stacey, close your mouth. We are not a codfish," Lilly said quietly, trying not to laugh.

Stacey turned and began to giggle. "Mary Poppins, right? Sorry, it's all kind of new. A real Lady. Wow!" she whispered.

"She's just a person, one with a title admittedly, but she's just the same as us. She's also someone I wouldn't mind frequenting my shop from time to time. It's bound to attract positive attention if she begins to purchase from me."

"Right, got it," Stacey said. Turning and getting on with restocking the shelves.

Lady Defoe was, as expected, perusing the high end tea sets Lilly displayed in a locked art deco style cabinet. Since opening the shop, Lilly had only sold one single item from that cabinet and it had been an individual twenty-four carat gold rimmed teacup, for a lady wanting to replace one in a set she already owned.

"Now these are sublime." Naturally, her friends all agreed with her. "I *have* been looking for a new set..."

"I can see why you wanted to come here," one of the others said. "I must tell my husband about this place when I get back to London."

As Lilly eavesdropped on the conversation, she realised Lady Defoe was hosting a number of out-of-town friends. Among them a fashion designer, and the wife of a foreign diplomat from Paris. Lilly made her way over and smiling politely asked if there was anything she could help them with?

"I do so love this set," Lady Defoe replied, indicating the set in the cabinet. "Though I'm looking for something not quite so dark. Do you have anything similar but in a lighter shade?"

"Not in stock, but I do have an extensive catalogue you can look through. Perhaps something in there will catch your eye?"

Lady Defoe agreed and followed Lilly back to the counter. The other ladies electing to continue browsing.

"Lilith, look at these napkin rings." One lady exclaimed.

"These silver teaspoons are precious..."

"This is a beautiful linen tablecloth. Just look at the thread count."

Lady Defoe settled on one of the stools at the counter, taking in the array of fine teas displayed in the cabinet on the back wall.

"Would you like to sample one of our teas, ma'am?" Stacey asked.

Lady Defoe raised an eyebrow. "Oh, you're an American. How delightful. Where are you from?"

"Well, my mom's work meant we travelled a lot, but I spent a good bit of time in Georgia."

"I just love the southern united states. I visited Key West last year. Do you know it?"

"I do, actually. Mom and me vacationed there a lot when we were in Georgia. The last time I visited the Earnest Hemingway house."

"Oh!" Exclaimed Lady Defoe, clasping her hands together in delight. "I adore the Hemingway House. Do you know, I tried to adopt one of the polydactyl cats that live there but they wouldn't let me." She laughed. "They were offended I'd had the cheek to ask, but there were so many and so adorable, I thought they wouldn't miss one if I made a donation to the museum, but no. They wouldn't countenance the idea."

"I know, right?" Stacey said, laughing along with her. "They're the cutest things. After the tour, I sat in the garden and one hopped right in my lap and fell asleep. I wound up hanging around for ages because I didn't want to disturb it. So I sat and read *Old Man and the Sea* while one of Hemingway's cats slept in my lap."

"How romantic," Lady Defoe said before turning to Lilly with a smile. "I like this girl. Very cultured. Wherever did you find a young American who knows her teas?"

"As a matter of fact, she found me and she picked up the knowledge very quickly."

"I'll brew you up something," Stacey suggested.

"Your favourite, my dear," Lady Defoe insisted, and Stacey beamed in response, reaching for the chamomile.

Then the genial, relaxed atmosphere was spoiled.

"*L*ADY DEFOE!" MRS Davenport shrilled as she materialised out of nowhere to stand at her side. "Always such a pleasure," she continued, almost performing a curtsy.

Lilly couldn't help but notice Lady Defoe cringe briefly before relaxing her face into a polite smile. She was the epitome of good breeding and manners.

"Hello, Elizabeth. It's been a while. What brings you here?"

"The same as you, it seems. I'm looking for a new tea set."

Lilly busied herself with arranging the new gift hampers on the counter, fully aware of the reason for Mrs Davenport's change of mind. She'd gone from just browsing and possibly picking up something small to now wanting something extravagant and costly. There were no prizes for guessing why.

Stacey had finished brewing the tea and poured out for both ladies into bone china teacups with a background of vibrant green, on which were decorated an array of colourful spring flowers. Lady Defoe paused to examine and admire the china. "How pretty," she said with a smile. Everything in the shop seemed to impress the woman. Clearly, she felt as though she'd found a hidden jewel in Lilly's shop.

"Oh, I agree. Lovely colours." Mrs Davenport said, taking a sip.

"This tea is wonderful," Lady Defoe said.

"Oh, it is," Mrs Davenport agreed. "You have excellent taste, Lady Defoe."

"Oh, it wasn't my choice, Elizabeth. This young lady picked it out for me, and I'm most definitely going to need a box or two to go along with my new set." She pointed to a photograph in the catalogue, tapping the image twice for emphasis, and Lilly promptly found an order form.

It was an exquisite set, with a background of pale duck egg blue, decorated with Camellia blossoms in the palest pink, called Fairy Blush. A stunning bluebird completed the design, and it was all set off with a 24 carat gold rim around the edges of every individual piece. With a full set for six people, including side plates, teaspoons and infusers, it was the best single sale Lilly had ever had. Lady Defoe also insisted on paying in full there and then rather than just the normal deposit.

The other women also made their way to the till, each of them carrying something to purchase. They all had wide smiles and had obviously thoroughly enjoyed their shopping experience. The French diplomat's wife had bought a couple of single teacups to go with her eclectic set of mismatched ones, along with a silver-plated heart shaped infuser. The fashion designer had bought the linen tablecloth, matching napkins, and a set of six silver napkin rings. The others had selected various items, including two teapots, three gift hampers and sets of fine teaspoons.

"Mark my words, ladies," Lady Defoe said, rising from her seat. "This adorable shop is going to become a true staple of Plumpton Mallet."

Chapter Three

MRS DAVENPORT, WHO had been standing at the counter browsing the catalogue, cleared her throat. "I think I would like to order this tea set, here," she said, pointing to the exact one Lady Defoe had just bought.

"I see you and Lady Defoe have similar taste," Lilly said diplomatically. "Let me get an order form."

"Thank you, dear. It's a beautiful set, similar to the one in your cabinet I noticed, but I do love the design of this one just that bit more."

As Lilly was completing the form, the bell rang and glancing up she saw it was Fred Warren, a face she'd not seen for a while. He was a student at the local university who'd come into the shop for advice, just as the Carol Ann Hotch case began to pick up speed. He'd saved her a couple of times during that investigation.

"Fred, what a pleasure."

"Hi, Miss Tweed."

"Hey, Fred!" Stacey exclaimed enthusiastically.

Fred smiled and held up a paper bag. "I've got your lunch."

"You're the best. Thanks!"

"You can take your lunch break if you want, Stacey."

"Thanks, Lilly."

Lilly watched as Stacey and Fred made their way to the back storeroom kitchen where there was a table and chairs for breaks.

"Well, well, well..." Lilly muttered to herself. Could that explain the change in Stacey and her obsession with her phone recently? Were she and Fred dating? If they were, then Lilly was pleased for them, they made a nice couple.

"Is everything all right, dear?" asked Mrs Davenport.

"My apologies, Mrs Davenport. Yes, everything's fine. I'll put your order in this evening. Would like to pay in full or just the deposit?"

"Oh, in full is fine."

Lilly took her gold card and rang it through. Mrs Davenport may not be a member of the aristocracy but she was certainly on a par wealth wise.

"Now, Lilly. I hope you don't mind, but I have a proposition to put to you."

Lilly poured them both a cup of newly made Green Tea with Jasmine and asked Mrs Davenport what she had mind?

"Well, dear, as you are probably aware, I run one of the most popular book clubs in Plumpton Mallet." Lilly had had no idea, but she nodded anyway. "Well, our current read is a magnificent saga about a family owned tea plantation in

Africa. A beautiful, evocative story, and I happen to be the host this week."

Lilly continued to nod, patiently waiting for Mrs Davenport to get to the point, because she had no idea where all this seemingly irrelevant information was heading.

"Now, from what I hear on the grapevine, you know your teas very well."

"Yes, I do. I've always had an interest and had gained a vast knowledge even before opening The Tea Emporium. It was a natural transition for me to make after I left the paper."

"Well, Lilly, I would like you to come along and give the book club a talk on your teas and a demonstration of how to make a perfect cup using your various samples. You've become rather famous around here, haven't you?" she added, revealing her true motivation. "So, how does that sound?"

Lilly sipped her tea while she thought. Mrs Davenport had a reputation for being a bit pretentious and a bit of a snob. She liked to surround herself with important people, and it was apparent that Lilly had garnered her attention thanks to her sudden rise in popularity as a sleuth. A part of Lilly didn't want to be used in such a way, but on the other hand she recognised what a good opportunity it would be for her business. It would be foolhardy of her to bite her nose off to spite her face.

"It sounds very interesting, Mrs Davenport, although I've not done anything like that before, so don't have a fee off the top of my head."

"A fee?"

Lilly realised the woman had expected her to do it for free, no doubt for the supposed PR benefit.

"Well, if you're wanting your group to be able to sample the teas, then it will cost me in merchandise. Not to mention my time in preparing and presenting, which will take me away from my business."

"I see," Mrs Davenport said, looking crestfallen.

"How many are in your book club?"

"Usually, we have at least five or six in attendance."

Lilly thought for a moment, then nodded as she worked out a suitable compromise.

"How about seventy-five pounds for the fee? but I'll bring along a selection of my merchandise to sell. If I do well and manage to sell a few items and it's enough to cover the fee, then I will waive it completely. I will take care of everything. All you'll need to do is inform your members they'll need cash deposits if they wish to buy anything, but receipts will be given. How does that sound?"

"Oh yes, that's much more agreeable." Mrs Davenport said, suitably buoyed again.

"Wonderful, here's my business card. You can send me all the details and I'll be sure to prepare a good presentation for you and your club members."

"Thank you, my dear. I do believe my guests will enjoy it very much. After all, your shop is truly on its way to becoming a town staple." With that regurgitation of Lady Defoe's parting words, Elizabeth Davenport sailed out of the shop like a tug boat.

"OH, I JUST love the sets you've picked out for this!" Stacey declared as she helped pack the merchandise that would be part of the first outside event Lilly had done.

"Thanks, Stacey. I wanted to make sure I had something for every budget," Lilly said, passing her a dusky pink coloured teacup with a single dark pink rose and turquoise leaf design. It was part of the vintage range and one of her favourites. Lilly had planned everything down to the last second and was determined to provide an entertaining and interesting presentation for the ladies Elizabeth Davenport was hosting at her book club.

"Do you think there will be a lot of important people there?" Stacey asked. She'd certainly lived up to her name this week, as she'd peppered Lilly with questions about the Defoe family non stop ever since the family matriarch had visited the shop. She was interested in learning more about British history and culture since it was a strong part of her identity despite having grown up the states.

"Not a lot, there's usually only half a dozen or so apparently, but knowing Mrs Davenport they will certainly be influential I should think."

Lilly passed Stacey several tea infusers and a set of teaspoons with ceramic Alice in Wonderland decorated, handles. "I'm quite sure she only invited me because Lady Defoe complimented my shop and due to my newfound fame as a sleuth. Ridiculous as that is."

"Seems a bit shallow," Stacey said.

"I suppose it could be conceived that way, it's all about social games though, isn't it? It's common the world over, not just in rural England. I mean, you only need to look at the news and social media to see it in action."

"Yeah, I suppose you're right. It's a bit sad though, right?"

Lilly nodded.

"Well, I've got the shop today. Earl will help me hold down the fort."

Earl meowed from the doorway when he heard his name, he'd been watching proceedings with an avid interest. Probably wondering when he could commandeer an empty box. "We're still here, Mr Grey," Lilly said, scratching his ears, before taking the last of the boxes out the back door to her car.

Before she left, she returned to double check the till float and saw Stacey was once again glued to her phone, a giddy smile plastered across her face.

"You know, Stacey," she said gently. "I really like Fred, and I'm glad you've become friends. But, I'd appreciate it if the phone stayed in your pocket during working hours."

Stacey's face went scarlet. "Oh," she said. "Um... of course. I'm sorry, we're not..."

"You don't have to tell me, Stacey, it's none of my business. But I do know how exciting the beginnings of a relationship are, I've been there myself. The odd text is fine providing it doesn't affect productivity."

"Thanks, Lilly," she said with a weak smile.

The worried expression caused Lilly to pause. "Is there something else worrying you?"

Stacey put her phone in her pocket and sighed. "Fred wants to introduce me to his family."

"Does he? Well, I'd say that's a very good sign. But it's not something you're ready for, is that it?"

"No, I'm totally fine with meeting his family, it's just I haven't told him about my family drama. You know, with my dad. I'm a bit embarrassed, if I'm honest."

"Stacey, everyone has family drama of one sort or another, it's nothing to be embarrassed about. Your experience is a lot more common than you'd think, and I'm sure Fred would understand if you explained it to him. He's a sensible young man with a good head in his shoulders."

"Yeah, it's just that things with my dad are so strange right now, and bringing a boyfriend into the picture, well it would be nice to be able to keep those things separate for a while, you know?"

"I do know. And if you explain it to Fred, I'm sure he will too," Lilly assured her.

"Thanks, Lilly."

'No problem. If you want to talk, Stacey, I'm happy to listen," she said, checking the till as she'd intended to before she left. "But for now, I really need to go if I'm to make this book club meeting on time."

❦

ELIZABETH DAVENPORT HAD given Lilly comprehensive directions to her house: across the bridge that went over the tunnel she rode through into the park, when she took her bike to work. Continue up the road until it reaches the top of the woods and then take a left. Her house, a very large detached in an acre of grounds, was the second on the left. Named Dovecote Grange.

The weather was glorious, very hot with brilliant sunshine in a sky of bright blue. Not a cloud in sight. Elizabeth had told her the book club would be meeting in the garden, under the rose covered pergola, and Lilly could set up in the garden room. A glass covered orangerie style area with wicker seating, brightly coloured soft furnishings and a huge array of plants. Lilly thought it sounded perfect. The demonstration would be at a seating area on the outdoor patio area, alfresco style.

As she pulled up outside, the double wrought-iron gates opened automatically, and once Lilly was through, closed behind her. She continued down the gravel drive, flanked with blossoming rose bushes, Dahlia and marigolds, until she reached the front of the house. Elizabeth Davenport was there to meet her.

"Ah, Lilly, perfect timing. Are you excited to present?"

"Do you know? I am, as a matter of fact. Thank you for the opportunity, Elizabeth," Lilly replied with a smile.

"I'll show you where you can set up. Follow me."

Lilly was led through the hallway to the rear of the house and into the garden room. The back of the house was as beautiful as the front, with a well landscaped garden consisting of verdant lawns, established trees and colourful beds. Set in the distance were several ornate white dovecotes, which obviously gave the house its name. In the room itself, against one wall, a sideboard was available for her to display her wares and next to that a table adjacent to the wall outlets for the kettles. Water, Elizabeth said, could be obtained from the kitchen inside to the left.

"And I thought," she said, taking Lilly out onto the terrace. "That this is where we could sit while you're serving the tea and explaining their benefits."

It was a large wrought-iron chair and table set in white, adorned with red, white and blue striped cushions, very French looking and perfect for the occasion. There was also a huge free-standing garden umbrella in royal blue for much needed shade.

"I also have a table cloth should you need one?"

"This is lovely, Elizabeth, thank you. I have brought my own cloths. A pale blue with a yellow and white embroidered daisy design for out here, I thought?"

"Oh, how perfectly summer!" she exclaimed, glancing at the small, neat gold watch on her wrist. "Now, my guests will be arriving shortly and will most likely walk straight through the house to the pergola, over there. We'll keep it short and sweet this week so you'll probably have three quarters of an hour or so to get ready before your presentation."

"That should be plenty of time. I'll just go and get what I need from the car."

"Wonderful. You can use the gate at the side of the house, it will save you having to walk through. Now if you'll excuse me, I have biscuits in the oven to serve with the tea."

Lilly smiled as Mrs Davenport scurried back inside. She was absolutely in her element playing hostess. It took Lilly six trips back and forth to get everything she needed, and twenty minutes later the display inside the garden room was complete. She'd added vases of faux greenery and artificial but very realistic tea roses in creams and pinks, then finalised it all with sprinkles of rose petals. She was very pleased with the end result. And when Mrs Davenport entered, so was she.

❦

"OH, LILLY, HOW gorgeous. You've clearly put a great deal of work and imagination into this," she said. "It looks like something the Savoy or Claridges would do.

Lilly turned and smiled, seeing her host now had a guest in tow.

"Lilly, let me introduce you to Jane Nolan," Mrs Davenport began, indicating the woman who had already moved away to examine Elizabeth's orchids. She turned to Lilly and said in hushed tones, "Jane's just inherited two of Plumpton Mallet's best hotels and a number of other properties around the town from her father." She dropped to a lower whisper. "She's now one of the richest single women in town to come from new money. Her family is all new money, you see, but they've made quite a splash, nonetheless." She turned to Jane. "Jane, dear, this is Lillian Tweed. She owns that precious new tea shop in the market square."

Lilly nodded politely.

"How do you do?" Jane said, without meeting Lilly's gaze. She had what Lilly recognised as a supercilious hauteur. Very aloof and unfriendly, as though Lilly were so far beneath her she mattered very little. She wandered over to the display table as a tea set caught her eye.

"How pretty. I've not seen one quite like this before."

It was the darkest blue one with gold accents, not a rare colour scheme, it was the peacock design that made it unusual. Lilly was about to give her more information on the artist, when Jane excused herself and wandered out into the garden. Lilly frowned, hoping she wasn't going to be treated like 'trade' by all of Elizabeth's guests just because she hadn't been born into wealth and privilege.

"I'll come with you, Jane," Mrs Davenport called out, then quickly turned back to Lilly. "If Lady Defoe arrives, would you mind calling me?"

"Of course, I didn't realise she would be coming."

"Well, I naturally invited her and explained you would be attendance to do a bespoke presentation. I didn't hear back, but of course she's very busy."

Lilly nodded. She doubted Lady Defoe would turn up, but privately wondered if half the reason she'd been invited in the first place was to see if it would be enough to lure the biggest fish. There was no doubt it would be a coup for Elizabeth Davenport to have a woman of her standing attend her little function.

When Elizabeth had gone, Lilly started on the table outside. It was a meticulous process setting up an elegant table, but Lilly knew the type of women who were attending would expect the fine details. Not only that, they would also be able to identify immediately if anything was out of place. She was just placing the sugar bowl and tongs on the central tray when she heard a familiar voice, "Lillian Tweed."

Lilly couldn't believe it, it was none other than Abigail Douglas.

Chapter Four

ABIGAIL DID NOT look pleased at Lilly's presence. Lilly had thought the two of them were on better terms, but the glower of hostility suggested otherwise. She really hoped Abigail wasn't going to ruin the day.

"What are you doing here?" she demanded. "Please, don't tell me you've joined Elizabeth's book club?"

"No, I haven't joined the book club. But you could sound a little more grateful, Abigail."

"Grateful? What on earth should I be grateful for?"

Lilly was aghast. "Are you serious? What's wrong with you?"

After Lilly had stopped her getting arrested and then helped her get the job to write the biggest headline article the area had seen, she thought this antagonistic attitude would be dropped. Unfortunately, it seemed as though things were worse than before. She was now beginning to think the little note of thanks Abigail had scrawled on the newspaper and dropped in Lilly's letterbox, had been written because she'd been told to, rather than because she was genuinely thankful for Lilly's help.

"I don't know, Lilly, maybe it's because your agony aunt box has turned my job into a complete joke."

"Oh, will you please change the record, Abigail? I thought you'd got over that."

"I'm still the paper's agony aunt," Abigail hissed. "And my column took yet another blow after that article came out."

Lilly very nearly laughed. *Oh, the irony,* she thought. *She wrote that article herself.*

"You think it's funny," Abigail snapped. "You are so childish."

"I don't really think it's funny, but you've only got yourself to blame, Abigail. You were the one who wrote the article, so you can't blame me for the situation you find yourself in. You should try giving better advice if your column isn't doing well. And that's a free bit of advice from the gazette's most popular agony aunt."

Abigail's jaw fell open. "I... well, how utterly rude!" she spluttered and stormed off across the lawn towards the pergola.

With the tables complete, Lilly took her two kettles to the kitchen to fill. As she returned, she noticed a new face had joined Elizabeth, Jane and Abigail, it was Lady Meredith Gresham, another prominent town resident. Lilly smiled, it looked as though Elizabeth's desire to have a member of the aristocracy in her circle had been answered.

"Ooh, what a heavenly display!" A jolly and very cultured voice said behind her, causing Lilly to jump.

"Oh, hello."

"Sorry, I didn't mean to startle you," the woman said, holding out her hand. "Isadora Smith."

"Lillian Tweed, but you can call me Lilly," she said, shaking hands with the eccentrically, but beautifully dressed woman in a large straw hat. "Are you here for the book club?"

"Yes, I'm a little late, one of the dogs ran off and I couldn't find her for ages. Turned out she'd gone home by herself and was waiting at the door when I got back." She giggled.

Lilly laughed with her, then indicated the pergola where the others were waiting. Isadora tripped across the lawn to the sound of Jane Nolan's slightly sarcastic voice, "Fashionably late as always, Isadora." Lilly noticed the final guest didn't reply but shook her head slightly in annoyance.

While the women were discussing the book Lilly sat and waited in the garden room, she'd brought a book of her own to read, which made the time fly. Eventually they all started to saunter slowly back across the lawn and made their way to the outdoor table. She joined them on the terrace just as the last of them took a seat.

❦

"LADIES, WELCOME," LILLY started by saying. She could tell Abigail was looking at her with unconcealed judgment, no doubt hoping she would fail miserably. "Thank you for having me here today, especially our host Elizabeth for the idea and the invitation."

There was a chorus of agreement along with a smattering of applause, and Elizabeth beamed in delight.

Lilly settled a teapot on the table and lifted the lid to give it a final stir.

"Oh, what a lovely scent," Jane said, sitting upright.

"This is lemon infused nettle tea, one of my personal favourites," Lilly began, pouring each of them a sample. "We'll be trying lots of different tea types today and I'll go through some of the health benefits of each. This nettle tea, for instance, is an excellent source of both iron and calcium. When I first opened the shop, I started to cycle into work and chose this tea because it helps to prevent leg cramping and relieves rheumatism. It can be also be flavoured with lime and honey. Having a cup each morning has helped my legs and knees no end."

"Really?" Lady Meredith asked. "So, it's potentially beneficial for those who suffer from arthritis?"

"Indeed. The joints could benefit greatly from having a regular dose of nettle tea, and it's also known to decrease blood sugar and lower blood pressure. With this tea it's better not to exceed four cups a day, that's if the tea is made from the leaves. If made from the root, then a single cup is the recommended dose."

"My mother-in-law suffers from dreadful arthritis," Lady Gresham said, taking another sip. "Perhaps I should suggest some of this for her to my husband when he returns from Asia..."

While Elizabeth Davenport handed round her biscuits, Lilly rinsed the tea cups at the table, pouring the dregs into a pansy decorated china pot made for the purpose, then returned to the garden room to brew the next sample. She'd chosen a green tea this time and after pouring continued with her lecture. As she talked and the ladies sipped, nodded and asked questions, she handed out various catalogues and leaflets, and the conversation soon turned to the tea sets she had available.

"I adore that one you have over there," Jane said, waving her arm in the general direction of the display table. "Is it available to buy?"

"Yes," Lilly confirmed. "All the items and the sets you see here today are available, including the one we're using for the samples. What's in the catalogue can be ordered specifically in whatever size you require. Mrs Davenport just ordered one recently in fact."

"Page twenty-two. What do you think, ladies?"

"It's beautiful, Elizabeth. You have such exquisite taste," Lady Gresham said.

"I agree, it's quite beautiful," said Jane. "And this demonstration was a wonderful idea."

"Yes it was," Abigail muttered, albeit reluctantly.

Lilly went back inside to get another sample, one of her finer mint teas, and returned to the table pouring for Isadora Smith first. "Oh, what a lovely hatpin."

The large sun hat Lilly had noticed when Isadora had first arrived was pinned in place by a silver pin with an ornate butterfly design.

"Thank you, Lilly. I know they are probably thought old fashioned nowadays, but I do so adore them. They speak of history and more genteel days, I feel."

"It is beautiful, Isadora," Lady Gresham said, leaning over to get a better look. "Personally, I wish the style would come back, although I'm not sure I'd be brave enough to wear them. I'm not really suited to hats except for weddings, and Ladies Day at Royal Ascot, of course."

Suddenly Mrs Davenport zeroed in on the subject. "Once Lilly has finished, Lady Gresham, I'd love to show you my collection."

Isadora frowned slightly.

"You collect hatpins, Elizabeth?" Lady Gresham asked in surprise.

"Oh, I do. I simply adore them. I have quite a few, although I imagine they're a bit older than the one Isadora is wearing."

"Antiques then?"

"That's right. Some nearly one-hundred and fifty years old."

"As is mine, Elizabeth," Isadora said, with a tight smile.

Lilly could immediately feel the tension between Elizabeth and Isadora. Mind you, a lot of people had strong feelings when it came to Elizabeth Davenport, she had a real knack for stepping on toes. Attempting to diffuse the situation before it got out of hand she spoke about the tea they were drinking. "This is one of my mint blends, excellent for calming nerves and is a wonderful choice for evening as it promotes restful sleep."

"I could use a whole pot of this before bed," Jane said, and the others laughed.

"Any other health benefits to this one?" Abigail asked.

"It's certainly one of the best teas for relieving tension headaches as well as easing digestive upsets."

"Isn't this one of the samples you gave me in your shop the other day, when we were with Lady Defoe?" Mrs Davenport said.

It wasn't but before Lilly could correct her, Jane spoke.

"Oh, you saw Lady Defoe, Elizabeth?"

"Why yes, we sampled tea together in Lilly's shop," she replied, giving Jane a snide look, which Lilly noticed. Why Mrs Davenport was friends with so many people that she seemed to have ill will towards, Lilly couldn't understand.

"I think I've found a teapot I'd like to order," Isadora said, marking the page in the catalogue.

"Wonderful, I'll get some order forms after I bring the last pot."

Lilly hurried inside to fetch the last sample of the day, a superior chamomile blend. After sampling, it proved to be a popular choice and nearly all of them ordered a box. They all bought other items too. Jane, the tea set she'd been admiring since her arrival. Lady Gresham a tea set from the catalogue as well as a box of nettle tea for her mother-in-law, and the mint for herself. Mrs Davenport chose the mint. Even Abigail bought a box of mint to go with the chamomile she'd also liked. All in all, it had been an excellent day for Lilly and Mrs Davenport's fee had been covered several times over. Perhaps she should start to provide this sort of service officially?

Although the demonstration was over, the ladies didn't seem to want to leave. They stood on the terrace talking while Lilly cleared and packed everything away. Elizabeth had brought out glasses of champagne. Jane had slipped inside a few minutes before, but the rest continued to discuss their purchases and the surprising health benefits of tea while sipping an obviously favourite tipple.

Lilly packed up carefully, but efficiently and made the several trips through the gate at the side of the house to load up her car. After she'd stowed away the last of her items, she made her way back round to the terrace to say her final goodbye.

Elizabeth, Abigail and Isadora were the only ones left on the terrace when she returned. "Ladies, I just want to say thank you again for having me," Lilly began, but before any of them could respond they heard a terrified scream from inside the house.

ceಲಿ

THE SCREAM HAD been ghastly and sent all four of them dashing inside in time to see a ghostly looking Lady Gresham running towards them from inside the house. She let out a second shriek, almost colliding with Elizabeth Davenport as she reached out to her, grasping her shoulders. "Elizabeth," Meredith cried, tears streaking down her face. "It's Jane. In the powder room."

"Jane? What about Jane, Meredith?"

"She's hurt. There's blood. So much blood!"

"Call the police," Lilly shouted as she ran to the cloak-room. She flung open the door to find Jane Nolan lying on the floor, eyes closed and head resting in a small pool of blood. "Jane!" Lilly exclaimed, getting down on her knees next to the prone woman. Her lips were pale and Lilly quickly located a deep cut near her throat. Jane's hands were covered in blood, and Lilly imagined she'd tried to stem the flow before passing out. She lifted a wrist and attempted to locate a pulse. There wasn't one. "Oh, Jane..." she said, getting up in shock and looking away.

Her eyes fell on the white sink where a small pool of water sat in the basin, stained a pale pink as though someone had just washed their hands. Surely Lady Gresham hadn't paused to wash her hands before raising the alarm?

Lilly hurried out of the room where she was met with a sea of frightened faces. Isadora was on her mobile with the emergency services. "They want to know if she's breathing?" she asked Lilly, glancing behind her into the room, eyes widening in shock at the grotesque scene.

Lilly shook her head. "No, she's not breathing. I felt for a pulse. I'm terribly sorry, but I'm afraid she's dead."

Isadora stepped away from the others and repeated the grave news to the operator.

"I don't understand," Elizabeth stuttered. "What happened?"

"I don't know," Lilly said. "But there's a neck injury and quite a lot of blood."

Lilly saw Abigail fiddling with her phone and realised, unbelievably, that she was trying to take a sneaky photograph of the scene. She stepped in front of the door and snarled at her, "Have some decency, Abigail. Don't embarrass yourself." Abigail promptly put her phone away and disappeared from view. Lilly turned to the others, shutting the cloakroom door to try to give Jane at least some dignity in death and suggested they all move back to the garden room or the terrace and wait for the police. There was nothing more they could do. Jane Nolan was beyond help.

℘

THE DOORBELL RANG not long afterwards, and Elizabeth Davenport went to answer it. She returned with three police officers, one of whom was Sergeant Bonnie Phillips, an old friend of Lilly's. She'd known her since her old days at the gazette, having been introduced by Archie. Bonnie was Archie's contact at the station and fed him bits of information as and when she could.

The first thing Lilly noticed when she walked over to greet her friend was that she wasn't in uniform. "Plain clothes today, Bonnie?"

Bonnie smiled. "I did tell you I was moving to detective work. I've got my exams coming up shortly. So what are you doing here?" taking in the other women sitting in silent shock in the garden room.

Lilly explained briefly the reason for her presence, then the more important information about Jane Nolan's death. Bonnie sent the other two officers to assess the scene while she stayed with Lilly.

"So who found her?"

Lilly pointed to a very pale Lady Gresham. "Lady Gresham did. She screamed, and we all came rushing in

223

from the terrace. She was on the verge of passing out due to the shock."

Bonnie nodded and made her way out to the small group. Lilly followed and took a seat in one of the spare wicker chairs.

"I don't understand," Lady Gresham was saying, wringing her hands. "How did it happen? Did she fall?"

"I'll get you some water, Meredith," Mrs Davenport said, rising to get a pitcher and some glasses from the kitchen.

Bonnie watched her as she went, and could see one of her officers had stopped her briefly to ask some questions. Abigail also stood, looking as though she was about to follow but was prevented with a severe look from Bonnie who was positioned in the doorway. Bonnie beckoned her over and they spoke in hushed tones for several minutes, while Bonnie took notes.

Lilly rubbed her eyes as she felt a headache coming on. She could hardly believe something like this could have happened. She tried to picture the cloakroom to see if she could work out what Jane had hurt herself on. There didn't seem to be anything present that would cause the injury she'd seen. Then a horrifying thought occurred to her. What if someone else had hurt Jane? But that would mean... oh no! Please not another murder in Plumpton Mallet.

Chapter Five

*L*ILLY SHIVERED AT the dreadful thought, but glancing over to where Abigail was still deep in conversation with Bonnie, she realised she wasn't the only one thinking in this way. It was why Abigail had tried to photograph the scene; she saw the story of a possible murder laid out before her and, for once, she had beaten Archie Brown to the scoop. Bonnie too, with the way she was studying each of the women in turn, was clearly looking for a suspect among them, wondering at possible motives and plausible, but faked shock and remorse. Lilly eyed the women present, but all of them looked to be as shocked and stunned as she was.

"Lilly, can I speak with you now, please?" Bonnie asked as she escorted Abigail back to her chair.

"Yes, of course," she said, rising. She passed Elizabeth, who was returning with a tray of iced water for her guests, especially Lady Gresham who was looking worse by the minute.

"Elizabeth, might I suggest hot sweet tea for Lady Gresham?" Lilly said quietly. "It's very good for shock."

"Oh, yes. What a good idea, Lilly. I'll see to that shortly."

Lilly, along with Bonnie and another officer, stood just inside the kitchen out of hearing range of the other women. "Is everything okay?" Lilly asked, then realised instantly what a stupid question it was. "Sorry, I don't mean okay, of course it isn't. I just mean..." she sighed. "What can I do to help?"

"Lilly, Constable Steel here, has just been speaking with Mrs Davenport, and as you know I've just had a chat with Abigail. We're trying to pinpoint the time of death and sequence of events as they happened. How long would you say Jane Nolan was away from you all in the cloakroom?" Bonnie asked, notebook in hand.

Lilly frowned in concentration. Now she thought about it, Jane had been gone for quite a while. "Let me see... she headed inside right after she filled in an order form for a tea set she wanted... oh, she gave me a cash deposit for it, Bonnie. I have no idea who to return that to?"

"You can give it to me, Lilly. I'll give you a receipt for it. Go on."

"Okay, thanks. The others also took a few minutes to fill out their order forms. They then finished off their tea, which took another few minutes.

"And Abigail said she went inside briefly to wash her hands?"

Lilly nodded. "Yes, I think that's right. Once everyone had finished, they moved to the terrace, freeing up the table so I could clear away. Elizabeth Davenport returned to the kitchen with her tray of biscuits. She was gone for a minute or two as well. She must have returned with champagne at some point as they were drinking that when I came out from the garden room to start clearing the table."

Constable Steel nodded, also taking notes. "Right, and then?"

Lilly thought for a moment longer. "I started packing everything up at that point. Mrs Davenport came back, that might be when she brought the champagne out come to think of it. Isadora went inside and kindly collected one of my teapots from the kitchen where she'd taken it and rinsed it out."

"Would you say everyone was inside for at least a few minutes by themselves prior to Lady Gresham finding Jane?" Bonnie asked.

Lilly frowned. "Yes, I suppose that's true."

"All except you, it seems, though you were walking back and forth down the side of the house loading up, Mrs Davenport informs us," Constable Steel said. "She commented you were working so quickly she doubted you had time to go inside."

Thank you, Elizabeth, Lilly thought, realising the woman's statement was the only reason she wasn't being treated as a suspect. "So, just so I'm clear, Bonnie, are you saying one of these women deliberately hurt Jane?"

Constable Steel and Bonnie exchanged a brief glance. "You go ahead, Steel, the pathologist, and the ambulance will be arriving shortly. Best if you meet them at the front." Bonnie said, and he left, moving to the front of the house near the cloakroom, leaving the two of them alone in the kitchen. Bonnie sighed. "This isn't good, Lilly."

"I know. What did you find? It's obvious to everyone here you're treating this as a murder inquiry."

"I'm not sure exactly, but her carotid artery was severed," Bonnie said. "She lost consciousness within a minute or two, I would think, then bled to death."

"Oh, Bonnie, that's awful," Lilly said, her hand instinctively reaching up to her neck. "What sort of weapon was used?"

"I don't know, we're looking for a possible murder weapon now, but this sort of attack should have resulted in blood splatter, and looking at all these women there's no blood on any of them."

"There was blood in the sink, I think," Lilly said. "I caught a glimpse of it when I went to see if Jane was breathing. It looked like someone had washed their hands."

Bonnie nodded. "Yes, we noticed that too. I'm guessing whoever it was came up behind her and reached round, otherwise they would have had a hard time avoiding getting blood on their clothing. It was quick and efficient, Lilly. We spoke to Elizabeth Davenport and apart from the guests at the book club there was no one else here. I asked about security, but she says there's only a house alarm, which was obviously switched off. Do you know if there was anyone else here?"

"I agree with Elizabeth. There wasn't anyone else here at all apart from us, Bonnie."

Bonnie sighed in frustration. "This is going to get nasty quickly, Lilly. Not only was Jane Nolan a prominent and very wealthy citizen, but she was found by Lady Gresham. People are going to be all over this, the press especially. Abigail being here is only going to make matters worse. We need to solve this crime quickly before people start to speculate about what happened. There's no doubt about it, Lilly, there were a number of very important people here today, and now one of them is dead under extremely suspicious circumstances.

*L*ILLY WAS RELIEVED when Bonnie told her she could leave. She'd already packed everything up before the police had arrived and had been itching to go for a while. She couldn't believe she was caught up in yet another suspicious death so soon after the previous one. There was naturally a terrible feeling of dread in the air, but unbelievably alongside that were undertones of glee and gossip which made Lilly feel nauseated. They were all distraught over Jane, of course, but there was a suggestion of thrills, almost as if they couldn't wait to tell others about what had happened in order to give themselves a sense of importance. No doubt they would be dining out on this macabre story at social functions for years to come. Lilly didn't want to be a part of it, and had an almost frantic need to distance herself from all of them.

She exited via the path at the side of the house and pulling on the door handle of her car, found it was locked. Reaching into her pockets for her keys, she frowned when they weren't there. "Oh, no," she muttered, peering in through the window to make sure she hadn't left them in the ignition or on the seat and locked herself out. She had an annoying habit of losing her car keys. She should put them on a chain around her neck or something.

"Miss Tweed! I say, Miss Tweed. Lilly!" Isadora Smith called from behind her, one hand holding her hat, the other lifting the voluminous skirt of her ankle length tea dress, as she tripped daintily down the steps like a princess coming to greet her subjects.

"Isadora," Lilly said with a smile. "Can I help with something?"

"I think you dropped these out on the terrace," she said, dangling a set of car keys. "They are yours, aren't they?"

"Oh, yes," she said, relieved she wasn't going to have to go searching for them. "I was just wondering if I'd managed to lock myself out of my car. Thanks so much. I didn't really want to go back to the terrace to look for them."

"Of course," Isadora said, dropping the keys in Lilly's outstretched hand. "Are you all right? I imagine you're terribly flustered considering what's happened, aren't you?"

Lilly was momentarily surprised that Isadora had bothered to ask, not that she'd pegged her as being self-absorbed, but Lilly herself wasn't part of this group's circle, didn't know any of them in fact apart from Abigail. She hadn't expected anyone to wonder how she was feeling.

"I'm a little shaky, but okay. I didn't know Jane personally but am very upset for her. Such a tragic thing to have happened, I can't quite believe it."

"I imagine this was not how you envisaged today ending," Isadora said with a dramatic sigh. "None of us did. I mean, how could we possibly? It's ghastly. Utterly ghastly. But, just so you know, I was very impressed with your demonstration and knowledge. I hope you won't let this awful experience deter you from doing similar events in the future? It would be such a shame if you didn't continue."

"Thank you, Isadora, I was just wondering about that exact thing."

"Really, you mustn't mind too much if you feel a little put out at all your hard work ending in such an awful way. Don't berate yourself for being upset for *you*; it's your livelihood after all."

Lilly was surprised at how astute Isadora was, she'd been feeling guilty and selfish as those very thoughts had flitted across her mind. Her ruined day couldn't compare to the loss of Jane's life.

"How are you, Isadora? Obviously you knew Jane much better than I did."

Isadora nodded. "I think I'm still in shock. It's as though I'm watching a film or a play as opposed to actually being part of it. It's a very odd feeling. I must admit, I was surprised to see Jane here when I arrived, though."

"Surprised?" Lilly asked, fiddling with her keys. She was torn between wanting to leave and wanting to hear what Isadora had to say. "Why was that?"

Isadora sighed melodramatically. "Well, I don't want to tell tales out of school as it were, but she and Elizabeth were not on the best of terms I'm afraid."

This was news to Lilly. She had picked up on the fact that Elizabeth Davenport had butted heads in one way or another with most of the women in her group, but she hadn't noticed any particular animosity towards Jane Nolan. "Why? Had something happened?"

Isadora shrugged, as though the incident wasn't really of significance. "Jane had rather a tactless way with her at times. She embarrassed Elizabeth terribly in front of Lady Defoe recently."

Lilly cast her mind back to that day in her tea shop. Mrs Davenport made no secret of the fact she wanted to be in Lady Defoe's good graces. She'd almost curtsied and her manner had been overly obsequious. She couldn't imagine how she'd react to being made to look a fool in front of her.

"Oh, dear. What happened?"

"It was at a lawn party Lady Defoe held for Easter a few months ago. A lavish affair naturally, as all her soirees are, and Elizabeth was trailing around after her like a little puppy, as she does. I'm afraid she was being a bit of a bother actually, as well as leaving her poor husband to entertain himself. Jane caught on to Lady Defoe's annoyance and accused Elizabeth of being, in veiled terms, but the implication was there for everyone to hear, a desperate little social climber. I witnessed the whole exchange, and truly, Lilly, it was mortifying for all of us, but especially for Elizabeth. Lady Defoe, gracious as ever, gently admonished Jane for her harsh tongue, but we all saw the amusement for a split second in her face. It was quite dreadful for poor Elizabeth."

"I can imagine," Lilly said. "What an awful experience that must have been for her."

"Oh, it was. She really took it to heart, poor thing. Our book club took a hiatus as a result," Isadora explained. "Today was our first meeting since Easter because no one wanted to bring Elizabeth and Jane together. We all made excuses for not hosting, but eventually Elizabeth reached out to us to start it back up again. I had assumed she simply would omit Jane, but I obviously thought too little of my friend, it seems. She did invite her and treated her perfectly well. I thought that was very brave and courteous of her."

Lilly nodded. "Yes, I'd have to agree. When Jane first arrived, Elizabeth was very kind and introduced us. I never would have guessed they were on poor terms."

"No, of course not, reputation is everything you see. But it was very accommodating of Elizabeth, nonetheless. Jane, in her usual undiplomatic way, was trying to give Lady Defoe some space, I think. It worked, but it was very poorly done, and Lady Defoe values good manners above all else. While she did momentarily let slip her amusement, she certainly wouldn't put up with one of her guests insulting another. She handled it well, I thought."

"I'm sorry to hear Elizabeth has had such a difficult time with some of her friends lately," Lilly said.

"Don't feel too sorry for her, Lilly. Elizabeth makes a rod for her own back. She and I have been known to come to verbal blows occasionally; it wasn't just a problem with her and Jane. Although we don't hold grudges. Anyway, I probably should be getting back; Lady Gresham was looking very pale when I left. I really should check on her, too."

Lilly thanked her again for returning her keys then got in the car ready to leave. As the engine roared into life, she looked up to find Abigail Douglas standing in her way.

"OH, FOR CRYING out loud," Lilly muttered, winding down her window and leaning out. "Abigail, what on earth are you doing? Get out of my way I want to leave." She noticed Abigail had a notebook under her arm and a pen in her hand.

She walked to the driver's side window and leaned in, glaring at her. "I wanted to make it clear that I would be handling this investigation, and your assistance this time will not be needed."

"You are not a police officer, Abigail," Lilly said wearily. She really was fed up now and wanted to go home.

"And neither are you," she hissed back. "I'm an investigative journalist, unlike you."

"No, you're not. You're an agony aunt."

Abigail's nostrils flared and her face turned an ugly shade of scarlet. She pointed a finger at Lilly, wagging it as she spoke. "I am a reporter. I work for the paper. You own a teashop. This does not concern you, Lillian Tweed, and I insist this time that you leave it to the professionals. Your head has become far too big since that last article, but you have absolutely no reason to be involved. Stay out of it."

Lilly rolled her eyes. Her patience with Abigail was wearing dangerously thin, but she just didn't have the energy to argue with her. "Whatever you say, Abigail. Now get out of my way otherwise I promise, I'll run you down."

Abigail's jaw fell open, but she moved so Lilly could drive out. Lilly glanced in her rear-view mirror while she waited for the gates to open. She could clearly see Abigail staring at her. *She is definitely a sandwich short of a picnic,* Lilly thought as she made her way back to town.

As she drove, her mind involuntarily turned to the image of Jane Nolan's body lying dead on the floor of the cloakroom. It was a picture she wouldn't be able to forget for a long while. The previous case she'd been involved with, the death of Carol Ann Hotch, she'd learned about second hand so hadn't seen the body at all. This time, not only had she been there when it happened, but she was a witness and had been the one to check for signs of life. You couldn't get much closer than that, and it was hitting her very differently.

Abigail, on the other hand, was almost feverish with excitement. An abnormal reaction for someone who'd just seen her friend killed. But not as bad as trying to photograph the scene with her phone. That was despicable and a far from normal act for anyone in their right mind to attempt. Then another, far more horrific thought occurred to her, and she had to pull over to calm down before she ran herself off the road, or worse.

Archie Brown had already let slip he thought Abigail was writing agony aunt letters to herself because no one else was. She was also frantic that her column would be done away with altogether, leaving her unemployed. And if what she had intimated during the last case was true, possibly homeless as well. Her idea of moving to crime reporting was to try to keep a job and a roof over her head.

Was Abigail so desperate to prove herself that she'd actually created a story to write? Would she really go as far as that?

Lilly wasn't so sure if she knew the answer.

Chapter Six

*L*ILLY TRIED HARD to forget the incident at the Davenport house that night when she got home. Stacey had already closed up for the day when she'd returned briefly to drop off the items she'd taken to the demonstration, and to pick up Earl, who was fast asleep in the window.

She'd taken a long soak in the bath, then immersed herself in a book to take her mind off things, and thankfully it had worked. The whole experience had become surreal, like being in a Jane Austen novel but with murder as part of the plot. She'd not even dreamed about it, which was a great relief because she had expected a restless night.

However, she and Bonnie had made plans for lunch the next day, ostensibly to catch up. With both of them having busy lives, they hadn't managed a get together for some time, but in reality Lilly knew the main topic of conversation would be Jane Nolan's murder.

She left Stacey to man the shop and rode her bike to the cafe in the park where they'd decided to meet. Choosing to sit outside, but in a shady corner where they wouldn't be seen or overheard, they waited until a waitress brought the menus before turning to the murder.

"You're on the case full time, then?" Lilly asked, nodding at the file Bonnie had brought with her, now sitting on the table.

"I am. I've got my exams in a couple of weeks, so although I'm not fully qualified, I'm expected to pass with flying colours according to my boss. As a consequence, they've thrown me in at the deep end with this one."

"Well, they must have a tremendous amount of confidence in you, Bonnie, considering how important all the players are. Well done."

"Thanks," she said. "A cappuccino, please," she said to the waitress who'd arrived to take their drinks order.

"I'll have the same, please," Lilly said, and the server disappeared. "Are you feeling up to the challenge?"

"Absolutely. When have you ever known me to pass up a challenge? The difference with this one is that I'm the lead on the case. Before I was always working under a superior officer, so it's a bit more stressful trying to make sure I've covered and documented every stage and possible angle. And Abigail Douglas is unfortunately involved in the whole thing, so she won't leave me alone. That, I could really do without. She thinks I'm going to be her inside woman at the station."

"Doesn't she know you've been Archie's contact at the station for years?"

"Obviously not," Bonnie said. "I'll probably drop his name next time she contacts me. That ought to persuade her to leave me alone. She won't want Archie to find out she's going behind his back, I understand he's already furious with her for a number of other transgressions."

When the waitress returned with their coffee, they ordered toasted sandwiches and a side salad to share.

Lilly's eyes shifted to the file. "So, is that..."

"Don't even think about it, Lilly. As a soon to be fully qualified detective, I can't possibly let a member of the public read a file pertaining to an ongoing murder inquiry."

"What?" said Lilly, confused. "Then why did you bring it if I can't see it?"

"All I'm saying," Bonnie said, leaning closer and dropping her voice. "Is that my reputation and job are very important, I could get myself in serious trouble if anyone thought I'd showed you this file."

"Riiiight," said Lilly in exaggeration. "So, are you letting me look at it or not?"

"I'm not *letting* you do anything," Bonnie replied, casually pushing the file nearer to Lilly. "Right, I must go to the bathroom. Back in minute."

"Ah, I get it, plausible deniability," Lilly muttered to herself, snatching up the file when Bonnie had gone. It was Jane Nolan's autopsy report. It made for gruesome reading, and Lilly quickly scanned the text, then turned the loose page over to find an x-ray of Jane's head and shoulders.

"Oh wow," she breathed. There was something long and thin lodged in the side of her neck. The previous typed report sheet had said an unidentifiable metal rod, approximately two millimetres in circumference and just over ten centimetres in length, had been thrust at an angle through the windpipe and pierced the carotid artery. It stated the victim would have passed out through lack of oxygen within a minute before bleeding to death.

Lilly looked up in time to see Bonnie exiting the cafe and making her way back to their table. She grabbed her phone and took a quick picture of the x-ray before sliding the file back into place.

"So," Bonnie said, picking up the sandwich Lilly hadn't realised had arrived. "They found a length of metal in her neck."

"You don't say?" Lilly replied in sarcastic tones. Bonnie frowned and Lilly grinned. "Sorry. So what do you think it is?"

"I was hoping you could venture a guess. Anything come to mind?"

"A very thin metal rod about ten centimetres long? I honestly have no idea."

"Actually, the metal broke off in her neck," Bonnie explained. "So the murder weapon would most likely have been longer, although how much longer we can't say until we find the missing piece. I searched the immediate scene for the rest of it but came up empty. I honestly can't figure out what it is, it's even got my colleagues at the station and the morgue people scratching their heads."

"So that's why you wanted me to look at the file," Lilly said.

"I don't know anything about that," Bonnie said, and Lilly gave her a look. "I've got to be careful, Lilly. Not only could you seeing this file risk the chain of evidence, but I could lose my job. I need to be able to plead innocence if needed. So, I didn't share this with you, okay?"

"I do understand, Bonnie. You being up for promotion is complicating things."

"It's not as though I knew what you were up to last time. You never told me you were investigation the Carol Ann Hotch case. I assumed you were asking questions because she'd written to you. If I had known what you were doing, I probably would have tried to stop you."

"What about this time?" Lilly asked, curious. She hadn't made up her mind whether to pursue the question of what happened to Jane herself yet. "If I do decide to look into things, and I am not saying I will at this stage, the whole thing has left a sour taste in my mouth if I'm being honest, but if I do will you try to stop me?"

"I'll pretend I didn't hear that. I'm going to deny everything," Bonnie said. "Because you're a grown woman who is going to do what she wants anyway. I do however greatly value your opinion, Lilly, although this isn't me asking you to get involved. I just wanted to see if you had any idea what the implement in her neck was?"

"I'm afraid not. I wish I could be more help."

"Don't worry. But if you think of anything remotely plausible, can you let me know?"

"Of course I will," Lilly assured her, and they finished their lunch talking about anything and everything else but murder.

⌒⌒⌒

AFTER LUNCH WITH Bonnie, Lilly felt a bit weighed down with responsibility. While her friend hadn't made a big deal out of it, nor asked her outright, Lilly assumed that Bonnie really wanted her involvement. She obviously couldn't come right out and ask her, but the subtle hints had been there, and this was her first real case, and it was a big one. She needed to solve it and as quickly as possible. But did she need Lilly to help her do that?

The police were in a bit of a predicament. This case was a highly sensitive one with the women of the book club all being prominent, wealthy and influential residents. Every step of the process would have to be meticulously dealt with, every 't' crossed and 'i' dotted. To accuse any one of these women, they would need to have all the necessary evidence at their fingertips to back it up. Lilly didn't envy Bonnie her job, it was a political nightmare.

As she cycled back to the shop, her mind was in a whirl trying to work out what Bonnie had actually meant. *Does she want me to get involved because she knows I could ignore the red tape? Could I get myself into trouble if I start snooping around? I certainly came close last time. She kept saying she didn't want me to get involved, but the way she was acting suggested otherwise. What if I'm misreading her signals?*

By the time she got back to the shop she was no nearer working out what Bonnie really wanted and was almost tempted to ring her and ask her to come out and say it plainly one way or another. But that was a stupid idea.

She parked her bike in its usual spot, chained it to the post and put the flower baskets in place. It had become a recognised staple of the shop front display now, and she regularly found tourists posing and taking photos beside it. She tapped on the glass and Earl opened his eyes, gave a huge yawn which showed his needle-like teeth, then turned over and went back to sleep.

She grabbed the lunch she'd brought for Stacey and entered the shop, finding her pouring a sample for a male customer at the far end of the counter.

"Here's your lunch, Stacey," she said, putting the bag on the counter just as the man turned his head. It was James Pepper, Stacey's father.

"Oh, Mr Pepper, what a surprise, I didn't realise it was you."

"Miss Tweed," he said with a nod before turning back to his tea.

"Thanks, Lilly," Stacey said, turning to her father. "I'm just going to have my lunch. I'll be back down in a bit."

Stacey had got into the habit of taking her lunch upstairs to her flat, where she'd quickly do the laundry or the washing up while she ate. The young woman was pleased with the convenience of living above where she worked, and Lilly couldn't blame her. She had, for a brief moment, considered moving up there herself, but she loved her cottage too much to leave it. Besides, she really needed a garden, not just for her but for Earl.

As Stacey left out of the back door, Lilly made her way behind the counter, secretly wishing another customer would walk in so she could avoid having to have a conversation with James. For some reason, and not just because of his lax attitude towards his daughter, Lilly hadn't really taken to him. Admittedly, she didn't really know him well enough to judge him, but she couldn't shake off the way she felt.

"How was your lunch?" he asked once she was settled by the till.

"It was very nice," Lilly replied. "A perfect day to sit outside and enjoy the sunshine."

"That's always nice," he said. There was a long, increasingly awkward silence as he sipped his tea and Lilly sorted through her tea samples. Eventually to fill the void, he started to make small talk. "I'm surprised Stacey knows as much about tea as she does. Her mother certainly was never much of a tea drinker. Americans seem to think you have to drink the stuff cold and sweetened with so much sugar it would rot your teeth just by looking at it."

Lilly smiled at him. He was trying hard to make conversation. She felt a bit ashamed at her feelings towards him and was sure he could tell she wasn't a fan. Usually she prided herself on her discretion and manners. She really should make a better effort. She wondered for a moment if Dr Jorgenson was right, that her ill feeling stemmed from the possibility that she was viewing his daughter as the one she had never had, or worse that Stacey would leave. This was something she would have to work through herself. She shouldn't take it out on a man who appeared to be honestly trying to better his relationship with his daughter.

"How did the two of you meet? Stacey mentioned her mother travelled a lot."

"Yes, she was a writer. And a painter. Sometime musician and did a bit of acting, too. Even had interest in the sciences. She was a true Renaissance character. She went where the work was. We met in London at the university where I teach."

Lilly nodded. "Yes, I remember now, Stacey mentioned you were a professor. What do you teach?"

"History," he said, smiling. "I dabble in a bit of everything, but I specialise in American History. You can imagine how meeting Stacey's mother, a beautiful American artist, caught my attention. She dreamed of writing the next great American novel. The two of us actually worked together on a book for a while before we separated. It was never finished."

"I'm sorry. Do you mind me asking how Stacey ended up at university here, when the London one is so prestigious? I'm sure you could have helped her get accepted there."

The question evidently struck a nerve. James Pepper tensed up for a moment, gripping his teacup so tightly Lilly thought he might break it. When he returned it to its saucer, he let out a deep sigh.

"You don't like me very much, do you?" he said, confirming Lilly's suspicions.

"What makes you think that?" she replied, neither confirming nor denying, but feeling dreadful that she'd been so transparent.

"Look, I can tell you mean a lot to Stacey and I'm grateful you've been a source of support for her while she's so far from home. I do hope you and I can get along."

"I would prefer it."

"Then to answer your original question, I didn't want Stacey going to the school where I was teaching. I'm a bachelor, stuck in my ways I suppose, and didn't want the interruptions and change of lifestyle having a daughter nearby would mean. I avoided her phone calls when she began talking about coming to England, and I believe I hurt her. She came anyway and was accepted up here."

Lilly couldn't think of anything to say, which wasn't either barbed or sarcastic. *You should be ashamed of yourself,* and *how selfish can you get?* Were absolutely not the correct responses. As an agony aunt she should have been able to give impartial advice, but with Stacey involved she found she couldn't. She kept her mouth shut.

"I know what you're thinking," Mr Pepper continued. "I realise I've been very selfish and I'm trying to make up for my behavior. There's nothing you can say to me that I haven't already said to myself a hundred times, Miss Tweed. I've been an awful father and I don't expect her forgiveness. But I'd like to make amends and be there for her if and when she does need me."

For Lilly, this was the best response she could hope for. "I shouldn't judge you, but I will say that you have a wonderful daughter, Mr Pepper, and I do hope it's not too late for you to get to know her and see for yourself what you've missed."

He looked down, running the tip of his thumb around the rim of his cup. "I hope so as well. And you can call me James. There's no need for us to be so formal, is there?"

Lilly took a cloth and began to polish the counter. "James, it is then. And you can call me Lilly."

He smiled at her. "Thank you. If there's anything I can do, Lilly, please let me know. I imagine losing both an employee and a tenant will be difficult once Stacey transfers to London."

✺

"EXCUSE ME?" LILLY said as her stomach clenched. James realised he'd said something he shouldn't have. "I apologise. It's just you asked why Stacey wasn't at school in London. I assumed you meant I should be using my position to help her get the best education possible. I was therefore going to talk to her about transferring in the Autumn. I'm sure she'd be glad to be studying in the city at one of the finest universities in the country."

Lilly threw the cloth under the counter and stiffened. "That's up to Stacey, don't you think?"

"Naturally. But I intend to give her the option I denied her before," he said reasonably.

Lilly nodded. "Yes, of course. What tea did Stacey brew for you?" she asked, eager to change the subject. Whatever decision Stacey made, she would support her, although it would be a dreadful loss if she left.

"A Chamomile. It's very nice."

"I think I'll have a cup."

Stacey returned from lunch just as she'd finished pouring. "How did your lunch with Bonnie go," she asked, joining Lilly behind the counter.

"It was interesting. I think Bonnie wants my help with the case."

"Wow, really? Dad, Lilly's got quite famous round here since she solved a case in the Spring. People are always coming in asking how she did it."

"Yes, I read the article on-line. It was impressive. So, there's already a new case, is there? What is it this time?"

Lilly sighed. "It's a bit complicated. I was asked to attend a book club meeting recently to do a talk and demonstration of my teas. Unfortunately, at the end one of the women was found dead in the cloakroom. Murdered."

There was a sharp intake of breath from James.

"The police are having a difficult time identifying the weapon even with half of it still buried in her neck."

"That's interesting," James said. "They have half the murder weapon to hand, but still can't identify it? It must be something unusual."

Lilly nodded. "While Bonnie was in the bathroom, I took a picture of the case file," she added, pulling out her phone. "There was an x-ray of the victim's head and neck."

"Now that's better than being a cat burglar," Stacey teased. "Let me see, maybe we can help?"

Lilly showed Stacey the x-ray. "If you read the description, it's very odd. A Thin piece of metal with a pointed end. The other end snapped off so they don't know what the rest of it is or what it looked like. But it would have been longer."

Stacey looked puzzled. "I have no idea," she admitted. "Dad, what do you think?" she asked, spinning the phone round.

"Do you mind, Lilly?"

"No, go ahead."

James took the phone and peered intently at the image. "Mmm, I can't say for sure, but you know what this reminds me of?"

"What?" Lilly asked, suddenly alert.

"Have you ever heard of The Hatpin Panic?"

Stacey giggled. "No, but it sounds hilarious."

"Well, it was in a way. In other's not so much. He slid the phone back to Lilly. "I wrote a paper on it in my undergraduate years for an American Women's history course. It was an event that took place in the late eighteen to early nineteen hundreds. A woman named Leoti Blaker, a young Kansas woman visiting New York, was the victim of street harassment. Instead of putting up with the man attempting to take liberties with her, she elected instead to rip out her hatpin and stab him in the arm."

"Ha!" Stacey exclaimed. "Good for her."

"It started a movement," James continued enthusiastically, and Lilly could see the professor in him shining brightly. "More and more reports of women defending themselves from attacks using hatpins started cropping up with increasing frequency, all over the United States. In fact, one plucky woman in Chicago stopped a train robbery with her hatpin."

"That's incredible," Lilly said. "And very brave of her."

"Honestly, it was fascinating to study. The trend even spread here and to Australia. It was a fight for a woman's right to defend herself, but of course it became a hot topic political issue and was twisted into the safety of men. Should women be allowed to carry something so dangerous on their persons? After all, according to the politicians of the time, women were crazy and prone to hurt innocent people if given too much power."

"You're kidding me," Stacey said.

"I'm not," James said, shaking his head. "Things have changed now, thankfully, but it was very different back then. Men had never before experienced a time when women could and would defend themselves from attackers. They wanted to make hatpins illegal. There was a lot of debate and some laws were passed forbidding hatpins of certain lengths, but the whole movement was overshadowed with the break out of the war. Women's fashion shifted drastically after that, and they stopped using hatpins. The legal battle ended."

"I'm glad I didn't live in those times," Stacey said, with feeling. Lilly agreed with her.

"Sorry, that was a rather long-winded way of saying the picture reminded me of a hatpin."

"Don't apologise, dad, it was fascinating."

"Yes, but no doubt irrelevant. Women don't wear them anymore."

Lilly blinked. "Not usually, but..." she paused, thinking of Isadora and trying to recall if her hatpin was still in place after they'd found Jane. She couldn't remember.

"What is it, Lilly?" Stacey asked.

"One of the women at the book club was wearing a hat, and it was secured with a pin." She looked at the image again. "James, I think you just gave me my first lead."

"Yay!" Stacey cried. "Way to go, dad!"

Chapter Seven

AFTER THE SHOP had closed for the day, Lilly collected the teapot and tea blend Isadora Smith had ordered the day of the event. She'd long ago made it a habit to hand deliver, if possible, all orders for people living in Plumpton Mallet. It was a personal touch her customers appreciated, so it wasn't out of the ordinary for her to do it this time. Of course, her real motive was to make sure Isadora still had the hatpin she'd been wearing at the book club meeting.

Earl had already gone upstairs to the flat with Stacey, who'd volunteered to look after him while Lilly made her deliveries. Picking up the boxes, she went via the front door and unchained her bike. It was a beautiful evening, perfect for a leisurely bike ride.

As she rode she tried to think of a scenario whereby she could ask about the pin without it seeming obvious what she was up to. She also wondered what possible motive Isadora could have for the murder, but couldn't come up with anything. She didn't know Isadora or Jane at all, having met them both for the first time at Elizabeth's house, so being objective wouldn't be a problem. But at the same time, she didn't have any insider knowledge either. There had obviously been tension between Isadora and Elizabeth, Isadora herself had told her that. And then there was the spat at Lady Defoe's house, where Jane had been very rude to Elizabeth and made her look like a fool in front of everyone. Could Isadora have come to her friend's aid? Then there was Lady Gresham, the one to have found the body. But why would she have wanted to hurt Jane? Finally there was Abigail, who, at that moment, was the only one who appeared to have anything to gain from Jane Nolan's death. But it didn't seem to be the likeliest of motives.

It didn't take long to reach Isadora's home. It was a more modest abode than Elizabeth Davenport's, or the other women in the book club, apart from Abigail's, but it was still in the top tier of expensive homes in the area. She was just about to ring the bell on the gate, when the front door opened and Isadora waved. She must have seen her approach from the window and come to greet her.

"Lilly, what a lovely surprise," she said, unlocking and pulling open the iron gate. She was dressed more casually but still expensively in a floor-length skirt, silk blouse and with a designer scarf holding back her hair. "I wasn't expecting you so soon. Did my teapot arrive?"

"It did," Lilly replied, pushing her bike down the short drive towards the door. "I thought I'd deliver it to you myself."

"Oh, how lovely of you, I do so appreciate the personal touch. It's so rare nowadays. If you're not busy, would you like to come in for a cup of tea? I can christen my new pot."

Lilly smiled, she had been banking on Isadora's sense of hospitality. She was certainly the friendliest of all the women in the book club. "I'd love to, thank you." It would give her a chance to try to work the hatpin into the conversation.

She leaned her bike against a small tree and followed Isadora through to a large kitchen where she gave her the boxes. Isadora tore into the one containing the teapot like a child on Christmas morning. She held it up to admire before rinsing it out and opening the tea.

"I just love this Chamomile. I've been craving a cup since the book club."

While Isadora made the tea, Lilly asked how she'd been since the death of her friend.

"As well as can be expected in the circumstances, I suppose. I spoke with her boyfriend yesterday, he's absolutely distraught. He told me he'd been planning to ask Jane to be his wife."

Lilly frowned. "Oh, how awful, I didn't realise she was in a serious relationship. Is it anyone I would know?"

"It's Lady Gresham's brother, Theodore. Lord Gresham. Yes, they were besotted apparently."

"Oh," Lilly said, making a mental note. She hadn't realised Lady Gresham had been so close to Jane that she was about to become her sister-in-law. It seemed the members of the book club were more intimate than she'd initially thought. "Poor man, no wonder Lady Gresham was so distraught if

252

Jane was to become part of the family. I realise now it was a double shock to find her as she did."

"Yes, it is terribly upsetting to all of us who knew her," Isadora said, wringing her hands. "Jane really was such a lovely person."

This was definitely a different tune to the one she'd been singing during their private chat at Elizabeth's house. The way she'd talked about Jane's incident at Lady Defoe's house at Easter hadn't shown Jane in a good light at all. But perhaps it was simply a case of remembering only the good things and conveniently forgetting the bad when someone had died. Or not wishing to speak ill of the dead. Nonetheless, Lilly got the impression Isadora had some conflicting feelings towards Jane.

"Were you and Jane on good terms? I don't mean to be rude, I just got the sense there was some tension the other day."

Isadora laughed. "Dear Lilly, there's always some tension in our circles; it's just the way it is. We were on excellent terms. If anything, I've been locking horns with Elizabeth more these days. While I hate to condone Jane's crude behaviour at Easter, she did have a point when she called Elizabeth out that day. But that's how it goes in friendships, isn't it? We snip and snipe at each other occasionally, then a few days later we're at the book club, or luncheon, or a dinner dance and everything is as right as rain again."

Lilly wasn't sure she agreed. It wasn't anything like the friendships she had, it sounded exhausting truth be told. But she didn't argue. The kettle began to whistle and Isadora brewed the tea the same way Lilly had shown them all, then poured them both a cup. "Oh, heavenly," she said.

"I'm glad you've found a tea to enjoy."

"Oh, I adore many teas. I usually order them from a shop in London, but I will certainly be purchasing what I need from your Tea Emporium from now on," she said. "You really do know your stuff."

"Thank you. And talking of shopping," Lilly said, hoping she was making a smooth transition and not sounding bonkers, or worse, suspicious. "That hatpin you were wearing the other day? Would you mind if I had another look at it? I thought it was just stunning and would like to show it to the local antique shop owner in town and ask her to be on the lookout for something similar for me."

"You wear hats with hatpins?" Isadora asked. "How lovely, there's not many of us left, you know. Yes, I'll just go and get it."

Lilly kept smiling until Isadora had left the room then sighed deeply. If she still had her pin and in one piece then it obviously wasn't the murder weapon. A moment later she arrived back with the butterfly pin, along with another, its match. "I love these," she said. "I tend to collect sets, but these really are my favourites."

Lilly took a picture with her phone. "They are very pretty, so intricate. I hope I can find something as nice for myself."

They finished their tea and Isadora walked Lilly to the door. "Thank you again for delivering my order, and so promptly."

"You're very welcome. Thank you for your hospitality," Lilly replied. They said goodbye and Isadora went back inside, saying she'd see to the gate later.

Lilly was a bit disappointed. But looking at the hatpins again, she felt sure it was more than similar to the item Jane Nolan had been stabbed with. Perhaps it wasn't so far-fetched after all to believe a hatpin was the murder weapon, even if it wasn't Isadora's. *I think I'll talk to Bonnie and see what she thinks...*

Lilly walked over to her bike deep in thought when a car came speeding up the drive, clipping her bike wheel and knocking it over. "No!" Lilly exclaimed in surprise, just as Abigail Douglas got out of the car screeching about what a stupid place to park a bike.

"My car," she wailed, but Lilly could tell this time it was an act.

"My bike," she countered, glaring at Abigail.

Abigail walked to the front of her car to examine the bumper. "You're lucky that bike didn't damage my car."

"You're the one who hit my bike. It better not be damaged, Abigail." Lilly snapped.

They glared at each other for a moment, then realised where they both were.

"What are you doing here?" they both said at the same time.

※

"ACTUALLY, ON SECOND thoughts Abigail, there's no need to tell me. I know exactly why you're here, to interview Isadora."

"Of course I am. I'm writing the story on the case."

"And I suppose Archie knows what you're up to?"

"First of all, what happens at the paper is no concern of yours. Secondly, he is well aware I am covering this story. I was there when Jane was killed. I have insider, first-hand knowledge and the powers that be have agreed I should be the one to take the lead on this. So you don't need to worry about your little friend. I'm interviewing all the ladies who were present. Not you though, Lilly. I mean all the *important* ladies."

Lilly picked up her bike, checked there was no damage and mounted, ready to leave. "Well, good luck, Abigail."

"You didn't tell me why *you* were here," she said, stepping in front of the bike and blocking her path. "You're not looking into this case, too, are you? I've told you to leave it to those of us who are qualified."

"Oh, grow up, Abigail. If you must know I was delivering Isadora's order, it arrived today. I always personally deliver orders to customers in Plumpton Mallet. Now, if you'll get out of my way, I'd like to leave..."

As she manoeuvred the bike around Abigail and passed the side of her car, she caught a glimpse of the side light and couldn't help but laugh.

"What? What is it?" demanded Abigail, stalking to the side of her vehicle. "My car! You've ruined my car."

"It was patently obvious, even to a blind man riding a fast horse, that you hit my bike on purpose, so you have no one to blame but yourself. Goodbye, Abigail," she said, and she sped off up the drive, eager to be away.

As she cycled back to town, she spotted the local antique shop, still doing a brisk trade with tourists. *They must open later in the summer, lucky for me.* She parked her bike at the front and peered through at the window display to see if she could spot any hatpins for sale. There weren't any, so she went inside.

"Hello, welcome to Rosie's Antiques," the elderly lady behind the counter said.

"Hello, I was wondering if you sold hatpins?"

"I do indeed," she said, leading Lilly toward the back of the shop where a number of antique pins were on display, sitting on red velvet inside a locked display case. "As you can see, I have quite a few. Most of them dated just prior to the turn of the twentieth century."

Lilly leaned forward and looked more closely. They were beautiful and obviously old, but more to the point they were very similar to the metal on the x-ray. Lilly felt a surge of hope that she'd found the identity of the murder weapon. She walked back towards the counter where the owner had returned.

"You have a lovely selection. Do you get a lot of people in here looking for hatpins?"

"Oh, yes, they don't stay on the shelves very long. It's amazing how popular they are considering they aren't used much nowadays. There are quite a number of collectors around Plumpton Mallet, actually."

Hearing this, Lilly made her excuses and went back outside to call Bonnie.

"Lilly? What can I do for you?"

"Bonnie, I'm at Rosie's antiques in town, do you know it?"

"Yes, why?"

"Well, I'm feeling reasonably confident that the murder weapon used to kill Jane Nolan was an antique hatpin.

I've already spoken to Isadora Smith, I had to go anyway to deliver her teapot, and the one she was wearing that day she still has. But I'm thinking any one of those women could own them. According to the shop keeper here there are a lot of collectors around town."

"That's very interesting, well done, Lilly. I spoke to the pathologist earlier, and he was still at a loss, he was swaying toward the idea of it being a broach, but apart from his feeling that it would be too difficult to wield in the way needed in order to pierce the victim's throat, he also felt the back pin wouldn't have been long enough. I'll throw the hatpin theory his way and see if he can confirm. In the meantime, I'll do a follow up at Rosie's Antique shop and see if she has a list of local customers that have bought these pins. I'll check with other shops in the area too. It's all a bit of a long shot as the murder weapon could have been a family heirloom, or bought abroad or something, but it needs following up."

"Good idea," Lilly said. "I'll go back inside and take some pictures of the ones here. I'll send them to you to pass on to the pathologist."

"I appreciate that, thanks Lilly."

"Okay, speak soon." Lilly hung up and returned to the display case inside the shop. "Do you mind if I take a few pictures of these?" she asked, holding up her phone.

"Not at all."

Lilly took several images of the whole array of pins and forwarded them on to Bonnie, then something in another case caught her attention. "Oh, this is nice." It looked to be French porcelain although there was no marking and had a hand painted cherry blossom design finished with a gold rim. It was an unusual triangular cup with triple foot and a matching saucer. Definitely a cabinet piece and would look fabulous in the shop. She decided to buy it and put it on the counter just as her phone rang. It was Stacey.

"Hi, is everything all right."

"Yeah, fine. Just wanted to let you know that Lady Defoe's tea set has arrived."

"Are you in the shop?"

"No, Earl and me were upstairs when I heard knocking. I went downstairs and signed for it."

"Perfect, Stacey, thank you. I might come back and pick them up. Do you think Lady Defoe would mind me delivering this evening?"

"No, I don't think so, she'll be glad to have them, I'll bet. Besides, she's too polite to refuse you and if she's not there, you can always go again another day."

"Yes, you're right, Stacey, but it's..." she looked at her watch, "Nearly half-past six. Could you do me a favour and ring her to see if it's all right? Her number is on the order form in the storeroom. Text me back and let me know, would you?"

"Sure, no problem, give me a couple of minutes."

Lilly hung up and turned back to the shop owner. "Sorry about that. I'd like to take this cup and saucer, please."

"It's lovely, isn't it? No maker's mark, hence the price, but it's an unusual and very pretty little piece." As she wrapped it up, she looked at Lilly with a smile. "You know Lady Defoe?"

"Sort of. She ordered a tea set from my shop recently."

"She's a lovely woman. She was in here just this morning as a matter of fact with her husband and Lord Gresham and his sister, Lady Gresham. Well, there you are, my dear. Enjoy it."

Lilly took the well wrapped china from her, paid and left the shop with a promise to return when time allowed. Just as she put the parcel in the bike's basket, a text from Stacey came through to confirm Lady Defoe would be very pleased for Lilly to deliver her tea set. She mounted her bike and returned to the shop.

✑✑✑

THE TEA SET Lady Defoe had ordered was too large to fit in the bicycle basket, so Lilly picked up her car from home and drove to the Defoe house. Although on the same side of the river as the homes of the other ladies, it was by far the largest. With the drive being twice the length and the well maintained and well established gardens, set over several acres, it looked like a painting. Once again Lilly was reminded of a setting for a novel, this time Ferndean Manor from Charlotte Bronte's Jane Eyre, although it wasn't quite as large. It had apparently been in the family for at least five generations, with each generation adding to the house to make it bigger and grander.

There was a turning circle set outside the house with a central fountain surrounded by box hedge. Lilly parked and was retrieving the order from the boot of her car when she heard the sound of footsteps coming down the flight of stone steps. It was obviously the housekeeper.

"Good evening, Miss Tweed, let me help you with those boxes. Lady Defoe is expecting you, if you'd like to follow me."

"Thank you."

She was taken through the large foyer with its enormous central chandelier, marble floor and stained glass windows, along a panelled hallway and through to the rear of the house. Lady Defoe and her guests were gathered in a large sun room which overlooked swathes of manicured lawn, woodland, the river and finally the edge of the town itself before taking in the sweeping moorland at the opposite side of the valley.

Lady Defoe and Lady Gresham were seated on a large cushioned sofa talking, while two men she assumed were Lady Defoe's husband and Lady Gresham's brother Theodore were sitting at a green baize card table, playing what looked to Lilly's eagle eye, poker.

"Miss Lillian Tweed, Ma'am," the housekeeper announced, depositing the boxes she had carried on a nearby table, then departed.

"Lilly, welcome," Lady Defoe said, rising gracefully from her seat and coming to greet her. "Come and have a seat. I believe you know, Lady Gresham? And this is her brother, Theodore and my husband."

Lilly said hello to the two men, then took a seat opposite the ladies, handing the largest box to Lady Defoe. She carefully opened it and withdrew the teapot first, holding it up to the light to admire it, just as Isadora had done with hers. "It's simply beautiful, isn't it?" she asked the room at large.

"Very beautiful," Lady Gresham agreed. "It's the same set Elizabeth ordered the other day, if I'm not mistaken. You must have similar tastes."

Lady Defoe raised an eyebrow. "Yes, I'm sure that's what it is, Meredith. Now Lilly, will you stay and have tea with us? It would be lovely to have you share my set's inaugural outing."

"I'd love to. Thank you," she replied, hoping she wouldn't be expected to serve.

Lady Defoe rang a bell and at the housekeeper's return gave her explicit instructions, then turned to the men. "Gentleman, we're having tea on the patio shortly. We'll meet you there."

Lord Defoe smiled fondly at his wife's joy in her newest acquisition. "Lovely," he said. "I could do with some tea. Theo's wiping me out and I'm afraid I'm about to lose the family silver."

The ladies made their way outside to a comfortable seating area under an awning where the warmth of the evening sun and the fragrance of the surrounding roses made Lilly feel as though she were on holiday somewhere exotic. Moments later the housekeeper returned with the tray and the gentlemen joined them shortly after.

"Shall I do the honours?" Lady Gresham asked, lifting the pot and filling their cups.

"Do you know," Lady Gresham said to the men. "Lilly has an amazing knowledge of teas. She's quite the expert. The talk and demonstration she gave at the book club was fascinating. I never knew there were so many health benefits and remedies."

Theodore Gresham shifted uncomfortably in his seat, catching Lilly's eye briefly then glancing away.

"Are you all right, Theo?" Lady Defoe asked.

"It's nothing," he said, fixing a smile in place, but only a few minutes into their tea he excused himself and went indoors.

"Oh dear, Meredith, perhaps you should go and check on your brother? He's obviously not well."

Lady Gresham sighed. "It's Jane. I should have known better than to bring up the book club in front of him. Excuse me." She rose and followed her brother inside.

Lord Defoe shook his head. "Your friend has a nasty habit of upsetting her brother, my dear." He said to his wife.

Lilly sat sipping her tea and keeping quiet, watching and listening as the drama played out. Perhaps she'd learn something interesting.

"It's not her fault. Theo is hurting terribly, which is only to be expected. But I'm sure she didn't mean any harm."

"He's in an awful state, poor man," said Lord Defoe. "He was in love and was going to ask the girl to marry him from what he's been telling me."

Lady Defoe nodded. "Yes, that's what Meredith thinks, too. Of course, she wasn't very happy about it."

"Now don't start gossiping, my dear," Lord Defoe said, with a quick glance at Lilly.

"Oh, Lilly was there, darling, and took control while the others were too shocked to do anything remotely helpful from what I heard. She's one of us now. Isn't that right, Lilly?"

Lilly nodded. "It was a dreadful thing to have happened. I didn't realise Lord Gresham was so close to Jane. He must be heartbroken, especially if his sister didn't approve. That must have made things much more difficult?"

"You're right on every count, Lilly. Meredith was not very happy at Theo's interest in Jane. She always had something negative to say whenever they'd spent time together. You see, Meredith never thought Jane was good enough for Theo. She came from new money, with no status as it were, and unfortunately she just couldn't look past it."

Lord Defoe scoffed. "Honestly! Who really cares about that nonsense nowadays? It's ludicrous. Poor Theo feels as though he can't talk to his sister about this tragedy because he knows how she really felt about Jane. He's feeling very alone at the moment. I've told him he can come here and drink my scotch and get it off his chest whenever he wants."

"That's good of you, dear. I feel as you do about the whole thing. It's hard enough to find love these days as it is. I do feel it very hypocritical of Meredith. If Jane was good enough for her to befriend, then why not her brother? I mean, look at the members of the book club. None of them apart from Meredith are titled, yet she spends all her time with them."

"Exactly," Lord Defoe said. "If they're good enough for Meredith, then they ought to be good enough for her brother."

Lilly lifted the tea pot and refilled their cups, wondering if Meredith Gresham's motive for surrounding herself with the untitled was because she would therefore always be the queen bee among them.

"Thank you, Lilly. You know, out of all those women who made up Elizabeth Davenport's circle, I always liked Jane the best."

"Why is that?" Lilly asked, taking a biscuit the housekeeper had brought with the tea tray.

"Jane Nolan was a woman who knew who and what she was, and what she wanted from life. There were no airs and graces, what you saw is what you got, a terrible cliché but perfectly true. When Theodore first showed interest, she turned him away. Remarkable, isn't it? Now if the shoe was on the other foot, any one of those other women would have snapped his hand off and dragged him down the aisle before he knew what was happening simply because of his title, but not Jane. She didn't have a sycophantic bone in her body. She honestly didn't care about any of that. She wanted to take her time, let the relationship grow naturally to make sure they were compatible before committing. Do you know he tried the ultimate grand gesture once, offering to fly her to Paris for dinner? She turned him down and said she rather go to the movies. In my book, that was the mark of a woman comfortable in her own skin but genuine at the same time."

"I think that's partly the reason he was so fascinated by her," Lord Gresham added perceptively. "She made him work a bit harder than any of the others."

"Yes, I believe you're right there."

They continued with tea and the subject changed to less serious matters. When some time had gone by, and it was apparent that the Gresham's would not be returning, Lilly made her excuses.

"Thank you for your hospitality, it's been lovely."

"You're very welcome, Lilly, and thank you for coming all this way yourself to deliver my wonderful china. No doubt I will see you again soon. I have every intention of purchasing my tea from you in the future."

Lilly said goodbye to them both and assured them she could find her own way out. In the hall, she found Meredith Gresham returning.

"Oh, are you leaving?"

"Yes, I have to get back."

"That's a shame. I apologise for the interruption. It was rude of us to disappear like that, but I'm afraid I inadvertently upset my brother and had to check on him. He's a little better now, but isn't up to coming back for tea."

"I understand." Lilly said, and Meredith smiled and went on her way to rejoin her hosts.

As Lilly ascended the steps, she spotted Theodore Gresham at the fountain, fiddling with a small cigar and a lighter. Seeing Lilly, he stuffed them in his pocket. "Leaving so soon?" he asked.

"Yes, I'm afraid I have things to be getting on with." She paused for a moment. "I hope you don't think I'm speaking out of turn, but I've just come to understand how close you and Jane actually were. I'd like to say how very sorry I am for your loss."

Theodore blushed. "Kind of you. Thanks."

"I hope you have someone to turn to, to talk things through with? It helps to have that kind of support."

"Yes. Actually, Jane's friend Isadora has been very kind. We've spoken a few times since it happened, which has helped."

"I'm sure it would help your sister to be able to talk things through too. She's obviously upset for you, but I suspect because she's been critical of your relationship in the past, she now feels as though she can't help you because her intentions might not be welcomed as genuine. She doesn't want to overstep, I think. But she does care."

"You're very astute."

Lilly nodded and smiled. "I was the agony aunt at the paper for years. I've seen my fair share of heartache and loss."

Lord Gresham nodded. "That explains it. Well, I better be getting back."

Lilly watched him stride towards the house wondering at the odd relationship Jane Nolan had had with the Gresham's; loved by one sibling, loathed by the other. Could it have had something to do with her murder?

Chapter Eight

*T*HE NEXT DAY was Stacey's day off, so Lilly and Earl were alone in the shop. It seemed a long time since it had just been the two of them and she had to admit she was looking forward to it. Stacey was a godsend to her business, but the recent immersion in the world of the rich and aristocratic of Plumpton Mallet had left her feeling grubby, and she wanted time alone to process it all.

As she set the shop up and brewed herself a pot of mint tea, she thought about what she'd learned since Jane Nolan's death. Apart from Jane, who hadn't been friendly when they met, and in hindsight that could have been her response to Elizabeth as opposed to her, and Abigail who wasn't worth mentioning, she had, on the surface at least, been made to feel very welcome by all the woman. On the face of it they were all good friends, but now she knew there was an underlying current of cattiness and one-upmanship between all of them, it muddied the waters in terms of finding a motive and the person responsible for killing Jane.

Meredith, while proclaiming friendship to her face, didn't like Jane due to her relationship with her brother Theo. Would she have gone so far as to get rid of Jane to prevent the marriage? Elizabeth had been acutely embarrassed at Easter by Jane's acerbic tongue. Perhaps it wasn't the first time she'd been on the receiving end of such an insult and had decided enough was enough? Isadora, while agreeing with Jane's comments, admitted she came to the defence of her friend Elizabeth, but then said she and Jane had also butted heads. What about? And would it be enough of a motive for her to get rid of Jane? If she was right and a hatpin was used as a murder weapon then Isadora was probably out of the equation because she still had hers. But if it wasn't hers then where did it come from?

Lady Defoe, while not a suspect due to her not attending the book club meeting, admitted she liked Jane the most due to her non sycophantic behaviour. But she intimated her thoughts ran to believing the rest of them were little more than social climbers. Did anyone in this group genuinely like the others? It seemed not.

And then there was Abigail. How she had managed to become part of this social circle, Lilly didn't know. Possibly with promises of favourable articles in the paper, an uncharitable thought perhaps, but she wouldn't put it past her. Abigail was definitely the one person in that group who had ideas above her station. The epitome of the social climber the others had been accused of. But would she have committed murder in order to prove herself and keep her job? A job that she had admitted was her last chance. Somehow Lilly couldn't see it, but at this stage she had to keep an open mind. So far every single one of the woman was a suspect with a motive. How on earth could she narrow it down?

*I*T APPEARED EARL was in an unusually social mood that day as he jumped onto the counter and lay down near the till. The customers found it adorable, and he received many strokes and ear scratches, as well as quite a few cuddles as the day went by. Several people had insisted on taking photographs with him, so no doubt he would also be all over the Internet before the day was out. She made a note for Stacey so she could add them to The Tea Emporium's social media sites. Perhaps her former stray would become a viral sensation?

It was mid afternoon and Lilly was just contemplating shutting the shop for five minutes while she went out to grab a sandwich, when the bell above the door rang and James Pepper walked in. Lilly wondered when he had time to teach, considering he was in her shop so often. Or maybe he'd taken some of his owed holiday?

"Hello, James."

"Good afternoon, Lilly. Is Stacey about?"

"No, it's her day off today."

"Is she upstairs, do you know?"

"I think she's out actually."

James looked a little annoyed at this. *Surely if he wanted to see his daughter he would be better making a specific arrangement rather than just turning up and expecting her to be here?* Lilly thought.

"Have you tried phoning her?"

"Of course. There was no answer. Honestly!"

Lilly sighed, which was a mistake as James Pepper immediately took it as a criticism.

"Do you have something to say, Lilly?"

"No, James, I have nothing to say."

Good grief, this man was unbelievable. One minute he was nice and calm, friendly and helpful, the next irritated and on the verge of exploding. It reminded her of Abigail.

"It looks as though you do. Go on, what is it? I'm interested in what you have to say."

James Pepper was obviously looking for a fight. She took a deep breath, willing herself to stay calm.

"Honestly? I don't think you should expect Stacey to be constantly at your beck and call. She's an adult with a life of her own."

"She's my daughter."

"I'm not disputing that, but she has her own life to lead, too."

"But I am her father," he said, raising his voice.

"I know," Lilly said, raising hers in response and causing Earl to sit up, ears twitching.

"Then please stop interfering in the relationship between me and my daughter. It's nothing to do with you."

"Fine," Lilly said, raising both hands. She did not want this to escalate; James Pepper was obviously in a foul mood for some reason.

"Now, let's start again. Do you know where Stacey is?"

"No, I don't. She doesn't take many days off, so I imagine she had plans. If she turns up then I'll let her know you're looking for her. Now, I think you'd better leave. With Stacey absent there's no reason for you to stay."

He snorted but did not raise his voice this time. "I know you feel threatened by me."

"I'm sorry?"

"You know Stacey will be leaving and coming to London soon," he said. "And you're naturally worried about losing both an employee and a tenant. But there's no need to be so aggressive whenever I turn up."

Lilly was stunned for a moment and just stared at him. "Me? Me, aggressive? You come into my shop and start shouting at... you know what? Never mind, James. I have no intention of arguing with you."

James tutted, shook his head and left.

Lilly picked up Earl, giving him soothing strokes. "Don't worry, Earl, he's gone, thank goodness. And I have no idea what that was all about."

It was almost closing time before Lilly had a spare moment to herself. The height of summer had brought tourists and locals out in force, and nearly all of them had walked into her shop. She was just finding her keys to lock the door when it opened.

"Good evening, Lilly. I've got that paint you ordered."

"Oh, Jim! I'm so glad you caught me before I closed because I had completely forgotten you were coming with it today."

She had ordered some specialist paint as the shop sign needed a touch up and she had intended to do it before she went home.

"Didn't you need it today?" he asked to confirm.

"Yes, I did. Thanks so much for dropping it in, I really appreciate it."

"Are you about to close?" he asked, putting the paint cans inside the door.

"I was. Why, did you need something?"

"The kids had an accident and broke the teapot. I thought maybe you could have fixed it, but my wife said she'd like a new one. I told her I'd come and have a look at what you've got when I brought the paint. Do you mind? If you're going to be here for a while painting, anyway?"

"Not at all," Lilly said. "Let me pay you for the paint and you can have a look round while I'm working outside. I'll put the closed sign up so no one else comes in while I'm trying to paint." She went to the till and paid with cash, taking the paid invoice from Jim, then went to the storeroom for ladders.

On the way back through the shop, she found Jim playing with Earl rather than looking at tea pots and laughed. "Caught you," she said on the way out the door. Jim laughed. "Well, he's a very nice cat."

With paint and brushes in hand, she climbed the ladder while Jim browsed. It was a very good job he was in the shop as she would be in need of a witness very soon; Abigail Douglas had just pulled up outside and as was her wont she did not look pleased.

*L*ILLY'S ENTIRE BODY tensed at the sight of Abigail Douglas. She truly was fed up to the back teeth of her constant appearance and petulance. She seemed to take great joy in getting Lilly's back up and deliberately goading her. It was bad enough meeting her on terra firma, but at the top of a ladder, paint can and brush in hand, it was more than a little nerve-wracking, because you just never knew what she would do. She slammed her car door and stomped over to Lilly, seething with so much rage she was practically vibrating.

"Good evening, Abigail," Lilly said, trying to be sincere but failing miserably. Between Abigail Douglas and James Pepper, her patience was wearing so thin as to be almost transparent. It felt as though every time she met Abigail she ended up on the receiving end of an unwarranted tirade. Her natural response to the woman now was to tense up and become defensive and she didn't like the feeling. She'd never felt this way before meeting Abigail, and wondered if her shortness with James earlier was due to having to be constantly on guard and defending herself.

"Don't you *good evening, Abigail* me! You're at it again, Lillian Tweed."

She remained at the top of the ladder, her back to Abigail, while she continued working on the sign. She'd rested the paint can on the narrow top step of the ladder where she could dip in her brush easily. *If I hurry up and finish, I can leave. It's not likely she'll follow me home to harass me.*

"What am I supposed to have done this time?" she asked, without looking down. She didn't want Abigail to realise she was actually beginning to get to her.

"You had tea at Lady Defoe's house, and with the Gresham's there!" Abigail circled the bottom of the ladder, trying to catch Lilly's eye.

Lilly snorted, swallowing the mirth that had begun to bubble up. She couldn't help finding it amusing. "That's what you're concerned about? The fact I had tea with our titled locals? I can't believe how shallow you are, Abigail. Or are you moving into gossip columns now?"

"How dare you? I am not a gossip columnist." She exclaimed. But Lilly knew from Archie that Abigail had pitched that very idea to the senior executives at the gazette not long after she'd arrived. The idea had been shot down. They wanted to remain a professional paper, not a rag whose primary type of journalism was to report on whom had been seen with whom among the most notable of the Plumpton Mallet residents.

"So, what exactly is your problem now?"

"You know very well what it is. You are constantly step-ping on my toes and trying to play detective. Well, I am not going to put up with it any more. This is my story. You are a menace, Lillian Tweed."

Lilly finally snapped, all vestiges of the previous mirth vanishing in an instant. "Right! That's it, Abigail Douglas. I refuse to be the punching bag for your ludicrous insecurities any more. You need to take a long hard look at yourself and ask why people no longer write to you? Stop harassing me or I will get an injunction taken out against you. You are borderline insane, Abigail. Get a grip on yourself before you do or say something that will get you into serious trouble. Trouble you may not get out of."

Lilly was surprised at herself, she'd never lost her temper like this before, but she'd absolutely reached her limit. Abigail hadn't expected it either, and true to form reacted badly to what she perceived as insults rather than the home truths they actually were. She approached the ladder and gave it a swift, hard kick.

"Ah!" Lilly wailed as the ladder wobbled dangerously. She grabbed the sign to prevent it falling completely, but the paint can was now balanced precariously with no support. It fell, hitting Abigail on the shoulder and splattering thick black oil paint all over her clothes, one side of her face and her hair, before bouncing to the ground where it covered her shoes.

Abigail stared at the mess in absolute horror. Then gave Lilly the blackest look she ever had. *Literally*, Lilly thought as she watched the ink coloured paint drip off Abigail's chin.

"You'll pay for that, Lillian Tweed," she hissed through clenched teeth. "Do you hear me? I'm calling the police and you are going to pay for assaulting me!"

Lilly was about to give Abigail a piece of her mind for even suggesting this was her fault, when Jim exited the shop. "I saw that, Ms Douglas. What did you think you were doing? You're lucky Lilly didn't fall off the ladder and break her neck! This was all your doing and if you dare suggest otherwise, *I* will be the one calling the police.

Abigail clearly had not expected there to be a witness to her abhorrent behaviour and started stuttering.

Lilly climbed down the ladder on shaking legs, looked at Abigail and shook her head. *What a mess.* She turned to Jim, "Thanks, Jim, I appreciate your support. Abigail," she said.

"Jim is right, what you did was dangerous and could have resulted in me having a serious accident, or worse. I refuse to deal with your tantrums anymore, and if you do anything remotely like this again, I'll see to that you are prosecuted. Do you understand me?"

Abigail nodded; seemingly mute as it suddenly dawned on her how serious the situation was.

"Now, if you walk round to the back of the shop, I'll let you in through the storeroom to use the bathroom and get cleaned up as much as you can."

"I'll go with her," Jim said, still frowning. "I suggest you thank Lilly, Ms Douglas. She is being far more magnanimous than I'd be in the same circumstances."

"Thank you," she said in a small voice.

Lilly nodded curtly. "Did you find a teapot, Jim?"

"Yes, I put it on the counter."

"All right, I'll deal with that while you're escorting Abigail."

Lilly went back inside with the ladder, a now empty paint can and the brushes, putting them in the storeroom before opening the back door. Back in the shop, she rang up Jim's sale and wrapped it. A moment later, with Abigail using the bathroom, Jim reappeared with her bag, which he'd carried for her to prevent it getting covered in paint. He put it on the counter.

"I'll bring some sand round shortly to cover the paint on the pavement. It should soak most of it up and make it easier to clean. I'll pressure wash it for you first thing."

"Thanks, Jim, you're a life saver."

"Are you all right, Lilly?"

"Yes, I think so. Still shocked that Abigail would go so far. We have an interesting history, to say the least. Perhaps I shouldn't have snapped at her."

"Don't feel guilty about snapping at her, Lilly. From where I was standing, she deserved it and more. It's not normal behaviour you know. I honestly think that woman needs professional help. Do you need me to stay until she leaves?"

Lilly shook her head. "No, I'm fine, Jim, but thank you. Abigail has completely embarrassed and shocked herself, and I think she'll calm down in order to save face. How long she remains in the bathroom is another thing. But I've got a good book with me so I'll be fine."

"All right, well, I'll start the clean up outside. Thanks again for the teapot. Look after yourself, Lilly, and remember I'm not far away if you need me."

❦

WHILE ABIGAIL WAS in the bathroom, Lilly decided to call Archie. If anyone knew the true story about Abigail being put on the murder inquiry legitimately it would be him.

She stood behind the counter, one hand on the phone pressed to her ear, the other scratching an ecstatic cat who was purring very loudly.

"Archie Brown," said a harried voice at the other end of the line.

"Archie, it's Lilly," she said, keeping an eye on the back of the shop in case Abigail appeared. "Have you got a minute to talk?"

"Hi, Lilly. Yes, what is it?"

"Nothing new, just being harassed by Abigail Douglas for a change," she said, and Archie grunted. "Listen, she's been telling me she's been put in charge of the Jane Nolan story and I wanted to double check with you to see if that's right? I've come to the point where I don't believe a thing that comes out of her mouth."

"I wouldn't either, the woman's a pathological liar," Archie said. "She's not been put in charge of that story at all, and I'll tell you why that would be inappropriate; because she's a prime suspect. Personally, I don't believe she did it, but the police are interested in her for obvious reasons."

"Really?"

"Of course. I spoke with Bonnie earlier and it looks as though they haven't managed to narrow it down much at all. She's under a lot of pressure from the higher ups to get this sorted out quickly. You really are the only person out of all the attendees they have crossed off their list, because you didn't have any opportunity to kill Jane. Everyone else was inside alone at one point or another while Jane was in the cloakroom. Any one of them could have walked in on her, quickly stabbed her and returned to the party without being detected."

"Including Abigail," Lilly said. Silently thanking Elizabeth Davenport for informing the police that she had been outside or in the garden room the entire time, therefore keeping her off the suspect list.

"Exactly. It's a conflict of interest at the very least, so we would never have even contemplated putting her on the story. This is just another incident of Abigail trying to secure her currently precarious position at the paper," Archie explained. "She's continually trying to make a splash. She was hired as an agony aunt but has completely ruined it. The column is a disaster, as is her advice. Nobody is writing to her, Lilly. Her job security really isn't looking good. I don't think she had this kind of problem where she was before, even though it's the same owners, but of course they didn't have you to compare her to. And her previous paper wrote a different type of news if you get my drift. People appreciated and believed in your advice, Lilly, they still do, which of course is part of the problem. But it's not yours."

"Thanks, Archie, I appreciate you saying so," Lilly said, double checking Abigail wasn't listening to the conversation. "So, Abigail, really is a suspect?"

"According to Bonnie she is, and even if I don't agree, I understand why. There's no proof she isn't for one thing. In fact there's barely any proof at all to say who committed the crime. Everyone knows Abigail is desperate for a story and a little unhinged..."

"I'll say," Lilly replied with feeling, the near miss on the ladder fresh in her mind.

"Yes, but it means there's potential there for her having *created* the story, if you know what I mean? It might be far-fetched, but it's no weaker a motive than the ones they're thinking about for the others. It's one of the reasons Bonnie is having such a difficult time with this case. They can't pin down a motive."

Lilly felt a fluttering in her chest. The same thought had occurred to her, but could Abigail really have killed Jane just to get a story? She'd just tried to kick a ladder out from underneath her so she obviously had some pent up rage, but surely that would be one step too far? "Thanks for the information, Archie," Lilly said, suddenly remembering Abigail's handbag was on the counter. "I'll let you go. Talk to you soon."

"You will do. Bye, Lilly."

Lilly hung up and checked the storeroom door. Abigail was obviously still in the bathroom, so she pulled the bag closer and opened it. Immediately she found a large spiral notebook, she took it out and began to read.

She had a number of notes on Jane's murder, specifically those involving Elizabeth Davenport. *If Abigail is compiling legitimate evidence on the case, then it seems unlikely that's she's the guilty party,* Lilly thought.

"What do you think you're doing?" Abigail shouted. "What gives you the right to go through my bag?" She marched across the room, hair a glutinous mess and a dirty shade of grey dripping with oily water and reeking of turpentine. She snatched the notebook from Lilly's hand before she'd had a chance to read any of the notes.

"What gives you the right to try to cause me serious injury by knocking me off a ladder?" Lilly countered. This drastically changed Abigail's tune.

"Fine," she said. Sighing and taking a seat at the counter and putting her head in her hands. She'd done her best with turpentine and soap and water, but the stains of black paint were still unmissable. She looked an absolute fright.

"Do you want a cup of tea?" Lilly said, beginning to feel a little sorry for her. Abigail nodded. "Then, perhaps we can call a truce and share what we know? To be frank, I'm sick of fighting with you. It's exhausting and dispiriting and I have better things to do with my time. Are you agreeable? Because if not, you can leave now."

Abigail nodded again.

"Right, then in the spirit of our new found détente, I need to tell you you're being thought of as a suspect by the police, Abigail." She said, spooning leaves into a pot and switching on the kettle.

Abigail looked up. "What?"

"I was looking to see if I could find anything incriminating."

"I'm a... what are you talking about? Why would I be a suspect? Who told you that?"

"Apparently the police have no reason to rule you out. You were there on the day..."

"So were you."

"But I never went into the main house apart from when I first arrived, and that was before anyone else had turned up. The next time was at the end when Meredith screamed. The furthest I went during the day was the garden room, other than right at the beginning when I went to the kitchen to fill the kettles. All of you, including Jane, were in the pergola then. So you see it couldn't possibly have been me. Now, since you had time to be alone with Jane, the police can't rule you out as a suspect. You had the opportunity and the police feel you also have a motive. While the other women also had the opportunity, the police are struggling to find a decent reason for any of them to kill Jane."

"I don't have a motive. But I have evidence."

"None that I saw," Lilly countered, pouring them both a tea and sliding Abigail's cup and saucer to her across the counter.

Abigail glared for a moment, but didn't lash out. Eventually she calmly said, "I didn't hurt Jane. I'm trying to find out what happened to her. She was my friend, Lilly. I joined the book club quite soon after I moved here, and I am very upset about what happened to her. All I'm doing is trying to find out what happened to my friend."

Lilly was sad to realise she still didn't believe Abigail was being sincere. The way she'd tried to take a picture of Jane's dead body had been callous in the extreme. It was difficult to believe she had any genuine friendships at all.

"I saw in your notes you were writing about Elizabeth Davenport. I can't imagine what sort of motive she would have."

"I thought the same thing at first. Elizabeth certainly wouldn't have wanted her party ruined," Abigail said. "She's all about reputation and standing. But, I got a glimpse of Jane's phone during the book club meeting and there were some rather alarming messages from Elizabeth warning Jane not to embarrass her in front of Lady Gresham."

"When did you go through her phone?"

"After she was found dead. My first instinct was to go through her bag before the police got there to try to find a clue. I sneaked away for a minute while we were all waiting."

Lilly then remembered Abigail had disappeared immediately after she had stopped her from photographing the scene.

"What did you find out?"

"I looked at her text history and found a conversation between her and Elizabeth," Abigail said, grabbing her own phone from her bag. "I took some pictures. Here, look."

Now that Abigail was in a sharing mood to prove she was innocent, she was happy to let Lilly see her phone. The text read;

> **ELIZABETH:** *Just a word of warning you better watch that vicious mouth of yours today*
> **JANE:** *?*
> **ELIZABETH:** *Don't act as though you don't know what I'm talking about*
> **JANE:** *I don't*
> **ELIZABETH:** *Honestly! After the way you acted in front of Lady Defoe you are lucky to get an invitation at all*
> **JANE:** *Don't be so dramatic*
> **ELIZABETH:** *I'm not being dramatic. You were childish and mean and you'd better watch what you say today in front of Lady Gresham*
> **JANE:** *I've already apologised*
> **ELIZABETH:** *It makes no difference. What I want is to be able to move on so don't you dare act that way again and try to embarrass me in front of my friends or you will be sorry*
> **JANE:** *Such a drama queen like always, Elizabeth*

"Good grief! They were on worse terms than I thought," Lilly said.

"Exactly. They were at one another's throats the entire time during the discussion about the book too, because Jane contradicted something Elizabeth said and she in turn was mortified about how Meredith Gresham was viewing the whole discussion and her in particular. It was thinly veiled snipes almost from start to finish."

"I can't understand why she invited Jane in the first place, if they felt like this about one another. Have you told the police you've got this?"

"Not yet, but I will. They took Jane's bag and phone, so I expect they've found the texts by now."

"Well, you may be onto something here, you know?" Lilly said.

"Of course I am," Abigail said, with no modesty at all. She put her phone and notebook back in her bag. "I think Elizabeth had a motive. For all we know, she planned the whole book club meeting just so she could get Jane into her house to kill her."

"In revenge? Do you not think that would be a little far-fetched? I mean, at a tea party there would surely be easier ways to murder someone. She could have poisoned the tea for one thing."

"What and let you get the blame? I don't think so, Lilly. Besides you were the only one in charge of the pots and the brewing. You brought all your own cups as well. I don't think she'd have been able to do that without being seen. But I do think revenge could have been on her mind."

"Yes, I suppose you have a point there. It wouldn't have worked that way, thank goodness."

"No. But it was a messy way to do it, wasn't it? Whoever the murderer was, they were extremely fortunate not to get covered in blood. That would have been an immediate giveaway."

"It's easy than you think actually, as she was attacked from behind and very quickly. So, you know all these women fairly well, Abigail?"

She nodded. "I've been part of the book club for quite a while now."

"If you don't mind me saying so, you don't really seem to fit the mould for the type of woman Elizabeth Davenport... well..."

Abigail laughed, sounding almost friendly. "You mean I don't seem to fit into her little collection of titled and wealthy?"

"Yes, I suppose I do, although I wasn't going to describe them in quite that way."

"It's true. Elizabeth is a collector. Her favourite thing to collect is people, odd as it sounds. She doesn't so much make friends as add them to her group as a way of adding interest to herself. Me? I was the new agony aunt at the newspaper. A professional woman who was part of a large and well-known national company. I was established and my name was recognised with my former paper, so she invited me along when I first moved here. I think she initially thought I was going to be quite famous here too then it all turned out... well not quite how I expected. She ignored me for some time after; until I wrote that front page article with Archie, then suddenly I was her best friend again. It's obvious she thinks that by making important connections she in turn will be made to look important. Not that I'd ever accuse her to her face. I'd be on her radar like Jane and Isadora before I could say old news."

Lilly frowned. "I understand Elizabeth's confrontation with Jane, but what do you mean about Isadora being on her radar?"

"Oh, didn't you know? It is one-upmanship and competition just about all the time with those two. I've just told you Jane annoyed her intensely at the meeting, but you should have heard Isadora. She put a lot of work into sounding smart and ingenious in front of Lady Gresham, cleverer than her host especially. She and Elizabeth are always trying to outdo and outshine each other," Abigail explained. "It's just the way they are. If I'm honest, one of the main reasons I attend these functions is because they're a huge source of entertainment. I hardly ever read the books."

Lilly laughed.

"Well, Lilly, I need to leave. Thank you for the tea and for letting me clean up," Abigail said, picking up her bag and exciting through the back door.

Lilly watched her leave. Earl let out a small meow and Lilly absently scratched his ears. "Do you know, Earl, that was almost civil towards the end. If only she made a bit more of an effort, then I'm sure she would make more friends and become better at her job. I wonder what her story really is?"

Chapter Nine

*T*HE NEXT MORNING, while Stacey and Lilly were busy in the shop, a special delivery arrived. It was the tea set that Elizabeth Davenport had ordered.

"Hey, Lilly," Stacey said, as she'd been the one to greet the driver. "It looks like that second fancy tea set has arrived."

"Perfect," Lilly said, as Stacey set the large box on the counter for her to inspect. "I had hoped it would arrive at the same time Lady Defoe's did, considering they were ordered on the same day. But never mind."

Lilly opened the box and carefully took out each piece to ensure there were no cracks or chips or full-blown breakages which had occurred in transit. Everything was perfect, so she carefully wrapped and repackaged it all, ready to take to its new owner.

"Okay, that's all fine, let's get it wrapped in The Tea Emporium gift wrap and I'll drive over and deliver it."

"Do you always make home deliveries when orders arrive?" Stacey asked.

"I try to. If it's something small that I can fit in my bicycle basket and for someone who lives close by, I'll bike over."

"But this is neither. Mrs Davenport lives miles away, and it's too big for your bike."

"Yes, that's true, but it's a beautiful set and one of the most expensive I have to offer. Something like this deserves a special delivery. If the customer lives in Plumpton Mallet, I usually try to make a personal delivery, even if it means taking the car. It brings back repeat custom if they have a good experience."

"And it gives you a chance to ask Mrs Davenport some more questions about what happened at the book club meeting," Stacey teased. Lilly had already brought Stacey up to date with everything that had happened, including the incident and subsequent conversation with Abigail the evening before. In typical Stacey fashion she had turned the whole thing into a running joke, constantly asking Lilly whether she was setting up as a private investigator and if she was attempting to ruin Abigail's life and car in the process. She finished by saying if Abigail was forced to dye her hair black to disguise the paint, then it wouldn't matter if she lost her job, because she could make loads of money standing in for Cruella de Vil. Lilly had had to pass that little gem on to Archie, who laughed uproariously. Luckily Jim had been true to his word and there was no sign of the mess outside the shop now. What Abigail looked like was another thing entirely.

"Well, yes, there is that too," Lilly now said. "Could you help me put this in my car so I can deliver it today?"

"Sure."

They shut the shop for five minutes while they traipsed back and forth through the storeroom to the car park with the boxes, and very carefully put them in the boot.

"It seems to me like the more expensive the china, the more delicate and breakable it is," Stacey said, as they loaded the last of the boxes.

"That's absolutely right. Fine porcelain like these are fired at a higher temperature and will allow bright light to pass through. But because of the firing method, they are much more expensive to produce. The downside is despite its strength, it does chip more easily. When I first opened, I felt as though I was having to replace something every other day. It took me some time to get used to the fact that no matter how excited I was to see the new stock, I shouldn't rush to unbox it, otherwise I'd ruin all my merchandise. Now, are you okay to run the shop for a while if I make this delivery now?"

"Absolutely fine, don't worry," Stacey assured her, so Lilly got in the car and drove out of town to the Davenport home.

It was the first time Lilly had been back to Elizabeth's house since Jane had died, and it brought back an eerie sense of deja vu as she made her way down the drive. The gates, once again, had been opened by some unknown method.

She parked and went up the steps and was about to knock on the door, when it was opened by Elizabeth Davenport.

"Lilly, how lovely to see you again, please tell me my gorgeous tea set has arrived and you're here to deliver it?"

"Got it in one,"

"Fabulous," she said, following Lilly to help carry the boxes into the house. "I told my husband that I had a charming little tea set coming. He thinks I spent too much, of course, but I believe when he sees the design and the superb quality he'll agree it was worth it. I intend to have an afternoon tea for him this week to show it off."

Lilly followed Elizabeth through to her kitchen and they chatted while they gently unpacked. It was a set of tea cups and saucers, Teapot, side plates and various accessories. "This is all so wonderful," Elizabeth said, holding a cup up to the light. "And thank you for delivering it, you didn't have to."

"I wanted to. A special tea service deserves a special delivery."

"It's kind of you, dear. What can I say? I have a refined taste."

Perhaps because of Stacey's teasing earlier, or possibly the result of being back where the murder took place, Lilly had a sudden, alarming thought. She'd just remembered that during the course of conversation at her demonstration, Elizabeth had mentioned having a hatpin collection to rival that of Isadora's! With the shock of the murder, she'd completely forgotten about it. She needed more information. Anything she could gather for Bonnie was sure to help, especially as the police were now working on the hatpin angle.

"You most certainly do, Elizabeth. You definitely have a skill for identifying good quality." Elizabeth Davenport positively preened. "In fact, I wonder if you would mind giving me some advice on hatpins? I remember you said you had a lovely collection when I remarked on Isadora's. It piqued my interest. Do you think I could see it?"

"Oh, you're thinking about starting a collection too? You won't be disappointed. They are so very interesting and quite beautiful. Some plain and some ornate, but all with such lovely history. I always wonder what sort of woman would have worn the ones I now have. Come along and see." She beckoned Lilly to follow and led her through to the drawing room where a display cabinet on ornate legs was filled with a small, unique collection of trinkets, including several hatpins.

"Goodness, how lovely," she said, admiring the sparkling items. She noted the case appeared to be locked, but there was some damage to the surrounding wood. "Oh dear, did something happen to the case?"

"It's been like that for a few days," Elizabeth said with a huff. "I'm not sure what happened to it. It's quite aggravating because it ruins the look, doesn't it? My husband has been promising to fix it, but he's a businessman rather than a handy man, I'm afraid. I think I'm going to have to call in a professional to see to it. I do so hate to see it looking this way, it rather spoils things don't you think?"

Lilly nodded. "Well, your collection is lovely." She looked at all the hatpins, noting the display didn't appear to have a gap where something was missing. Of course, it would have been easy enough for Mrs Davenport to rearrange the items to hide the space. "Would you mind if I used your cloakroom before I left?"

"Not at all, you go ahead. I was going to make some tea to break in the new set. Would you like to join me?"

"That would be lovely, thank you. I never turn down a cup of tea."

"Neither do I. It's always teatime here at the Davenport's."

Lilly headed to the bathroom as Elizabeth returned to the kitchen. The whole place had been thoroughly cleaned since Jane had been found, and there was no sign at all of the tragedy that had occurred. Lilly took her time scouring every inch of the place anyway, even though she knew it was unlikely she'd find anything helpful. She was feeling discouraged when she re-entered the hall, then for a split second, as the sun shone through the glass panel in the front door, a brief sparkle caught her eye. It came from a large pot housing a huge potted palm in the entrance foyer. She approached and leaned down, reaching into the pot, and gasped. She pulled out a diamond encrusted jewel in the shape of a letter E, a snapped stem at the back. It was the missing decorative end of the hatpin! "E for Elizabeth..." she breathed, realising the woman must have commissioned a personalised hatpin for herself.

Lilly didn't waste any time and darted back into the cloak-room to hide from Elizabeth, the missing part of the murder weapon still in her hand, and called Bonnie. When she informed her what she'd found, Bonnie told her to remain in the cloakroom and wait for her arrival. She was on her way immediately. Under no circumstances was she to let anyone at all know what she'd found. And that included Elizabeth Davenport.

A moment later there was a knock on the cloakroom door and Elizabeth called out. "Are you all right, Lilly? The tea is nearly ready. I thought we'd have it on the patio?"

"Yes, I'm fine. That sounds lovely," Lilly called out. "I'll be there in a moment."

Almost immediately, she heard the doorbell. Bonnie must have either driven like a rally driver, or more likely been quite close to Dovecote Grange already when Lilly had called her. Or it was someone else entirely. "Oh, there's someone at the door, dear, I won't be a minute."

She heard raised voices muffled behind the closed cloakroom door, followed by an insistent knock. "You all right, Lilly?" Bonnie asked.

"Fine," she said, opening the door and showing her the broken hatpin she'd found only moments before.

Bonnie took it carefully and nodded. "Yes, that's definitely a match. I don't suppose you thought about fingerprints?"

"Oh, Bonnie! No, I never thought. I just grabbed it and called you. I'm so sorry."

"Doesn't matter, hopefully we'll get something from it."

"Where's Mrs Davenport?" Lilly asked.

"In the back of the car, in cuffs, she's protesting her innocence, of course. She'll be taken to the station and questioned. Well done, Lilly."

Lilly nodded. "I'll just go and check everything's all right in the kitchen. I'd hate for her to have left the kettle boiling away on the cooker top and burn the place down."

◈◈◈◈◈

THE NEXT MORNING, the front page of The Plumpton Mallet Gazette carried the story of Elizabeth Davenport's arrest for the murder of Jane Nolan. It had been written by Abigail Douglas and was sensationalism at its finest. Lilly found this surprising considering Archie had only recently told her the bosses at the paper didn't want Abigail anywhere near the Jane Nolan story. Either she'd pitched something so compelling to the editors that they were willing to overlook her involvement and conflict of interest, or now that someone had been arrested for the crime she'd been let off the hook.

Lilly stood on the pavement outside her shop reading the article and shaking her head. It wasn't that it was badly written. Compared to Abigail's recent articles it actually was a vast improvement, but the entire thing was full of speculation and assumptions that a half decent reporter would have either worded differently or most likely, omitted. Of course, the word 'allegedly' was sprinkled liberally throughout to avoid getting the paper into serious trouble and on the wrong end of a lawsuit. Even so, the tone was highly accusatory, and Lilly found herself quite offended by it. She was surprised the chief editor had given the go ahead for it to be printed.

"I can't believe it," she muttered, shaking her head and folding the paper in half, tucking it under her arm. She leaned down and picked up the watering can she'd abandoned after discovering the paper tucked under one of the plant pots. She watered the plants, tall red geraniums surrounded by a waterfall of delicate blue, pink and purple lobelia that decorated her bike and returned inside.

Stacey was busy assisting a customer who was trying to choose a new tea, selecting sample after sample in an attempt to find the perfect blend. After returning the watering can to its place in the cupboard and setting the newspaper down by the till, Lilly took the selected leaves from Stacey and offered to brew a pot. "I think you'll really like this one," Stacey said to the young man. "I'm a huge fan of all the Chamomile teas, but this one is the absolute best."

"Thanks," he replied. "I've been feeling a bit stuck in my ways recently and decided it's time I tried something new. My mum always made mint tea, so it was something I grew up with, but I'm just discovering there's so much more to try."

"I've been expanding my own palate a lot since I started working here," Stacey said while they waited for the tea to brew. "I'm from the states, which you can probably tell from my accent. I spent most of my time in the south where their tea is pretty much just black, iced and filled with sugar."

Both Lilly and the young customer wrinkled their noses. "Sounds dreadful," he said.

"I ought to make you a southern belles sweet tea some-time, Lilly," Stacey offered with a huge grin.

"Please don't," Lilly said, and the three of them laughed just as the tea was ready to pour. Truth be told, Lilly was usually willing to try just about any type of tea, but black iced tea sweetened with so much sugar was just too much. Not to mention her teeth probably wouldn't thank her for it as James Pepper had said.

Stacey poured each of them a beverage, using the vintage mix-matched cups Lilly kept on display behind the counter. She smiled when Stacey handed hers over in the new teacup she'd bought from Rosie's antique shop. Stacey knew Lilly had wanted to try it out. Luckily it didn't leak, which had been Lilly's main worry.

"Wow," the young man said when he took a healthy mouthful. "This is excellent. Okay, you've sold it to me. I'll have a large box, please."

Stacey rang his order up and he departed with words of thanks and promises to be back, leaving Lilly and Stacey alone in the shop. "Been kind of slow this morning," Stacey said. "He's only the fifth customer we've had. It's weird how random the influx of customers is round here. You can't keep track of it."

"Don't worry, I'm sure it will pick up soon." Lilly said with confidence. "Mid week is always slower, while the end of the week and the weekend is always busier because of the extra buses full of tourists that turn up."

Stacey picked up the newspaper Lilly had left by the till, reading the front page with interest. "You told me about the police taking away Mrs Davenport," she said, speed reading the article with a frown. "It's a bit judgmental, isn't it? It's as though she's already been found guilty."

"I know," she said, wondering what Stacey's thoughts were. Stacey had no journalism experience and was young, probably not an avid news reader, but even she could see the blatant faults in the article after only a brief read. She was interested in her take on it all. "All the evidence found was circumstantial. Even though the decorative E on the hatpin was a little telling."

"Yeah, but, Lilly, it's too obvious. I mean, that just tells you who it belonged to not who used it. And would Mrs Davenport use the only one that she could be linked to like that?" Stacey shook her head. "Ever since you told me what happened at her house yesterday, I've been thinking about it. That broken bit you found was stashed in a plant pot after one of the women, supposedly Elizabeth Davenport, stabbed and killed Jane Nolan. They washed up in the cloakroom sink and then we're supposed to believe they ditched the broken part in a pot and left it there, right?"

"Right."

"But I was thinking, if it was Mrs Davenport, why would she leave the murder weapon in the plant? She *lives* there. Jane was killed days ago, so that means she's spent all this time in her own house knowing the key piece of evidence that could pin, sorry that wasn't meant as a joke, the key piece of evidence that could *connect* her to the murder, was sitting right there a couple of metres from the crime scene. She had plenty of time to go and remove it and dispose of it somewhere else. Somewhere better, where no one would *ever* find it. Instead she chose to leave it there, knowing sooner or later someone would be bound to come across it? That's all kinds of stupid, Lilly, and Mrs Davenport doesn't strike me as being that much of an idiot."

Lilly nodded. "I agree with everything you've said and have been thinking along those lines myself. If she is the guilty party, then it wasn't the wisest move. Unless she's double bluffing, but I don't think that's the case at all. Elizabeth Davenport is far from stupid."

"That's what I'm saying. If she did it, then she'd have got rid of the letter E part of the murder weapon as soon as she could. It makes me think she couldn't possibly have known it was there. Which means she isn't the one to have killed Jane at all. I'm pretty sure the police are going to figure that one out too before long, if they haven't already. I bet they're annoyed they didn't find the head of that pin."

"I agree," Lilly said. "But, just to play devil's advocate here, Elizabeth cares very deeply about her reputation. Jane put a not inconsiderable dent in it, in front of a lot of people she called her friends, and Elizabeth was both angry and mortified. But, would she really have risked her reputation and standing in the community by committing murder? The scandal would have been off the charts in a small town like this. Well, it is now actually since the article came out."

"Mm, maybe, but not this way," Stacey said.

"What do you mean?"

"I mean, I don't really know this woman or anything, but it seems to me if she was going to commit murder she wouldn't have done it like this. She would have made a good plan. She acts like a planner, you know? Like the day she ordered the exact same tea set on the exact same day as Lady Defoe happened to be here. I think she knew Lady Defoe was coming. It was her first time here, remember, and planned to be in the shop just before she arrived so she could accidentally bump into her."

"Actually, that's more than possible. I've learned all these women play little games like this. But planning to bump into someone is a far cry from planning to bump them off, Stacey."

"Yeah, well, I still don't think she did it," she said, getting up and stretching her back. "It's all a bit too convenient. Which means one of those ladies she calls her friends has set her up!"

"Yes, I know. And sadly, I believe you're right."

"Okay, well, there was a bunch of deliveries came in yesterday, so I need to go through the boxes and get the teas organised in the back. Since there are no customers in right now, do you mind if I go ahead and make a start?"

"No, that would be great. I'll watch the shop and let you know if I need you."

⟨ℰℰℓℰℯ⟩

*L*ILLY DECIDED TO use the uncommonly quiet time to go through her accounts. She gathered the receipts and her ledger and set to work, sitting at the counter with a freshly made cup of ginger and honey tea, needing the boost to her brain. She preferred to do things by hand initially, then transfer it all into her accounting software. She'd been caught out before when her laptop had died, taking with it all her accounts information. It had been several days before she could find someone to fix it and retrieve the information. She wouldn't be caught out again. She'd been working for a couple of minutes when Earl left his spot in the window and jumped into her lap. For a former stray, he'd certainly adapted to domesticated life quickly.

She'd hardly put pen to paper when she was interrupted a second time. This time it was the phone.

"Hello, Archie. You're calling to complain about a certain Ms Douglas, I take it?"

"You saw the article then?"

"I did. It wasn't good, was it? How did it get the go ahead, Archie?"

"The chief editor made a bad call on that one," he said. "You should have seen the original version Abigail turned in, though. It stated Elizabeth Davenport was the murderer no question, even though she hasn't even been charged yet. She's just in for questioning under caution from what I understand while the police gather all the evidence. She was told to fix it and what you read was the result. I think he only approved it because we were so close to the deadline, and he's already regretting the decision. He's been stuck in his office with the phone ringing off the hook all morning. There's been complaints from several quarters, not least from Mr Davenport, who is absolutely furious and threatening to sue. I can't blame him I'd do the same thing if I was in his shoes."

"Well, if it's any consolation, I though the writing itself was much improved. I even detected your voice in some places."

"I've been teaching her as you suggested. She's a pretty good pupil actually, until she decides that she knows best, which is most of the time, unfortunately. She's ruining everything, Lilly."

"I'm sorry, Archie, I know how much you care about the paper's reputation. We all should, it's been around for years and is as much a part of the town as the church or the town hall. The chief should have put you in charge of the story until Abigail was ready."

"Isn't hindsight a wonderful thing," Archie sighed heavily. "If they keep letting Abigail run wild like this, then I have no doubt the paper will turn into a gutter rag, or worse have to fold. It's already a laughingstock. I think for some reason they're afraid of sacking her. She came from the big suits side of things during the merger and has connections we don't have. I've told him to start documenting every single screw up, no matter how small, so when the time comes he'll have the proof he needs to get rid of her once and for all."

"You don't think that's a bit over the top, Archie?"

"Absolutely not!"

"So, what are your thoughts about Elizabeth Davenport being the murderer?" she asked, eager to change the subject. Abigail Douglas was going to cause Archie to have a stroke one of these days.

"Nonsense," he said immediately. "Jane Nolan embarrassing her once in public is not a motive for murder. It's ludicrous. And her hiding the weapon in her own home and leaving it there? It makes no sense."

"Stacey and I were just saying the same thing," she said, just as the shop door opened. "I've got to go, Archie, I've got a customer. Chin up, my friend, it will all work out, and I'm here when you need your dose of tea and sympathy."

"Thanks, Lilly. Talk to you later."

She ended the call and lifted Earl onto the counter, just as Fred Warren walked in.

"Hi, Lilly."

"Good morning, Fred. Do you want me to let Stacey know you're here? She's in the back."

"Actually, I'm looking for your help," He said, lifting a brown paper bag. "I have a broken teacup and Stacey told me you do repairs?"

"I do. Bring it over to the repair station and I'll see what I can do."

She unrolled the thick red velvet cloth and plugged in her magnifying light. Taking the cup from Fred, she placed it on the cloth and inspected it closely.

"It belonged to my Grandma, part of a set and mum's really upset about it. But Stacey said you were a miracle worker with this sort of thing."

The cup was obviously old and not in good shape. There were two cracks running its full length and a missing v-shaped chip from the rim. The delicate handle also had a small chunk missing from the bottom. She switched off her light and turned to Fred. "It will definitely be a challenge, but I believe I can repair it. It will take some time as it's neither easy nor quick, but I think I can make it look almost as good as new."

"Brilliant!" Fred said. "Doesn't matter how long it takes, mum just wants it back in one piece and looking like the rest."

The shop door opened again, and Lilly glanced up to see James Pepper walk in.

Chapter Ten

*L*ILLY'S GAZE WENT from James to Fred, then back again. James walked up to the counter paying Fred no attention and addressed Lilly. "Good morning," he said in his friendliest tone. "Is Stacey in?"

She saw Fred glance in James' direction. "She's working in the back at the moment. There are a few deliveries to unpack and put away, but she shouldn't be too long."

"Thank you, Lilly."

"How have you been, James?" Lilly asked, keen to keep the equilibrium going.

"Quite well. I've been staying at a nice hotel just out of town. It's been lovely staying in Plumpton Mallet in between summer courses."

"Ah, so the universities in London are taking a break at the moment?" Lilly asked pleasantly, and the question evidently caught Fred's attention. She assumed Stacey had told him her father taught at a London university, but she'd confessed she was uncomfortable with the two of them meeting just yet. Lilly suspected her father being so far away had been a good excuse to avoid an introduction. *And now here they are, both together in my shop*, Lilly thought.

"How do you know Stacey?" Fred asked pleasantly, now his suspicions had been raised, and Lilly cringed, wishing she'd never asked about the university.

James shot him an annoyed glance. "I'm her father."

Fred went quiet and turned away to avoid eye contact. James stared for a moment, but before he could question the boy's strange behaviour Stacey came back into the shop.

"Hey, Lilly, I've finished with the unpacking, but..." she froze when she saw the two men standing together at the counter.

"Thank you, Stacey." Lilly said.

"Hi, babe," Fred muttered, and James' eyebrows disappeared into his hairline.

Lilly felt as though she were watching a soap opera, or more aptly an American sitcom. She turned the light on and went back to studying Fred's damaged cup. She didn't want to appear to be eavesdropping, but she wanted to be within easy reach if things became heated.

"Did you two meet?" Stacey asked awkwardly.

Fred shook his head. "No, he's just arrived."

"Right. Well..." Stacey said, taking a deep breath. "Fred, this is my dad. Dad, I didn't know you were coming by today?"

James Pepper nodded, turning to Fred. "And you are?"

"I'm Frederick Warren, Mr Pepper," he said, sticking out his hand. "I'm Stacey's boyfriend."

James hesitated for a second, then shook the proffered hand. "Nice to meet you, Frederick." Then turned back to his daughter. "I came to bring you the application for London."

"Huh?" Stacey asked, confused.

It was then that Lilly noticed the file tucked under James' arm, which he passed to Stacey. "You'll see I've already written you a letter of recommendation, but feel free to review it. With that and your impressive grades, there's a very high chance you'll be accepted." He looked at Fred for a moment, then turned back to Stacey. "I hope having a boyfriend here won't interfere with your decision to pursue a better educational opportunity?"

Stacey opened the folder and briefly read the contents before laughing and putting it on the counter. "Why didn't you talk to me about this before spending time writing a recommendation, dad?"

James folded his arms, annoyed. Clearly he had expected gratitude as opposed to hilarity. "I beg your pardon?"

"If you'd asked me, I would have told you I wasn't interested in attending your school. I mean, don't get me wrong, studying in London would be an awesome opportunity for the right person, but I've got plans for my future and London isn't part of them."

"Stacey," James Pepper countered. "Plumpton Mallet is a small town with minimal opportunities. It has a reasonably good university, but it pales in comparison to London. With a degree from London you could..."

"Do you even know what I'm studying?" Stacey interrupted, becoming a bit annoyed.

James obviously didn't know the answer. "Well..." he began, but Stacey cut him off again.

"It's not on the curriculum where you teach, dad, so would never be part of my plan. And, since you don't know and have never bothered to ask, I'll tell you; I'm majoring in sports science. My goal is to become a physical sports therapist. And, guess what? St John's University, here in this small town, has one of the best programs in the country." She softened her voice. "Dad, I didn't reach out to you because of your connections, or to attend a London university. I never needed you to do that for me. I reached out because I wanted you, my father, to be part of my life. I thought we could at last get to know each other properly."

James Pepper was completely lost for words. Part of Lilly was relieved to hear that Stacey would not be leaving for London after all, but the other part felt rather sorry for James. He obviously believed he was putting his daughter first for once, but now he didn't know what to either say or do.

"James, perhaps you'd like to visit St John's? See what the university has to offer. Take a tour," she said, looking at Stacey and getting an encouraging nod. "I'm sure Stacey would love to show you around and tell you about the program she's studying. With your background, I expect you'll have a lot in common with the professors there and they would welcome an exchange of knowledge. Perhaps you might even know some of them?"

James slowly nodded in response, "Actually, I'd enjoy that," giving Lilly a brief smile of thanks. "Stacey, would you be willing to show your old dad around the place?"

"Yeah, sure, that'd be great. I get off at five, maybe we could get dinner?"

"Yes, we can do that," he turned to Fred. "Nice to meet you, Frederick." Then, with a final nod to everyone, he left.

"I can't believe your dad tried to get you to change schools without even knowing what you were studying," Fred said. "That was weird."

"That's my dad for you," Stacey said. "Sorry, Fred, I didn't plan on you meeting him like that the first time."

"He seems okay," Fred said with a smile. "I mean, he did all that work to try to help you, even if it wasn't what you wanted. You know, his intentions were good."

"Yeah, I guess."

Lilly's phone buzzed as Stacey and Fred continued to talk together at the end of the counter. It was a message from Archie asking her if she had time for lunch. She messaged back to confirm.

"Stacey, that was Archie asking if I could meet him for lunch. Will you be okay to hold the fort here for an hour or so?"

"Yeah, of course. I'll get Fred to do some dusting," she laughed.

"That's fine by me," Lilly said.

"Well, I hope you're insured, Miss Tweed, my mum says I have butter fingers."

"Ah," Lilly said, looking at the broken teacup.

Fred nodded. "Yep, why do you think I'm so keen to get it mended?"

"In that case, I think Stacey needs to find you something else to do if you're planning on staying for a while."

"No problem, there's lots of stuff needs doing in the store-room which doesn't involve delicate items. Don't worry, Lilly."

"All right, in that case it's all yours. I'll pick you both up some lunch on the way back. Anything in particular?"

Fred and Stacey looked and each other then both said, "Pizza!"

Lilly laughed. "Pizza it is. I know I don't have to tell you, but please keep it professional while I'm out."

*L*ILLY TOOK HER bike to the pub where she had arranged to meet Archie in the small beer garden at the back. It was a place familiar to them both, as it was where they used to go for lunch, if their schedules allowed, when she'd worked at the paper. She wheeled her bike through the side entrance to the garden and got a strange sense of déjà vu when she spotted Archie at the back table underneath a tree. It was like stepping back in time, as though they were about to discuss office politics and deadlines as opposed to two friends catching up. She leaned her bike against the tree and took a seat opposite. Archie had already ordered drinks and lunch for them both, and when they were delivered to the table, they spent a few minutes talking about her shop and other things before the conversation drifted to Elizabeth Davenport.

"I spoke with her husband this morning," Archie said.

"Oh? How is he?"

"He's furious about the article as you'd expect, but he's absolutely adamant his wife is innocent, and he's worried things are going to go wrong for her very quickly if the real culprit isn't found. He seems to believe the police have stopped trying to find anyone else now they have his wife in custody. Poor man is really going through the wringer."

Lilly nodded, finishing a mouthful of chicken salad. "I'm not surprised. The so called evidence is all circumstantial at best. What are his thoughts about it being Elizabeth's hatpin that was used as the murder weapon?"

"The police have told him a hatpin was the murder weapon and that they believe it belonged to his wife, but he doesn't know which one. They're playing it close to their chests at the moment. He did admit that he probably wouldn't recognise it anyway. He doesn't take a lot of notice of his wife's collections. Just lets her get on with it if it makes her happy."

Lilly nodded. "Bonnie made me swear not to tell anyone exactly what I'd found, too. Unfortunately, I let it slip to Stacey. But she's promised not to breathe a word, and I trust her to keep her promise. Did Mr Davenport say anything else?"

"Yes. He said anyone could have taken it and stabbed Jane. It was on public display to all those who ventured into the drawing room, and the display case had been tampered with. He also pointed out that as his wife had the key, she wouldn't have needed to break it open."

"He makes a good argument," Lilly said. "And I really can't see her damaging her own furniture. When I visited her, she was genuinely upset about the damage. She's very house proud, you know."

"The police thought perhaps Mr Davenport was so desperate to prove his wife's innocence that he broke into the cabinet himself to point the finger at it being someone else. Which I suppose is feasible, but I doubt it."

"No, he didn't do that," Lilly said, shaking her head. "It was already damaged when I was there, which was just before I found the missing piece of the hatpin. I saw it myself. Elizabeth told me it had been broken for a few days. It's what we've all been thinking, you, me and Stacey. Someone else murdered Jane Nolan and threw the end of the hatpin in the plant pot in a panic, not expecting it to snap, maybe? And possibly with the thoughts of going back and retrieving it once things had settled down."

"The police will side with the Davenport's eventually, they have to," said Archie. "There are too many holes and not enough evidence in the case against her."

"Which means Jane's killer is still out there. Maybe it's time I spoke with Mr Davenport myself."

Just as Archie was downing the last of his pint, he received a text. "Oh well, duty calls. I've got to get back to the office, Lilly."

"Oh dear, not more crime?"

He shook his head. "No, it's some follow up pieces on Elizabeth Davenport and her life here in Plumpton Mallet. With no further news on the case, the boss wants to keep the momentum going with some background pieces. You know the sort of thing; old garden parties and charity events showing her rubbing shoulders with the town's elite."

"Yuck."

"Yes, but it sells papers. Lunch has been paid for by your old employer. Sorry to have to run."

"Don't worry about it. And thanks for lunch, we should try to do it more often. Bye, Archie."

Once Archie had left, Lilly sat alone for a while, deep in thought while she finished her apple juice. Then her phone rang.

"Hi, Bonnie, is everything all right?"

"I've just a bit of an update. Are you free for a chat?"

"Yes, of course. I've just finished having lunch with Archie, so I'm at the pub."

"Right, I'm on my way, see you in five minutes."

It was nearer ten when Bonnie put a glass of orange juice on the table and took a seat opposite Lilly.

"Bonnie, don't take this the wrong way, but you look awful. Are you all right?"

"Thank you for the boost to my confidence there, Lilly."

Lilly giggled. "I'm sorry. Is it the case?"

"The case, the whole case, and nothing but the case," Bonnie replied. "It's driving me to distraction that I'm putting in all these hours yet don't seem to be getting any further forward."

"Well, not getting enough sleep won't help. Drop by the shop and I'll mix you up a special tea blend. So what was it you wanted to tell me?"

"The end of the hatpin. Forensics have been studying it carefully and are now convinced, beyond a shadow of a doubt, that it was deliberately filed through to make sure the end snapped off when it was used to stab Jane Nolan."

"What?" Lilly said in astonishment. "But that makes no sense. Why would they do that?"

Bonnie shrugged. "Beats me, Lilly, nothing about this case makes sense to me so far."

"Well, what does Elizabeth Davenport say about it?"

"And that's the most mysterious part, Lilly. Elizabeth Davenport is adamant the hatpin is not hers."

❦

*L*ILLY DECIDED, AFTER her confusing conversation with Bonnie, there was no time like the present to visit Elizabeth's husband. After a brief text to Stacey letting her know of the changed plans, she said goodbye to Bonnie and set off to cycle to the Davenport's home.

It was a fairly long bike ride, but the weather was perfect, with the sun beating down from an azure sky and just enough of a cooling breeze to make the journey extremely pleasant. Her head was filled with thoughts of Elizabeth Davenport, currently sitting in a jail cell and probably extremely frightened. The whole experience must be dreadful for her, and now convinced of her innocence, Lilly was determined to prove it.

The gates opened automatically when she arrived, and wheeling the bike down the drive she saw an unfamiliar car. A top of the range deep bronze coloured Bentley in immaculate condition. *Probably Mr Davenport's* she thought. No doubt leaving it in a handy spot if he needed to get out quickly to see his wife or his solicitor.

She leaned her bike against the wall and ascending the front steps knocked loudly on the door. It was flung open a second later by a red faced harried looking gentleman. She had never met Mr Davenport before, but from the gossip around town she understood Elizabeth only dusted him off and took him to important events when she needed an arm to hang onto. He worked away a lot, so was hardly ever home. It seemed to her, Elizabeth filled her days with the likes of afternoon teas and book clubs to stave off the loneliness.

"May I help you," the man said now, making no attempt to conceal his irritation.

"Hello. Mr Davenport?" asked Lilly, just to make sure.

"Yes. Who are you? What do you want? You'd better not be from that damned paper."

"No, I'm not. My name is Lilly Tweed. I've..."

"You're the one who found that blasted hatpin!" He snapped, looking as though he wanted to push her down the steps. "What are you doing here? Thanks to you, I've been on the phone with the police and solicitors for the last twenty-four hours. Not to mention having to fend off those so called reporters. I was supposed to be leaving for an important business meeting this morning, but now I'm left dealing with this nightmare. Who do you think you are coming here? Don't you think you've caused enough trouble? My poor wife is currently languishing in a jail cell thanks to your interference. God only knows what it's doing to her mental health."

Lilly hadn't expected such a malevolent tirade and was a little nonplussed. "With all due respect, Mr Davenport," she began. "Yes, I found part of a murder weapon in your house and reported it to the authorities. It was not, however, with the intention of casting suspicion on your wife. You do realise that a young woman was savagely murdered in your cloakroom?"

Mr Davenport seethed for a moment, turning crimson, before taking several deep breaths in an attempt to calm down. "Yes, well, I apologise. This has been the worst twenty-four hours I've ever had."

"I'm sure it has been, and I'm terribly sorry for disturbing you again today, but I was hoping I could ask you about the relationship your wife had with Jane?"

"You and everyone else in this town," he said bitterly. "I'm going to tell you the same thing I told the police, Miss Tweed, Elizabeth had no reason and nothing to gain from hurting Jane Nolan. The so called evidence the police think they have is a joke. Anyone present that day could have taken that hatpin from the display, and if it had been my wife, she wouldn't have needed to break into her own cabinet to get it. Anyone with half a brain can see my wife has been made the scapegoat."

Lilly nodded. "I understand, Mr Davenport. And for what it's worth, I agree with you completely. I don't believe your wife murdered Jane. She doesn't have a solid motive for one thing."

"And Jane, of all people," the man continued not hearing Lilly's declaration, shaking his head in disbelief. "There are plenty of women my wife has clashed with, but that nasty little spat with Jane at the Defoe's would not have been enough for her to stab the woman to death. If she was that unhinged, and believe me she is not, I would have put my money on her getting rid of Isadora Smith."

"Isadora? Really? Why her?"

"Because after that particular incident Isadora deliberately poured salt onto the wound, she jumped on the bandwagon and continued to speak ill of Elizabeth to Lady Defoe. It made the situation a lot worse than it already was, and Elizabeth was hurt to the quick. I'm no fool, Miss Tweed, I know my wife better than anyone. Yes, she has snobbish tendencies and a wish to be seen in the best company and an almost childish desire to belong to the best circles. She's not particularly clever and her social skills aren't terribly subtle, but she is a good and kind person. Suffice to say Isadora, in my opinion, is not. Why Isadora's offensive behaviour was let slide and my Elizabeth cruelly picked on, I'll never know. But Isadora has always been a master of manipulation and has an innate ability to pull the wool over people's eyes so they don't recognise her spite for what it is. Personally, I think being sneaky and underhanded is far worse than being upfront."

"I had no idea," Lilly said. "I was informed that Lady Defoe gave Jane a dressing down for the way she'd treated Elizabeth that day. Did she not therefore scold Isadora too?"

"She did not. As I've just told you, Isadora is very subtle with her insults. Lady Defoe keeps her around because of her wit. She can be very amusing and entertaining, but she's one of the worst social climbers there is. Now, if you'll excuse me, I have several phone calls to make. I cannot let my wife squander in that cell a moment longer."

Mr Davenport shut the door and Lilly sloped back to her bike, deep in thought and feeling despondent. What had she really learned from that conversation? Naturally he would plead his wife's innocence, and Lilly agreed with him. But what about the rest? Was it all just sour grapes? Him grasping at straws in eagerness to point the finger at someone else? Isadora had been the only one who had greeted Lilly with anything remotely akin to friendliness. She'd found and returned her car keys when she'd dropped them. She'd also been honest and open about her spats with her friends, but had Lilly really been manipulated to the extent Mr Davenport had suggested Isadora was capable of? She didn't like to think of herself as being that gullible. She put the idea to the back of her mind and set off for the ride back to town, hoping she could unearth a real clue and a way forward very soon.

O N THE RETURN journey she suddenly remembered she had promised to pick up lunch for Stacey and Fred. Firing off a quick text to see if they still wanted something, she got a reply almost immediately in the affirmative and stopped at the Italian cafe on the outskirts of town, the best place for pizza. She ordered herself a cappuccino and sat at a free table in the corner behind a large plant while she waited for the pizza's to be made.

Her phone buzzed, indicating there was a text. Opening it, she found it was from Archie and it was marked urgent. Looking at her call history she'd realised he'd tried to phone her when she was cycling to the Davenport's but she hadn't heard it. She rang him back immediately.

"Archie, what is it?"

"I think I've just found the mother of all clues. I'm going to forward you some pictures from Lady Defoe's Easter garden party. We covered the event. See if you can spot what I did. Give me a call back as soon as you've seen them."

Lilly waited with bated breath for the images and pounced to open them the minute they arrived. At first she had no idea what Archie was getting at, it was images of the guests laughing, talking and drinking. She recognised a few of them; Lady Defoe obviously, her husband, the Gresham's, Jane, Isadora, Elizabeth. Mr Davenport standing alone by an Azalea bush nursing a glass of champagne and looking lost. Even Abigail was in a fair few of them. It wasn't until she read the text from Archie which accompanied each individual shot that she made the connection.

"Oh my god!" she breathed. She rang Archie back. "How did we miss it, Archie?"

"Well, how would we have known? She doesn't use that name, does she? I've spent every minute since you and I had lunch getting confirmation. I've called in every favour I had owing to me, and some I didn't. She hid it well. I doubt even her so-called friends know."

"Have you told Bonnie?"

"I'm just about to. She needs to go to the woman's house and see if she can find any other pins that would make up a set."

"She'll need more evidence, won't she, to be able to do a search?" asked Lilly.

"Possibly, but at least she can get the ball rolling based on that photo. It definitely counts as probable cause."

"Well done, Archie."

Lilly ended the call and continued to study the images. She now almost certainly knew the 'who', it was the 'why' she needed to work out. She looked up sharply when the door opened and she heard a voice she recognised.

"Oh, Theo, darling, I'm so glad you've not lost your sense of humour. It's so important to move on."

Lord Gresham and Isadora Smith and entered the cafe together. The casual flirtation caught Lilly's attention. Isadora was all batting eyelashes and smiles, Theodore much less so.

"I wasn't trying to be funny, Isadora," Theo said. "Why are we here? I would much rather have stayed at home. I haven't got much of an appetite, anyway."

"You needed to get out of the house," she replied, rubbing his arm. "And you must keep your strength up, Theo. I know you're still grieving, but staying inside and hidden away alone, is really not going to help. You needed some fresh air and a change of scenery. It will help you get out of this melancholy state of mind. It's not healthy, dearest."

Theo sighed deeply. "Yes, I suppose you're right. Thank you, Isadora."

Lilly had a good view of the pair but remained unnoticed by them. She studied them carefully. Isadora was standing much closer to her companion than necessary, and any excuse to lay a hand on his arm or stroke his shoulder, she took. She couldn't help but feel her behaviour was vulgar. It also wasn't being encouraged by Theo himself. The poor man had just lost the woman he had intended to make his wife, and while she didn't know this group of friends well, she thought Isadora was acting in poor taste. Theo seemed to expect it though, so perhaps it was typical Isadora behaviour. But the more she watched the interaction, the more she questioned Isadora's real motives.

Mr Davenport had suggested all the women to some extent were social climbers, but none more than Isadora Smith. Lilly also recalled the conversation she had had with Theo in Lady Defoe's garden. He commented on how concerned Isadora had been about him and had been checking up on him regularly. Even Isadora herself had told her she'd contacted him after Jane's death, and in tones that her affection for him was obvious.

A cold shiver suddenly went down Lilly's body and her heart began to thump. The pieces of the puzzle were at last beginning to come together. Had Isadora seized the opportunity to take out a romantic rival and frame Elizabeth Davenport in the process?

ℰℯℓℯ𝒟

*L*ILLY'S ORDER WAS ready and brought to her table by a bubbly waitress who caught the attention of Isadora and Theo. Their heads turned and Isadora locked eyes with Lilly.

"Oh, Lilly," Isadora called out from where they both stood holding take away coffee cups.

Lilly picked up her order and walked towards the couple. "Lord Gresham, Isadora," she greeted them with a forced smile.

"Have you heard the news, Lilly? Elizabeth Davenport has been arrested for Jane's murder! Isn't it simply dreadful?"

Isadora said, while Theo cringed next to her. Any mention of the case was naturally difficult for him.

"Yes, I have heard," Lilly replied. Then decided to see if she could get a reaction. "Although between you and me, the police are saying there's not sufficient evidence."

"Oh, really? I hadn't heard that. From the newspaper report it all seemed cut and dried to me."

"I have a friend working on the case," Lilly replied, matter-of-factly. Then decided to put the cat among the pigeons by coming up with a complete fabrication to see what the response would be. "But," she said, lowering her voice conspiratorially. The other two leaned in, wide eyed and expectant. "Between the three of us, they may have found additional evidence that points to someone other than Elizabeth Davenport as being the murderer."

Lord Gresham stood upright. "What additional evidence? And points to whom?"

"My friend couldn't say," Lilly said, watching Isadora fidget. "But apparently Mr Davenport had a new security system fitted recently and it included several discreet cameras around the house, one of which showed the front door and the cloakroom. Elizabeth was totally unaware they were switched on and recording the day of Jane's death. The police are reviewing it all now."

"Security cameras," Isadora whispered, looking extremely sick.

"Yes. By the end of today they should be able to confirm it wasn't Elizabeth who killed Jane."

"And who did," Lord Gresham said, sounding relieved and frightened in equal measure.

Lilly kept her eye on Isadora, hoping to see something that would confirm what she now knew to be true. Isadora was avoiding all eye contact and swaying. It seemed so obvious now and Lilly was annoyed she hadn't seen it sooner.

"Exactly, Lord Gresham. I think it will be very interesting to see what they find, don't you, *Isadora*?"

Theo caught Lilly's tone and emphasis immediately and turned quickly to his companion. "Isadora?" he said in puzzlement.

Isadora dropped her coffee and pushed through them both toward the door, hands raised. "I'm not... I'm not going to stand here and listen to this. You think I don't know what you're insinuating? It's repulsive. How dare you!"

"Isadora!" Theo shouted, in such an authoritative tone it startled her. She stopped inches from the door and turned to face him. "Did you kill Jane?"

Lilly took a step towards her. "I know it was you, Isadora. Or should I call you, Elsie?"

Isadora gasped, "No!"

"You wanted Jane out of the way so you could have Theodore all to yourself," Lilly continued. "As long as she was around he wouldn't look twice at you, isn't that right? So you seized the opportunity to kill Jane and aggressively pursue Theodore while he was at his lowest ebb. All while making sure Elizabeth got the blame. You used one of your own hatpins. One you had brought with you with the sole intention of using it to kill Jane that day at the book club meeting. That's premeditation. You have three, don't you? All part of an identical set using your initials. E I S. Elsie Isadora Smith."

"No, that's a lie. Don't listen to her, Theo, she's making it up."

"I have a picture of you wearing the letter 'I' in your hat on the day of Lady Defoe's Easter party, Isadora. It's identical to the letter 'E' that was used to kill Jane. Thanks to the skills of a superb investigative journalist, your full name has been confirmed. No doubt the police will find that 'I' and the letter 'S' when they search your home. And what's more, the police have discovered the letter 'E' was deliberately filed through so the end would easily snap when it was used. Allowing you to throw it in the plant pot where it would easily be found, incriminating Elizabeth."

"Is that what happened, Isadora? Did you take Jane's life just so you could have me?" Theo asked. He sounded shocked and incredulous. "The cameras will tell the truth, Isadora. So tell me now, did you do it?"

Isadora reached for the door. "You were too good for her," she cried, ready to bolt.

Lilly started to move, but Lord Gresham charged past her, reaching for Isadora. But she was too fast and out of the door before he could get there. He bolted outside, with Lilly quick on his heels. She made it outside in time to see Theo dive forward and rugby tackle Isadora to the ground. She hit the pavement hard.

"Help me!" he cried to Lilly, and she threw the pizzas on a nearby table and rushed to his aid, grabbing Isadora's left arm and pulling her to her feet.

"You're not going anywhere," she said. "We know you did it. It's over."

"Fine," Isadora screamed. "Good riddance to her, that's what I say."

"So you admit you killed Jane and tried to frame Elizabeth all so you could have Lord Gresham to yourself?"

"Yes, I killed her, and I don't regret a thing! You were going to throw your life away for that nasty mouthed trollop, Theo. I couldn't let you do it. You would have been happy with me."

Lilly pulled out her phone. Some sixth sense had told her to start recording the moment Isadora had spotted her in the cafe. "I've got her confession recorded."

"Between that, the photograph and the camera footage, the police will have an undisputed case against her," Theo said.

Lilly smirked. "What camera footage?"

Isadora's eyes widened at the realisation she'd been tricked, and Theo barked out a laugh.

"It serves you right, you monster!"

Lilly called the police and Isadora was promptly arrested for the murder of Jane Nolan, thanks to the statements and evidence she and Lord Gresham were able to provide.

Chapter Eleven

*L*ILLY WAS SITTING at the shop counter, a smile on her face as she read Archie Brown's latest newspaper article. Not only did it go into full detail about the investigation, including interviews of multiple witnesses, first-hand accounts of the murder and Isadora's arrest, but also included a wonderful correction notice and apology from the paper for Abigail's previous article.

"Reading Archie's article?" Stacey asked as she hurried past with a small box of handkerchiefs to put near the till. It was a new product one of Lilly's wholesalers had given her to try out in the shop. The handkerchiefs, superb quality silk in colours suitable for both men and women, had The Tea Emporium logo embroidered on one corner in gold thread. Lilly intended to give them away as a thank you gift for those whose orders were over a certain amount. Or they could be bought individually. But she doubted she'd include them in her range. They weren't quite in keeping with the ethos of her shop.

"How did you know?"

"By that big grin on your face," Stacey replied, laughing. "I read it earlier. It's great. You're mentioned by name again. You know what that means, don't you? You're going to get more customers in here wanting to meet the famous celebrity sleuth of Plumpton Mallet."

"I had thought that was going to die down," Lilly admitted, folding up the paper and putting it on the counter. "But I suppose this latest case has just re-lit the flame. Honestly though, I don't mind, it's been very good for business. But really Archie is the star of this one. He found the main the clue I just happened to be where Isadora was at the time."

"You think you're going to have any more trouble with Abigail over it?"

"I'm not sure, but I don't think so. Abigail and I reached a truce during that paint fiasco. I think she understands I am doing nothing to harm her reputation or risk her job. She's managing that quite well all by herself. The chief editor asking Archie to add the retraction notice was a bit harsh, I thought, though. Abigail didn't actually write anything that was blatantly untrue it was the tone that was wrong. However, I'm sure Mrs Davenport is relieved the gazette is attempting to right the error."

"She most certainly is!" Mrs Davenport's voice boomed across the shop as the door swung closed behind her.

Lilly rose from her seat while Stacey focused on arranging the new merchandise. "Elizabeth, welcome back, I'm so glad to see you walking out and about again."

"And it's all down to you, dear Lilly. I came by to thank you. I could have been in the most dreadful trouble if you hadn't pursued your own investigation and obtained Isadora's confession. I read the article this morning and thought it was so clever the way you did it, and had the brains to record it all too. It would never have occurred to me to do that. I must admit I am seriously considering having security cameras put up in my home, though. I never thought this dear little town could be so dangerous."

"I'm relived you're not angry at me for calling the police in the first place when I found the rest of the hatpin in the plant pot."

"I won't deny that being in that cell was the worst experience of my life, Lilly. But you were doing what was right," Mrs Davenport said, patting Lilly's arm. "I certainly don't blame you for that. I'm sure I would have done the same thing had I been in your place. Even my husband said so."

"I'm glad to hear that. He wasn't very pleased to see me last time we spoke."

"It was worry and stress. He's not normally so abrupt. He's just glad I'm out of jail now. As am I. You did me a great service, Lilly Tweed."

Lilly shrugged. "It wasn't that much."

"You got a murderess to confess and clear my name. My good reputation, which means a lot to me, has been restored. And far from my horrible experience being a disaster, I have since been invited to tea by Lady Defoe. She's absolutely dying to hear all about it directly from me. She called it the story of the year when she telephoned."

Lilly smiled. She knew an invitation from Lady Defoe was a huge deal to Elizabeth Davenport and she was pleased for her.

"Just so you know, Lilly, you will be receiving my patronage, and that of Lady Defoe, a lot more in the future. She wants to hear all about your marvellous presentation. Take it from me I will be giving you a dazzling review. Now, my dear, if would be so kind, could you get me a box of Lady Defoe's favourite tea? I need to be sure I have it in next time she comes to visit."

Lilly watched happily as Elizabeth Davenport scurried out of the shop, head held high again and clutching two boxes of tea. She was still standing there when another familiar face entered. "Hello, James."

He nodded his head. "Lilly. I just came to say goodbye to Stacey before I head back to London."

"Hey, dad. You're leaving already?"

"I feel as though I may have overstayed my welcome in Plumpton Mallet," he said sadly.

"Is this because I told you I wouldn't be coming to London?"

"No, not really," although he sounded far from convincing.

Lilly made herself scarce while father and daughter continued their personal conversation. She decided to empty the agony aunt box. There were several letters, and she was busy outside the shop flipping through them when James exited. "Goodbye, Lilly. Hope to see you again soon." He certainly sounded happier.

"You too, James," she said, returning inside.

"Did that go well, Stacey?"

"I think so. I told him I knew he'd really tried with the letter and everything. And that I really appreciated the effort, but I needed him to stop trying to make up for the past. What I wanted was for him to get to know me *now*. For us both to get to know each other now, actually. I think the talk went well."

"I'm glad, Stacey. Hopefully you can both build a new relationship."

She was still holding the letters when Stacey asked, "What's that one? Doesn't look like the normal letters you get?"

She was right. Lilly opened it. "Oh, it's a wedding anniversary invitation. How lovely."

"Who from?"

"A few years ago, while I was still working at the paper, I received a letter from a widower. He was attracted to a widow but had been out of the dating game for so long he didn't know how to approach her. I wrote back giving him some advice."

"And?"

"And they've been married for nearly five years."

"And they want you to celebrate with them? That's so cool. You're going, right?"

"Well, it's out of town, what about the shop?"

"Lilly, I can handle it, you know I can."

"Well, I really could do with a holiday. And it's the south coast, a beautiful place where the sea is warm and with a private beach."

"You deserve a break after what you've been through these last few months. And I'll be on the other end of the phone. Earl will be very happy at my place, and it's a great excuse to hide from the busloads of tourists who are probably on their way right now to speak with the town's famous lady sleuth, thanks to this latest case."

"Do you know, Stacey, I think you've talked me into it."

"Great. Just relax and have fun. And stay well away from mysteries and murder."

Lilly laughed. "I doubt very much there'll be anything like that where I'm going."

ᘓᘓᘓᘓᘓ

If you enjoyed *A Deadly Solution*, book two in the Tea & Sympathy series, please leave a review on Amazon. It really does help and you'd make the author very happy.

Tiffin &
TRAGEDY

A Tea & Sympathy Mystery

BOOK 3

ABOUT THE BOOK

**Meet Lilly Tweed. Former Agony Aunt.
Purveyor of Fine Teas. Accidental Sleuth.**

Invited to celebrate the wedding anniversary of two close
friends, Lilly jumps at the chance. Not only is there to be a
party, but as the family owns a luxury seaside bed-and-breakfast she's looking forward to a well-earned break.

Unfortunately, nothing goes to plan. Beneath the happy,
carefree exterior, lurk secrets and lies, and as the tension
mounts somebody reaches breaking point.

The party ends in a tremendous storm which causes a
power cut and fells trees across the only access road, and
the inhabitants of The Palms find themselves trapped with
no way to call for help. Then a body is discovered and Lilly
realises the danger outside is nothing compared to within.

There is a murderer among them.

Chapter One

$\mathcal{S}$UMMER WAS NOW in full swing in the small town of Plumpton Mallet, and Lillian Tweed was busying herself at her Tea Emporium with a sudden though very welcome intrusion of a town tour group. Usually when the coach holiday company brought day trippers through, it was a relatively small crowd containing only two or three people actively looking to purchase. Today, however, the group was full of Americans who all wanted an authentic British tea set and various selections of teas to take home from their European holiday, and it was an absolute madhouse.

Lilly and her shop assistant, a young college student named Stacey who also happened to be from the states, were doing their best to ensure each of the nearly thirty customers were being taken care of. From explaining the history of tea, to brewing numerous samples and explaining their health benefits. From demonstrating how to set the perfect tea table to acquainting them with the manufacturers and artists who designed and hand painted the china. Lilly was determined that each and every customer received the full experience and left her shop happy and full of additional knowledge. Earl Grey, former stray and now official shop cat, had bolted for the back room to hide from the crowd almost as soon as they'd made an appearance.

This exposure was something fairly new and Lilly was still getting used to it. Her business had been open for less than a year, but the coach company had only added her shop to the stopover in the past spring. So far, the groups had been small compared to what they were now getting during the summer months.

Several of these first-time customers wanted their orders shipped back home to the states while others were trying to choose something that would be a bit more durable and safer to take on board the aircraft. Lilly and Stacey did their best to help them pick out something for their specific needs and taste, since most of the group did not appear to be regular tea drinkers. It was more being able to return home and show off their quintessential British collectables, Lilly supposed, but if it was also about introducing a bit of additional knowledge and culture to the group as well as making a good sale in the process, she was more than happy to go the extra length.

A total of sixteen complete tea sets were purchased by the time the group was ready to move on, along with a number of collectable tea cups and saucers, six teapots and numerous sundry items such as the hand embroidered tablecloths and napkins. The tour guide, who had become a familiar face over the previous months, gave Lilly a thumbs up as he shuffled his group out of the door. He knew this had been the most profitable crowd to have come through so far. He was still grinning at Lilly and Stacey through the large front window as the last of his tour goers trickled out of the shop to catch up with him.

"Whoa," Stacey said, collapsing on one of the bar style stools that lined the front of the main counter. She looked dizzy and a bit shell-shocked from the whirlwind that had just gone through. The shop had occasional bursts of customers, but nothing like what they had just experienced. Usually it was half a dozen or so at a time and half would be merely browsers.

"You're telling me," Lilly said, laughing and taking a seat herself. "I don't think the shop has ever had as many customers at the same time. All requiring attention considering they had very little knowledge about teas and teapots. You did a brilliant job of keeping your head and not getting flustered or overwhelmed. Well done, Stacey."

"After that, I see what you mean by my fellow countryman's abrasive personality," Stacey said, laughing at herself as much as the recent customers. "I've got so used to dealing with the locals, I'd almost forgotten how loud we Americans can be. Gosh, am I really that loud, Lilly?"

Lilly laughed. "I've never once said you're abrasive. And no, you're not that bad, Stacey."

"I feel like you wanted to add *anymore* to the end of that sentence."

Lilly chose to remain quiet, neither confirming nor denying Stacey's statement. It was true when Lilly had first met the young woman, she had nearly burst her ear drum with her constant peppy chatter. Stacey had marched into the shop almost demanding a job, partly for the same reason the American crowd had just bought half her merchandise, hoping for a truly British experience. But also to help with her college education and rent. Since then, though, Stacey had become as much of a tea drinker as the average Plumpton Mallet resident. Not to mention exceptionally knowledgeable about the teas. She was a godsend to Lilly and her business. And now that she was living in the flat above the shop for a much reduced cost, she was also on hand whenever Lilly needed her.

"After a crowd like that, I admit to having second thoughts about whether I should go tomorrow," Lilly said, thinking of a celebration she'd been invited to. She'd been hesitant all week about leaving the shop for the weekend trip, and after the crowd they'd just dealt with, her hesitancy had only grown. It was summer, and the number of customers would only increase.

"Lilly, come on," Stacey groaned, clearly having grown a bit fed up of the agonising back-and-forth Lilly had been experiencing all week. "You've been talking about how much you're looking forward to seeing your friends Robert and Joanne for almost a month now. Don't you go getting cold feet just because we had one day that was a little busier than usual. I seriously doubt we'd get another crowd in like that while you're away for just a few days, and even if we did, I could totally handle it."

Lilly smiled at her young assistant. It was true she was very much looking forward to the visit. "I know," she said. "And I also know you're more than capable of dealing with whatever is thrown at you. That crowd was just a lot to handle, that's all."

Earl Grey came meandering out of the back room, obviously having sensed the large crowd had finally dispersed. He effortlessly jumped up onto the main counter where they were both sitting, enjoying a well earned cup of tea. It was the remains of one of the sample pots brewed for the tourists, and neither one wanted to see it go to waste.

"And besides," Stacey continued, reaching out and scratching Earl behind his damaged ear, his favourite spot, "Earl Grey will be here to help me hold down the fort. Won't you, buddy?"

Lilly laughed and rolled her eyes. "Oh, well, that completely puts my mind at rest. I appreciate you being so willing to look after the shop and Earl during my absence. Though I don't know how much help he'll be if he runs away and hides, like he did today. It will be really nice to see Robert and Joanne again, it's been ages since we were together. I don't think I've seen them in person since their wedding, and that was five years ago. We've just talked on the phone or sent the occasional email or card for birthdays and Christmas. They haven't managed to get back to Plumpton Mallet since they got married and I know I haven't been anywhere."

"Wow, five years is a really long time without a break, Lilly. You can't work all the time, it's not good for you," Stacey said. "So, how do you know these people exactly?"

"It was from my Agony Aunt days," she replied, giving their cups a refill.

Prior to opening her shop, Lilly had been the advice columnist for the Plumpton Mallet Gazette. The paper had been taken over by a larger concern and as they already had an Agony Aunt on staff, she was made redundant. Her redundancy money made up part of what she had used to open her business. She'd written a lot of advice columns in the days leading up to the takeover.

"Oh? Did they work at the paper as well?"

"No, actually, Robert wrote a letter in to the paper," Lilly explained, thinking back to the occasion with fondness. "It was anonymous, which is par for the course with an advice column, so obviously I didn't know who had written it at first. He needed some advice about a woman he was interested in, a divorcee, because he'd been out of the dating game for so long. He was a widower and a single father. He didn't know the best way to approach it without making a mess of things, or appearing too keen and desperate, so I helped him. A few months later, they both turned up at the paper to thank me and show off the engagement ring. We've been friends ever since. I was invited to their wedding which was beautiful, they have great taste. I think that's the last time I saw them face to face, though. I got to know them both well during their engagement period and ended up helping with some of the wedding preparations."

"That's so sweet, and so romantic. It was you that got them together," Stacey said approvingly. Earl had now moved from the counter to her lap, and she was continuing to stroke his back while they chatted above the audible purring.

Lilly nodded, smiling. "That's what they both say, although I'm sure Robert would have worked it out on his own, eventually. Now they have a bed-and-breakfast on the coast down south and are celebrating their five year wedding anniversary. It's a family occasion, so I was a bit surprised to get an invitation, although I think Joanne wants some help with the planning and decoration, and my teas."

"No surprise, as far as I'm concerned. They probably think of you as family. Besides, you do make a great cup of tea."

◦◦◦◦◦

HE BELL ABOVE the shop door chimed, so Stacey stood up and Earl hopped down to the floor, giving a languorous stretch of each individual leg before making his way to his favourite spot in the window, where he curled up and went to sleep. Lilly turned and smiled.

"Archie," she said, happy to see her old friend Archie Brown paying a visit.

"Good afternoon, ladies," he said, tipping his old-fashioned hat. "I understand my teacup is ready?"

"It is indeed," Lilly said. She was particularly proud of this repair. It had been in a sorry state when Archie had first brought it to her and had taken much longer than she'd expected due to its delicate nature. "Stacey, would you bring it through?"

"Sure will," she said, disappearing into the back room while Lilly stepped back behind the counter and Archie took the bar stool she had just vacated.

"So, how have you been, Archie?"

"A lot better, actually. Ever since Douglas had a personality transplant and started calming down. She must have visited Stepford recently."

Lilly laughed. Abigail Douglas was the new Agony Aunt at the paper and had been banging heads with Archie since day one. Archie was the senior crime reporter at the gazette, a position Abigail had set her sights on once she realised her column was all but dead, and was quite vocal about how much he missed Lilly at work, particularly considering the type of personality who'd taken over her job.

"You two are getting on better, then?"

"As well as can be expected, I suppose," he said. "She even asked me to pass on her regards to you. Can you believe that? I suppose she's having to adjust her attitude considering the results from your last case."

"Case? Good grief, Archie, you're making me sound like detective."

"You're two for two, my friend," Archie responded, referring to the hot water she'd managed to get herself into over the previous few months. On two separate occasions Lilly had managed to solve a local murder and earned herself a bit of fame in the process. The gazette had even done a couple of stories about her, deeming it front-page headline news both times. The first article had been co-written by Archie and Abigail, on the second Archie had taken the reins himself, which was how it should be. Lilly had enjoyed being interviewed by her old friend, especially as the articles had meant a spotlight had been shone on her business to positive effect.

"She's not still upset about my Agony Aunt letterbox, is she?" Lilly asked, referring to the one she had had fitted at the shop for people to continue to drop off advice requests. It hadn't been intentional to continue giving personal guidance once she'd left the paper, but people had reverted to contacting her at the shop, much to Abigail's chagrin. She'd feared the paper would nix her column completely if people didn't start writing in, causing her to lose her job. It was a fear Lilly admitted had some merit. But she couldn't stop people writing to her, nor could she ignore their requests for help.

"She hasn't mentioned it in a while, actually," Archie said. "So we'll see. I'm hoping she'll continue on this pleasant path at work. She's starting to get along with several other members of staff now she's stopped harassing and bad-mouthing you. You're still popular among the staff at the paper so her antagonism toward you wasn't doing her any favours. Quite the opposite, in fact. At least she's seen reason now, thank goodness."

Stacey arrived back, holding a small box that she gingerly placed on the counter between Lilly and Archie. Lilly grinned and opened the package, carefully lifting out the contents, and placed it before Archie for him to examine.

"So, what do you think?" Lilly asked, as he picked up the teacup with a grin as big as the one Lilly was wearing.

"Absolutely incredible," he said. "I'd just about destroyed this poor cup. I honestly didn't think you'd be able to repair it at all, Lilly. Now look at it. It's like magic. You can't even see where it was damaged. I have no idea how you managed to do it, but I really am very impressed, my friend. The real question is whether it will do its job. Will it hold my tea?"

Lilly smiled. "Only one way to find out, Archie. Let's test it. I have some mint tea already brewed, how about that?"

"Perfect, I love mint tea. Do the honours, would you?" He said, placing the cup on its saucer and sliding it towards Lilly.

She swilled it out, then poured the tea. As she expected, and much to Archie's delight, it worked perfectly. For much of the afternoon, in between spells of serving customers and taking in deliveries, the three of them laughed and swapped stories before Archie realised how much time he'd let sneak by. He once again thanked her profusely for the repair as he departed, and before Lilly knew it, the day was over.

It felt very strange leaving Earl behind with Stacey, who lived in the flat above the shop, but she had to go home and pack ready for her early morning start. She had a long day of driving ahead of her tomorrow. She rode her bicycle home to her little cottage on the outskirts of town and realised how much she was looking forward to a rest and a fun weekend with her friends.

Unfortunately, the celebrations wouldn't go according to plan and if she'd known what was about to happen, she would never have gone.

Chapter Two

ALMOST SIX HOURS after she had set off from home, Lilly finally joined the winding back road that would lead her to the bed-and-breakfast. She'd never had the opportunity to visit before, but Joanne had sent her pictures, and she thought she had a rough idea of what the place was going to look like. However, nothing had prepared her for the extravagance of the building and its striking setting. The photos really hadn't done it justice.

The bed-and-breakfast was located on England's southern coast, perched on a coastal cliff with a panoramic view of the sea. As she stepped out of the car, stretching her back to get the kinks out after the long drive, she could taste the tang of salt in the air and smell the warm sand and the kelp. The balmy weather was perfect and she could already envisage daily trips down the private steps to visit the beach below the cliff.

"Wow," Lilly breathed softly, trying to take it all in.

She glanced back the way she had come. The long drive was as picturesque as all the other parts of the property she could see from where she stood. Numerous trees, probably older than she was, grew majestically alongside a smaller, more recently planted orchard, filled with apple trees and other assorted specimens she couldn't name. The more formal gardens, which she could see from where she had parked, were accessed via an ornate white archway leading to a little path flanked by large, colourfully flowering shrubs. Rhododendron and Hydrangea she thought. As well as several Palm trees which gave the bed-and-breakfast its name.

The property itself was of a moderate size. Her friends had told her it hosted ten separate guest suites along with a private lounge and bedrooms for the owners, and smaller suites for the live-in staff. It was an older house built in the late eighteen hundreds in a timeless Art Deco style and painted an opaque white. It looked incredible against the deep blue of the summer sky. *It almost glows,* Lilly thought as her friend came rushing down the steps, arms outstretched, to welcome her.

"Lilly!" she exclaimed, her long sun dress flowed behind her as she ran, and a sneaky breeze nearly whipped the large beach hat from her head.

She looks incredible, Lilly thought. The last five years had obviously been good to her friend.

"Joanne, gosh it seems like forever since I last saw you."

Joanne threw her arms round Lilly in dramatic fashion, laughing like a school girl.

"Lilly, I am so glad you're here. Thank you for coming, it's going to be great to catch up this weekend. And you must tell me all about your tea shop."

"Try to stop me," Lilly said with a smile. "This place is absolutely amazing, Joanne. You and Robert must have worked so hard to get it looking this beautiful. The pictures you sent must have been when you first took over?"

"Yes, we've painted the whole place inside and out since then, as you can see," she said with a broad sweep of her arm. "It gave the place a much needed face lift. Come on, let me help you with your bags and get you settled in your room, then I'll give you the grand tour. So, how was the drive?"

"Long. Six hours," Lilly said with a slight groan. "Although I did stop for lunch."

"You really should have caught the train, you know. Robert would have picked you up at the station. You could have been here two hours ago."

"I know, but I had too much luggage. I've brought a full tea set with me. One of my best."

"You didn't have to do that," Joanne exclaimed. "We've got perfectly good sets here. I just wanted you to bring along some of your speciality teas. We have nothing like your shop down here."

"Well, I did that too, but the set is an anniversary present for you both," Lilly explained, opening the boot of her car.

"Lilly, that's so kind of you. You really didn't need to bring us anything, you're already coming early to help us get ready for the party."

"I wouldn't dream of coming empty handed, Joanne. Besides, I wanted to get you something special."

Lilly pulled her suitcase out.

"Here, let me get that," Joanne insisted, taking the case from Lilly's hand. "Now, let me show you to your room."

⁂

*T*HEY ENTERED THE bed-and-breakfast through the main front door, and Lilly gazed up at the crystal chandelier that was causing a dazzling light display, thanks to the influx of sunlight from one of the higher windows.

"That's absolutely stunning," Lilly said. "It's like being in the foyer of a fabulous cruise ship from a hundred years ago."

"I know, I love it. Although it's a bit of a dust gatherer. We have to clean each individual glass droplet every six months, otherwise it loses its shine. It's worth it though."

A woman in a beige calf length shirt dress and matching espadrilles came hurrying to the door when she heard it open.

"Welcome to The Palms," she said in a soft and quite sultry voice.

"Natalie," Joanne said. "This is my very good friend Lilly Tweed. She's going to be staying with us for a few days and has generously offered to help with the party. Lilly, this is Miss Natalie Sampson, our housekeeper. And a very good one at that."

Natalie put out her hand. "Nice to meet you, Lilly. Joanne has been telling me about your shop. You're the person to go to when it comes to tea, apparently. We provide Tiffin for the guests every afternoon at three o'clock, so I would love to pick your brains at some point, if I may?"

"A pleasure to meet you, too. And yes, of course, I'd be happy to help," Lilly said.

Miss Sampson escorted both ladies upstairs and along the hall to one of the suites. Lilly was delighted to find her room had a glorious view of the sea and the private beach.

"Oh, this is absolutely beautiful. What a gorgeous place to live," she said, gazing out of the window as Natalie Sampson carefully placed Lilly's bag by the door.

"I'll just go and get you your room key," Natalie said before disappearing.

"I don't know what I'd do without Natalie," Joanne said to Lilly. "She runs the place like clockwork."

"So, where's Robert?" Lilly asked, gazing around the beautiful room she'd been given. It was a timeless luxury in an Art Deco style, with much of the features obviously original. An antique double bed with matching wardrobe and dressing table were the main pieces of furniture. But in the bay window sat an occasional table with two club chairs in teal velvet. She was really going to enjoy staying here.

"He and Chloe went to have a father daughter early dinner in town," Joanne replied, already half way out of the door, eager to show Lilly around the place.

"Gosh, I haven't seen Chloe since your wedding. How old is she now?"

Lilly had never got to know Chloe very well. She'd been quite young and very shy when she'd first met Robert.

"Sixteen. Can you believe it? And let me tell you, she has really come out of her shell."

"I bet you had a lot to do with that. How do you like being a step mum?"

"I honestly love it, Lilly. Admittedly Chloe makes it very easy, she's such a sweetheart."

Lilly smiled as she followed Joanne down the hallway, where her host showed off a number of the rooms, each with their own unique and stunning design. She opened up the final door leading to one of the larger guest suites and almost crashed into a young man.

"Oh," she yelped.

"Sorry, Aunt Joanne," he said. "I was just putting new sheets on the bed."

"No, that was completely my fault, Dominic. I should have knocked before charging in like a bull. Lilly, this is my nephew Dominic, he works with us, too."

"Looks like it's a family affair around here," Lilly said. "Nice to meet you, Dominic. Do you like working at The Palms?"

"Absolutely," he said with a pleasant smile.

Dominic was quite young, in his mid twenties, Lilly thought, but she got the impression he was a dedicated employee and more mature and serious than a lot of his contemporaries.

"How long have you worked here?"

"A couple of years now. My brother Edward and me got summer jobs after we'd finished school, but I stuck it out a little longer than him. You'll get to meet him, though. He and mum are coming to help Aunt Joanne and Robert celebrate their anniversary. We're all really happy for them, he's a really nice guy. You're the one he wrote to asking for dating advice, is that right?"

Lilly laughed. "Yes, that's me. But how on earth did you know?"

"Are you kidding? Aunt Joanne's been staring out of the window for the past hour waiting for you to arrive," he said, earning him a playful thump on the arm from his aunt. "Hey, I'm just saying you're really excited to have your friend here. She showed me the articles about you in the Plumpton Mallet Gazette."

"Really? Wait, surely you don't get the gazette all the way out here? Their circulation isn't that big, unless it's changed a lot since I left."

Joanne shook her head. "No, we have a subscription. They send it on to us by post. Plumpton Mallet is our home town, so it's lovely catching up and seeing what everyone is up to. Especially when it's one of my closest friends. Besides, we have a bit of a soft spot for the paper because it was your agony aunt column and advice that brought us together."

"Oh, by the way, Aunt Joanne, did Natalie tell you about the little mishap?"

Joanne raised an eyebrow. "What mishap?"

Dominic sighed. "I don't know whose error it was, but one of the rooms has been booked for a guest this weekend."

"What? Oh, no. I thought we blocked this weekend off for friends and family with no overnight guests apart from Lilly so we could have the party?"

"I'm sorry. I don't know how it happened, but the guy is already here. I showed him to a guest room. I wasn't sure what to do, but I didn't think it was right to turn him away, considering he'd booked and paid for the weekend. Especially since he'd travelled all the way here. We had the room available, and it is just one guy. I don't mind looking after him."

Joanne didn't look too happy about this turn of events, but she sighed and shrugged, resigned to the fact there was nothing she could do.

"It's fine, Dominic. You did the right thing. I would be furious if I'd shown up at a bed-and-breakfast I'd booked and paid for in good faith, only to be turned away because the owners were having a party. You're right, it is only one guest, but I was hoping we'd be able to have a relaxed weekend without any work."

"Actually," Dominic said. "I did tell him what was going on and he said he wasn't expecting anyone to be at his beck and call. He just wanted to enjoy the private beach. He seems pretty low maintenance."

"That doesn't sound too bad," Lilly said. "You have a whole compliment of staff and only one guest. It could be worse. Especially if he's being so understanding about the mix up."

"Yes, you're right. And there's certainly enough people to help him so Robert and I can enjoy our celebration. Come on, let's continue the tour, then I'll mix us a gin and tonic."

Lilly followed Joanne downstairs while Dominic continued his duties.

❦

NATALIE SAMPSON MET them at the base of the stairs and gave Lilly her room key, saying she was looking forward to learning more about tea over the weekend. She then disappeared to help Dominic with the room preparations. Even though they weren't to be used over the weekend, as soon as the festivities were over The Palms was booked solid throughout the whole of the summer and well into the autumn, Joanne told Lilly. Preparing it all now meant everyone would be able to take some much needed time off.

Lilly and Joanne made their way to the dining room, where she met the elderly cook, Morris.

"And who is the gorgeous young lady?" he said by way of a greeting, which included quite a naughty wink.

Lilly laughed. "It's nice to meet you, Morris," she said, shaking the old man's hand.

"You too, my dear," he chuckled, as he continued to clean and polish the large oak dining table. "Joanne, have you heard from your husband about Jack? Is he coming this weekend?"

Joanne nodded. "Yes, he is coming, Morris, but I don't want you to get your hopes up too much."

"Who's Jack?" Lilly asked curiously.

"Robert's father," Joanne said. "He and Morris served together in the army." She smiled affectionately at the old cook.

"So, Jack has lost some more marbles then?"

"Morris!" Joanne exclaimed. "That's no way to talk about your old friend."

"Nonsense, Joanne. That's exactly what Jack would have said if the roles were reversed and I had Alzheimer's. You know I love that man like a brother and would do anything for him. Besides, you can't take life too seriously when you get to our age."

"You always seem to bring Jack out of his trances when you're together, Morris. I hope you manage it this weekend. I know it would make Robert happy if he could see a bit of the father he remembers shining through."

"Challenge accepted," he said before giving both women a salute, collecting his cleaning supplies, and disappearing into the kitchen.

"He seems like a fun person to have around," Lilly said. "I'm sorry to hear about Robert's father. Is it serious?"

"I'm afraid so. His moments of lucidity are very rare now. I don't think he's going to be with us for much longer," Joanne admitted. "But he did tell Robert he was looking forward to coming here this weekend, which is a lot more conversation than we usually get from him. Robert obviously caught him on a good day. Now, let's see, you haven't seen the gardens yet. You need to meet Walter. He's our gardener, handyman, and can turn his attention to most things. Which is a godsend when things break for no apparent reason. You'll like him. I think he's outside. Come on..."

Joanne took Lilly out of a side entrance which led straight to the formal flower gardens where guests had Tiffin each afternoon. It went right up to the edge of the cliff, a white picket fence being the only thing separating them from the sheer drop to the beach and sea below. In the midst of the garden were a number of tables with large umbrellas where they would be having the celebration over the course of the weekend. In one corner of the large oasis, she spied a man crouched over the dirt, putting in some colourful Azaleas.

"Oh, Walter, these are going to look stunning when they've grown a bit," Joanne said, approaching the man who, upon hearing his name, stood up to greet them.

"I think so too. I'm sorry we lost the old ones over the winter. I wasn't expecting the ground frost we got. Killed the roots off." He then noticed Lilly and offered her a warm smile. "Walter," he said, introducing himself.

"Lillian. But everyone calls me Lilly."

"One of my favourite names," he said, putting a soil laden gloved hand to his chest in dramatic fashion. "It's the gardener in me, I can't resist a girl named after a flower." He pointed to the tall slender stems with vibrant purple, orange and yellow flowers adjacent to the fence. "Those are our lilies. They've been strong this season and have lasted long past their normal blooming time. They're positively glowing this year, so you're getting a special treat."

"They are very beautiful," Lilly said. "Especially against the white of the fence."

"Joanne? Where are you?" a familiar voice called.

"Oh, brilliant. Robert and Chloe are back." Joanne said excitedly, making her way round to the front of the house. Lilly followed after complimenting Walter on his handiwork in the garden.

As she walked, Lilly pulled out her phone, intending to send a text to Stacey.

"There's no mobile service out here, I'm afraid, Lilly," Robert said when he spotted her.

Lilly put the phone back in her pocket. "It's all right, I'll send an email later."

She took in the sight of Robert as she approached. He looked like he'd lost a bit of weight and grown his hair slightly since she'd last seen him. He was a family man at heart and it was clear the intervening years had been as kind to him as they had to Joanne. They both looked as though they were thriving at The Palms.

She smiled when she saw Joanne hurry to her husband and give him a fierce hug, as though they'd been apart for days rather than a few hours.

"It's so good to see you, Lilly," Robert said, giving her a brief hug, too. "I'm really glad you were able to come this weekend." He turned towards a young lady who was just getting out of the car. "Chloe, do you remember, Lilly?"

The teenage girl's eyes widened slightly. Then she grinned. "Yes, I think so," she replied, getting pulled into a hug by her father as she walked past.

"Let me tell you, Lilly," Robert said. "I feel as though I've been living in paradise these last few years, with my two favourite girls."

"Dad..." Chloe groaned, embarrassed. But Lilly could see she was fighting back a smile.

"Seriously, I don't know what my life would be like right now if I had written to you."

Lilly beamed. "I'm sure you would have worked it out, Robert. But I'm really happy to be here to celebrate with you. This place really does look like paradise."

The four of them made their way back inside, chatting about the plans for the upcoming party.

Chapter Three

WITH THE BED-AND-BREAKFAST almost deserted, apart from staff and family members due to the party, Lilly spent her time enjoying what it had to offer. Plenty of strolls on the beach, swims in the sea, afternoon tea and board games in the evening for them all. It almost felt like old times, Lilly recalled, as during their early engagement Joanne and Robert would frequently hold small social gatherings like this.

Because of the relaxed atmosphere, Lilly felt as though she'd come to know the staff quite well, which would have been almost impossible if it had have been full of guests. Natalie Sampson was lovely, with a great personality, as well as being a very attractive woman. She kept the place clean and tidy, but was far from being a stickler. She played a few practical jokes on Chloe as the two of them seemed to be in the middle of a prank competition.

Walter, still enamoured by her name, brought her flowers. On her first morning she found he'd even taken the time to put a display of lilies on the breakfast table. He was certainly a hard worker, but very thoughtful, too. Constantly wandering the gardens in an attempt to make every flower pot, hanging basket, shrub, bush and patch of lawn perfect. He was managing it too, Lilly thought. It all looked absolutely stunning, and the fragrances were gorgeous.

Morris entertained them all with war stories during dinner. They'd obviously been told many times before, but Lilly's presence was a good excuse to repeat them. Apparently, Robert's father Jack had taken a bullet during the time they'd served together, a bullet meant for Morris thus saving his life. It was a riveting tale of bravery and survival against the odds, and Lilly was enraptured.

And Joanne's nephew Dominic, handsome and sprightly, decided to erect both a volleyball net and a boules pitch on the beach as additional entertainment for Lilly. She had the impression all the staff were as much a part of the family as the real members. They all got along well and truly enjoyed one another's company.

The day before the party, Lilly and Joanne scurried about putting up decorations and displaying the elegant and very stylish tea set Lilly had brought for them. It was being used mostly as decor, displayed on the garden table.

"Oh, Lilly, you know me so well. It's just beautiful. Thank you so much."

The design was one Lilly knew Joanne, with her love of vintage, would like. The teapot had a pale pink body with a lid, spout, and handle, all in white and decorated with vintage roses. Gold accents completed the look and Lilly had to admit, along with the coordinating tea cups, milk jug, sugar bowl and spoons with matching handles, it looked stunning as the display centrepiece.

"You really have an eye for this sort of thing, Lilly," Joanne continued. "And Walter is going to add displays of tea roses and lilies. I'll serve champagne cocktails and Pimms in the other teacups I have, and I thought Morris could do some cupcakes using the colours of your tea set. What do you think of pale pink butter-cream with a darker pink icing rose on top?"

"They sound perfect. It's going to be amazing, Joanne," Lilly said as the two of them made their way to the front of the house, where they heard the sounds of a car pulling up.

"Robert," Joanne called out. "It looks like your sister is here, with your dad."

They met the large car as it came to a stop and parked on the front drive, with Robert and Chloe joining them a moment later, just as the driver stepped out.

He was a tall, heavily built man with a sour expression and for some reason Lilly immediately felt unnerved. The deep frown lines on his forehead and the sullen set of his mouth seemed to suggest that smiling was a rarity. Robert and his family seemingly ignored the man's mood, so she suspected this was his usual countenance. They greeted him, sounding as friendly as they always did.

"Hi, John, how was the drive?" Robert asked with a smile.

John just huffed in response. Robert shook his head and moved to the passenger side, opening the car door for his sister, Sarah. Lilly smiled. She remembered meeting Sarah at the wedding five years before. Sarah yawned and thanked her brother for opening the door.

"Gosh, it's good to be home," she said. "Can you help me with dad, Robert?"

Lilly stood by, watching as John, evidently Sarah's husband, lurched up the steps to the front door of the property without offering any assistance, while Robert retrieved the wheelchair from the boot. John let the house door slam shut without so much as a glance behind him. He hadn't even bothered to introduce himself to Lilly. He'd just walked past, ignoring her.

Granddad Jack was in the back seat of the car. Robert had slid open the side door, but Jack didn't seem to have noticed the car had even come to a halt, let alone that his children, Robert and Sarah, were gently trying to manoeuvre him out and into the waiting wheelchair.

"Is there anything I can do to help?" Lilly asked Joanne softly while Chloe stood next to the car talking animatedly to her granddad. Jack, in return, gave no acknowledgment that he either understood or was aware of what was happening around him. Just a confused and vacant stare in her general direction.

Joanne shook her head. "It's better if they do it. Robert and Sarah have it down to a fine art now. He's old, Lilly, with both a body and a mind that's failing him. He's mostly confused and hardly knows if he's on this earth or Fuller's most of the time. I'm surprised he wanted to come, actually. But I'm glad he has." She lowered her voice. "Robert's mother was going to come too, but honestly, it's been very hard on her recently, both physically and emotionally. She did want to be here to help us celebrate, but Robert and Sarah decided to surprise her with a spa weekend break. It was Morris's idea, actually. It's a full-time job taking care of her husband now, so we're all pitching in to help with Jack so she can have a bit of a breather. She's had her hands full, especially lately as unfortunately he's taken a turn for the worse. I think it will be good for her to have some time for herself."

Lilly nodded. She had always thought Robert was a good and caring person, so to hear he and his sister had planned something nice for their mother didn't come as a surprise. She glanced back at the house with a slight frown, which Joanne immediately interpreted correctly.

"That's typical John for you. Don't take anything he says or does personally, he's all talk and no walk if you know what I mean, and doesn't get on with anyone, really."

"It was a long drive," Sarah said, obviously having over-heard the comments about her husband and not looking pleased about them. "You know how John hates long car journeys."

"Well, we appreciate you both going to get Jack, Sarah. It was very kind of you," Joanne said, then looked down at the old man in the wheelchair. "Hello, Jack, I'm so glad you're here." She bent to give him a kiss on the cheek.

"Veronica," he replied breathlessly, using the name of Robert's first wife, Chloe's mother.

Chloe frowned. "No, Granddad, this is Joanne. Mum's not with us anymore, remember?"

"It's all right, Chloe. Let's get inside, shall we? We were about to start lunch so your timing is perfect."

THEY ALL MADE their way inside to the dining room where John was already seated and stuffing his face with some of the food Morris and Dominic were bringing out from the kitchen.

"Honestly, John," Sarah said in exasperated tones. "Couldn't you have waited just five minutes for the rest of us?"

"Oh, shut up, I'm hungry." John scowled as everyone else started to take seats. Dominic started to sit, but John waved a hand at him. "Before you sit down, get everyone a drink. You work here, remember?"

Dominic frowned, and his face reddened slightly. "Yes, okay. Sorry," he said.

By the look on Dominic's face, Lilly suspected this was John's typical behaviour and attitude.

"I'll do it, Dominic," Morris said. "You sit down with your family."

John glared at Morris. "I told Dominic to do it, Morris. He's got to learn that just because he's Joanne's family doesn't mean he's not one of our employees. He doesn't get special treatment just because he's related to Robert's wife."

Lilly had almost forgotten that Robert's sister was part owner of The Palms and by extension her husband obviously had some authority over the staff. They weren't present when she'd arrived and it had slipped her mind. From what she understood, Robert and Sarah had taken over the place from their father and their spouses had come to work alongside them.

"It's fine," Dominic said quickly, and Lilly was under the impression he wanted to avoid a confrontation with John at all costs. And glancing around the table, it was obvious no one else seemed to want to get involved either. "I'll get drinks for everyone, don't worry, Morris," Dominic finished.

The atmosphere was filled with a mild tension while the drinks order was filled, but Morris tried valiantly to diffuse the situation by chatting to Jack about their time during the Falkland's conflict. Jack managed the odd smile, but his responses were slight, apart from the odd nod of his head. According to the whispers from Joanne, who was seated next to her, this was more than they had expected. As Morris continued regaling them with humourous stories of their time together, he managed to make the old man smile, and once he laughed at an inside joke. Morris's presence seemed to bring a bit of light to Jack's eyes, as though he were snapping back into reality, if only for a brief moment.

"It's down to Jack that you came to work here. Do I have that right, Morris?" Lilly asked while the group was enjoying their lunch.

"Yes, that's right, Lilly," Morris said with a grin. "After Sarah and Robert took over, along with their partners, they were looking for a new cook. The Palms was a little under-staffed at the time because Jack did most of the work himself. Jack put a good word in for me. Isn't that right, Jack?"

Jack smiled and nodded, although Lilly could see he was nodding at the sound of his name rather than any under-standing of the question. He slumped back into his wheelchair and was once more lost in a world of his own.

"I was going through a bit of a bad time then," Morris continued. "I was homeless. War does bad things to a man and I couldn't settle when I got back. If it wasn't for Jack's recommendation and Robert and Sarah's kindness in offering me a chance, I don't know where I'd be right now. This place saved me. It's life changing having the right sort of people in your corner."

"Well, you are obviously good at what you do, Morris, and I can see you love working here," Lilly said.

"More than anything. And I get to see this old reprobate once in a while, too," he said, squeezing Jack's shoulder. "Didn't you mention some new medicine Jack's trying, Robert?"

John scoffed. "For all the good its doing. He's about as alert as ever. It's like talking to a wall most of the time."

"John, don't... please," Sarah muttered, looking both mortified and weary at her husband's attitude.

"I'm just telling it like it is, Sarah. Your mother is spending all that money on experimental drugs and it's obvious they aren't working. I'm not trying to upset you, but he's getting old, and it's time to face facts."

Chloe sighed loudly, staring daggers at her uncle.

"Something you want to say, Chloe?"

"No."

"No, what?"

"No, I haven't anything to say," Chloe responded defiantly, folding her arms and meeting John's steely gaze with one of her own.

John rolled his eyes. "Stop trying to be clever, Chloe. It doesn't suit you. And have a bit more respect for your elders.

Right, I'm exhausted after that drive, I'm going to crash out for a while." He stood, and throwing his napkin on his plate, left the room to an audible sigh of relief from Robert.

"I hate him!" Chloe announced to gasps from Robert and Joanne.

"Chloe!" they both exclaimed at once.

"Well, I do. I don't know why Aunt Sarah married him, he's horrible."

"That's enough, Chloe. Apologise to your Aunt," Robert said.

Sarah shook her head. "It's all right, Robert. Chloe, I married him because I love him. You'll understand when you're older. I know he's difficult sometimes, but he's had a long day and is tired. try to understand, okay?"

Chloe nodded. "Okay. And... sorry."

Sarah leaned across the table and squeezed her niece's hand.

"So, do you and John live here too, Sarah?" Lilly asked. "I know Robert, Joanne and Chloe have their own suite here."

"Yes, we have our own suite, too. John oversees the hiring and purchasing. I do most of the bookings and scheduling. And Robert and Joanne do almost everything else, if I'm honest," she laughed. "They are actually the brains behind the whole operation. I don't think John and I would have been able to make it such a success on our own."

"Speaking of bookings," Joanne said. "We currently have a guest staying. He arrived earlier. I don't suppose you accidentally took a booking, did you?"

Sarah covered her face. "Oh, no. Please tell me I didn't do that." She groaned at that thought of making such a slip up on what was supposed to be her brother- and sister-in-law's special weekend.

"Honestly, it's no problem, Sarah, I was just trying to work out how it happened."

"Yes, it might have been me," Sarah admitted. "Last week was a bit chaotic. There was more than our usual amount of enquiries for summer bookings, which is great for the business, but that one might have slipped through. I'm so sorry."

"Seriously, it's fine. One guest won't be a problem to look after. Don't worry about it."

Sarah sighed, brushing off the error with a wry smile, then turned to Dominic. "So, I hear your mum and brother are coming this weekend?"

"Yes. They'll be here tomorrow. Mum's really looking forward to seeing you."

Joanne explained to Lilly how Sarah and her other sister-in-law, Fiona, Dominic's mother, became close when Joanne's brother died. "Sarah became a real tower of strength and support for Fiona, when I was in the midst of grief myself."

Dominic nodded in agreement. "You and Robert getting together did a lot for both families, Joanne."

Lilly smiled. She was glad to realise she had had a hand in the resulting happiness of this lovely group of people.

Chapter Four

IT WAS THE morning of the anniversary celebration and Lilly was very much looking forward
to it all. She had a shower and then put on shorts
and a loose fitting tee shirt suitable for the heat of the day,
before trotting downstairs to the dining room. She knew it
would be a busy few hours to get everything ready before
she could relax and enjoy herself, so she wanted to make the
most of a hearty breakfast to set her up in case they needed
to work through lunch.

When she arrived, there was only one other person seated
and she didn't recognise him.

"Good morning," he said pleasantly, flipping casually
through a newspaper while enjoying tea, freshly squeezed
orange juice and a delicious-looking continental breakfast.

"Good morning," she replied, sitting down just as
Dominic appeared by her side.

"Good morning, Lilly. Did you sleep well?"

"I did, Dominic, thank you. That bed is the most comfortable one I've ever slept in. And it was lovely listening to the sound of the sea gently breaking on the shore. Almost hypnotic. It certainly put me to sleep."

"It has that effect on a lot of guests. Now, what would you like for breakfast?"

Lilly glanced at what the stranger had chosen. Muesli, fresh fruit, croissants with homemade jam and creamy butter, a pot of tea and a tall glass of juice.

"I'll have what this gentleman is having, please. It looks delicious."

Dominic disappeared, and Lilly turned to the other guest. He'd put his paper down and was smiling at her.

"I don't believe we've met," Lilly said. "How do you know Robert and Joanne?"

"I don't. Not really," he said with a wry smile. "I'm the guest who booked a room during a family weekend celebration."

"Oh," Lilly said, with a laugh. "I'm sorry. I didn't mean to bother you. I assumed you were here for the party."

"It's quite all right. I'm just doing my best to stay out of everyone's way. As well as feeling very grateful I wasn't asked to leave as soon as I got here."

Lilly shook her head. "They would never have done that. It's hardly your fault, you didn't know. It was an oversight by one of the owners, I believe. You've been very understanding about the whole thing. It's very kind of you."

"It's a special weekend, and they have been very accommodating. I'm, Sam, by the way," he said, reaching across the table to shake her hand.

"Lillian, but please call me, Lilly, everyone does."

"A pleasure, Lilly. It's actually fun being here with a celebration planned. Robert was even kind enough to invite me to this evening's festivities, considering I'm not on the official guest list. I think he feels a bit awkward and doesn't know what to do with me. I've told him not to worry. I'm here to get away for a while, to enjoy the private beach and generally relax. I'm quite happy with my own company and don't require any special treatment."

"Is it the first time you've stayed here?" Lilly asked, pouring milk onto the cereal Dominic had just brought to her.

"Oh, no, not at all. As a matter of fact, I've been holidaying here since I was a boy. I've seen the place go through a number of owners over the years. I can remember coming here with my grandparents as a child and collecting shells, building sandcastles on the beach and catching minnows in the rock pools. I don't come as often as I like nowadays, but it's nice to take a trip down memory lane every now and again."

"That's a lovely story," Lilly said. "And talking of stories, I bet you could tell a few about this place, considering you've known it for so long?"

Sam grinned. "I could probably tell you more than you'd care to know." He ate the last bite of his croissant, dabbed his mouth with the napkin, then rose. "But, perhaps another time. I'm going to enjoy the beach this morning while I have it to myself. Enjoy your stay, Miss Tweed. And be careful if you explore the place on your own. It has many little secrets. We wouldn't want you to get lost now, would we?"

And with that friendly, but strangely ominous part-ing shot, Sam left the room. Lilly stared after him as a thought struck her. She hadn't told Sam her last name was Tweed.

🙘🙙

WHEN DOMINIC BROUGHT the rest of her breakfast, Lilly asked him what he could tell her about Sam?

He shrugged, laying assorted dishes in front of her. "Not much really. He's a regular customer. Comes a couple of times a year in the summer and once in the winter, too. Although I think it's been a little while since his last stay. I know he's mentioned knowing the owners before Robert's dad bought it, which was years ago."

"I see. He's a bit, I don't know, odd."

"A little, maybe, but he's harmless," Dominic assured her. "I think he likes being in the know about the building and its history. He's really sentimental about the place. He knows a lot more about it than Robert or Sarah."

"Dominic." A woman's voice said from the door.

Lilly turned in her seat to see a slim woman enter, wearing crop jeans and a blue and white striped tee shirt. Navy deck shoes and sunglasses nestled in a riot of short dark curls com-pleted the look. She looked extremely weary from travelling. Right behind her was a young man who, apart from a few minor facial features, looked exactly like Dominic. It was such a startling similarity Lilly paused for a moment, doing a double take. She vaguely recognised the woman from the wedding, but not the young man with her, although it was obvious who they both were.

"Mum, you made it," Dominic said, giving her a hug. "Have you both eaten? I can ask Morris to get you breakfast."

"Sounds great," Dominic's brother said. "You know what I like."

"The usual, mum?"

"Please, dear. Can you join us?" she asked, then in an added whisper, "John's not around, is he?" which seemed to suggest to Lilly she knew about the man's difficult disposition. Especially when it came to staff taking time off. Even when it was supposed to be a friends' and family weekend.

"Forget him, mum. I don't think *Robert* would mind, considering our only guest has just finished," he replied, clearing Sam's breakfast things away and returning to the kitchen.

The woman and her son sat at the table and she turned to Lilly. "I don't believe we've met?"

"Lilly Tweed. You must be Fiona, Joanne's sister-in-law?"

"Yes, that's right," Fiona said. "And you must be the agony aunt who brought our two love birds together?"

"Yes, that's me."

"You've obviously met Dominic. This is my other son, Edward."

"It's nice to meet you. I hope you don't mind but I have to ask, are you and Dominic twins?"

"Irish twins," Edward said. "I'm the eldest by ten months."

"Wow, you must be superwoman," Lilly said to Fiona.

Fiona laughed. "I can tell I'm going to like you, Lilly," she said.

Dominic arrived back a few minutes later with breakfast for himself and his family. He sat across from his brother and smiled. "Good to see you, Ed."

"You too, little brother. You'd better be careful John doesn't see you sitting with us when you should be working."

"John can go to..."

"Dominic! John is as much your boss as your Aunt Joanne."

"Am I right in thinking it was Jack who first bought The Palms?" Lilly said.

"That's right," Fiona said. "He bought it shortly after he left the army. Fixed it up and was running it almost single handedly for a while, with his wife helping part time. Unfortunately, he didn't have it for long. He damaged his back falling off a ladder while working in the grounds, and he hit his head on a rock as he landed from what I understand. He wasn't able to keep up with it after that. Robert, Sarah, and John took over and hired Walter to help. He's been working here ever since Jack had his accident."

"It must have been quite a while ago?" Lilly said.

"About ten years now. Robert and Sarah have worked wonders here. I've seen pictures of what it looked like before and you'd hardly recognise the place. Then five years ago Robert married Joanne and with her background in marketing and her eye for interior decorating she really helped it grow. Needing additional staff as it became more and more popular, my boys came to work here."

"So, you used to work here too, Edward?" Lilly asked, to bring him into the conversation. She already knew he had from Dominic.

Edward huffed. "Yeah. I was fired."

Fiona squeezed his arm. "Let's not rake over old coals, Edward. It's done. How about we forget about it?"

"So, I understand you and Joanne are sisters-in-law?" Lilly said, trying to get the family relationships straight in her mind.

"Yes, Joanne's brother is my late husband."

Lilly nodded. "I'm sorry for your loss."

"It was a few years ago. Cancer. It was a really hard time for me and the boys. But I think we're finally beginning to bounce back a bit."

The clicking of the silverware on plates was the only sound from the brothers as they ate, each with their own thoughts at the mention of the father they'd lost.

"I understand you and Sarah are good friends?"

Fiona smiled. "The best. I got to know her when the boys started working here, but she was an absolute godsend and a tower of strength when my husband was sick. I don't know how I would have managed without her."

"I'm glad you had someone to turn to," Lilly said, buttering her last croissant.

"You know, I really should thank you for helping Robert and Joanne find each other. I would never have met Robert and his sister otherwise. And I've become such good friends with Sarah over the years. Your advice not only resulted in a perfect match, but an important friendship as well. Plus Edward and Dominic have become close to Robert, and I know Dominic adores working here. So, thank you, Lilly."

"My pleasure. It's a shame I'm just now playing catch-up with them both. I haven't seen them both since the wedding, although we've spoken on the phone and exchanged emails and cards. It really is wonderful being here and seeing them both and Chloe, and what a fantastic job they've done with this place. It's really beautiful and very sympathetically restored."

"It is. Although truthfully it's been a while since I've been here myself."

"What mum means," Edward said. "Is that she has been avoiding the place ever since John fired me."

"Oh, Edward, please can we not do this now, darling? I know you're angry and frustrated, but this weekend is supposed to be about celebrating with Joanne and Robert. It's not about you or what has gone on in the past, wrong as it may have been."

"I know, mum, I'm joking. *Mostly*," he added.

Dominic grinned and made a few sarcastic, but humourous comments about his brother not being able to keep his job, which was responded to by Edward issuing a warning that it was only a matter of time before Sarah's grouchy husband got rid of him too.

ᖇᖇᒪᕯᕯᕯᕯ

AFTER BREAKFAST, LILLY went in search of Joanne to see what else needed doing in preparation for the party. She had a small list, but it seemed for the most part Lilly's role was already completed. Joanne asked Lilly if she'd help Walter in the garden, selecting flowers for the arrangements accompanying the displays and the central table decorations, but after that small task was completed Joanne insisted she relax.

"I want you to be able to enjoy the party and your break too," Joanne said. "I know I asked you to come early to help a bit, but that was mainly so I could spend some time with you before everyone else arrived. We've got most of it done now. Why don't you have the rest of the day to yourself, explore the place?"

Lilly admitted she'd love to, but on the proviso that should there be anything else she could help with, Joanne was to promise to let her know.

She decided to take a walk through the grounds and enjoy the scenery. The Palms was situated in isolation with no near neighbours, on several acres of land stretching for a few miles from its perch on the cliff. The beach with its ocean vista was only one of many stunning scenes the Bed and Breakfast had to offer.

Further from the more orderly and structured recreation gardens there were orchards providing seasonal fruits for the kitchen, and a kitchen garden and greenhouses tucked out of the way provided vegetables and salad stuff. She loved the self sufficiency of it all. But beyond that, Lilly found herself on a wilder path leading to a large woodland area, which reminded her of home. She walked for several minutes through the dappled shade of the trees before realising if she continued, it was very likely she would get lost. There was talk of providing a woodland trail for guests at some point in the future, so Joanne had told her, and Lilly imagined it would be a success, however it would be foolhardy for her to continue today without a guide.

She turned to retrace her steps and as she was approaching a small grassy glade she spied two white-tailed deer, a mother and fawn. She hid behind a tree and quietly took several photographs on her phone. After several captivating minutes of watching them munch on the grass, a sound which Lilly didn't hear spooked them and they bounded away.

Lilly continued her journey back to the bed-and-breakfast, thrilled to have witnessed such a unique and beautiful sight. She attempted to send a picture of the deer and a quick message to Stacey, knowing she'd be interested, but frustratingly there was no mobile phone signal. She made a mental note to email her later from her room.

For the rest of the day, friends started trickling in to help Robert and Joanne celebrate their anniversary and to enjoy the beach and other amenities The Palms offered before the party began in earnest that evening.

Chapter Five

HE FORMAL GARDENS looked absolutely amazing. Joanne and Lilly had strung up paper lanterns around the picnic table umbrellas, fairy lights in among the trees, bushes and along the fence cordoning off the drop to the beach. Candles were placed on the tables in small cranberry glasses and torch effect solar lights edged the lawns and pathways. Festive fabric bunting was strung up on just about every available surface. It looked like the set of a fairytale.

Lilly had changed into a calf length dress for the evening festivities, cream cabbage roses with Myrtle and Moss green leaves on a pale tea green background, and paired it with cream sandals. The look was finished by a three strand necklace of pearls and matching ear-rings.

Joanne's sister-in-law, Fiona, had surprised the couple with a beautiful cake, a smaller replica of their wedding cake.

Lilly had set it in pride of place on the display table, which now housed numerous gifts to be opened by the couple in private. It made for a perfect addition and really brought the whole thing together.

There was a slide show Chloe had put together of her dad and step mum during their last five years together, and judging from the laughs and whispers, some of the images Robert and Joanne had never seen. It made the show more personal and enjoyable. It was very special.

As people began to move to the dance area, a large wooden floor with several posts strung with fairy lights, to take advantage of the music playing through the speaker system Walter had set up that afternoon, Lilly stood and made her way over to the cliff side.

"The weather has been perfect for their celebration so far, hasn't it?" Sam said as Lilly joined him to gaze across the expanse of water. "Though I did hear it was due to change. I'm afraid we could be in for some high winds before long."

"I think we can cope with a bit of high wind as long as it doesn't spoil their anniversary party," Lilly said. "I hope you're not feeling too out of place here, Sam."

"Not at all. I don't know the owners well enough to have merited a legitimate invitation, but I can't fault their hospitality. Free drinks, a fabulous buffet and some excellent tea. What more could a man wish for?" he said with a laugh. "Although I do think it's time I called it a night, it's getting late. I'm looking forward to a bit of quiet time in my suite. I came here to relax after all."

As Sam wished her goodnight and retired to his rooms, Lilly returned to the main party. It had been a huge success, although she noted, as Sam had predicted, the wind was beginning to pick up. Guests, realising the weather was about to turn, said their goodbyes and thanks to the happy couple and hastily began to depart.

As they waved to the last of them, the wind increased substantially and the rain started. Not a soft trickle, but a huge sudden downpour that took everyone by surprise and drenched them through within seconds. It was all hands on deck as they rushed around, trying to salvage the equipment, food, crockery and gifts before it was ruined.

Chloe rushed to bring in the apparatus from the slide show while others snagged decorations. Walter and Morris made light work of taking down the sound equipment and getting it safely into storage in the barn.

A tablecloth escaped as Lilly was running towards the terrace, taking to the air like an out-of-control kite and heading towards the cliff. She and Sarah both darted after it, though Sarah managed to grab it first before it was lost forever.

"Close call, Sarah. You were very quick there."

"Would you believe I used to be a runner? It was a long time ago though."

Lilly could hardly hear a word she was saying due to the howling wind. "I'm getting soaked. Come on," she shouted, grabbing Sarah's wrist and trying to make herself heard.

The two of them threw the tablecloth over their heads in an attempt to shield themselves from the deluge while they sprinted back to the building. They were the last ones to come running through the door into the main living area, laughing at themselves for putting so much effort into saving a tablecloth, and assuming a sodden piece of fabric would prevent them from getting wet.

"Oh, very smart, Sarah," John said with an unpleasant scowl. "You got yourself soaked chasing after a stupid tablecloth."

Lilly immediately felt indignation at John's comment. If he was casting aspersions on Sarah, then he was inadvertently accusing her of being a fool too.

"You're just as soaked as we are," she said, a tad sarcastically. "Look at the puddle you're standing in."

John looked down and swore under his breath. "These are new shoes. Now they're ruined."

"I can't believe this storm," Sarah said. "It was supposed to be a few high winds, but nothing like this deluge."

"Those weather people never get anything right, you know that," John said, bending to remove his shoes. "They should be ashamed of themselves."

"I suppose it's just a freak storm," Lilly said, handing the cloth to Sarah to wring out ready for the laundry. It was then she noticed the bruise around her wrist. "Oh, Sarah, how did that happen? It wasn't me when I grabbed your wrist, was it? I'm so sorry."

Sarah pulled her sleeve down and shook her head. "No, don't worry, it wasn't you. I'm a bit accident prone, that's all." She laughed.

"I keep telling her to be careful, she bruises easily," John said.

Lilly frowned, noting that John was staring at her intently, as though challenging her to contradict him. Sarah, on the other hand, was busying herself with the cloth and doing everything she could to avoid meeting her gaze. It left an unsettling feeling in the pit of Lilly's stomach.

But before anything more could be said, a deafening roar of thunder followed immediately by a bolt of lightening, which seemed to light up the whole world for a second, made everyone jump in fright. Then the place was plunged into darkness as the power went out.

"Ow. Blast it," Morris said, bumping into a coffee table.

"Oh no, the power has gone off," Edward groaned.

"Well done, Ed. You have a real knack for stating the obvious. I tell you, if brains were bird droppings you'd have a clean cage."

"John, please," Sarah said.

"Everybody stay calm," Robert called out over the increasing noise of family members coming to Edward's rescue. "I'll go and have a look at the fuse box and see if I can get the lights back on."

"I'll try to get the fire going. It will give us some light as well as warmth. It's getting a bit chilly in here now." Joanne said.

Someone else volunteered to find candles and with action being taken, Lilly found herself a seat near the fireplace. A moment later Fiona took another by her side.

❧

"JOANNE, I WAS hoping I could talk to you about Edward," Fiona said. "About the possibility of him getting his job back? I know I said I wouldn't bring it up, but things have been a bit difficult at home lately. You know how much he loved working here. And he was good at the job too. The customers all loved him."

Joanne sighed and poked at the fire. "He's having a difficult time finding a job still?"

"He doesn't want to work anywhere else he wants to be with his family and his brother. Come on, Joanne, you and I both know Edward shouldn't have been sacked in the first place. John's just being his usual obnoxious self. Throwing his weight around to make himself appear the big man."

"I can't disagree. John's getting worse, actually." Joanne said. "I'll talk to Robert about it, but John does most of the hiring and firing now, unfortunately. His isn't the final call, that's up to Robert and Sarah as the owners, but you know as well as I do Sarah always takes John's side and does what he wants, which means Robert is always outvoted. My vote of course means nothing as far as John is concerned. It helps keeps the peace for Sarah, I suppose. Leave it with me, Fiona, I'll talk to them and see what I can do. But I can't promise anything, okay?"

"Thanks, Joanne. I really appreciate you trying."

By the light of the candles and the now blazing fire, Lilly watched Fiona rejoin her sons. Her curiosity piqued.

"Do you mind me asking why Edward lost his job, Joanne? I've heard it mentioned a few times since I arrived."

"I don't know all the details myself. It was a silly mistake. Something and nothing, but John decided he had to go and with Sarah taking his side, there wasn't much we could do. John would have made all our lives very difficult if he didn't get his own way, which was bad enough, but Robert was concerned he'd take it out on Sarah. To be honest, Edward is better off out of it for the moment."

"Are you and John part owners of the business, too?"

Joanne shook her head. "No, it belongs solely to Robert and Sarah. But after Robert and I got married, it was only natural that I would start working here too. I live here, Lilly, so it's my home as well. And I love the work, I really do. John didn't want anything to do with the place until I turned up. He was happy to let Sarah and Robert do all the work and just reap the benefits. But for some reason, as soon as I arrived he decided he wanted to be a part of it. Maybe he felt intimidated, or left out. I don't know."

"I see," Lilly said. "I hope you don't mind me saying, but John isn't very friendly, is he? It's as though he doesn't particularly like anyone and actually deliberately goes out of his way to antagonise them. Not a good trait for the hospitality industry, I wouldn't have thought. If I treated my customers like that, I'd lose my business pretty quickly."

"I don't mind you saying it. We all think the same. John doesn't get along with anyone." She gestured to the back of the room where he and Natalie Samson were talking and laughing. "Though Natalie has a knack for bringing out his friendlier side, as you can see. I wish she'd share her secret, it would make life a lot easier."

"Yes," Lilly said, under her breath.

Robert returned, but with the power still off, it was obvious he hadn't managed to rectify the problem.

"I'm sorry, everyone, but it looks as though we're going to be without power for the foreseeable future. I've brought torches for us all. Dominic, could you go and check in with our guest upstairs? Let Sam know we'll keep him informed, but at the moment all we can offer is company and warm fire. Take him a torch. We don't know why the power is out at the moment."

"Obviously the storm caused it, genius," John said, with a sly grin at Natalie, who grinned back as though he'd said something clever. He forced Dominic to edge past him on his way to see to Sam.

"I know that, John," Robert replied with a patience Lilly couldn't help but admire. "I just don't know what we can do about it at the moment."

"I was hoping we could play some games tonight," Joanne said.

"We still can," Chloe said. "It'll be fun in the dark with just candles and torches."

"That is not my idea of fun. I'm going to bed. Sarah, are you coming with me or are you going to sit in those soaking wet clothes and catch your death?" Lilly noticed his tone suggested it was a rhetorical question.

Sarah looked as though she wanted to stay, but reluctantly followed her husband upstairs. Other staff followed until it was just Lilly, the family and Morris left. Dominic returned shortly after, and a game of Jenga was set up at a small table beside the fire. Halfway through the game, Sam appeared.

"I'm sorry about your weekend, Sam," Robert said. "What with us booking the place for a family party and now this power cut it can't be what you hoped for."

"You can't blame yourself for the power, Robert. It's the storm. But it was getting a bit chilly, so I came to avail myself of the fire."

"Of course, help yourself. And if you want to join in the games, you're very welcome. It's almost time to get out the poker chips," Joanne said.

"Jenga!" Dominic cried as the wooden tower came crashing down, nearly knocking over a candle in the process. Edward managed to grab it just in time.

"Probably not the best game to play with candles everywhere," Sam said with a grin.

Lilly laughed. "Yes, I think it's time we moved onto cards before we burn the place down."

Robert nodded. "I agree. Joanne, could you get the cards? I think a game of blackjack is called for."

"Absolutely. Now that's what I call a proper game."

THE LATE NIGHT card games were well under way, with Lilly surprising herself by winning and amassing quite a few matchsticks and poker chips, when John came staggering back downstairs. He'd been woken by a massive crash outside. A tree had fallen as the storm picked up pace.

"There's going to be a mess for you to clear up tomorrow, Robert. I can't believe Sarah's sleeping through this racket. That tree falling nearly gave me a blasted heart attack."

"You like playing cards, John?" Lilly asked, trying to be friendly.

"Only if those poker chips are actually worth something. I play for cash."

"You know we don't play for real money, John. It's just for fun. Gambling can lead to addiction and ruin," Robert said from his seat at the card table with a quick glance at Chloe.

John had sat down on a nearby settee and now rolled his eyes. Leaning over, he tapped Jack on his arm to get the old man's attention. "What about you, Jack? I bet you had some good card games going in your army days, eh? How is it you sired such a goody two shoes son, that's what I want to know? He won't even throw a little cash on the table to play cards with his brother-in-law."

Jack glanced in John's direction and managed a half smile. John wasn't satisfied with his response, even though it was more than Jack had managed for the last few hours, Lilly thought, watching the exchange. John gave a snort. "Thanks for the support, you're a great conversationalist, you know that, Jack?"

"Don't start," Morris warned, glaring at John.

John stared him down. "Why don't you go and make us all something to eat, Morris? We've still got gas so you could do some soup. The temperature's dropped with this storm and I'm hungry."

Morris snorted and continued looking at his card hand.

"I'm not joking, Morris," John continued, with a steel edge to his voice. "You're the hired help, remember, and I'm the boss. Go and make the soup. I'll not tell you again."

Morris flushed. With anger or embarrassment Lilly couldn't tell, but he laid down his cards and headed toward the kitchen in silence. She avoided looking at John because she knew he would see the disgust in her eyes. She didn't know him, yet he'd been rude and vile to just about everyone so far. She couldn't imagine guests returning if this was the way they were treated, but she supposed he was fine with people who paid, he just reserved the vitriol for those who couldn't answer back. He was nothing more than a bully.

"Perhaps you should calm down a bit, John," Walter said, seated to Lilly's left and with a scowl she was sure matched her own.

"You too, Walter?" John snapped. "Robert, Joanne, this is what you get when you treat the help as your friends. They aren't, they are employees. This is how we get taken advantage of."

"Stop calling them 'the help' would you?" Robert snapped. "We're not living in a Victorian novel. You've got a bad attitude, John, and are spoiling the end of what has been a great day. Perhaps you'd better go upstairs. Or better still, go and help Morris in the kitchen. If you really want something to eat after the huge buffet we've just served and during a power cut, then the least you can do is hold a torch for the man." And with that, Robert picked up a torch and tossed it in John's direction.

John caught it and smirked. "What a good idea, Robert," he said, before storming away to the kitchen.

Lilly exhaled. "Blimey," she said with feeling.

"I'm sorry you've had to see John at his worst this weekend, Lilly. He wasn't happy Joanne and I planned our anniversary celebration here and lost money from paying guests. He felt we should have made plans to do it elsewhere. Though he's obviously not bright enough to realise the place would still have had to close because there'd be no one here to run it."

"I'm still here," Sam said, laughing.

"Apologies to you too, Sam. I'm more than happy to give you a full refund."

"This probably isn't what you expected from your relaxing weekend away," Joanne said.

Sam waved off the apologies. "It's all right. I've had a wonderful weekend and there's no need to refund me. It's been nice getting to know you both better for one thing. And it's your business, there's nothing wrong with using it for a family weekend. Well, I'm going to call it a night, again. I'm sure whatever Morris is cooking is delicious, but I'm exhausted."

"If you need anything, let me know," Dominic said.

"I will. Thank you. Good night, everyone."

Just as a new game of cards was starting, there came a series of almighty crashes from the kitchen.

Robert sighed and put his head in his hands. "Oh, for Pete's sake, what now?"

❦

MORRIS CAME STORMING out of the kitchen, followed by a furious-looking John.

"Sod you, old man," John yelled, and Lilly could see he was drenched in a wet red substance. For a moment she panicked, thinking it was blood, but as he drew closer, she realised it was tomato soup.

"No, sod you, John. I've had enough. I'm leaving," Morris yelled back. "I'm going home."

"Morris!" Robert exclaimed, jumping up. "What happened?"

"Your brother-in-law is the nastiest piece of work I've ever met. You mark my words, Robert, he's going to run this place into the ground if you're not careful. And I refuse to sit here and listen to him bad mouth your father anymore. He served this country and very nearly lost his life in the process. He deserves respect. John treats him like rubbish and I'm surprised no one's bashed his nose in before now considering the vile things that come out of his mouth."

"What did John say, Morris?" Joanne said, laying a soothing hand on his arm while Morris searched in his pocket for his car keys.

"He called your dad a stupid vegetable," Morris angrily told Robert. "One of these days you're going to man up, Robert, and give the foul-mouthed pig what's coming to him. And I hope I'm here to see it."

"Morris, you can't leave. Can't you hear how bad the storm is?"

"Let him go. He just poured a pan of soup over my head, that's assault," John snapped. "We ought to sack him."

"No." Joanne shouted, turning on John. "Go and clean yourself up and go to bed, John. No one wants your nasty attitude anymore. We are not sacking Morris, and what's more I think my nephew deserves a second chance here too. You should never have sacked him in the first place. You had no good reason."

"You're out of your tiny mind. Listen, I've been part of this family a lot longer than you have, missy, and I've been through the ringer with the lot of them. You don't get to take on your family members just because you feel like it."

"Get lost, John," Joanne retorted. "Morris, Dominic and Edward all do a lot more work around here than you do."

"Joanne, calm down," Robert pleaded.

"See, that's what I mean, Robert," Morris said. "You let your brother-in-law walk all over you when you should get rid of him. He's a bad apple and one day someone will have the guts to get rid of him. I'm leaving."

"Good riddance!" John shouted.

"For heaven's sake, go upstairs and get cleaned up, John, you've done enough damage for this evening," Joanne said.

John huffed and threw up his hands. "I don't want to sit down here with you lot, anyway. Natalie, get me some towels and bring them up to room four. I don't want to wake Sarah getting cleaned up."

Natalie nodded and dashed off to do as she was ordered as John took the stairs two at a time, leaving drips of red soup on the carpet.

"Morris, please don't leave," Fiona begged, worried. "There is a violent storm raging outside. It's dangerous and the roads could be flooded. Not to mention you could be hit by a falling tree. John's not worth risking your life for. Stay here safely tonight and if you still want to leave in the morning, no one will stop you."

"Mum's right, Morris," Edward said, coming to stand by the older man. "It's really bad out there. John's gone now. Why not have a drink and play another hand with us?"

"No, I'm sorry, but that was the final straw. I refuse to stay a minute longer under the same roof as that man. I'll take my chances. I'm leaving," Morris declared, at last having found his keys. He stormed out, slamming the door in his wake.

Lilly looked out of the window, just barely able to see, as Morris's green car disappeared down the drive. She hoped he would be all right.

Chapter Six

THE FIGHT BETWEEN John and Morris and the older man's sudden departure had left an uncomfortable tension in the air, not to mention grave concern for Morris's safety. The festivities were well and truly over. After listening to several apologies from both Robert and Joanne, Lilly assured them she was fine and not to blame themselves, before retiring. The party broke up and everyone else decided to go to bed, too. Frankly, she was relieved to be alone in her room.

She felt as though she'd only been asleep for a few minutes when she was awakened by shouting. As she came out of her sleep induced haze, the shouting grew louder, accompanied by banging, and she wondered what on earth was happening. She hurriedly got out of bed, flung open the door and ran down the hall, where she found Sarah pounding on a door.

Lilly wasn't the only one who'd been awakened by the racket Sarah was making. Robert, Joanne, Chloe, Walter, Fiona, Dominic and Edward were all standing in the hallway with torches, trying in vain to calm her down.

"What's going on?" Lilly asked Chloe

"Aunt Sarah thinks John is in there with Natalie," the girl whispered.

"Really? Oh, dear..."

"Sarah, for crying out loud, please stop, you're going to wake dad up," Robert pleaded. "Not to mention our only paying guest."

"My husband is in there with our housekeeper, Robert! What do you expect me to do?" Sarah yelled. "This does it, John. I swear, you had better open this door, this minute." She shouted, pounding on the door even harder. "I knew you were having an affair. I just knew it! Natalie Sampson, when I get my hands on you I'm going to ring your cheating neck. Do you hear me? Open this door, you cowards."

"Sarah?" a voice said from the end of the hall.

Lilly turned and saw Natalie Sampson in her nightgown, walking towards them with a torch of her own. She looked as though she'd just woken up.

"What's going on?" she asked, stifling a yawn.

Sarah's face turned scarlet, and Lilly heard Joanne mutter, "Oh, Sarah," under her breath.

"Wait a minute," Natalie said, as the words Sarah had been shouting suddenly registered. "You thought I was in there? With your husband? I dropped off the towels hours ago, Sarah."

Sarah shook her head. "I... I thought you were. If you're not in there, why won't John answer me?"

"You thought I was having an affair with your husband? How dare you? How could you think such a thing?"

"I'm sorry," Sarah said tearfully. "Why won't he answer? I know he's in there." She resumed the banging on the door, shouting for John.

Lilly glanced at the number four artfully painted on the door, recalling John had gone in there to clean up after Morris had thrown soup at him. Had he not returned to his wife all night?

"Do you think something has happened?" Lilly whispered to Joanne and Robert.

"I don't know," Robert said. "Let me get the master key from reception and we'll find out."

He was gone less than a minute. He unlocked the door, only to find the security chain was in place.

"John, let us in," he shouted. When there was no reply, he rammed the door hard with his shoulder, breaking the chain and they all plunged inside.

John was laid out on the bed, multiple stab wounds apparent in his chest, blood seeping through his pajamas and onto the sheets below. Sarah screamed, her legs giving way as Dominic and Edward grabbed her and gently lowered her to the ground. Natalie shrieked and ran out of the room, collapsing in the hallway, back against the wall, in complete shock.

"John!" Robert cried out, dashing to the bed and pointlessly checking for vital signs. "He's... he's dead," he gasped, sharply pulling his hand away and turning in wide eyed shock to the others. "Dear god, what happened?"

"Looks as though someone has killed him," a voice said from the doorway, startling everyone.

Sam's eyes slowly took in the room as he observed the scene. Walking to the figure on the bed, he frowned. "Very recently too, by the looks of it."

"I'm going to call the police," Chloe said.

Sarah was sobbing. "I don't understand... what happened?"

Sam was now carefully walking around the room. Lilly watched as he tried the window. It didn't budge.

"The door was locked?" he asked the room at large. It was Fiona, from her place crouched by Sarah's side, who answered.

"Yes. Robert went for the master key then had to break it down when he discovered the security chain was in place."

Walter was pacing by the doorway. "Who would stab John?" he asked.

Sam shook his head. "I have a better question for you, Walter. How did someone manage to murder a man in a room that was locked from the inside?"

⸎

CHLOE CAME DASHING back into the room just as Sam's revelation hit home. Because the room wasn't in use for guests, the window had been locked and the key put safely in reception. The door had been locked from the inside. The key, Lilly saw, was sitting on the dresser to the left. The security chain had been put in place, presumably by John, in an attempt to keep everyone out. There was obviously no plausible way this could have been suicide, and considering the chaos the sheets were in, it appeared as though he'd been thrashing about in an attempt to defend himself from his attacker.

John had been murdered and the perpetrator had somehow then left a locked room. Lilly shook her head. It was utterly impossible.

Robert pulled the sheet over his brother-in-law as Chloe entered the room, not wanting her to be exposed to the gruesome scene any further.

"Dad, the landline is dead. I couldn't call the police," she said anxiously. "And there's no mobile signal or internet."

"All right, Chloe, thank you for trying," Robert said, glancing outside the window. "The storm is letting up a bit. If the phone lines are down one of us needs to get to town and bring the police back urgently."

"I'll go, Robert," Walter said immediately. "My jeep is much better in this weather than any of your smaller cars. It's likely the roads will be either washed out or slick with mud and the jeep will handle those better."

Robert nodded and clasped the man's shoulder. "Thank you, Walter. Come on, everyone, there's nothing more we can do here. We need to keep everything as it is for the police."

It was a stunned and very subdued crowd of people that made their way downstairs. Lilly was in disbelief that she had once again become embroiled in a murder investigation, and mentally made a note to arrange an appointment with Dr Jorgenson when she returned to Plumpton Mallet.

"Does anyone know what time it is?" she asked as they reached the lounge.

"About half-past three," Walter said, shrugging on his coat. "Wish me luck. It's still pretty bad out there."

"Please, be careful, Walter," Joanne said. "Don't take any risks and if you don't think you can make it turn round and come straight back."

"I promise, Joanne," he said. And taking a deep breath ventured out into the raging storm.

Lilly shuddered, imagining a roaring, violent sea churning below the cliff. One wrong turn or a loss of control on a slick road with practically no visibility, and Walter and his vehicle could easily go tumbling down into the water. It was dangerous outside, and she wondered if Walter's attempt to get to the police was foolhardy. Then she remembered the danger inside. She had to concentrate on what was happening here and hope Walter's driving experience, knowledge of the area and steadfastness would see him through.

"This is a nightmare," Sarah said, collapsing on the sofa. "I just can't believe it." She covered her face with her hands and shook her head, sobbing and trying to make sense of what had happened.

"Natalie, perhaps you'd be good enough to make us all some tea?" Sam said. "Hot and sweet for Sarah to help calm her nerves?"

For a second Natalie looked at him blankly. "There's no power?"

"A pan of water on the gas hob will work," he replied gently.

"Yes... yes, of course," she stammered. "I could do with one too. I can't stop shaking."

"Use the mint tea I brought with me, Natalie. It soothes the nerves."

"Could you help me, Lilly?"

"Of course."

The kitchen was a mess when they entered. After the altercation they'd witnessed between Morris and John, no one had remembered the soup and the hob and floor were drenched with the congealing mess.

Lilly started to clean it up while Natalie found a tray for the teapot and cups.

"Do you have any honey, Natalie? It's better than sugar."

"Yes, I'm sure we do. In the pantry. I'll go and look."

By the time Natalie came back with a jar of honey, which she put on the tray along with a spoon, Lilly had cleared up the mess and had put a pan of water on to boil.

"Are you all right, Natalie?"

"I'm not sure. I think so. Just... it's such a shock. I went from being accused of having an affair with a man, only to find him moments later murdered and covered in blood. It's a lot to take in. I'm not sure it has yet, it's unbelievable. Who would do such a thing?"

"You're doing well, Natalie. Take some deep breaths, it will help. If you don't mind me saying so, you seemed quite close to John."

Natalie wiped away a tear as she spooned mint leaves into the pot.

"If I'm honest, Sarah's accusation isn't completely without merit. John and I had become quite close recently, but not in the way Sarah suggested. Their marriage has been quite rocky, especially lately, and I think she was becoming paranoid. He wasn't the kindest of men, particularly to her, and I think her seeing him treat another woman respectfully and kindly wasn't easy. I should have kept my distance."

"I could tell their relationship had its difficulties," Lilly said, lifting the pan of boiling water and pouring it into the teapot.

With the kitchen clean and the tea made, the two women made their way back to the lounge and began to dispense the tea. Jack had now joined them. Robert had apparently heard his father stirring, having been awakened by the commotion, and had fetched him down to join the others. Lilly handed Jack his tea with a smile.

"Thank you, Daisy," he said politely.

"Close. It's Lilly," she said with a warm smile.

"Don't tease. I know you're my Daisy," Jack replied with a wag of his finger and a dazed look.

"Who is Daisy?" Lilly asked Robert quietly as she handed him a cup.

"An old girlfriend. Sorry about that, Lilly, he gets mixed up a lot nowadays."

"It's fine, Robert. I understand."

"Where's Morris?" Jack asked suddenly.

"He left last night, dad. You were here, remember?"

Jack looked momentarily confused. Then the frown turned to a vacant smile as he sipped his tea. All thoughts of Morris forgotten.

Sarah thanked Natalie and Lilly for the tea and sipped the drink slowly.

"Try to drink it all, Sarah," Fiona said.

"What the heck happened?" Robert asked, pacing back and forth. "And how? Like Sam said, the room was locked from the inside. How did someone get in there, stab John to death, then get out of the room?"

"Robert," said Joanne. "You're upsetting your sister."

"I'm all right, Joanne. It's just... well, I can't take it in, it seems unreal. Natalie, I am so sorry. I was out of line. I shouldn't have spoken to you the way I did. I wasn't thinking straight."

"There's no need to apologise, Sarah," Natalie said. "You were distraught. I honestly don't know what happened. I saw him a few hours before when I took him the towels. He seemed fine then. But what happened after that I just don't know."

They all sat quietly in the lounge sipping tea, each with their own thoughts. Trying to work out what happened and who was responsible. After about half an hour, the door opened and Walter walked in.

"It's bad news. I couldn't get to town. There are trees down all over the place and several have blocked the road. We're stuck here, I'm afraid."

❦

"YOU'RE KIDDING ME," Robert groaned, returning to his seat next to Joanne. "How bad is it, Walter?"

"As bad as it can be. I tried going around but got the jeep stuck in the mud. It took me twenty minutes to get it out again, and I was lucky. The other side is a sheer drop off the cliff, as you know. We won't be able to clear the trees until the storm dies down. It's just too dangerous."

"Thanks for trying, Walter," Robert said. "I'm glad you got back safely. That's the main thing."

"So," Chloe said from her position next to her father. "Let me get this straight. We've got a body upstairs, murdered in a room locked from the inside, no mobile phone service, the landline is down, the police can't get here and we're trapped. Trapped with someone who killed John. Have I got all that right?"

Lilly immediately noticed a change in the atmosphere as the tension began to build. There was silence as everyone glanced suspiciously at each other, attempting to read reactions to Chloe's succinct summary of their predicament. It was true, they were trapped with a killer among them. And a clever one at that. Lilly was still getting over the shock of seeing John's dead body and she didn't even know him. She could only imagine what everyone else was thinking.

Suddenly a comment was made. Lilly didn't even know who had said it, but that was the fuse that lit the room on fire. Soon everyone was shouting accusations at one another, long held grudges, for every perceived slight, innocent or not, were dredged up and aired. Even Lilly was accused. She realised she needed to try to solve this mystery quickly before everything got out of hand and the damage to this family ended up being beyond repair. Looking at them all, she could hardly believe this was the same fun-loving group of people from the day before.

"But, Sarah," Natalie was protesting, "I already told you I didn't hurt him. How can accuse me again?"

"Well, you heard Walter, we are trapped here with a killer. It could be any one of us, including you," Sarah said, looking at Joanne for help. But Lilly could see she'd get no help there. Joanne was distraught herself, looking at her family with tears in her eyes and shock on her face.

Lilly walked over, and taking Natalie by the arm, gently guided her away from Sarah. There was a possibility this could get physical, and that was the last thing Lilly wanted to happen.

"And you," Sarah suddenly said to Lilly. "You had no right to speak to John the way you did tonight. You didn't know him. He was a wonderful husband. In fact, none of you really knew him. All of you are suspects as far as I'm concerned."

Lilly took a deep breath and held her tongue. Sarah had been through a lot this evening and it was natural she should lash out. It was also natural that at the moment she should only remember the good times rather than the violence and the abuse. She was in denial. Lilly moved to the outer edges of the family group. The better to observe. Straight heads prevailed in situations like this and she knew she must remain calm. Dominic and his brother looked to be arguing. She wondered what it was about, but going over to find out meant walking past Sarah, who was just getting into her stride.

Lilly remained in the shadows, pondering what to do as she watched another argument break out between them all.

Chapter Seven

AS LILLY WATCHED Sarah stretch to put her tea on the table, her sleeve moved and once again revealed the bruise she had noticed earlier. She realised now, due to the colouration, it was at least a few days old and she was almost certain it had been John who had been the cause. Could Sarah have been the one to kill her husband having had enough of the abuse? If that was the case, then she was doing an excellent job of acting as the bereaved wife. And how did she get out of the room?

Dominic and Edward had stopped arguing and were looking miserably at the others. Robert and Walter were discussing a plan to remove the obstructions in the road, allowing them to get to the police. And Fiona and Joanne were now trying to comfort Sarah, who was sobbing. She looked worn out and beaten down, the reality of John's death having just hit home. Pain and guilt were the next stages of grief. Natalie was standing to one side, alone and upset.

But there was one person missing.

In her peripheral vision, she saw movement and turned to find Chloe sneaking upstairs. Quietly, Lilly followed. Chloe was undoubtedly mature for her age, but she was only sixteen and still impressionable. The last place she should be was in the room with the body.

Lilly got to the top of the stairs just in time to see Chloe sneak into room four. She hurried down the hallway and stepped over the threshold.

"Chloe!" she hissed, causing the girl to jump. A guilty look on her face.

"Oh, hi."

"What are you doing in this room? Your father would be furious if he knew you'd sneaked in here. What do you think you're playing at?"

"I know, but please, Lilly, just let me explain."

Lilly looked at her for a moment, then gave a small nod. "Go on."

"Well, I thought I might be able to find something that could tell us who stabbed John. I mean, no one even looked round the room, did they? Everyone was just shocked and crying and stuff. Then we all left. I thought it would be a good idea to see if I could find some clues."

"Chloe, this isn't a game."

"I know it's not," she said, glancing quickly at the bed. "But you have experience and I know you can't be the murderer because you didn't even know him. I've read about the last two murders you solved. They were in the Plumpton

Mallet Gazette. What you did was amazing. Don't you want to try to solve this too? It could be ages until the police can get here. I could be your Watson!" she finished, eyes shining with the expectation.

"I'm not Sherlock Holmes, for goodness' sake. I'm a former agony aunt who now owns a tea shop. The cases you're talking about were mainly dumb luck, and I nearly got myself in dreadful trouble, as well as injured. I'm not a detective, Chloe, this is serious and we really need to leave it to the professionals."

Lilly was trying to work out how to get Chloe out of the room. If Robert happened to come upstairs and see them in the room together, he would be furious. And who would get the brunt of the blame? The impressionable teenager or the middle-aged adult who should know better?

"I know it's serious, that's why I came up here. No one else is doing anything except arguing and blaming each other. It's a complete nightmare downstairs. This is a total mystery, Lilly. A murderer gets away with killing someone inside a locked room and then vanishes. Please, can't we just have a quick look round and see if we can find something that would help? I've already seen the body, so it's not like you're shielding me from anything. And dad has already covered him up. Please, the quicker you help me, the quicker we can leave."

"Oh, for heavens' sake," Lilly muttered, both annoyed and reluctantly admiring the emotional blackmail. "Five minutes and no more. And if someone comes we leave quickly. Deal?"

"Deal," Chloe said with a serious nod.

Lilly sighed. She didn't know if she wanted them to find a significant clue or not. But Chloe was right, they needed to do something. The family was tearing strips off one another downstairs.

<center>ceeleo</center>

*T*HEY SET TO with earnest and started searching the room for anything, no matter how small, that might help them work out who the perpetrator was. Lilly didn't want Chloe anywhere near the body, so suggested she started by searching the dresser. With no guests in residence, there wasn't much in it, but Lilly was impressed by Chloe's methodical and diligent approach. She removed all the drawers, checking through the meagre contents, upended them to see if anything was stuck to the base, and looked inside the empty carcass in case something had fallen inside. There was nothing. She then moved to the wardrobe and searched it just as assiduously, but once more came up empty-handed.

Lilly searched the bedside tables and a built-in bookcase, but she too came away with nothing to show for her efforts.

"So, how did you solve your other two cases?" Chloe asked.

"They weren't my cases, but the first, like I said, was more luck than anything. I just had a feeling it wasn't the suicide the police thought it was. The second one, with some considerable help I might add, I managed to work out what the murder weapon was, which led me in the right direction."

"So we need to find the murder weapon, don't we? That would be a good start. Do you think the killer left it behind?"

"I really don't know, Chloe. It seems unlikely to me, but I suppose it would depend on how much of rush they were in and how careless. Especially if they were disturbed."

Before Lilly could stop her, Chloe rushed for the bed. She could almost hear Robert blaming her for Chloe's subsequent nightmares, but she was already too late. The girl was on her hands and knees, searching underneath.

"Wow! Look, I found something."

As it turned out, the murder weapon had indeed been left behind, thrown or kicked under the bed.

"Don't touch it, Chloe! There will be fingerprints on it. Let me find something you can use."

Lilly dashed into the bathroom and tore off a length of toilet paper, which she handed to Chloe.

"Here, use this and very carefully."

Chloe did as instructed and pushed the weapon into the open by the top edge of the pommel. Lilly could see it was a dagger of some sort, still bloodied from recent use. At the top of the blade, just below the quillon, was an engraved royal emblem; crossed swords, a crown, and a lion displayed prominently.

"An army knife?" Chloe breathed in awe.

Lilly had to agree. It was definitely military and most likely army.

"Chloe, did your granddad have this or any other army knives displayed around The Palms where someone could have just helped themselves?"

Lilly picked the knife up by the cross-guard using the paper and carefully laid it on the bedside table.

Chloe stepped closer and shook her head. "Not that I know of. I've never seen one before. But granddad wasn't the only one in the army, was he? Maybe Morris had one?"

"Morris said he was going home last night," Lilly said. "I thought all the staff lived in?"

"They do. Morris does as well most of the time, but he also has his own place in town. I think he meant he was going there." Chloe turned toward the bed and suddenly let out a gasp.

"What is it?"

Chloe reached toward the bed, and very carefully lifting up the pillow, gingerly extracting a pair of women's briefs; bright pink with black polka dots. She dropped them on the floor and looked at Lilly, aghast. "Aunt Sarah was right. He was having an affair."

While Chloe went to the bathroom to wash her hands, Lilly used her phone to take pictures of the evidence they had found so far. Thinking about the knife made Lilly sad. Morris seemed like such a nice man, very good to Jack and a hardworking and loyal member of staff. But it was John that had made Morris furious enough to leave. Had he been so angry he'd come back and killed him? She hoped not, but if there was anything her recent experiences had taught her, it was to keep an open mind.

She went to see how Chloe was doing.

"You okay, Watson?" she asked, eliciting a small smile.

The girls shrugged. "Yeah, I'm fine."

"You know we can stop and leave this to police, Chloe. We've found evidence that we can pass on and let the authorities do their job."

"No, we need to keep going. We will solve it. I know we will. We have to."

"Maybe, but you need to understand you might not like what we find out. Someone in this house is responsible, Chloe. If it's not a member of staff, then it has to be a member of your family. That's going to be traumatic enough without getting involved. If we carry on and find the evidence we need, we will ultimately be responsible for unmasking a killer. The last thing I want is for you to get hurt, and I don't think you're fully prepared to deal with the fallout."

"I am, honestly. I know it's someone here, but whoever it is has to answer for what they've done, don't they? And if we can find out who it is, then maybe everyone will stop blaming each other."

The girl had a steely look in her eye, which Lilly recognised. She was not going to back down from investigating. If Lilly didn't help her, then she'd just do it on her own. The best Lilly could do was be with her and support her along the way. No matter what they found out.

"Yes, they do. All right, we'll keep going, but any time it gets too much you must tell me and we'll stop. Do you promise me?"

Chloe nodded. "I promise, Lilly."

"All right. Now, let's get out of this room and decide what to do next."

409

"SO, WE'VE FOUND the murder weapon," Chloe said once they were back in the hall. "It's an army one, so either belongs to granddad or Morris. Granddad doesn't live here so I don't think it's his, and he's really ill and in a wheelchair. I also don't think he would have kept his knife here. Why would he? So I think it belongs to Morris."

"Well, Morris left last night before it happened," Lilly said. "So, who would have been able to get hold of his dagger?"

"Anyone with access to the rooms the staff live in. Which is pretty much everyone in this house."

"All right, while everyone is arguing downstairs, perhaps you and I could do a little snooping?" Lilly suggested, coming round to the idea of letting the girl help. She'd found both the murder weapon and a rather telling piece of evidence, so clearly had a keen eye as well as a determination to solve the crime. "Maybe we can see if there is anything that would indicate a quick clean up? Whoever stabbed John must have got blood on them so would have had to clean up quickly in order to get back into the hall with the rest of us. I just wish I could remember where everyone was standing, then perhaps we could work out who turned up without us noticing. But everything happened so quickly."

"Whoever it was must have killed him and got back to the hall without any blood on them or we'd have seen it. Having to do it in a rush means they could have made a mistake. There might be blood in one of the bathrooms. Come on, let's go," said Chloe.

Lilly followed Chloe to the rear of the building where the owner and employee suites were situated.

"I think we should check Natalie's room first."

"Why?" Lilly asked.

"Because it's obvious John was having an affair. It's not going to be with Joanne, so she's the only one left. But besides that, no one got along with him apart from Natalie. You must have seen the way they were with each other?"

Lilly nodded.

Reaching Natalie Sampson's room, Chloe turned the door handle but found it locked.

"We'll have to find a key," Lilly started to say before Chloe produced one from her pocket. It looked to be a master that would open all the doors in an emergency.

"Are you supposed to have that, Chloe?"

She grinned. "Nope."

Natalie's room was beautifully decorated in an ornate French style. Very feminine in blue pastel shades with cream, antique style furniture and numerous gilt-edged mirrors.

"Does it have an en-suite?" Lilly asked.

"Yes, just through there," Chloe said, pointing to a door on the left of the stunning hand decorated walnut double bed.

"I'll start there and see if there's any sign of blood. See what you can find in here."

The bathroom was relatively small, with a white suite. Lilly checked the bath, sink and shower but there were no tell tale red spots anywhere. Nothing in the waste paper bin or in the laundry basket. The cupboards above and below the sink revealed nothing more than cleaning products and cosmetics. There was no tell tale smell of bleach or other disinfectant. This was not the room where an urgent clean up had happened.

"I've found something," Chloe called out, and Lilly entered the main room to find her holding up a pink bra with black polka dots. A perfect match to the underwear they'd found under John's pillow. "It looks like Aunt Sarah was right after all."

Lilly took a photo with her phone. "So it's probable Natalie was in the room with John last night."

"Maybe they had a fight or something and she killed him?"

"But that doesn't explain how she came to have Morris's knife or how she managed to get out of a room that was locked from the inside."

"Yeah," Chloe said, frowning. "And she came up behind us in the hall, remember? If she killed John, she would have had to find a way to lock the room and get out without any of us seeing her. It's impossible. How could she have done it?"

"I think I may have the answer," a voice said from the doorway, causing Chloe and Lilly to nearly jump out of their skins. They spun round to find Sam leaning nonchalantly against the door frame.

"For crying out loud, Sam," Lilly said, breathing heavily and willing her heart to slow down.

"Sorry, I didn't mean to startle you. I've been thinking about how this could have been accomplished, and I believe I have the answer."

"You do?" Chloe said.

"Come with me," Sam said. "And be prepared for a surprise."

*L*ILLY AND CHLOE exchanged quizzical glances, but followed Sam down the hall. The opposite way to room four.

"Um, you know, John was killed in the room the other way?" Chloe said.

"Yes, I'm aware of that. But I believe Natalie exited the room from here," Sam replied, stopping in front of a large built-in bookcase.

"What?" Chloe and Lilly said together.

Sam pulled one of the lower shelves, and they all heard an audible click. The entire shelving unit then slid into the wall, leaving an opening into a tunnel. It was a door. Lilly's jaw dropped.

"A secret door!" Chloe gasped in excitement. "Oh, wow! I had no idea this was here. This place has been in my family since before I was born. How come I never knew about this?"

Sam smiled. "Like I said, this place has many secrets. I discovered it when I was a child, much younger than you Chloe. Long before your granddad bought the place." He walked inside, and Lilly and Chloe followed.

It was only a short passage and ended with another bookshelf which opened up like a regular door into room number four.

"This is amazing," Chloe said. "So this is how she did it. Natalie had some sort of argument with John. She stabbed him, but probably heard Aunt Sarah shouting and banging on the door, so slipped into this passage, cleaned up somewhere and then came walking up behind us looking like she'd just woken up."

"It's certainly a possibility," Sam said. "Although it's too early to say for sure without any proper proof."

"Well, let's go and see what she has to say about her underwear being in here, then," Chloe said, dashing back through the passage.

"Chloe, wait!" Lilly said, as she and Sam hurried after her.

The others were all still in the lounge arguing when Chloe marched up to Natalie, pointing an accusing finger.

"We know what happened. She killed John."

"Chloe," Robert admonished. "You can't just go around accusing people of murder."

Lilly bit her lip to keep from pointing out that this was exactly what he and the others had been doing for the last hour.

"There is some possible evidence," Sam said calmly. "Perhaps you could let Chloe explain?"

Robert and Joanne exchanged worried glances. Sarah got up from where she'd been sitting. "I would certainly like to hear what she has to say."

"We found your underwear under John's pillow," Chloe said. Natalie's face went white. "We know it's yours because we found the matching bra in your room."

"I knew it!" Sarah spat. "You were having an affair with my husband."

"I... we... No..." Natalie stammered as Sarah launched herself at the shaking woman and slapped her across the face. Immediately a hand shaped red welt began to bloom across Natalie's cheek.

Fiona dashed over to her friend and grabbed her arm. "Don't, Sarah. She's not worth it. And you're better than that."

Robert inserted himself between Natalie and his sister. "Calm down, Sarah. We don't know exactly what's been going on as yet."

"Natalie," Lilly said, turning to the shaken housekeeper. "Now is not the time to deny the affair. Someone killed John last night and at the moment you're the prime suspect because we know you were in the room with him."

"But I didn't kill him. Yes, we were having an affair, I'm sorry. But he was alive when I left. I promise."

"I don't believe you," Sarah yelled. "Why should I? You've been lying about the affair you could easily be lying about killing him. You're sacked. When this storm clears, I want you to pack your belongings and get out."

"Sacked?" Natalie cried and turned to Robert, expecting him to come to her defense.

"I'm sorry, Natalie, but I agree with Sarah. We can't keep you on after this. But if you are responsible, then you'll need to stay until the police can get here."

"But I didn't kill him. How could I the room was locked? And you all saw me arrive in the hall."

"That's a good point," Joanne said.

"We worked that out too," Chloe said. "There's a secret door and a passageway. You knew about it, didn't you, Natalie?"

Natalie covered her eyes and, after what seemed like an age, gave a slight nod. "But he was alive when I left. I swear."

"A secret door? Chloe, what are you talking about?" her father asked.

"Come on, I'll show you," she said, leading everyone upstairs.

Jack was left sitting in his wheelchair in front of the fire, oblivious to what was going on around him.

Once again, a flock of people descended on room four. Lilly noticed Sarah remained in the open doorway where she could still hear what was being said, but as far away as she could be from the body of her husband. Chloe showed them the bookshelf that led along a passage to the one out in the hall.

"So, I think Natalie had some sort of fight with John and stabbed him. Then left through the passage, making it appear as though she was never here," Chloe explained.

Natalie was still white and shaking but Lilly now noticed beneath the fear anger was beginning to show.

"I didn't do it. How many more times must I tell you. Yes, I slept with him, but he was alive when I left. I heard Sarah in the hall and used the passage to leave. I'm sorry I didn't mention it before, but I was terrified you'd accuse me of killing him. Just like you are now."

"I've worked here for years," Robert said. "How is it I didn't know about this passage? How did you even find it?"

"Your father showed it to me when he hired me," Natalie said. "Before his accident."

"I'm shocked at your behaviour, Natalie," Walter said.

"Oh, be quiet, Walter. I'm not the only one who knew about the passage." She turned, looking pointedly at Dominic and Edward. "I know Jack showed you two the secret doors, yet neither of you bothered to say anything when John was found. So why the silence?"

"Now wait a minute! I hope you're not trying to lay the blame for John's murder on my sons, Natalie Sampson?"

Fiona said angrily. "You're just trying to weasel your way out of this. You were sleeping with John. You were the last one to see him alive. You've got a motive. What happened? Did John try to break it off with you so you decided to kill him?"

"Let's all just take a deep breath and calm down, shall we?" Sam said in a firm tone. "I'd like to point out another piece of evidence which Chloe found. If you turn your attention to the bedside cabinet, you'll notice the murder weapon. An army dagger. Now why would Natalie have had that on her? How would she have come to be in possession of that knife? Robert, perhaps you could identify it?"

The room grew quiet as Robert made his way over to the dagger. "I remember dad having something like this when we were children. But I honestly can't say if this is his or not. I haven't seen it in years. It's definitely an army knife though. Perhaps it belongs to Morris? Sarah," he turned to his sister. "Could you have a look?"

From the doorway, Sarah shook her head. "I don't want to come in, Robert. But I wouldn't recognise it, anyway."

"Could your father identify it?" Sam asked. "As belonging to either him or Morris?"

Robert shook his head sadly. "I really don't know. The times when he is lucid are rare now. He can't walk anymore, can't dress himself. He doesn't know what's going on around him or even what day it is. He doesn't have long left, Sam. Even if we caught him on a good day and he did identify it, how would we know what he says is true? His judgment and recollections just aren't reliable. We could try I suppose, but we couldn't take what he said as fact."

Lilly had been aware of Edward's awkward shuffling since they'd entered the room. She had the feeling he was trying and failing to keep his mouth shut about something. She was proved right a moment later.

"You know, Walter knew about the passage too."

Walter glared at him, but remained silent.

"What?" Sarah said from the door. "You mean all the staff knew about this but never bothered to tell us, the owners?"

"It's always been kept as a staff secret," Walter admitted. "The Palms has been through a lot of owners over the years, as well as staff. I was told of it by Eliza, the housekeeper who retired before Natalie took over. It was her grandmother, who also worked here, I believe, who showed it to her when she was a little girl. The previous owners never knew about it either. In the olden days staff were supposed to be seen and not heard. It was a way of hiding if guests were in the hallway, or a shortcut to room four for cleaning. Many old hotels and grand houses have them."

"As I said," Sam whispered to Lilly. "There are quite a few secrets here at The Palms."

Chapter Eight

ODDLY, AS NIGHT spilled into morning and the first signs of dawn appeared outside, the tensions began to rise rather than fall. Lilly had expected everyone to begin to calm down through sheer fatigue, if nothing else, but the opposite was true. The discovery of the affair and the secret doors had added to the strain and Lilly, as an outsider looking in, could see it clearly. Unfortunately, Natalie Sampson, having now lost her job, was forced to stay as they were trapped. Trapped with a murderer and a corpse. Her presence was making the others, not least of all Sarah, irrational and resentful. It was a powder keg of emotional pressure just waiting to blow.

As the sun began to rise, a plan was worked out to attempt to clear the road in order to gain access to the town. The consensus had been that the local council were, in all likelihood, dealing with several clear ups around the area and were making the busier roads a priority. The single track up to The Palms wouldn't be high on the list, even if the authorities realised the access road was impassable. A quick check revealed the telephone lines were still down so they couldn't even call anyone to let them know.

After breakfast, leaving Chloe behind to take care of her granddad, the rest of the able-bodied adults left with various tools to help make the job easier. Armed with a couple of chainsaws, axes, handsaws and hefty ropes, they loaded up the vehicles and set off.

Lilly had thrown on a pair of jeans and a sweatshirt. Luckily, she'd found a pair of old walking boots in the back of her car. She was to accompany Walter in his jeep, the interior of which was redolent with fuel from the can in the boot for the chainsaws. Before they'd even travelled for five minutes, she felt a headache coming on and opened the window for much needed fresh air.

"You seem to enjoy your work here, Walter," Lilly said as he pulled out of the immediate property grounds, leading the convoy.

"I do. Very much," he said, concentrating on the road. It was littered with fallen branches and assorted debris, making the journey a slow one. "They are a good family to work for. I'm relatively new compared to the others. I didn't start working here until after Jack got hurt falling from a ladder."

"Yes, you mentioned that," Lilly said. "It sounded traumatic not just for Jack but for the whole family. How bad was it?"

"He hurt his back quite badly, from what I understand. But he also suffered from a head injury of some sort. It was before the Alzheimer's set in. I often wonder if that was the starts of it. It's not my place to ask though. I'm sure the family looked into the possibilities of head trauma. Robert and Sarah and Jack's wife have looked after him well. If I'm honest, I was hoping to see him looking better this time after he started the new treatment, but if anything he seems worse. It's a real shame to see a man with such vigor and vitality as I'm told Jack had, reduced to a mere shell of himself. He was always such good company, apparently."

They remained silent for a while as Walter concentrated on navigating the hazardous road, then Lilly asked Walter just how bad the blockage they were attempting to clear actually was.

"It looked pretty bad last night, but with the rain lashing down and the wind it was difficult to tell. But you're just about to find out. We're here."

They parked on the left of the road, the other two cars stopping behind them. Strewn right across the road were two enormous oak trees, completely wrenched free of the ground, a mass of tangled roots, some as thick as a man, exposed to the air. To the left was the dense wood the trees had once been part of, and to the right the cliff dropping down to the sea below. Lilly could see there was no way any sort of vehicle could drive round them. So armed with the tools they'd brought, the group started to cut the trees into more manageable pieces, which could then be dragged or carried to the verge.

An hour later, hot, sweaty and itching, there wasn't much to show for all their hard work. The trees didn't seem any smaller than they had when they'd arrived. It was going to be a very long job.

"You'd have thought the council would have sent someone up here to clear the road by now," Edward said, swinging an axe.

"We're too far out," Robert said. "I doubt anyone even knows there's a problem up here."

"It could take days for us to clear all this," Fiona said, voicing Lilly's thoughts.

A few more days trapped in a bed-and-breakfast with a murderer was an horrendous thought. There must be a way to get to town and get help, Lilly thought.

"Is it too far to walk into town?" she asked.

"I wouldn't try it," Fiona said. "Who knows what the road ahead looks like? Or the wood for that matter. These trees won't be the only ones to have come down. Besides, you'd end up walking in the dark. It's too dangerous even for those of us who know the area well."

"And we couldn't get a vehicle through those woods?"

"Not on your life," Sarah said, dragging a coil of rope from Walter's jeep. "It's full of massive rocks, gullies and streams. Not to mention the amount of mud there'll be considering the storm."

Lilly realised just how right Sarah was when she stepped into the woodland and sunk up to her ankles. But she was determined to find a way. She wanted to get the police to the house as soon as possible. They were all on edge, with a killer among them. No one felt safe and everyone was leery of the others, which could spill over into something far more serious the longer it went on.

Sleuthing with Chloe had turned up some clues, but they had provided more questions than answers. Freeing her boots from the mire, she decided to go a little deeper into the wood in the hopes the mud would thin out a bit considering the protection of the overhead canopy. She was right, the ground was more solid, but it was still slick and she found herself sliding several times but luckily managed to stay upright by grabbing onto the underbrush. Her immediate goal was to try to get to the other side of the fallen oaks. If they could tackle the obstruction from both sides, it might make the whole job quicker.

She'd not gone too far in when she saw a sight that made her heart skip a beat. In the midst of the trees was an overturned vehicle.

"Robert. Joanne. Everyone!" she shouted, scrambling to get to the car she recognised. "It's Morris, he's in trouble."

ﬗﬗﬗ

*L*ILLY CLAMBERED TO the driver's side of the car, but Morris was nowhere to be seen.

"Oh no, Morris," Dominic cried, first at the scene of the accident.

The rest caught up quickly and with no sign of Morris, began to spread out and shout for him.

"He must have driven straight off the road in the storm and hit that tree," Joanne said, close to tears. "I told him it was too dangerous to go out. He could be lying in the woods somewhere hurt. Or worse. Is there any blood in the car?"

"I don't see any blood," Robert said. "But the windscreen is smashed in, and the driver's side window. We need to find him. He must be lying hurt somewhere after the impact."

Lilly froze. "Maybe not," she said as a sickening thought occurred to her. Everyone turned to face her.

"The dagger," Natalie gasped.

"Did Morris know about the secret passage?" Robert demanded.

"Yes," Dominic said. "All the staff knew about it."

"If Morris made his way back..." Joanne said, unable to finish the sentence.

"Oh my god, Chloe!" Robert cried, spinning on his heel and scrambling back to the road as fast as the conditions would allow.

Everyone else followed, hurrying to their vehicles. Lilly jumped into Walter's jeep as he gunned the engine, spun the car around, and sped up the road just behind Robert and Joanne.

"You don't think Morris killed John, do you?" Walter asked frantically. "He's a nice old man, I just can't imagine him killing someone like that."

Lilly wasn't sure, but the evidence, circumstantial as it was, didn't look good.

"He had a bad altercation with John last night, and it was his dagger we found. You know how loyal he is to Jack, Walter. I don't know either of them, but it's apparent even to me how much Morris cares for Jack. Maybe he thought he was defending him. He said he owed his life to him, remember?"

Walter shook his head in despair as he pulled up in front of The Palms.

"Yes, he and Jack were close, like brothers, in fact," he said, opening the door and jumping out. "But to kill someone over, what? A foul mouth and a bad attitude?"

"Let's not jump to conclusions just yet, Walter. We've no proof it was Morris. We don't even know where he is yet."

Walter nodded, and they both ran inside, just behind the others, listening as Robert called out his daughter's name.

Inside, Lilly was relieved to find Chloe and her grand-dad sitting at the dining table tucking into sandwiches and fruit juice.

"What's going on?" Chloe asked, eyes wide as everyone charged into the room.

Robert grabbed his daughter and gave her a hug, exhaling with relief.

"Dad, what's happened?"

He let her go and sank into a chair next to her. "It's Morris, Chloe. He crashed his car in the woods not long after he left here last night. We found the car but there's no sign of him."

"Morris," Jack said dreamily. "Where's Morris?"

"I don't know, Dad," Robert said. "He's missing."

The group decided the best thing to do would be split up and search the house, then the outbuildings. Dominic, Edward and Fiona took one half of the ground floor, Walter, Natalie and Sam the other half, while Robert, Joanne and Sarah went upstairs. Lilly was going to join in the search upstairs, but Robert asked if she would stay and keep an eye on Jack and Chloe, a task she was more than happy to do.

While she sat and ate the sandwich Chloe had made for her, Lilly thought about Morris. If he'd staged the accident and doubled back to the house during the night, he could easily have killed John, then disappeared with no one being any the wiser. He knew the house like the back of his hand, having worked there for so long, including the secret passageway. The murder weapon looked to be his, and his argument with John certainly gave him a motive. John was not well liked by anyone, but he had been particularly disparaging towards Morris and had obviously pushed him too far.

The question was, where had he gone?

*L*ILLY HADN'T REALISED how long it had been while her thoughts whirled with the murder until Chloe spoke. She'd been wondering if it really was Morris who was guilty.

"You're not convinced it was Morris who killed John, are you?"

She smiled. The girl was adept at reading her thoughts.

"I'm just worried we're trying to fit the person to what we know rather than having proof. It's dangerous to do that, Chloe. It could ruin lives. We have no evidence to speak of and the facts as we know them could easily fit Natalie as well as Morris. It's all pure conjecture at this point."

"But Morris is missing."

"I know, but he could be hurt and found shelter somewhere. There's nothing to say he came back here at all. The opposite, actually. For one, I've noticed the stairs make quite loud creaking sounds when anyone is on them. Surely someone would have heard them if Morris had come back? Especially in the dead of night when every little noise sounds louder."

"But there was a massive storm outside. Really loud. Maybe it covered it up?"

"Okay. But Natalie was in there with John not long before he was killed. Do you think Morris was really lurking in the shadows, waiting for her to leave? It would take someone a lot braver than me to kill someone in a room while we were all outside the door."

"He could have hidden in the passage."

"Perhaps. But it would have been cutting it extremely fine, considering that was the way Natalie left the room. And what about the mud?"

"What mud?"

"Exactly. I've been down to where his car was crashed, Chloe. The place is like a quagmire. It would have been much worse last night. If Morris sneaked back in, surely there would have been signs of mud and water. Yet there's nothing."

"I suppose," Chloe said, munching her sandwich thoughtfully. "But he could have cleaned up or got changed before he came in. John made him really angry last night with something he said about granddad. They never liked talking about the war. Maybe something happened that John knew about and he brought it up when they were in the kitchen?"

Lilly sighed. "I wonder if anyone else overheard the argument? Morris said it was the derogatory way he spoke about your granddad, but he didn't really go into any detail, did he?"

Chloe shook her head.

There were sounds of footsteps filtering through to the dining room and Lilly realised everyone was gathering in the lounge.

"Give me a minute, Chloe," Lilly said, rising.

"I'll make some more sandwiches. I'm sure everyone will be getting hungry by now."

Lilly nodded. "That's a good idea."

⚬⚬⚬

AS LILLY ENTERED the lounge, she could immediately see everyone had broken off into groups. Sarah, Fiona, Dominic and Edward were seated together on the sofa. Robert and Joanne had separated themselves and were in deep discussion in a couple of armchairs. Sam was on his own, seated in front of the fireplace, occasionally jabbing the embers with the poker. And Natalie and Walter were standing in a corner whispering. Lilly felt drawn to them. As staff members, she wondered if their insight and perspective might be different to that of the family.

"Morris wasn't to be found, then?" she asked.

Natalie shook her head.

"I'm wondering if he managed to make it back to town somehow last night," Walter said. "And we're jumping to conclusions."

"Please, Walter," Natalie said. "I've finally got everyone off my back. Let's not give them a reason to start accusing me again."

"You were found in John's room," Lilly said pointedly. "Did you see anything in the passage when you left?"

Natalie's face turned crimson, and she shook her head. "No. But honestly, I was in a rush. That's part of the reason why I had to leave my underwear behind. I didn't have time to look. I was worried about getting caught. When I got back into the hall, I immediately came round the corner to greet all of you. I wanted to make sure I was seen outside the room by Sarah. I knew she didn't know about the passage, and even though I was aware Dominic and Edward knew about it, I was hoping it wouldn't occur to them. I had no choice but to pray they wouldn't bring it up."

"I'm surprised no one at all thought to bring up the secret route to room four," Lilly said, looking at Walter. "What's your excuse, Walter? You could have mentioned it the moment Natalie appeared from that direction, or at least when we found out John was dead. Instead it took Sam, a guest, pointing it out to Chloe and me, while you, Edward and Dominic remained silent. At least Natalie had a genuine reason not to say anything, since she was trying to keep her relationship with John under wraps."

"Yes, well, my job is outside, as you know, Lilly," Walter replied, testily. "I've no reason to be in that part of the house. In all the years I've been here I've used it maybe twice, and that was when I was first shown it. To be honest, I'd forgotten it existed until last night. My first assumption was the same as everyone else's, that Natalie had just been woken up because of all the shouting. I didn't for one minute think she was having an affair with John." He glanced at Natalie as he said this. "I thought better of you, Natalie."

Natalie averted her eyes. "It's not one of my finer moments, and believe me I bitterly regret it now."

"I should think so. Especially with John, of all people. You can do better than that. So could Sarah, truth be told," said Walter.

"No one here seems to think very highly of John," Lilly said. "Except perhaps you, Natalie."

Natalie scowled. "I'm not talking about it anymore. I'll go and make us some lunch."

Lilly was about to tell her Chloe was already doing it when Natalie stormed off in the direction of the kitchen.

"I thought she had more sense than to get involved with the likes of John," Walter sighed, shaking his head.

"You didn't happen to hear any of the argument between Morris and John last night, did you? I know Morris mentioned it was about Jack, but he didn't say much more."

"No, I didn't hear them, but if it involved Jack, I can take a good guess."

"A regular argument?"

Walter nodded. "I'm surprised John hadn't tried harder to convince Sarah and Robert to sack Morris. Usually he got his own way, but they held onto the old man for Jack's sake."

"Why would John be so keen to get rid of Morris?" Lilly asked, intrigued. "Was he a bad cook?"

"No, nothing like that. Quite the opposite, he was a wonderful cook."

"Then why did John want him to leave so badly?"

Walter grew quiet. Then taking her arm pulled her as far away from the group as he could and lowered his voice.

"Listen, I don't know for sure what happened the day Jack fell from the ladder, but Morris... well... he had his suspicions."

Lilly felt a cold shiver down her back.

"Go on. What do you know, Walter?"

"I wasn't working here at the time, but Morris once told me in confidence he was convinced John had deliberately pushed Jack off that ladder."

Chapter Nine

"WHAT?" LILLY SAID, shocked. "Are you sure, Walter?"

"John, Morris and Jack were the only ones there that day, from what I understand," Walter said. "Jack was at the top of the ladder working on the guttering. John was standing on the roof itself, replacing broken tiles, and Morris told me he and John were having some sort of argument. The next thing Morris knew, Jack was on the ground. He didn't actually see it happen, but sort of sensed it, so he told me. He'd turned and saw Jack hit the ground, saw an instant look of satisfaction on John's face when he glanced up. But it was only for a split second. He didn't actually see John push Jack, so couldn't prove it. Jack hit his head hard and was rushed to hospital. When he regained consciousness, he couldn't remember anything at all about what had happened."

"What about you, Walter? Do you think John was capable of pushing his father-in-law off a ladder from that height? He could have killed him."

Walter shrugged. "I'm not committing one way or the other. But I will say we're all better off without John in our lives. He treated all of us dreadfully, especially poor Sarah. She's in shock and upset now, but she'll come round and see him for the abuser he was in time. I can't believe Robert put up with him for so long. If he'd been married to my sister, I would have dealt with him a long time ago."

"Walter..."

He held his hands up in defense. "I didn't do anything, it's not my place. Nor do I think it would be the right thing to do. All I'm saying is John seriously mistreated Sarah and if she wouldn't or couldn't do anything about it... well, maybe Robert should have."

Lilly sighed. This was becoming more and more complicated, but she understood Walter's sentiments. As a former agony aunt she'd received letters from abused spouses and knew the long term emotional, mental and physical damage it caused.

"Walter, John is dead, so whether he pushed Jack or not is a moot point now. Can't you tell me in confidence what you think? Did John really push Jack?"

"No, I can't, but Morris certainly thought so, and he loves Jack. He's been holding onto pent-up rage over the incident for years. Maybe it just came to a head this weekend? It doesn't really matter whether John pushed Jack, what matters is that Morris believed he did. And with Jack out of the way, Robert and Sarah would get this place. Which ultimately they did."

"You think that's what it was about?"

"It wouldn't surprise me. You know, John was the one who originally hired me and that's been a problem. He's been holding it over my head from day one, subtly threatening me whenever he got the chance. Letting me know he could sack me at any time. It was a power thing with him. I think that's why he sacked Edward. He wanted the staff to know that if he could get rid of a member of Joanne's family, when she's married to one of the owners, then he could do it to any of us."

"You certainly paint an appalling picture of him, Walter."

"That's how he was. I miss the days when he only came up occasionally. I could stay out of the way then. It wasn't until Joanne came on board that he suddenly wanted to be involved with the business. He didn't like the idea of a new in-law, especially a woman, having more say than he did. He felt threatened by her and was worried she would voice what Robert should have been saying all along."

"Which was?"

"That Sarah should leave him. He hated his wife having supportive girlfriends and wanted to make sure he knew what Joanne was saying to Sarah about him. When Sarah and Fiona became friends, it began to get a lot worse. I think that's another reason why he fired Edward, to stir tension within the family and stop Sarah from getting too close to anyone. Fiona's not visited as much since then."

Lilly nodded. "I agree with you, Walter. I've seen it before where an abuser and a bully manipulates the situation, essentially to isolate the victim, meaning the only one they can turn to is the abuser."

"And that's why we're all better off without him, Lilly."

FTER LUNCH, LILLY volunteered to help Chloe with the washing up. She could tell Chloe had something on her mind and wanted to talk to her about what she'd learned herself from Walter.

With no power the dishwasher wasn't working, so they boiled pans of water on the hob, filled the sink and did it by hand.

Lilly embraced the job of doing something normal and mundane like washing dishes. It took her mind off what had happened and the tense atmosphere when the family were all in the same room together.

As she scrubbed and rinsed, she wondered about Robert and Joanne. Were two people she had known for five years and considered good friends capable of murder? She hated the thought and in her heart didn't believe it to be true, but she couldn't dismiss them as suspects. She let her mind wander, thinking through what they knew so far.

The fact there was a secret passage that no one had bothered to mention struck her as odd. Could those who knew about it be protecting someone? All those who knew the secret had despised the victim, but enough to kill him, Lilly couldn't be sure. There just weren't enough clues to point to one person. Morris certainly stood out in her mind, but there was no indication that he'd come back to the house that night. In fact, the absence of any traces suggested the complete opposite.

Chloe took a plate from the stack on the draining board, dried it, then put it back in the sink. Lilly glanced at her. She was in a daze.

"I've just washed that one. What's on your mind, Watson?" Lilly said.

"Oh, sorry. I'm just thinking about suspects."

Lilly chuckled. "I thought you might be. Want to tell me what you're thinking?"

She appreciated Chloe's thoughts. She had insider information she, herself, wouldn't be able to get from the family or the employees, and she was observant. Perhaps Chloe had some answers that she wasn't aware of, which could help Lilly sort out her own suspicions. "Let me make us some ginger and honey tea. It helps with brain function and mine is feeling very fuzzy at the moment."

"I think the most obvious suspect is Morris," Chloe said, putting down the tea towel and leaning against the counter. "He's missing. He argued with John only a few hours before he was murdered. And, he definitely blames John for what happened to granddad. I heard him talking to Walter ages ago about it. He knew about the secret passage and it was his dagger that was used. It all points to Morris, doesn't it?"

"It certainly looks that way, but I can tell you have other ideas."

"Yeah, I do," Chloe admitted. "I can't believe Morris could have got in without any of us hearing or seeing him. Especially as Natalie claims to have been in the room with John not ten minutes before we all came in and said he was still alive then."

"So, you think Natalie is the guilty party?"

"I think it's more likely than Morris," Chloe said. "But what's her motive? She doesn't have one, not really. The one with the most motive is Aunt Sarah. She thought her husband was having an affair, and she was right. Plus, John treated her really badly. I'll never let any man treat me like that. But I don't know how she could have done it and then been in the hall without Natalie seeing her. Unless they are working together. But that doesn't seem likely. Aunt Sarah doesn't like Natalie, especially now."

"It's good to brainstorm like this, Chloe. It helps you see things more clearly and work out what is possible and what's not. I'd have to say it's almost impossible for your aunt to be guilty. There wouldn't have been enough time."

Chloe nodded. "Yes, you're right. Now I think about it. The only one I can say was there the whole time was Aunt Sarah. And she didn't know about the secret door as far as we know. But there was a lot of commotion in the hall. Anyone could have slipped in and out then joined us. I can't say with certainty that any of the others were there the whole time, though. And let's be honest, just about everyone has a motive. Well, except dad and Joanne. They didn't like John but I know they didn't kill him."

Lilly nodded, she'd come to the same conclusion herself but she wasn't about to upset Chloe by explaining neither Robert nor Joanne could be eliminated from the suspect list just yet. Placing the tea on the kitchen table, she sat and Chloe joined her. "Walter said John held his job over his head often. He wasn't pleased about it."

"And Dominic and Edward totally hated him," Chloe said. "Ever since he sacked Edward, the two of them have had nothing but bad things to say about him. Same for Fiona. She always felt her sons were targeted by John because he never felt Joanne was part of the family, and therefore neither were Fiona, Dominic or Edward. And I know Fiona's been trying to talk Sarah into leaving John for years."

"You haven't mentioned that before," Lilly said. "Although when I spoke to Walter earlier, he suggested the same thing; that he was intimidated by Joanne and Fiona because he didn't want his wife having friends who would try to persuade her to see what her husband was really like."

"Fiona said he was abusive and I think she's right. Aunt Sarah always had a few bruises, from being clumsy and walking into stuff, she said. But I already guessed that wasn't true."

"Do you think Fiona might have killed John to protect Sarah?" Lilly asked.

Chloe shrugged, staring into her tea. "I don't know. Maybe. It's really hard wondering if someone in your family is a murderer."

"Chloe, we can stop this at any time. I don't want you upset. We should let the police deal with it."

"We can't wait that long. And I need to do something otherwise my family will all fall out and then what will happen?"

Lilly didn't have answers for her, but she knew Chloe was right. The arguments and the animosity among the family were barely below surface level now, and sooner or later words would be spoken that could never be taken back. She didn't want this family, who obviously loved each other dearly, to become estranged, with no chance of healing or making amends in the future.

And then there was Sam. He wasn't family, but he knew a lot more about the place than the owners. Just who exactly was he?

⁂

*L*ILLY AND CHLOE walked back into the lounge just as Robert announced his plan to go and search for Morris. Hearing this, Lilly volunteered to go with him. Whether he was the murderer or not, it was suspicious enough that he was missing. He needed to be found in order to be able to give his side of the story, one way or another. Assuming he wasn't lying injured or dead somewhere.

Chloe had naturally wanted to go with them, but Robert put his foot down. He wanted her safe in the bed-and-breakfast with the others, in particular her stepmother Joanne.

"I think you have a fan in my daughter, Lilly," Robert said as they left the building.

"She's a lovely girl, Robert. You should be very proud. She's also very astute and observant."

"She's been helping you investigate, hasn't she? She read the articles in the Plumpton Mallet Gazette and since then she's devoured Sherlock Holmes and Agatha Christie. She wants to be just like you. It's worrying me if I'm honest. She wasn't close to John and consequently I feel she's treating this more like a game. But it's real, and the fact is someone she knows and is probably close to, heaven forbid it's a family member, has committed murder. I'm terrified of what it will do to her when we discover who it was."

"It was my first thought, Robert. I've talked to her about it and I'm keeping a close eye on her. I promise if it gets too much for her I'll stop it. But at the moment she's frightened her family is going to fall out permanently, that's why she wants so desperately to find out who did it."

"Yes, I can understand that. It's got me concerned too, actually. Apart from John the whole family has always got on well with each other, but now we're constantly bickering and falling out. Not to mentioned blaming one another for what's happened. It's stressful and is ripping the family apart, Lilly. The trust is all but gone, and I don't want it to get to the stage where it can't ever be resolved. We need to find out who is responsible as soon as possible if the police can't get here to help us. Would you mind continuing to see what you can find out?

"Yes, of course I will, Robert."

"Thank you. And thank you for keeping an eye on Chloe too. Now, I think we should start looking in the outbuildings for Morris."

There weren't many external buildings to check; a couple of sheds, one Walter's domain, the other used for storage, and both were small with no sign of Morris. The other was a larger barn, which they tackled last.

They stepped inside and looked around the dim interior. There was some entertainment equipment on the ground floor which had been used for the party, along with old bits of furniture in need of repair, probably from the main house, Lilly thought, but not much else. Robert took the stairs up to the loft and Lilly followed, but there was no sign of Morris, nor any trace that anyone had been up here in a long time.

"Well, he's not been here," Robert said as they stepped back outside.

As Lilly turned, she spotted a lone figure walking down the path in the direction of the orchard.

"Who is that?"

Robert squinted his eyes and shook his head. "I don't know. Come on."

They hurried towards the figure, both of them half expecting Morris to turn round. Instead, as they drew closer, Lilly realised it was Sam outside by himself, hands in his pockets as though taking a casual stroll.

"Sam. What are you doing out here? I told everyone to stay inside, safe and together."

"I needed some fresh air. It's getting stuffy inside. Besides, I wanted to talk to you, Robert. I just remembered something from my childhood visits that may help locate Morris."

Lilly and Robert exchanged glances. Sam grinned and beckoned them forward. "Follow me," he said, continuing down the path.

"Where are we going, Sam?" Lilly asked, all too aware this man was as much a suspect as everyone else.

"I told you this place holds a lot of secrets."

"What do you mean, Sam," Robert asked. "Is there something else I don't know about?"

"I don't know what you know and what you don't, Robert. It is your business, after all. But I wondered how much exploration you've done of this place? Do you know about the old clubhouse?"

Lilly glanced at Robert. He looked totally confused.

"What? What clubhouse?"

"There's an old abandoned clubhouse not too far from where Morris's car was found," Sam said. "I'd forgotten all about it until I was just chatting with Chloe and reminiscing about exploring when I was a boy. Mind you, it was nearly thirty years ago so could very well be gone now."

"You didn't know about it, Robert?" Lilly asked.

Robert shook his head. "No. I've never heard about it until now."

"And you think Morris could be hiding in there, Sam?" Lilly asked.

"Well, he doesn't seem to be anywhere else, unless he managed to get to town, but I doubt he would have made it in the storm. No, if the place is still standing then I think there's a good chance he's taken shelter in there."

Once more they followed Sam, but Lilly felt uneasy. There was just something about him that was off. He knew far more about The Palms than even the owners did. First the secret doors and the passage, now a long abandoned clubhouse. It was too much. Why was he even here this weekend? Was it actually an accidental booking, like he'd said?

They walked for at least half an hour before Sam veered off into the thick woodland. A few yards away Lilly caught a glimpse of Morris's car, but the route Sam took them continued deeper into the trees and soon she lost sight of the car and the road altogether.

"We still need to move the trees in the road," she said to Robert to break the unnerving silence.

"I know. But I'd like to find Morris first."

Sam led them further through the woods, and Lilly began to feel more nervous with every step. Was there really a clubhouse this way, or was Sam taking them to a secluded spot to get rid of them? She hadn't noticed him carrying a weapon of any sort, but it could be cleverly concealed. She and Robert could possibly win in a fair fight, but against a weapon they would have no chance. Just as she was about to stop and turn round, she spotted the moss covered roof of a small wooden structure in the distance. Covered in brambles and surrounded by stinging nettles, it was so well camouflaged it was barely noticeable unless you were looking for it.

"You were telling the truth," Lilly said.

"You sound surprised," Sam said. "Why would I make up the existence of an old clubhouse?"

To get us in the middle of nowhere and bump us off, Lilly thought. But kept quiet.

"Right," Robert said. "Let's see if Morris is in there, shall we? I have questions for him."

*I*T WAS A modest size structure that had definitely seen better days. Thrown together with old wooden panels, most likely off-cuts from the time when the bed-and-breakfast or the barn was built. There was a square cut out in the side that once would have been a window. Now, no glass remained, and it was open to the elements. Lilly was amazed it was still standing.

Sam held out his arm. "After you, Robert."

Robert nodded, and took a step forward, but Lilly decided to stay just behind Sam in case he tried something.

The wooden door creaked a little as Robert pushed it open, but surprisingly, it moved quite smoothly on its rusty hinges. Lilly had expected it to fall in.

As they entered and their eyes adjusted to the internal gloom, they all saw the figure of Morris sprawled out on top of an old mattress in the corner, covered in an old tarpaulin and snoring loudly. An old empty whiskey bottle at his side.

Robert kicked the bottom of Morris's boot and the old man groaned.

"Morris, wake up!" Robert shouted.

Morris came to slowly, groaning and rubbing his eyes until he could focus.

"Robert? What are you doing here? What time is it?"

"It's two in the afternoon. What are you doing here?"

Morris slowly shifted to a sitting position, clutching his head, and Lilly could see a bump the size of a small egg on his temple just beginning to bruise.

"Crashed my car in the storm last night. I tried to make it back but lost all sense of direction. Then I remembered this place. Got soaked but at least it kept me out of the rain."

"Morris," Lilly said. "How do you feel? You've hit your head and could have a concussion. Drinking whiskey was a stupid idea after crashing your car."

Morris looked sheepishly at Lilly. "Yes, I expect you're right. I found an unopened bottle in here and couldn't resist. I obviously overdid it. Too late now, though. At least I woke up, although my head hurts."

"Get up, Morris. You need to get back to the house and get some warm clothes on, you've slept all night in wet gear," Robert said, hoisting the old man up by his arm and steadying him while he swayed a little. Once he was stable, they exited the clubhouse and began the slow journey back to The Palms.

Before she left, Lilly had checked inside the ramshackle shed for clues but had seen nothing. There was also no blood on Morris's clothes, but he'd had plenty of time to change them. Unlikely, but possible. However, if Morris did kill John, he was probably no danger to them now, hungover and exhausted as he was, he could barely put one foot in front of the other without help.

Once again Sam led the way with Morris next and Robert just behind him, ostensibly within easy reach should the old man stumble. But, Lilly could tell Robert no longer trusted Morris and had positioned himself in such a way so he could intervene should he suddenly take it into his head to attack or to make a run for it. Lilly brought up the rear, glad they were returning with Morris in tow. Maybe now they'd all get some answers.

Chapter Ten

IN AN ATTEMPT to sober Morris up and get rid of his hangover, Lilly offered to make him one of her special teas. However, Morris said he didn't hold with any of the newfangled stuff and preferred strong hot coffee. Lilly would have laughed if the situation weren't so serious. Tea had been around for hundreds of years.

Boiling a pan of water on the hob as the power was still off, she filled a small cafetière with the strongest grounds she could find. With the coffee tray complete, she took it to the empty lounge to wait. Robert had taken Morris back to his room to get washed and changed. He wasn't taking any chances that Morris would disappear again. Lilly hoped a cleaner and more sober Morris would return. Everybody else had dispersed, but she expected them all back once Morris made an appearance.

They began to turn up in ones and twos; Dominic threw a couple of logs on the fire, then took a seat, waiting in silence. By the time they were all gathered, with Morris sitting as close to the fire as he could and sipping the coffee Lilly had made, the questions began.

"Morris, what on earth happened last night?" Joanne said.

"I've already told Robert. I crashed the car in the storm. It was so dark out there I lost all sense of direction and went off course in the woods. Then I came across the old clubhouse and decided to take shelter until the storm blew itself out. I must have fallen asleep."

"A clubhouse I didn't even know existed, and I expect the whiskey helped put you to sleep," Robert said.

Morris shrugged. "I had to keep warm somehow. It worked."

"So you never came back here at all last night?"

"No. I've just said I got disoriented and ended up exactly where you found me, Robert. I apologise for my temper and my conduct last night, but John was out of order. I've never been so angry. Speaking of John, where is he? Not being his usual lazy self and still in bed is he? I'd have thought he'd have been here relishing the chance to tear a strip off me."

Sarah suddenly burst into tears and promptly rushed from the room. Morris, wide eyed, watched her leave.

"I didn't mean to upset her. What did I say? Did her and John have another argument after I left? If he hurt her, I swear..."

"John's dead," Fiona said, cutting Morris off before he could make things worse. "Somebody killed him."

Morris smirked, then glancing around at the sea of serious faces, realised this was no joke.

"What? Dear god, I didn't know. What happened?"

"John was stabbed in his sleep last night," Walter said.

Robert let out a huge sigh. "I'm going to check on Sarah. Morris, be careful what you say in front of her. She's in a delicate state at the moment," he said, hurrying after his distraught sister.

Morris looked at Joanne, understanding and sympathy etched on his face. "I didn't know, Joanne. I didn't mean to upset Sarah. I didn't know what had happened."

Joanne nodded. "I can see you didn't, Morris."

Lilly had been watching Morris intently while the conversation was taking place and she could see he was both sorry he had offended Sarah and seemingly genuinely shocked John was dead. But if he wasn't the one to kill John, then they were back to square one as far as suspects were concerned. Lilly waited to see what the family would ask next, keeping her thoughts to herself for the time being.

"Wait a minute, Aunt Joanne," Edward said. "Just because Morris was found in the clubhouse this morning doesn't mean he didn't sneak back here last night. It was his army knife that was the murder weapon."

Morris's eyes widened as the realisation dawned on him. "Hang on a minute! You don't all think I did this, do you? I wasn't even here."

"But you and John had a massive row last night," Dominic said.

"Yes, but I left," Morris shouted. "I didn't even know he was dead until you just told me."

"But we only have your word for that," Edward said. "It's not like you're going to admit it, is it? You could easily have sneaked back here. It makes sense doesn't it?" He asked the others. "We were all in the hallway when it happened, but where was Morris? We don't know for sure he left the property like he said. He could have pretended to drive off, parked the car out of sight and come back and murdered John. Then really left and made his way to the clubhouse after he crashed his car. I didn't even know the clubhouse was there, and neither did Robert from what he just said. It's very convenient Morris knew about it."

Immediately, the room erupted into an argument. With accusations flying and Morris vehemently protesting his innocence, Lilly, not wanting to get dragged into yet another family argument, slipped away unnoticed. She did, however, remain outside the door, listening to the drama unfold.

Both Dominic and Edward were convinced Morris had initially left the house and then returned to kill John. He had both the time and the motive. Joanne tentatively agreed to the possibility her nephews posed, but Morris fiercely objected, pointing out he was not the only one with a motive. He reminded Edward that John had sacked him and Dominic that he, too, had argued with John that day. Dominic disagreed, saying it was nothing more than a minor squabble. No more serious than any of the others they'd had in the past.

"And it didn't end up with John being covered in hot soup," he finished.

"After what he said about Robert's father, a soaking in soup was the least he deserved," Morris said.

The room grew quiet, and Lilly moved closer to the door.

"The least he deserved?" Edward repeated.

"Oh, for crying out loud, Edward. Stop putting words in my mouth. I didn't mean it like that. Surely you all know me well enough to recognise I would never kill anyone."

"What about in the army? You've obviously got skills and experience," Dominic said quietly.

"That's no one's business but my own."

"Dominic, that's enough," Joanne said. "Although," she said, turning to Morris, "It does add more fuel to the flames."

"Oh, Joanne," Morris said sadly. "I don't know what I can say to make you believe me. It's true, I didn't like John. He was not a good person. But can anyone here say, in all honesty, that they liked him? He was bad to the core, you all know that. A bully, a thug, and he had a vicious mouth. He was cruel to Jack and to Sarah, and treated everyone else like they were his personal servants. But I did not kill him. Why would I risk going to prison for someone like that?"

There was a lull in the conversation after Morris had finished speaking, and Lilly moved away to think more about the possibilities. She thought about the knife she and Chloe had found. If Morris had found out John was having an affair with Natalie, it could have been the final straw. He was already furious at the way John treated Jack, but what would he do if he found out his best friend's daughter was married to an adulterer? Perhaps this was what had driven him to kill John? If indeed it was Morris. Lilly realised she needed more evidence to back up her thoughts and wondered where she should search to find it?

Then it occurred to her that while she and Chloe had searched room four thoroughly, they had forgotten to examine the secret passage. Perhaps the perpetrator had left some sort of evidence behind that could point them in the right direction?

She headed upstairs, eager to try to piece this mystery together once and for all.

S LILLY REACHED the top of the stairs, she heard a creak behind her and spun round to see Chloe following her.

"What are you doing here?" she whispered.

"I know you're on the case again," she whispered back. "I want to help. I'm your Watson remember?"

"Fine, just keep your voice down, okay?"

Chloe scurried over, looking excited. "So what's your plan? Are you going to search some of the other staff rooms? I know we found some evidence in Natalie's room, but maybe there's something we missed? What about Morris's room? He looks really suspicious, doesn't he? We should probably search his room too and see if there's anything in there."

"Chloe, take a breath, would you? You're making me dizzy," Lilly said, amused. "Actually, I was going to take a look in that secret passage. We missed it last time."

"Good idea. Although it's not very long, what could we possibly find in there?"

"Probably nothing, but you never know. It needs checking either way."

They arrived at the bookshelf in the hallway and pulled it open. Lilly leading the way with the torch lit on her phone. As she moved down the short hall, the light caught the wall and Chloe grabbed her shoulder.

"What's that?"

Lilly took a closer look. "They're signatures. See the dates, Chloe? These go back to the time The Palms was built. I don't recognise any of the early ones, but look here, there's Sam's name. He must have written that when he was a child judging by the immature scrawl."

"He has been coming here a long time, like he said. Look here! That's Granddad's name. I think it was the year after he bought the place."

"And these are Dominic and Edward's signatures. That's when they first started working here, is it?" Lilly said, looking at the date.

"Yes," Chloe said, running her hand along the names. "Here's Natalie, and Morris and this one is Walter."

"This is consistent with what everyone's told us so far. I'm not sure there's anything to find in here, Chloe."

She started to turn to leave the passage when she kicked something. Looking down, she saw an object, small and metallic skitter across the floor.

"What was that?" Chloe asked, having heard the same sound.

Lilly crouched and picked up the coin sized object, turning it over.

"It's a military medal. The words say *For Bravery in the Field*. It's usually given to soldiers who sustained injury during battle."

"Morris," Chloe said, shaking her head. "I honestly was hoping we'd find the evidence we needed against Natalie. I don't like the idea of it being Morris, I like him. He's an old family friend and I don't want him to go to prison."

"I know, Chloe. But if he killed John, then it's what will happen, I'm afraid. You know there's not a speck of dust on this medal, that would suggest it was dropped recently."

"Like last night. Looks like we've solved it, doesn't it?"

"Not yet," Lilly said, tucking the medal in her pocket. "I think it's time we searched the other rooms."

Chloe nodded. "Okay."

"**I** THINK WE SHOULD start with Sam's room," Chloe said once they were back in the hall. "Why his room?"

"It's elementary," she said with a grin.

Lilly laughed. "Very good. Go on, Watson, dazzle me with your thought process."

"Because he knows too much and I think he's up to something."

Not exactly a scientific hypothesis worthy of Sherlock, but it was to the point and Lilly had come to the same conclusion. It was interesting to see Chloe arrive at the same assumption. However, she did wonder if there was more to it.

"Are you sure you're not just worried about what we might find if we start looking in your family's rooms?" she asked gently.

Chloe nodded. "Yes, I am. It scares me to think any of my family did this, Lilly. I was hoping we could do the staff and guest rooms first then if we don't find anything... you know, we'll have to search their suites. Is that okay?"

Lilly gave the girl a quick hug. "Yes, of course it's okay. And for what it's worth I think you're right about looking into Sam first. But you'll need to stay and keep watch in the corridor for me, okay?"

The girl nodded, and the two of them approached Sam's room. Once again, Chloe produced the master key from her pocket and gave it to Lilly. She carefully opened the door and entered quietly. The room was in semidarkness with the lights off and the voiles drawn across the windows, but Lilly could immediately see there was a table under the window which had been set up with a laptop computer. She reached it in three long strides and opened it but was unable to access anything, as it needed a password. To the side was a spiral-bound notebook filled with pages of notes. It was a detailed description of Robert and Joanne's time at the bed-and-breakfast going back several months.

Lilly was flabbergasted. "What on earth? She muttered, turning pages to discover Sam had not only been following her friends around the business, but on all their trips to town and elsewhere. *Why has he been following them?* Lilly wondered, taking her phone and photographing the pages. *He's been following Chloe, too! What is all this?*

She replaced the notebook and began opening the drawers. At the bottom of the right one she found an official looking manila envelope. Opening it, she discovered what looked like a contract and at the top was John's name. Before she could read further to discover what it was for, someone cleared their throat.

Lilly let out a surprised yell, and spun round to find Sam sitting in a corner, apparently having been there the entire time, watching her search through his private belongings.

"Sam!"

Sam grinned at her. "You are a very nosy person, Lilly Tweed. Although not very observant it must be said, considering you failed to notice me reading in the corner."

Having heard Lilly's shout, Chloe came bursting into the room, also startled at seeing Sam casually sitting inside the room.

"When did you come up here?" Lilly asked. "I swore you were in the lounge when I left."

"When you two were rummaging around in the passage. The constant bickering downstairs was giving me a headache, so I thought I'd come up here and read for a while. Then you came in. I nearly let on I was here but was intrigued as to what you'd come for."

"And I found it," Lilly said, snatching the notebook from the table and holding it up. "Just what is this, Sam? You've been stalking Robert, Joanne and Chloe. Making notes of their every move for the last several months. I think you'd better explain yourself."

"What?" Chloe said, snatching the journal from Lilly's hand and reading it for herself. "You've been spying on us? Why?"

"Spying, stalking. It all sounds so seedy and vulgar doesn't it? I prefer another term." He got up and started towards them.

Lilly instinctively tensed and held her arm in front of Chloe for protection. But Sam merely held out his hand for the envelope she was still holding. Reluctantly, Lilly passed it over.

"This," Sam began. "Is a contract. Several months ago John hired me to dig up some dirt on Robert and Joanne."

Chloe blinked. "What? What do you mean?"

"I'm a detective, Chloe. A private investigator, actually. About a year or so ago, during one of my visits, John and I got talking and when he found out what I did for a living, he hired me on the spot. Told me he wanted something on his brother-in-law."

"But why?"

"For leverage, apparently. As you know your father and aunt are the ones who legally own The Palms, Joanne and John just help out their spouses but have no legal claim on anything. It's deliberately and legally written in that way so if there's ever a divorce or a separation the business would remain in the family. Now, your step mother is perfectly fine with that. She and Robert have an excellent marriage and relationship. John, on the other hand, wanted more. Much more. He wanted control of the business and eventually to buy Robert out. Unfortunately for John, Robert had no intention of selling. He knew John was abusing Sarah, and he's been trying to persuade her to leave him for years."

"But John was worried that if Sarah began to listen and see him for what he really was, he risked losing everything. If they divorced he wouldn't get anything, especially if the abuse was proved. So he hired you to find something he could blackmail Robert and Joanne with?" Lilly said, immediately grasping the situation.

"Exactly that. Robert and Sarah, then latterly Joanne, put in a huge amount of work to get this place back on its feet. John wanted to take it from them."

"And you were going to help him do it, by investigating my family." Chloe said, seething.

"It's no different from what you're doing except it's my job and I get paid."

"But I'm not investigating my dad and step mum."

"You can't have it both ways, Chloe. Investigate someone you don't like in the hopes of finding incriminating evidence, but choose not to pursue someone you do like, purely because they're family or you think they are nice. Many seemingly nice people commit crimes too, you know, and they are all part of someone's family. But rest assured I don't have a horse in this race, Chloe," Sam said.

"And what's that supposed to mean?"

"It means," said Lilly. "He doesn't have a vested interest one way or another. He simply wants to get to the truth by doing the job he's been hired to do."

"Exactly. But if it's any consolation, Chloe, I had no idea what sort of man John was. He was always very friendly, polite and solicitous to guests."

"Because they pay."

"Of course. If there was one thing a man like John appreciated, it was money. Especially if he didn't have to earn it himself. But as I told him, there simply wasn't any dirt to dig up. I've followed them for months and as I know this place inside out it was easy. All I discovered is that they are good people. John still owed me money, two payments on the original price. He's the one who booked me in this weekend, actually, not Sarah. He'd tried to negotiate a lower fee, as I didn't find anything he could use. That's not the way it works of course."

"I knew Aunt Sarah wouldn't have made that sort of mistake. So John brought you here on purpose this weekend?"

Sam nodded. "He was hoping with all the family being present I'd be able to find something. One last attempt to dig up something he could blackmail them over. But then he was killed, and I had to change tactics. I've been trying to find out who is responsible ever since."

"So, you're an actual detective?" Chloe asked.

"A private investigator," Sam corrected.

"What have you found out, Sam?" Lilly asked. "Are you near to discovering who killed John?"

Sam smiled and shook his head. "Not yet, but I think I'm getting close. You see, I was up for most of the night John was murdered. I suffer from bouts of insomnia, particularly when I'm on a job. I may have a bit of intelligence for you amateur detectives."

"Well, tell us what you know," Lilly said.

Sam walked to the desk, picked up a pen, and took his notebook back from Chloe.

"Oh, no. You share first and then maybe we can work out together who killed John."

Chapter Eleven

*J*UST AS LILLY was beginning to feel she and Chloe had hit the detective jackpot by discovering a real private investigator to help them, Sam started bouncing in the hallway like he was on springs, almost ruining his credibility.

"You see," he said, pacing back and forth. He stepped in the middle of the floor and there was an audible creaking noise. "There's a loose floorboard."

"Okay," Lilly and Chloe said simultaneously.

"I told you I couldn't sleep. The loose floorboard at the end of the hall is unavoidable. In fact, all three of these boards creak."

As he explained, Sam proceeded to step back and forth making each board groan loudly in turn to make sure they understood.

"Now, my room is just there," he said, pointing to the door they'd all just exited. "If someone was attempting to get into the passage connected to room four, they absolutely would have stepped on these boards causing them to creak."

"So, are you saying you didn't hear anyone?" Lilly asked, not entirely sure what Sam was getting at.

"On the contrary, I distinctly remember hearing this sound shortly after Sarah began banging on the door for her husband. Presumably, it was Natalie Sampson sneaking away from the room just as you all started gathering outside the door. But, and this is the interesting part, I then heard it a second time as the rest of you congregated around Sarah. In other words, someone entered the passage while you were all otherwise engaged further up the hall."

Chloe frowned. "You think a creaking floorboard is enough to prove Natalie's innocence?" she asked. "She could have re-entered the room along the passage, standing on the loose floorboard just as easily as someone else could."

"Perhaps," Sam said. Then pointed down the hallway. "But everyone else's rooms are in that direction. They would have come from over there. It wouldn't have made sense for anyone to be in this part of the hall apart from Natalie, who was attempting to sneak away in order to come up behind everyone looking as though she'd just woken up. Besides, if Natalie's intention was to kill John, why not do it the first time? She was already in the room."

"So, let me get this straight," Lilly said. "You heard the floorboard creak after Natalie had left the passageway, but before we'd all managed to get into room four?"

"I heard three actually, but I've ascertained one was Robert going downstairs for the master key then returning, so we can eliminate those. Natalie had already left the passage, then she joined everyone in the hall. Robert went for the key and returned. It was at that point someone else entered the passage, while you were all outside room four."

"And that's when we're all assuming John was stabbed, while we were outside the door," Lilly said. "Unless it was Natalie who stabbed him."

"But Sam says he heard someone else enter the passage after Natalie left," Chloe said. "The only person who could have done that without being noticed by at least *someone* in the hallway was Morris, because we all thought he'd left."

"So where was the killer when we all charged into the room?" Lilly asked.

"Still in the passage," Sam said.

"You honestly believe the killer had the audacity to remain in the passage while we were all in the room discovering John's body?" Lilly asked.

"I'm almost sure of it," Sam said. "I should have pointed out the secret entrance there and then, and I suspect we'd have caught the killer literally red-handed. Too worried to leave and run the risk of being caught."

"Well, why didn't you?" Chloe demanded.

"Because, quite frankly, I was shocked at finding my client dead. The only thing I could think of was that someone had worked out that John had hired me, and if that was the case, then there was a good chance I would be next. I played the scenarios over and over in my mind while I was in that room and came to the conclusion my best approach was to remain quiet and investigate to see if I could unveil the killer myself before he or she got to me. I didn't put two and two together about the creaking floorboards and the passage until later."

"If you really believe the killer was in the passage while we were all in the room, it really only leaves one person who could have done this," Lilly said.

Chloe's shoulders slumped. "Morris," she said sadly.

Sam nodded. "Yes. I'm sorry, but it does appear that way."

❦

SAM MADE HIS way back downstairs, leaving Lilly and Chloe alone. No matter how straight-forward Sam's information and conclusion was, for some reason Lilly was still having doubts.

"I feel we still don't have enough to prove Morris is guilty, Chloe. If he really did kill John, then it makes absolutely no sense for him to be found on the property, even if it was quite far away. He wouldn't have sheltered in an old shed then drunk himself to sleep no matter how bad the storm, he would have taken the risk and kept running, getting as much distance between the scene of the crime and himself as possible."

Chloe was stunned, and stared at Lilly for a second before speaking. "Are you serious? All the clues point to him. It was his knife that was the murder weapon; we found his medal in the secret passage. He argued with John and then left giving himself a sort of alibi. But he could have easily come back."

"I know all that, Chloe, but what does it prove? We thought it was Natalie to start with."

"Well, surely we can't get it wrong twice?"

"I expect it's more common than you think. Look, I know it doesn't look good for Morris but we haven't actually investigated anyone else yet have we? Morris and Natalie aside, there are plenty of other people here and none of them liked John," Lilly said. "I just want to make sure we eliminate all other options before we jump to any conclusions. It's a man's life we're talking about, Chloe. We can't afford to make any mistakes."

"Okay," Chloe sighed. "What do you think we should do?"

"Finish snooping."

"All right. Let's get on with it."

They began to go through every room meticulously, but didn't find anything that could be considered interesting as far as the crime was concerned. In her granddad's room, Chloe found his Alzheimer's medication and a love note from his wife which apparently he kept by his side. It was very loving and sentimental, and both Chloe and Lilly were saddened by the fact he'd probably never be able to read it. Even if somebody else volunteered to read it for him, it was unlikely he would be able to concentrate long enough to understand the content. But it was a wonderfully romantic gesture and was obvious the two of them had been very much in love. Lilly took photos just to be thorough.

Nothing even remotely suspicious was found in Robert and Joanne's room, nor in what was now just Sarah's, though Lilly did learn Joanne had a bird watching hobby. There were several books on the subject next to the window, alongside a pair of binoculars. Lilly imagined on most days, when a violent storm hadn't just happened, there would be numerous garden and sea birds to watch outside.

Dominic's room was the smallest but yielded nothing of value except an interesting collection of action figures. Fiona and Edward's guest rooms drew a blank, as did Walter's.

They did, however, find something significant in Morris's room, which didn't help his situation at all. A matching knife to the one used as the murder weapon, suggesting he had a set. The drawer to his desk where they found it had been left partially open; signifying he'd probably grabbed one quickly and had failed to close it properly.

"Satisfied?" Chloe asked as they left the last of the rooms, having taken a picture of the army knife found in Morris's drawer.

"I suppose so. We've cleared everyone else, haven't we?"

"So, we're back to it being either Morris or Natalie, and the evidence against Morris is overwhelming."

"Unfortunately, I have to agree," Lilly said as they reached the top of the stairs. Suddenly the lights came on.

"Hurrah!" Chloe cried, taking the stairs two at a time.

"I'm just going to check my laptop to see if we've got internet connection," Lilly called after the speeding girl.

"Excellent!" she heard Robert say from the lounge. "The phone lines are working again. I'm going to call the police and get them up here as soon as possible."

Lilly gave a sigh of relief, glad this nightmare was finally over. The police would arrive as soon as the road was cleared, which Lilly expected would happen immediately once Robert told the police there was a murder victim currently in room four and the murderer staying in the house.

*L*ILLY WENT TO her room and sat on the bed with her laptop, relieved to see the Wi-Fi was back on granting her access to the outside world. She wanted to check in with Stacey to see how things were with the shop and Earl. While she had left Stacey to run The Tea Emporium before, she'd never been out of contact for this long and hoped Stacey wasn't getting worried over her lack of communication.

Checking her email, she opened Stacey's first, pleased to see that everything was fine and running smoothly. She'd even attached a few pictures of Earl sleeping in her lap, snoozing in his favourite spot in the window and on Stacey's bed. He was obviously getting spoiled.

"Good," Lilly said, satisfied. She replied quickly, then opened up a search engine.

She was still having misgivings about the information they'd garnered and the resulting conclusions they had come to. If Morris had killed John, he had been out in that raging storm having just been involved in an accident, and his shoes and clothes would be wet and muddy. Would that old man have been able to make it from the car, back to the bed-and-breakfast where he killed a man, sneaked back out and then made it back to an abandoned clubhouse a great distance away in time to drink himself into a stupor, all without getting any signs of mud and water inside the house?

Admittedly Morris was an army man, but that sort of stealth and speed at his age was extremely unlikely. In fact, a man half his age would have had trouble achieving all that. It almost felt as though someone was attempting to frame him, and Lilly wanted to make sure she wasn't missing anything.

She spent a long time on her computer doing research, and she was thankful she'd taken the time and opportunity. She was right. The evidence they'd gathered didn't add up. She shook her head sadly. *I know who killed John*, she thought and closed her laptop before hurrying back downstairs to join the others.

Chapter Twelve

HE ARRIVED JUST in time to greet the police with the rest of the household. Sam had taken charge, having announced to everyone that he was a private investigator, and was in the process of giving the police a blow by blow account of what had transpired in the previous few hours.

"We also eventually found Morris hiding out in the old clubhouse, a bit worse for wear due to a bottle of whiskey," Sam said, and Morris shifted uncomfortably in his seat.

"Morris isn't a killer," Robert said. "I just don't believe it. There's no indication he ever returned to the house after he left, and there would have been."

Once again Morris squirmed, but remained quiet.

"I agree," Joanne said, giving her husband a small smile. "It just doesn't make sense."

"Oh, so that's the way it's going to be, is it?" Natalie said, pointing a finger at them both. "You still think it was me. I'm telling you, I did not kill John."

"You were having an affair with him, Natalie," Sarah said angrily. "Maybe you were worried about getting caught?"

"Oh, of course, Sarah. I killed my lover to hide the fact I was sleeping with him, then left my underwear behind," Natalie said sarcastically. "That makes no sense at all. I ran from the room the moment I heard you knocking and hid at the far end of the passage until I was sure there was no one in the hall. I then left and came up straight behind you."

"Did you get the names of the police, Chloe?" Lilly whispered, coming to stand at her shoulder.

"Oh, hi. Yes, he's Officer Martins, and she's Detective Lacey. They're just trying to get the facts straight. I think the secret passage was a bit of a surprise."

"You sound as if you know them?"

"We all do, it's a small town."

"Okay," Lilly said. She decided to wait and keep the information she'd found on-line to herself for the moment. She didn't want to step on the toes of the police, and it would make more sense once the police knew everything else. There was also the fact of how devastating the news would be to all concerned. She was dreading it and could only hope the truth would be found before she had to speak.

"All right," Detective Lacey said. "Show me upstairs. And nobody leaves while I'm gone, understood? Officer Martins will remain here. We'll need to take a statement from each of you and I also have a crime scene team on the way."

"I'm not going anywhere, detective," Morris said quietly.

Robert led the detective to the next floor, followed closely by Sam, who volunteered to walk her through what had been uncovered so far.

Downstairs with everyone else, Lilly kept her eye on Morris, who was constantly fidgeting and wringing his hands. Unless they were being spoken to directly by the officer, the entire party kept quiet. Officer Martins was scribbling notes in his black book as the sequence of events was slowly unravelled. And he also announced that Detective Lacey would be speaking with everyone individually in the kitchen when she returned.

"This is going to be interesting," Chloe whispered to Lilly. "It's like an Agatha Christie book, isn't it? So, everyone will be interrogated one at a time by Detective Lacey? Do you think she'd let me help? I could be useful, don't you think? Maybe I should ask her."

"That's not a good idea, Chloe. Wait until it's your turn and help then."

Half an hour later, the detective was back with evidence bags dangling at her side. Lilly could see they contained the knife, the underwear, and the medal they'd found in the passage. She looked furious.

"Robert has just told me these items," she raised the bags. "Have been moved from their original positions. I'm sure you've all seen enough crime shows on television to know you never, ever tamper with a crime scene. Which one of you is responsible?"

Lilly sighed, and Detective Lacey's eyes immediately sought her out.

"I'm sorry, it was me. We were all trapped here and didn't know for how long. So, I looked around."

"I helped," Chloe suddenly said. Standing closer to Lilly in a show of alliance.

"And now your fingerprints are probably on everything."

"Oh, no, we were really careful," Chloe said.

Lacey held up the knife and the medal. "I assume these belong to one of our ex-servicemen?" she said, her gaze flitting from Jack to Morris and back. Jack smiled dreamily from his wheelchair, and Detective Lacey frowned. She pointed a finger at Morris. "I'll talk to you first."

celeo

*M*ORRIS NERVOUSLY SHUFFLED after the detective and followed her into the kitchen. All eyes watched him in silence as he went. He looked like a man being sent to the gallows.

While Morris was being questioned, the crime scene technicians turned up. Officer Martins met them and after explaining where the murder had taken place and giving directions, they trooped upstairs armed with various cases and bags.

One by one, each of the staff and the family were called into the kitchen to be questioned by the detective. All of them cooperated fully, none of them wanting to make themselves seem guilty as they all appeared to have some sort of motive brewing underneath the surface.

Lilly was called in last, and like the others told Detective Lacey almost everything from the day she arrived. She also included her observations as an outsider, which while not strictly evidence, the detective was still interested in hearing.

However, there was one pertinent discovery she kept to herself. Only time would tell whether she would need to share what she'd found.

Those couple of hours seemed to go by in a flash, and before they knew it, the detective was back in the lounge with them all, eyeing Morris with interest. It appeared to Lilly the woman had her suspicions already.

"Thank you all for your cooperation. We'll see what additional evidence the crime scene technicians find. They are an excellent team, so I'm certain we'll find what we need. I will of course require you all to submit to both DNA and fingerprint testing so we can eliminate those of you who are innocent."

Without warning, Morris jumped up.

"There's no need to do all that," he said. "I'm the one you want. I did it. I killed John. There's no need to put this family through any more, they are good people. I should have admitted it at the beginning rather than keeping quiet."

There was a collective gasp at the confession, and Sarah let out a shriek.

Lacey eyed him thoughtfully. "Let me confirm that. Are you confessing to the murder of John, Morris?"

"Yes, I am. I love this family, every one of them, and I've hated that man for years for how he treated them and the staff."

"All right," Lacey said. "Explain to me how you got in and out of here without leaving a trace and with no one seeing you."

Morris shrugged. "I was in the army. I know how to get in and out of a place without being seen. I know this place

471

like the back of my hand, including the secret passage. That's my dagger and my medal. What more do you need?"

Lacey nodded. "In that case, Morris, I am..." she began, obviously about to arrest him.

"Wait," Lilly said quickly. She had hoped it wouldn't come to this, but she had to intervene.

$$ \textit{celes} $$

"MORRIS, YOU CAN'T confess to something you didn't do, no matter what your reasons are. I know you didn't do it."

Morris glared at her. "Shut up. I told you I did it."

"What's the meaning of this, Miss Tweed?" Lacey asked.

"Lilly, what are you doing?" Joanne asked. "He just said he killed John and all the evidence says he did it."

"I'm so sorry, Joanne, Robert, Chloe. All of you. I've been wrestling with this ever since I found out. But Morris is protecting someone else. Morris, I can't in all good conscience let you take the blame for this. I know your confession comes from the heart, but I can't stand by and watch you get arrested for a murder you didn't commit. The person you're protecting should have the guts to stand up and tell the truth themselves. They are taking the coward's way out."

"Please, just shut up," Morris begged. "Let it go."

"Miss Tweed, unless you can explain what this is all about, I suggest you sit down," Detective Lacey said.

Then suddenly, Jack stood up. The shock in the room was palpable as everyone except Morris stared at the man, too bewildered to speak. Morris covered his face and collapsed into a nearby chair. "Dammit, Jack," he said softly.

Jack looked at Lilly. "I'm not a coward, Miss Tweed."

Robert and Sarah looked as though they would fall down at any moment, seeing their father upright and fully compos mentis. Lilly glanced at Chloe, who was staring at her granddad, bewildered and frightened as the truth suddenly dawned on her.

"Oh my god," Sam breathed, astounded. He too had thoroughly believed Morris had been the killer, and that Jack had been on his way to a fully vegetative state.

"Dad? Dad, sit down," Robert cried.

Jack shook his head. "I'm fine, son." Then he looked at the man who had been his best friend for more years than he could count. "It was the medal and dagger that helped you work it out, wasn't it, old friend?"

Morris nodded, tears streaming down his face. "Why did you get up, Jack? I was going to take the blame and would have done so happily. You saved my life once, it was my turn to save yours."

"I can't let you go to prison for something I did, Morris," Jack said. He turned to Lilly. "I understand how Morris worked out it was me. But what about you? How did you know?"

"Because of the Alzheimer's medicine that Chloe and I found. I've always had an interest in herbal medicine, particularly when it comes to tea. I recognised most of the list of ingredients on the bottle as being plant derivatives mixed with a sugar pill."

"Dad?" Sarah said.

Jack quickly glanced at his daughter, then looked away. "Go on," he said to Lilly.

"Your Alzheimer's isn't progressing as rapidly as you've led your family to believe. I realised what was happening when I saw the name of the doctor on the bottle. Your wife is a doctor, and she's the one who wrote the prescription. She's complicit too, isn't she, Jack?"

"Now wait just a minute, Lilly. What do you mean my mother's in on it? She's not even here," Robert said.

"No," Lilly said, feeling wretched at what she was having to do to her friends. "But she and Jack saw the perfect opportunity when his illness started to develop a plan to get rid of the man who was abusing their daughter."

"Oh no, dad," Sarah sobbed. "Tell me it's not true." The distress in her voice was obvious to everyone.

"I knew it wasn't Morris once we'd found the medal," Lilly continued softly. "Because he never received one. When I first arrived, Morris told me about you taking a bullet for him, Jack, saving his life. The medal was for your bravery. Once the power had returned, I made sure I was on the right lines by researching the recipients of that particular medal during the Falkland's conflict. There was no mention of Morris receiving a medal. But you were listed."

"That's right," Morris said quietly. "Jack's the hero."

"Is there anything else, Miss Tweed?" Detective Lacey asked.

Lilly nodded. "Yes, I'm afraid there is.

"Please, no more," Robert said, sinking onto a sofa, head in his hands. Joanne put her arm around her husband and laid her head on his shoulder.

"I'm sorry," Detective Lacey said. "But if there is more to this story, then I need to hear it. This is a murder investigation. Go on, Miss Tweed."

"There's no doubt Jack has Alzheimer's, but as you can see it's just not as advanced as was thought. Although it is getting worse and rapidly. It always struck me as strange that the murder weapon was left in the room. It was the one piece of pertinent evidence that would lead to the killer eventually, so why not remove it? It's certainly not a mistake a former service man would make."

"So, what do you think happened?" Detective Lacey asked.

"I believe Jack had some sort of episode, a seizure perhaps brought on by his illness and the stress of having just committed murder, where he forgot where he was for a moment and dropped the knife. When he came to, he heard all the commotion outside and realised he had to make his escape. In his haste, I think he accidentally kicked the knife under the bed. In the passage your medal probably dropped out of your pocket."

"Your lucky charm, dad," Sarah said.

There was a long pause as everyone let this revelation sink in. But Lilly wasn't finished.

"I'm sorry to have to say it, but I'm almost certain that Morris was in on it too."

"Don't you dare!" Jack warned, taking a step forward before Officer Martins took him by the arm, forcing him to remain where he was. "You've had your say, leave it at that."

"I can't, Jack. I'm truly sorry, but I need to tell the truth. You'd already put the plan into action by changing your medication and telling your family it was an experimental drug.

I assume when all of this was over and someone else was in prison for the crime, your plan was to begin to improve, citing your alternative medicine as being responsible? Anyway, you decided the murder weapon would be your military knife, a purely arrogant choice as it happens. I put it down to some sort of misguided poetic justice. But Morris also had one, so to save him from getting the blame you warned him what you intended to do and made sure he was away from here when John died. Morris deliberately picked a fight with John, then left, but he got stuck. He may not have wielded the knife, but he certainly knew what was going to happen."

"You know," said Sam. "I always thought Morris's excuse that he couldn't find his way back here strange. He's worked here for years and knows the place as well as I do. It didn't make sense, especially when the clubhouse is not only further away but much more difficult to get to."

Lilly nodded. "Jack did everything he could to make sure himself, his wife and Morris couldn't possibly be arrested for the murder. His wife stayed behind, ostensibly for a well deserved spa break, but it was Morris that gave Robert and Sarah the idea in the first place. He staged the severity of his illness and he got Morris to promise to leave somehow. The military evidence pointed to them, but how could that be if one had diminished capacity and the other was absent? But then Natalie threw a spanner in the works by having an affair with John, and it made a mess of your plan. Am I right?"

Jack chuckled. "You think that wasn't part of the plan?" Once again the room stilled as all those present waited with bated breath to hear what Jack would say next. "I knew she and John were having an affair. You'd be amazed what people will say in front of you if they think you're a drooling idiot."

"Jack!" Natalie cried in shock. "You were trying to frame me for murder?"

"You and John hurt my daughter," he spat at her.

"Dad," Robert said, his voice shaking. "This isn't right. What you did. It's not right."

"I know, son. I know. But John will never hurt my daughter or anyone else again."

"Or you, Jack," Morris said. "I know he pushed you off that ladder."

Jack shook his head. "He didn't push me, Morris. I slipped, it was my own stupid fault."

"What? No, that can't be right. I saw the look he had on his face when you were falling, Jack. He was pleased."

"Yes, he was. Because he could have saved me, but he didn't. He might not have pushed me, Morris, but he didn't save me when he could. That's just as bad in my book. He was a blight on my family and a blight on this earth. He didn't deserve to live."

Chapter Thirteen

WHILE JACK WAS formally arrested and led away in handcuffs along with Morris, and Officer Martins made arrangements to pick up Jack's wife, Lilly slipped away to the kitchen. She felt the beginnings of a headache and wanted to make a cup of tea before it got any worse.

She was just sipping a freshly brewed cup of chamomile, which would also help with the stress and anxiety she was feeling, when Joanne came in.

"Lilly, I..."

"You want me to leave?"

Joanne nodded. "I'm sorry, Lilly, it's just with everything that's just happened, we, the family that is, need to be on our own."

"I understand, truly. I'm so sorry, Joanne, if it's any consolation I really was torn between keeping mouth shut and letting Morris take the blame, and telling what I knew. I wouldn't have deliberately hurt any of you for the world. You do know that, don't you?"

"I do, Lilly. But it doesn't make it any easier to stomach. Robert's just lost his parents having found out they murdered their son-in-law, and Chloe has lost her grandparents. Sarah's lost her husband and her parents. The family is broken, Lilly, and I don't know if it will ever heal. I... I'm sorry, Lilly, but it's for the best."

Joanne left and Lilly finished her tea, then went to pack. As she was loading her car, Chloe came out and gave her a tearful hug.

"Thank you for letting me be your Watson," she sniffed. "The police have found granddad's clothes, covered in blood hidden in the toilet cistern in his room. There was also some blood in the passage that we missed."

"Oh, Chloe. I can't tell you how sorry I am that it worked out the way it did."

"It wasn't your fault. I told dad and Joanne you had to tell the truth. Dad has always told me to tell the truth and take responsibility for my own actions. This is the same thing, isn't it? You had to do what was right."

Once again, Lilly was struck with how mature and sensible Chloe was.

"Yes. I couldn't have lived with myself if I'd kept quiet. I just wish things had worked out differently," she explained, as tears welled in her own eyes.

Chloe nodded. "I know. I hope I get to see you again, Lilly. Maybe you could email me sometimes?"

Lilly promised she would, then watched as the girl ran back to the house, wiping tears on her sleeve as she went.

The drive back to Plumpton Mallet was long and silent. What had started as a happy celebration for two of her friends had ended in a tragedy so serious she didn't know if her friendship with Robert and Joanne would survive. It upset her deeply, and her mind was caught in a loop, replaying the sequence of events over and over. But she still came to the same conclusion. She couldn't have remained silent and let a man get away with murder. No matter who he was.

Two hours into her journey home, the phone rang. She answered automatically via Blue-tooth without checking who the caller was.

"Lilly, it's Joanne. Listen, I just want you to know we don't blame you in any way for what happened. I know you feel somewhat responsible, Chloe told us, but you shouldn't, Lilly. Jack made his choices and he'll have to live with them. Unfortunately, we'll also have to live with his actions. But Robert and I wanted you to know we both feel awful for how we let you leave. We're all reeling and distraught, but we should have behaved better."

"It doesn't matter, Joanne, honestly," Lilly said, full of relief that her friend was still speaking to her. "How are Robert and Sarah?"

"They've both suffered through every emotion possible since you left. Robert's just gone out with Walter to clear the remains of the fallen trees. The police arranged for a partial clearance so they could get through, but there's still a lot to do. I think doing something physical will help him. Sarah, as you can imagine, is blaming herself. If she hadn't married John, or if she'd had the strength to leave him, then it would never have come to this. That's what she's saying. But there's also a part of her that's relieved John is gone. I think when the dust settles I'll suggest she find a therapist to talk to."

"Yes, that's a good idea. What about Natalie?"

"She packed and left for good fifteen minutes ago. I'll give her a positive reference. She was excellent at her job after all and was very nearly made a scapegoat in Jack's scheme, but we can't employ her after what happened."

"No, of course not. Joanne, I know you all have a long road ahead of you and it will be difficult. If there's anything I can do to help you, will let me know, won't you?"

"Yes, I will. Thanks, Lilly. I've got to go and make a phone call now. Detective Lacey gave me the details of a specialist cleaning company for room four now they've all left. I was going to tackle it myself but I just can't bring myself to even go in there. What does it say about our society that there's a need for specialist companies who clean up crime scenes? Anyway, I'll be in touch. Take care, Lilly."

"You too, Joanne."

ℰℓℓℓℓ𝒟

*L*ILLY HAD SENT a quick text to Stacey informing her she was on her way home, but it would be late so she wouldn't be in the shop until the following morning, if she wouldn't mind looking after Earl for one more night. As expected, Stacey was more than happy to look after the cat.

The next day she was at The Tea Emporium, bright and early, but Stacey had still beaten her to it and was already setting everything up in readiness for opening.

When she entered, Earl jumped out of his usual spot in the window and came to greet her, purring loudly and weaving through her legs. She bent to pick him up. "I missed you too, Earl."

"Lilly, you're back," Stacey called, exiting the store room.

"I am. How were things while I was gone?"

"Really busy, but nothing I couldn't handle. Everyone asked where you were and when I told them, they all said you deserved a break. So, how was the party? Did you have a good time? I saw you had a massive storm down there. I hope it didn't ruin the celebrations?"

Lilly sighed. "Actually, it all started well then went horribly wrong," she said. And proceeded to tell Stacey all that had happened.

"Oh, Lilly, that's just awful. I'm so sorry. But I believe you did the right thing. What will happen to them?"

Lilly shook her head. "I don't know, Stacey. Jack may plead some sort of mental health breakdown due to his illness. I suppose it depends on how good his solicitor is. He may live out the rest of his days in an institution rather than prison, although there'll come a time when his memory will fail and he won't remember any of it, anyway. Regarding his wife and Morris, I don't know. It had been planned for a while so would be classed as premeditated, but there were extenuating circumstances because of John's abuse of Sarah and the fact he didn't save Jack from having the accident when he could have. There are plenty of witnesses to what a destructive and dangerous person John was. Morris was prepared to take the fall for a man who saved his life. It's a minefield which a good legal team will have to wade through. I suppose we'll have to wait and see what happens."

"Well, after all you've been through, I think a cup of tea is in order. The new lavender blend arrived yesterday, good for helping anxiety and calming you down. What do you say?"

"Make it a large one please, Stacey."

With the tea drunk and the shop ready to open, Stacey took a slip of paper from the message pile. "I have an interesting request for you. A couple came in, newly engaged and would like a fully vintage afternoon tea style wedding. They would like you to do it."

"Really? A wedding?" Lilly said, taking the note from Stacey. "That's a lot bigger than the small book club event I did at Mrs Davenport's."

"I know, right?" Stacey said excitedly. "I told you events were the thing. Mrs Davenport and Lady Defoe have been raving about your teas and tea parties. I guess word must have spread."

"A wedding would be interesting to do, actually. It sounds like fun, not to mention lucrative. But it would be a huge amount of work for just the two of us."

"Yeah, I know. They also want the catering doing."

"I only do teas, and special cocktails if asked which I would do for a wedding, but not food."

"I know, but I had an idea about that. What if we asked the owner of one of the local cafes to do that side of things? You know, like a joint venture. I'm sure one of them would be really interested in doing this type of event. You never know it could lead to lots more bookings."

"Hmm... you know, that's actually a really good idea, Stacey. Well done. I'll have a look round and send out some feelers later," Lilly said with a huge grin. "But for now, let's get this show on the road and open the shop. I've missed this place, Stacey. It's very good to be home."

If you enjoyed *Tiffin & Tragedy*, the third book in the Tea & Sympathy series, please leave a review on Amazon. It really does help other readers find the books.

About the Author

J. New is the author of *THE YELLOW COTTAGE VINTAGE MYSTERIES,* traditional English whodunits with a twist, set in the 1930's. Known for their clever humour as well as the interesting slant on the traditional murder mystery, they have all achieved Bestseller status on Amazon.

J. New also writes two contemporary cozy crime series:

THE TEA & SYMPATHY series featuring Lilly Tweed, former newspaper Agony Aunt now purveyor of fine teas at The Tea Emporium in the small English market town of Plumpton Mallet. Along with a regular cast of characters, including Earl Grey the shop cat.

THE FINCH & FISCHER series featuring mobile librarian Penny Finch and her rescue dog Fischer. Follow them as they dig up clues and sniff out red herrings in the six villages and hamlets that make up Hampsworthy Downs.

Jacquie was born in West Yorkshire, England. She studied art and design and after qualifying began work as an interior designer, moving onto fine art restoration and animal portraiture before making the decision to pursue her lifelong ambition to write. She now writes full time and lives with her partner of twenty-two years, two dogs and five cats, all of whom she rescued.

If you would like to be kept up to date with new releases from J. New, you can sign up to her *Reader's Group* on her website www.jnewwrites.com You will also receive a link to download the free e-book, *The Yellow Cottage Mystery*, the short-story prequel to The Yellow Cottage Vintage Mystery series.

Printed in Great Britain
by Amazon